RHYS BOWEN

Queen of Hearts

Constable • London

CONSTABLE

First published in the US in 2014 by Berkley Prime Crime, The Berkley Publishing Group

This edition published in Great Britain in 2016 by Constable

Copyright © Janet Quin-Harkin, 2014
Published by arrangement with The Berkley Publishing Group,
a member of Penguin Group (USA) LLC

1 3 5 7 9 10 8 6 4 2

The moral right of the author has been asserted.

A CIP catalogue record for this book
is available from the British Library.

ISBN 978-1-47212-082-3 (paperback)

Typeset in Berthold Baskerville by TW Type, Cornwall
Printed and bound in Great Britain by CPI (UK) Ltd, Croydon CR0 4YY
Papers used by Constable are from well-managed forests and other responsible sources

MIX
Paper from
responsible sources
FSC® C104740

Constable
is an imprint of
Little, Brown Book Group
Carmelite House
50 Victoria Embankment
London EC4Y 0DZ

An Hachette UK Company
www.hachette.co.uk

www.littlebrown.co.uk

Chapter 1

Kingsdowne Place, Eynsford, Kent
Monday, July 9, 1934

*Dear Diary: Weather fine but absolutely nothing to do. Dying
of boredom.*

I was sitting in a white wicker chair under a spreading chestnut
tree on a manicured lawn. Behind me the stately battlements
of Kingsdowne Place, seat of the dukes of Eynsford, were
reflected in the perfect mirror of the lake, its surface ruffled
only by a pair of gliding swans. Before me was a tea table,
groaning under tiers of cucumber and smoked salmon sandwiches, strawberries and cream, éclairs, Victoria sponges,
petits fours and scones with clotted cream. It was about the
most perfect afternoon one could wish for, one of those rare
English summer days when the only sounds are the buzzing
of bees among the roses, the clickety-clack of a distant lawn
mower and the thwack of ball on bat at the cricket match
down in the village.

I gave a long sigh. It should have been of contentment but

actually it was one of boredom. I have a confession to make. Being almost royal isn't always a piece of cake. For one thing it isn't always easy keeping that stiff upper lip in the face of royal relatives, lunatic suitors, and dead bodies. And it's certainly not easy doing nothing all day. I know that ordinary people who have to catch the eight-twenty to Waterloo every day envy our leisure, but frankly most of the time our lives are a battle against boredom. I'd love to be doing something useful. I'd love to be making money too. But alas there are no jobs for a young woman whose education has only equipped her to walk around with a book on her head and know where to seat a bishop at a dinner party. My royal relatives would certainly not have been amused if they learned I was working behind the counter in Woolworths or serving tea at Lyons. And in this horrid depression even people with strings of qualifications can't find gainful employment.

What I should have been doing was my duty by marrying some half-batty Continental princeling, thus ensuring the continuation of some outmoded dynasty (while running the risk of being assassinated by anarchists). So far I had managed to avoid all half-lunatic princes that had been thrust in my direction. And in case you think I was against the idea of marriage, actually I did have a candidate for marriage lined up, but he, like me, was penniless with no prospects. A pretty hopeless situation.

And so I did what other young ladies of my station do until they find a husband – endured long, empty days punctuated by meals, healthy walks through the countryside and occasional bursts of excitement in the form of hunts. And since the weather in England is usually bloody, even more days of sitting reading, doing jigsaw puzzles, writing letters and counting the hours until the next meal.

A few months ago I thought I had fallen on my feet for once when I was asked to educate the newly discovered heir to the Duke of Eynsford into the ways of polite society. Kingsdowne Place, seat of the dukes of Eynsford, was everything a stately home should be – impressively opulent and elegant with gorgeous grounds, a stable full of fine horses, and meals that were a succession of extravagant courses. There was no hint at Kingsdowne Place that the rest of the world was in a depression. But my stay had not exactly gone according to plan. There had been plots and a murder, and when the dust had settled I had stayed on out of duty to give companionship to the dowager duchess. My nanny and governess were very hot on duty. I had had it rammed down my throat since I could toddle. Rannochs prized duty above diadems. (Actually I'd have prized the diadems if I'd owned any.) Did I mention that I am Lady Georgiana Rannoch, and cousin to His Majesty King George?

I confess that my task had been made more pleasant because Darcy O'Mara, the man I hoped to marry one day, had stayed on with me. But Darcy never remained in one place for long. He was a true adventurer and was always off on strange missions to far-flung parts of the globe. Anyway, he had gone again, the younger members of the Eynsford clan had dispersed and I was left at a great house with a dowager duchess, her two half-dotty sisters and several dozen servants. I was longing for younger company and a change of scenery when my mother came to the rescue.

For those of you who don't know my mother, let me assure you that she is not the maternal type. But on that afternoon when I was having tea on the lawn with the three weird sisters the dowager duchess Edwina paused with her teacup raised on its way to her lips.

'That sounds like a motorcar coming up the drive,'' she said. 'How extraordinary. Whoever could it be?'

'We aren't expecting anybody, are we?' her sister Princess Charlotte Orlovski asked, swiveling around in her seat so that she could get a better look at the drive. 'My spirit guide didn't warn me of a visitor.' (The Princess Orlovski was heavily into spiritualism.)

'It's about time we had company,' the third sister, the naughty and poorly named Virginia, chimed in. 'It's been as dull as ditchwater since everybody left. I'm sure poor young Georgiana is dying of boredom and frustration. I know I am.'

'Oh, no, of course not,' I said hastily and untruthfully.

The sound of an approaching motorcar grew louder. Edwina put down her teacup and picked up her lorgnette, peering through the trees as the black shape of a motorcar came into view. It was an open-topped sports car, low and sleek, and it was being driven rather fast. My heartbeat quickened as I watched it come closer. Could it possibly be Darcy, home from foreign missions and coming to sweep me away?

Then I realized that the driver was certainly not Darcy. It was a small person, hatless, with blonde hair that blew out in the breeze. It was only when the driver spotted us and the car screeched to a halt in a shower of gravel that I recognized who she was.

'Who on earth?' Edwina started to say.

'It's my mother, Your Grace,' I said as a trim little person in bright red slacks and a white halter top climbed out of the car. She was wearing big sunglasses that hid half her face, and her hair, in spite of having been windswept, now looked perfectly in place. She waved then came toward us, tottering on high platform espadrilles.

'There you are, Georgie,' she called in that voice that had delighted theatergoers across the world. 'I've been looking all over for you. I telephoned Castle Rannoch but your brother didn't seem to know where you were. You weren't at the house in London where I left you a few months ago. I was quite despairing until I ran into your friend Belinda at Crockford's last night and she told me you were staying with the Eynsfords.' She had reached us now, picking her way carefully across the lawn. She seemed to notice the three elderly ladies, all sitting and staring at her in her flamboyantly modern outfit, for the first time. 'How do you do,' she said. 'Sorry to barge in on you like this.'

I intervened hastily. 'Your Grace, may I introduce to you my mother, the former duchess of Rannoch.' I thought it wise to give Mummy the only acceptable title she's ever had. I wasn't actually lying. She was a former duchess of Rannoch. It's just that since that time she had been a great many other things to a great many men. It was possible that the dowager duchess knew a lot of this, but as always her manners were impeccable.

'How do you do,' she said, extending a hand. 'Delighted to meet Georgiana's mother at last. Although I do believe we met many years ago when your dear Bertie was still alive. I was his mother's lady-in-waiting, you know. He was such a lovable little boy, such a sweet smile. So sad that he died too soon, just like my own sons. One should not have to outlive one's children.'

My mother, presumably not having heard of the demise of the Eynsford sons, wisely said nothing.

'Do sit down and have a cup of tea,' Edwina said, motioning to the maid who was standing nearby to bring another cup. 'Of course you must have been missing your dear daughter. And if only you'd let us know you were coming, we could have had a suitable room prepared for you.' It was the nearest to a reproach that manners allowed.

'Most kind, but I'm not intending to stay,' Mummy said, accepting the teacup and sinking into a wicker chair. 'I only came to collect Georgie.'

'To collect me?'

'Yes, darling. We're going on a trip together.'

'A trip? Where?'

'America,' she said, as if this was no more startling than a shopping expedition to London.

'America?' I blurted out.

'Yes, darling, you know that big place with the skyscrapers and cowboys.' She gave the elderly sisters an exasperated smile that her only child could be so dense. 'Why don't you run along and get your maid to pack your things while I have tea with these delightful ladies.' She was already helping herself to a cucumber sandwich.

'But I can't just leave like this, Mummy. It wouldn't be right. Her Grace has been through a most difficult time. I can't walk out on her when she needs me.' But even as I said the words a voice in my head was whispering, 'America! I'm going to America with my mother!'

Edwina reached across and patted my hand. 'You have been a wonderful comfort to me in my hour of need, Georgiana. Such a kind girl. But I wouldn't dream of preventing you from going away with your mama, especially not to America. Transatlantic crossings are delightful and a young thing like you needs to see life, not be cooped up here with three old women. Of course you must go.'

'Of course she must,' Virginia echoed. 'New York, such an exciting city. And they say that cowboys are wonderfully virile. In fact I remember a thrilling episode with a saddle and a particularly large whip. . . .'

Edwina cleared her throat. Virginia's sex life had probably even outdone that of my mother and she never minded recalling it in the most vivid detail.

'You'd better run up and pack, Georgiana,' Edwina said, 'if your dear mama is really intent on leaving this evening. Are you sure you wouldn't like to stay the night and leave in the morning?'

'Kind of you, Your Grace, but I'm afraid not,' Mummy said. 'We have secured passage on the *Berengaria* and she sails on Thursday from Southampton.'

'The *Berengaria*.' Virginia gave a sigh of envy. 'The ship of millionaires, they used to call it.'

'Still do,' Mummy said. 'Who else can afford to travel these days? Anyway, she sails on Thursday and there is so much to be done that I couldn't spare an extra minute. Do get a move on, darling.' She glanced at the motorcar. 'I don't see how we're going to fit in your maid and your trunk. Do you still have that ghastly girl who looks like a hippopotamus?'

'Queenie? Yes, I'm afraid I do.'

'She'll never fit into the back seat, darling, let alone with the luggage. Have her come up by train with your things. Brown's Hotel, of course. I wouldn't stay anywhere else.'

'Ah, Brown's Hotel. Such fond memories.' This time it was Princess Charlotte who gave her sisters a wistful look.

'Off you go, then.' Mummy clapped her gloveless hands impatiently.

'If you're sure, Your Grace?' I looked at Edwina.

'Don't keep your mother waiting, Georgiana,' Edwina said. 'We old ladies will carry on as we always have done.'

I put down my teacup, and tried to rise gracefully from my deckchair. Unfortunately I stepped on my skirt so that my graceful ascent turned into a stumble that nearly caught the tea table. I righted myself and set off, red-faced, with as much dignity as I could still muster.

'Typical Georgie. Always was a walking disaster area, I'm afraid,' I heard Mummy saying as I moved out of earshot. 'Has she wrecked your house yet?'

Oh dear. I'd actually done rather well until now with nothing broken and no elderly ladies knocked off their feet. But unfortunately she was right. I am rather accident-prone when I'm flustered – like the time I caught my heel in my train at my debutante presentation and was propelled rapidly toward Their Majesties instead of backing from the chamber.

There was no sign of Queenie when I entered my bedroom. I tugged on the bellpull and waited. No maid appeared. I tugged again and started taking items of clothing out of the wardrobe. After a few minutes there was a tap on the door and Edie, the head housemaid, came in.

'Did you ring, my lady?' She curtsied.

'For my maid,' I said. 'Have you seen her recently?'

'She was at tea,' Edie said. 'I'm afraid I haven't seen her since.'

'Then please have somebody find her. I need her right away.'

'I will, my lady.' She bobbed a curtsy and took off.

Why couldn't I have a maid like that, I thought. Willing, efficient, a joy to be around . . . Of course I knew the answer. Because I couldn't afford to pay her. Queenie had one advantage. She worked for almost no money, knowing that no gentlewoman in her right mind would employ her. The situation suited both of us most of the time.

I had emptied the contents of the chest of drawers onto my bed when I heard sounds resembling a stampede of elephants coming up the hall toward me. Queenie burst through the door, red-faced and disheveled.

'Bloody 'ell,' she said, observing the large pile of clothing on the bed. 'What the devil's going on 'ere?'

'We're leaving,' I said. 'I need my trunk retrieved and my clothes packed.'

'Leavin'? What do you want to go and leave for?' she demanded, hands on very ample hips. 'First decent food we've had in months.'

'And I see you've taken full advantage of it,' I replied, noticing that her uniform was now bursting at the seams. 'Where were you? I rang twice.'

'Well, I had three pieces of seedy cake at tea today and I felt a bit sleepy afterward so I just went up to my room to have a bit of a kip, and before you know it I was out like a light,' she said. 'So where are we going, then? Not back to that god-awful castle in Scotland.'

'Queenie, I've pointed out to you before that you should not criticize your employer or your employer's family. You should be glad you have a job in these hard times.'

'Oh, I ain't got nothing against you, miss,' she said. 'It's her what lives at the castle in Scotland. The ruddy duchess. She don't like me, does she? She thinks I'm too common.'

'Well, you are. You've seen how other lady's maids behave, haven't you? You haven't even learned to call me by my proper title yet.'

She sighed. 'I know you should be "my lady" but that sounds awful toffee-nosed, if you ask me. And you're so nice and normal and friendly that you're more like an ordinary miss.'

'Nevertheless, Queenie, society demands that an aristocrat should be addressed in the correct manner. My cousin Elizabeth is a friendly little girl but one still has to address her as "Your Royal Highness." Now please get a move on. My mother is waiting.'

'Your mum? We're going off with your mum? Oh, that's all right then. She'll make sure we eat properly. Where are we going? Back to London?'

'No, we're going to America.'

'Bloody 'ell,' she said.

Chapter 2

An hour later Mummy and I were speeding through the Kentish lanes on our way to London. Queenie and my trunk had been crammed into the estate car with much grumbling from her. What if she fell asleep and missed the station? What if a strange man got into her compartment and accosted her? And how would she manage all that luggage? I pointed out that the train terminated at Victoria and she should select a Ladies Only carriage. When she arrived all she had to do was summon a porter who would take her to a taxi. When last seen, she was heading to the nearest station and one hoped that she would eventually wind up at Brown's Hotel.

'So what on earth were you doing with those awful dreary old women?' Mummy asked as we drove through the impressive gateway and out onto a country lane.

'Keeping the dowager duchess company. She's had an upsetting time, you know. You probably didn't hear about it in Germany.'

'Oh, I think I did hear something about it, now that you mention it. Something to do with the heir, wasn't it?'

'It was. All rather horrible, actually.'

'Well, in that case I'm glad I'm whisking you away. We'll have much more fun where we're going.'

'Where are we going, exactly? And why are you taking me along?'

'That's obvious, darling. I didn't want to travel alone. A woman feels so vulnerable and those Americans can be wild and dangerous.'

Nobody in the world could take care of herself better than my mother. She might look frail and diminutive but she came from good Cockney stock and was as tough as old boots. She had been a leading lady on the stage when she had met and married my father, who was Queen Victoria's grandson, but she chose to forget those humble beginnings. She had actually enjoyed being a duchess and probably would have remained one longer if living at Castle Rannoch had not been part of the bargain. I looked at her face. She was now playing the part of a weak and helpless female – playing it really convincingly, as always. I had to laugh. 'There aren't any cowboys and Indians any longer, you know.'

'But plenty of gangsters,' she said. 'Al Capone, you know. I thought you'd be pleased and want to spend time with your mother.'

'I am. I do,' I said. 'It's just that it's rather sudden. When last seen, you abandoned me to that awful woman's cooking in London and went off with Max to Lake Lugano. Have you finally broken up with him?'

'*Au contraire*, darling,' she said. 'Max is insisting that he wants to do the right thing and get married. He's quite a puritan at heart.'

'But don't I remember correctly that you are still married to someone else?'

I should also add that my mother was a serial bolter, much married, and had worked her way through many men on all continents but Antarctica.

'Isn't he a Texan oilman?' I went on, 'And didn't he refuse to give you a divorce?'

'How was I to know he had a strange religious streak?' she said irritably. 'When I met him in Paris in the twenties he seemed quite gay and debonair, refreshingly naïve and ridiculously rich. It was only after I'd married him that I found that he didn't drink and he actually wanted me to live on a ranch in Texas.' She turned to me with a horrified face. 'A ranch, darling. In Texas. *Moi?* Can you imagine it. All those cows and oil wells. Castle Rannoch was bad enough but at least they could send up hampers from Fortnum's on a regular basis.'

'Is that why we're going to America? You're going to plead with him to set you free?' I asked. 'Or has he conveniently died?'

'Neither of the above,' she said. 'But I think I've found a way to circumvent him. I have been told that one can obtain a quickie divorce in Reno, Nevada, where anything goes.'

'But if he wouldn't divorce you in Texas, why would he agree to it in Nevada?' I heard myself almost shouting over the roar of the motor as we had now reached the London Road and Mummy had put her foot down.

'He doesn't have to agree to it. Given the right circumstances the other party doesn't have to show up.'

'Golly. Is it legal?'

'Perfectly, in Nevada, according to my authority. So I thought we'd have a nice little trip to Reno together. You'll enjoy the crossing on the *Berengaria*, won't you? And a train trip across America?'

'Oh golly, yes,' I said.

She turned to frown at me. 'You must learn to stop saying such schoolgirlish expressions if you ever want to be a woman of the world.'

'Sorry,' I said. 'They just slip out in moments of stress.' I cleared my throat. 'Thank you for your kind invitation. It sounds heavenly.'

'Jolly good.' She gave me a rare encouraging grin. A grin of co-conspirators. 'Now we only have two days to get you kitted out. You simply can't be seen on the *Berengaria* in a cotton frock like the one you are wearing. You look like an orphan in a reform school.'

'That's because I've owned this since I was a schoolgirl,' I said. 'One doesn't buy clothes if one has no money.'

'You really must find yourself a rich man, darling. I know that Darcy is quite delectable and I'm sure he's wonderful in bed, but he's not suitable husband material, is he? He'll never be able to provide for you properly.'

'I'd rather live in poverty with Darcy than with a rich man I didn't love,' I said hotly.

She smiled. 'So young. So romantic. You'll learn. And if you're smart you'll snag yourself an American millionaire on the ship.'

'Are there any millionaires in America these days?' I said, smiling at the absurdity of her suggestion.

'Of course there are. Live with him for a year, divorce him, and you'll be set up for life.'

'Like you did, you mean? And then have all the trouble of trying to divorce him? That's not for me, thank you,' I said.

'You're just like my father,' Mummy said, frowning. 'Too damned proud and honorable.'

'You've been to see Granddad?' My heart leaped at the mention of the man I loved almost as much as Darcy. My mother's father was a retired London bobby who now lived in a semi-detached in Essex, bought for him when Mummy was in the first flush of fame.

'I have, and he won't take a penny from me. Claims it's German money and he'll never forgive the Germans for the Great War.' I had heard him say the same kind of thing.

'How is he?' I asked, feeling a wave of longing for my grandfather.

'Not too well, actually. I offered to take him with us to America. I thought a sea voyage would do him good, but he refused.'

'I must go and see him before we sail,' I said. 'How long do you think we'll be away?'

'Not too long, I hope. A few days in New York – at least they've started drinking legally again. Those speakeasies were such a bore. And then a train ride across the country to Reno. Let's hope we have it all sewn up and back within a month. Max pines if I leave him too long.'

I turned to look at her. 'Do you really want to marry Max and live in Germany?'

'Darling, he's richer than God and the sex is divine. He's like a rampant stud bull and he wants it several times a night.'

I felt my face turning bright red at the mention of such things, having led a sheltered life so far.

'But you don't speak German and you don't like German food.'

She shrugged. 'I can stand a week or two in Berlin when necessary. It's really quite civilized if that nasty little Hitler man doesn't last long. Besides, when Max saw that I loved the villa in Lugano that we were renting, he bought it for me. So I now have a bolt hole in Switzerland. He's so generous. I may even learn to converse with him some day. I've promised to take German lessons.'

'Granddad won't like that,' I said.

'Then he'll have to lump it,' she said with true Cockney candor.

Brown's Hotel gave Mummy the sort of welcome she expected.

'Welcome back, Your Grace,' the doorman said.

'Welcome back, Your Grace,' the snooty young man at the reception desk cooed, bowing to her. 'We have champagne on ice, waiting for you.'

I followed Mummy up the stairs, feeling horribly self-conscious about my now-crumpled cotton dress. She had a lovely room on the first floor with French windows looking onto Albemarle Street. I had wondered why she always chose Brown's instead of the Ritz or Claridge's, but now I understood why she stayed here. They conveniently forgot that she was no longer 'Your Grace' but Mrs. Homer Clegg, if my memory served me correctly. And soon she'd be Frau von Strohheim. I wondered how Brown's would take to that?

I had been given a small but charming room facing away from the street. I was just realizing that I had nothing to wear for dinner when Queenie arrived, red-faced and panting.

'Some bloke's bringing up your trunk,' she said. 'I had a bleeding awful time getting the bloody thing off the train by myself. Do you think I could find a ruddy porter? No, I blinking well couldn't. I had to leave the guard with the luggage and go looking for one. "Now don't you let anyone nick that," I told him and the ruddy man wanted a tip when I came back. The cheek of it. "I'll have you know that these here bags belong to someone what's a cousin of the king," I told him. "You should consider it an honor to look after them."'

'Queenie, please hurry up and unpack,' I interrupted this flow. 'I have to go down to dinner soon and I've nothing to wear.'

'Where am I supposed to have me dinner, then?' she asked, opening the trunk and flinging garments onto the bed. 'I ain't half hungry after all that traipsing around.'

'I'll ask Mummy's maid where the servants dine,' I said. 'I think I'll wear the red one. We've been in mourning too long at Kingsdowne. I need cheering up.'

And as I said this I realized I was cheering up. A shopping spree with Mummy tomorrow and then a luxury liner across the Atlantic. What more could a girl want?

Chapter 3

At Brown's Hotel
Still July 9

Things are certainly looking up for G. Rannoch these days. Brown's and a spending spree with Mummy and then a transatlantic crossing. Golly.

The red evening dress was rather the worse for Queenie's packing and I saw Mummy's face when I went into her room to go down to dinner. 'Whoever told you that red was your color, darling?' she demanded. 'Don't you possess any decent clothing?'

'I have the outfit that Coco Chanel bought for me at the Galeries Lafayette,' I said, 'but that's up in Scotland. There wouldn't be time to telephone Fig and have it sent down to London, would there?'

'Knowing your sister-in-law, she'd probably flush it down the nearest loo and then claim she couldn't find it,' Mummy said. 'Let's just hope there are a few decent-looking outfits to be found in London tomorrow. Although God knows where we will find them.' She was prowling around me, examining me as if she were a tiger sizing up her next meal. 'It's a pity you are so impossibly large,' she said, 'or you could wear some of my things. Max loves me to buy new clothes and I never know what to do with the old ones. But I fear I have nothing you'd fit into.'

'You make me sound like a giant,' I said. 'I'm only five foot six. You're the one who is small.'

'Petite, darling. I'm petite. Too bad you inherited the robust physique of those Scottish ancestors. The royal side were small enough, just those wretched hearty Scots must be to blame.'

'Darcy seems to like me the way I am,' I said.

'I've found that men are often blinded by love,' she said. 'Never mind, we'll have you looking respectable, if not fashionable, by the time we leave.'

The next morning we set off right after breakfast. 'Might as well try Fenwick's first since they are just around the corner on Bond Street,' she said. But half an hour later she had declared them too impossibly frumpy. 'You'll be dining on the *Berengaria* with me, darling. They can't get the impression that I let my only child run around in rags.'

'You have until now,' I wanted to say. My mother had only popped into my life on rare occasions and it had never crossed her mind that I had no money and had been surviving on baked beans on toast.

She hailed a taxicab. 'Harrods might just have something,' she said.

'Selfridges is closer,' I pointed out.

She looked at me in horror. 'Selfridges is where typists and lower-middle-class housewives shop,' she said, conveniently forgetting again that she had been born in the backstreets of the East End.

So we went to Harrods where doormen leaped and bowed, murmuring, 'Welcome back, Your Grace. It's been too long.'

Mummy swept in, ordering a jar of her favorite face cream as she passed the cosmetics counter, a pair of red leather gloves and matching beret, suitable for a sea cruise, before she took the lift to ladies' dresses. A formidable woman bore down on us. 'And how can I assist madame?' she asked.

'You can find me an assistant young enough to have a feel for what is fashionable this season,' Mummy said. 'I'm taking my daughter on a sea cruise.'

'That young lady is never madame's daughter,' the woman said in her silky voice and gave a false titter. 'Your sister, surely.'

Since she had been one of the few people in the civilized world who had failed to recognize my mother and give her the appropriately groveling greeting, Mummy had taken an instant dislike to her. 'I should point out that "that young lady" is Lady Georgiana Rannoch,' she said. 'Cousin to His Majesty. She will be seen as an ambassador of her country when we visit America. We want to do Britain proud, don't we?'

The woman's face was now rather red. 'Oh, we do. We do. Forgive me for not recognizing you immediately. I will summon our Mademoiselle Dubois. She has recently joined us from Paris where she worked at the great couture houses. Allow me to escort you to a fitting room.'

'That told her,' Mummy muttered as the woman disappeared to find the fashionable Frenchwoman. 'Sorry, but that remark about you being my sister got my goat. And fancy not recognizing me.'

There was a tap on the fitting room door and the woman, still red-faced, put her head around it. 'Here is our young French assistant, madame,' she said. 'Mademoiselle Dubois, I'm sure you'll be able to find the perfect wardrobe for Lady Georgiana, won't you?' And she stood aside to usher in a svelte, dark-haired young woman.

'Bonjour, and 'ow may I assist madame today,' she started to say, then a look of horror wiped the smile from her face. I swallowed back a gasp. I think Mummy did too. I waited until the senior saleswoman had closed the door behind her before the young Frenchwoman let out a sigh of relief.

'Crikey,' she said. 'I thought you'd blow it for me.'

'Belinda!' I exclaimed. 'What on earth are you doing here?'

My best friend, Belinda Warburton-Stoke, put her finger to her lips. 'Shhhh,' she said. 'I'm supposed to be Mademoiselle Dubois.'

'But why?'

'Money, darling – why else? I'm rather broke at the moment and I saw this advertisement for a fashion assistant with knowledge of haute couture, preferably French.'

'Belinda, you're terrible.' I started to laugh.

'Not at all. I fit the bill perfectly. After all, I did work with Chanel and I designed my own line of clothing.'

'No, I'm sure you're perfectly qualified. Just not French.'

'Well, I had to claim to be French to beat out the other candidates. Also I wouldn't want word to get back to the family. Granny might cut me out of her will if she heard I'd gone into trade.'

'But what if you have to serve real French people?'

'I'll have you know my French is damned good,' Belinda said. 'We had three years at Les Oiseaux, didn't we, and then I worked with Chanel in Paris. And my liaison with Jean-Luc taught me all sorts of words I'd never learned in school.'

'Jean-Luc – was he the one who was Chanel's lover, and that's why you were dismissed?'

'How good to see you again, Belinda dear,' Mummy interrupted. 'I'd love to sit here chatting, but we have rather a lot to do in a short time. We need suitable clothing for a transatlantic crossing for Georgie. Silk evening pajamas, I think. She does have nice long legs. So maybe some linen slacks. A couple of decent tea dresses, although there won't be time for alterations and I'm sure nothing off the peg fits properly.'

Belinda was wonderful. Within an hour I was kitted out with the sort of clothes I'd so admired on others – the white Chinese silk evening pajamas, a backless midnight blue evening dress that made me look almost sexy, slacks and jackets, silky floral-print dresses and even a velvet evening cape.

'You are lucky, going to America,' Belinda said wistfully as Mummy went off to write a check. 'I can't afford to travel anywhere at the moment.'

'No sugar daddies in sight?' I asked, 'Or have you forsaken men for a life of respectability?'

'God, no,' she said. 'I'm positively sex starved, but any man worth looking at has fled from London this summer. And I have no funds for travel, alas, and I'm no longer welcome at home. America sounds divine. Do write and tell me about all your exploits there. Shall you be going to Hollywood?'

'Only Nevada, I think,' I said.

'But that's so close. You must go and see Hollywood. Who knows, perhaps you'll be discovered while drinking a soda on Sunset Strip.'

'Fat chance of that,' I said, laughing. 'Anyway, Mummy says she can't be away long. Max will be pining.'

'She certainly doesn't want to upset the applecart with Max,' Belinda agreed. 'There are so few people with his kind of money these days. I think I may have to go and visit her in Germany. You don't think Max might have any young rich relatives, do you?'

'I wouldn't know. Personally I'd rather stay in England and be poor. I don't like the sound of the way things are going in Germany.'

We broke off the conversation as Mummy reappeared. 'Well, that's done. They'll hem the trousers and have them delivered to Brown's by this afternoon. I must say the one thing one can count on from Harrods is efficiency. And I was pleasantly surprised by the quality of the clothing too. Quite chic. We may find you a rich man on the boat after all, Georgie.' And she winked at Belinda.

Before I could answer this she was making for the lift.

'Write to me, and don't forget . . .' Belinda started to say, then remembered she was supposed to be French. I blew her a kiss as I rushed to keep up with my mother. We emerged from the lift and Mummy swept grandly across the main floor, past bowing attendants and out to a waiting taxicab.

Chapter 4

We sail today! Dying to see the Berengaria. *America, here I come. Can't wait. But I do wish I could have told Darcy where I was going. He is so infuriating!!!!*

The next days were a whirlwind of Mummy doing her own shopping for essentials that apparently couldn't be obtained in America – like toothpaste, getting her hair done, getting my hair done, buying new luggage for me and new hats for us both. I must say it was rather exciting to be caught up in this shopping whirlwind. I hoped Max didn't have a fit when he saw the bills and decide not to marry her after all.

Then the day of departure dawned. It was almost like a dream as our bags were whisked downstairs and into taxi-cabs. Soon our train was steaming out of Waterloo Station, bound for Southampton. My only wish was that my hateful sister-in-law, Fig, might have been there to watch me depart in style. (Usually I have a nice nature, but Fig had certainly made my life miserable for quite a while and deserved comeuppance.) My other wish was that I could have told Darcy where I was going. As usual I had no way to contact him. Better still, I would have wished that he was coming too!

I had crossed the Channel plenty of times but I'd never seen an actual ocean liner. My jaw dropped as we pulled up beside the *Berengaria*. She was enormous, with three shiny red funnels, already puffing out wisps of smoke. It was like staring up at the Dorchester.

'Come along, darling, don't dawdle,' Mummy said, heading for the first-class gangway. 'And try not to gawp. You look like a country bumpkin.'

We were welcomed on board in the effusive manner that Mummy expected, and escorted up to A deck where Mummy was to have a suite. I had once had a cabin on an overnight Channel crossing from Ostend so I was expecting something like a railway sleeping car with bunks on one side and a washbasin. Therefore I was not prepared when the steward opened the door and we stepped into a spacious sitting room with a sofa and armchairs, a writing desk between two picture windows and thick pile carpeting. There were flowers on the table and champagne on ice.

Mummy nodded with satisfaction. 'Oh yes, this will do nicely,' she said. 'I suppose the bedroom is through here.' And I followed her through to a pretty bedroom with dainty white wood furniture and chintz covers. Two picture windows opened onto the deck. I observed there were two beds.

'Am I to be sharing this with you?' I asked.

'Good heavens, no.' She sounded horrified. 'Sharing with my daughter would definitely cramp my style. You never know whom I might want to invite up to visit me.'

I didn't like to point out that she was on her way to get a

divorce so that she could marry a rather puritanical German and news of shipboard antics wouldn't go down well with him. Also that he was paying for this little jaunt. The steward gave a discreet cough, making Mummy break off and grin. 'Thank you. That will be all,' she said. 'Please show Lady Georgiana to her quarters.'

My cabin was farther along A deck. Not a suite and not as grand but rather more to my liking with a big window looking onto the deck and the ocean beyond. It also had a lovely big bathroom and I was feeling extremely satisfied when Queenie arrived with the first of the luggage.

'They're bringing up the last lot now,' she said. 'Cor – this ain't bad, is it? You ought to find yourself a bloke what's got money like her German.'

'Queenie!' I wagged a finger. 'You can start unpacking while I go and explore.'

'Your mum's maid is right hoity-toity, ain't she? I had to travel all the way down in the train with her and she hardly gave me the time of day. And we've got to share a cabin for the next five days too – and I bet it won't be as big as this one.'

I had accepted Queenie's failings, knowing that I wouldn't find another maid for what I paid her, but enough was enough. It was about time I behaved like a proper lady of my class and didn't let my servant treat me as an equal. I took a deep breath. 'Queenie, I'm rather concerned about you,' I said. 'You seem to be doing an awful lot of complaining recently. May I remind you how lucky you are to have a job with a good family, and enough to eat and a roof over your head when frankly nobody else would employ you. If you were smart you would study Claudette and see how a good lady's maid behaves. She certainly doesn't speak to her employer the way you speak to me or she would be out on her ear in five minutes.'

She gave me an apologetic grin. 'Sorry, miss. You're right. My old dad said I was getting too big for me boots when I went to see them last time. He said pride comes before a fall.'

'Then listen to your old dad,' I said. 'And find an ironing board. Some of these things crumple easily.' I headed for the door. At the door I turned around. 'Oh, and Queenie, one does not use a hot iron on silk. It will melt.'

'Bob's yer uncle, miss,' she said. I sighed. She was never going to learn and I was stuck with her.

I left her to unpack and went out onto the deck. I stood looking down at the impossibly small people moving like ants on the dock below. The wind in my hair was fresh and had the tang of salt in it. I felt so excited that I did a little dance – a sort of hop, skip and jump as I went toward the railing.

'Very attractive,' said a voice behind me. I spun around, blushing, to see a young man leaning against the railing, smoking. 'I must make a note to secure you as my first partner in the ballroom.'

'I'm afraid I'm a hopeless dancer when it comes to ballroom,' I said. 'I hardly know a foxtrot from a two-step.'

'You prefer the more primitive sort of dance, like the one you just did?' His eyes were challenging me and I felt distinctly uneasy.

'That wasn't really a dance, just letting off steam after being cooped up with my mother for days.'

He came over to me. 'So you're traveling with your mother, are you? Off to find a rich American husband? I'm afraid there aren't so many of them these days.'

Under moments of stress I always seem to channel my great-grandmother Queen Victoria. 'You know, you're frightfully rude and we haven't even been introduced, so I shouldn't be speaking to you,' I said.

He threw back his head and laughed. 'We're on a ship. Anything goes. No outdated society rules here, and a lot of cabin hopping too.'

'Not to my cabin,' I said. 'I have a young man, thank you, and do not need a rich American.'

He opened his cigarette case. 'Do you smoke?' he said. 'I'm Tubby Halliday, by the way. And you are?'

'Georgiana Rannoch,' I said, accepting a cigarette although I'd never quite learned the taste for them and certainly had never inhaled the smoke.

'Are you? Good heavens. And your mother is the actress Claire Daniels? I thought I recognized her when she was being whisked on board. What are you going to be doing in America, may one ask?'

'Mummy has a spot of business. I'm keeping her company,' I said.

'A spot of business. How intriguing. Is she planning to buy land out West? There's plenty to be going for a song these days.'

'You really do ask a lot of questions,' I said. 'What will you be doing in America, then?'

'Amusing myself. It's what I always do. And things have become more amusing since I met you. It's usually only old fogies on board – the young rarely have the money to travel these days.'

I leaned over the railing and looked down. 'It's so big, isn't it? Like being at the top of St. Paul's Cathedral.'

'Is this your first time on the ship?'

'First time crossing the Atlantic,' I said.

'Good heavens. Then let me give you a tour so that you can find your way around,' he said.

I hesitated. I had been planning to explore the ship and I wasn't sure that I wanted to be too friendly with the chatty Mr. Halliday. But in the end I decided that having a tour would be better than wandering around on my own. 'All right. Thank you,' I said.

'We'll start at the top, at the promenade deck,' he said and led me to some outside stairs. 'There are just a few very swank suites up here.'

'Dear me. Mummy will be upset to know she's not on the most exclusive level,' I chuckled.

'They are usually empty. Reserved for royalty and millionaires.' He went ahead and helped me up the last stairs onto the promenade deck. 'The ballroom's also up here, and the first-class lounge. And the ladies' lounge where you and your mother will undoubtedly be sitting to escape from bores like me.'

'I don't think my mother is the ladies' lounge type,' I said.

'Ah, is that it?' he asked. 'She's going to America with a man? Or to meet a man?'

'You know, you're frightfully rude, either on or off a ship,' I said. 'My mother isn't meeting anyone and her private life is nothing to do with you.'

I started to stalk away. He came after me. 'I say, I'm awfully sorry. My father tells me I put my foot in my mouth every time I talk. I'm just interested in people's lives, that's all. I'm a writer of sorts.' He held out a meaty hand. 'Can we be friends? I promise not to mention your mother's private life again.'

I took it, reluctantly. 'All right,' I said.

We started to walk together, looking first into the ballroom and then the lounge, each with impressive stained-glass skylights. 'How long will the crossing take?' I asked.

'I think with this old tub it's usually five days,' he said. 'Other ships have done it in four but since the *Mauretania* retired the English don't really have a contender for the record. We'll have to wait until they finish the new *Queen Mary*. Then we should win back the Blue Riband from the Germans.'

He started down the grand central staircase. 'She used to be a German ship, you know. There was a big portrait of the kaiser on that wall.' He pointed to a nautical scene that now graced it. 'Their pride and joy. The *Imperator*, she was called – or should that be "he was called" since it's a male name? They had to hand it over as war reparations and it was rechristened *Berengaria*.'

'What exactly does "Berengaria" mean?' I asked.

'It's an old-fashioned female name,' Tubby Halliday said. 'I seem to remember I had a great-aunt called Berengaria. Phew, I'm glad that one's gone out of style, aren't you?'

'I'm not madly keen on Georgiana,' I said, 'but since my other names are Victoria, Charlotte and Eugenie they're all equally stuffy.'

'They're all royal, aren't they. You lot are always stuck with that sort of name. But my name is actually more hideous. I'm stuck with Montmorency. Nothing could be worse than that, could it? Which is why I go by Tubby.'

'I go by Georgie,' I said and rather wished I hadn't. He seemed nice enough, just a little too friendly.

Tubby guided me through the various decks, through the Winter Garden with its wicker furniture, the palm court with full-size palm trees and a stage for the orchestra, the first-class dining salon and finally into the bowels of the ship.

'What's down here?' I asked nervously as there was no sign of anybody else heading this way.

'You'll see. Best part of the whole ship.'

It crossed my mind that he was luring me down here to have his way with me. He didn't seem like the type of person who had his way with unsuspecting females, but then I'd been surprised in the past by frightfully proper English boys with horribly groping hands.

'This way,' he said and his voice sounded strange and echoing. I hung back. He disappeared through a doorway. I followed, stopped and said, 'Golly.'

It was a swimming pool. And not just any swimming pool – it was flanked by Greek columns, marble everywhere, subtle lighting in the ceiling.

'Pretty neat, wouldn't you say? Maybe you'll join me for a swim one day?'

'What happens if it gets rough?' I asked.

'The water slops around a bit. But it's no fun in a storm. You get tossed about like a cork. They close the pool if it's too rough.'

'Does it often get rough?' I asked, realizing that I had no idea whether I was a good sailor or not.

'All the time. The Atlantic's notorious for it. Haven't you noticed the furniture is all bolted down?' He saw my face and laughed. 'Just teasing,' he said. 'It should be fine at this time of year. No icebergs either. We'd better get back on deck. We'll be sailing soon and you don't want to miss the grand departure.'

When we came out onto the deck again it was lined with people, some with champagne glasses in their hands. Down on the quayside a band was now playing 'Anchors Aweigh.' The ship's siren sounded a great blast and they were just starting to release the great ropes that held the ship fast when I thought I spotted someone I recognized. Surely nobody else had that shock of unruly dark curls and that purposeful, confident, almost arrogant way of walking. He was forcing his way through the crowd still clustered around the last gangway. My heart did a complete flip-flop.

'Darcy!' I yelled but my voice was drowned by a second blast of the ship's siren. Smoke wafted across the deck and when I looked again I couldn't see him. The crowd had backed away from the liner and were now waving handkerchiefs furiously. We were inching away from the dock. I was leaning over so far that I felt a hand yanking me back. 'Don't want to lose you, young woman,' said an elderly military-looking man. 'It's a long way down, you know.'

'I thought I saw somebody I knew,' I said, giving an apologetic smile. 'I wanted to see if he was coming on board.'

'If he's on board you'll meet him soon enough.' The man gave me a kindly smile.

My new-found friend seemed to have disappeared. The throng of people on the deck began to thin out as the tugs pulled us away from the docks and out into the shipping lane. I stayed on deck, half wanting to go down and try to find Darcy, but then realizing what an impossible task that would be on a ship this size. I tried to tell myself that he couldn't have come on board, just as the ship was leaving. The man I had seen, forcing his way through the crowd, had no luggage with him, and the ship's officers wouldn't have let him board without a ticket. But then why couldn't I still see him among the crowd? I stood watching as the dock with its waving people receded and we were sailing down the Solent, skirting the coastline. I wished I knew whether it really had been Darcy, and felt a small thrill of pleasure that he had learned of my trip and come to see me off, even if he was too late.

And if by some miracle he had come on board, then he'd find me soon enough.

Chapter 5

At sea on the Berengaria
July 12

> *Golly, living the life of the rich and famous at last. About to get dressed and dine at the captain's table. Eat your heart out, Fig.*

As we reached the open sea and the passage around the Isle of Wight I felt the rise and fall of the water's swell for the first time. I hope I won't be seasick, I thought. It would be such a waste with all that fun and those lovely meals awaiting me. I decided to go down and change for dinner. If by some miracle Darcy was on the ship, I'd be bound to see him then, if he didn't find his way to my cabin first. I hurried eagerly along the passageway.

Queenie was standing looking out of my cabin window as I arrived. 'It ain't half going up and down, miss,' she said.

'You'll be fine, Queenie. You'll get used to it in no time at all. I see you've unpacked. Well done. Now I'd like to change for dinner.'

'What do you want to wear then? Them new pajamas what's all the rage?'

'No, I think I'll look sleek and sophisticated in the backless midnight blue.'

'Bob's yer uncle,' she said. Then she paused. 'Here. What kind of underwear goes with a backless dress?'

'Nothing, Queenie.'

'What, no vest? No brassiere?' (She pronounced it 'brazier,' like the fire.)

I laughed. 'Certainly no vest, and I'm afraid no brassiere either.'

'Blimey. You're being a bit daring, aren't you? What if yer boobs fall out?'

I laughed. 'Queenie, the dress is made so that they don't. Besides, I don't have your size breasts to worry about.'

She started to lay out clothes on my bed while I went to wash.

"Ere,' she called. 'What about my dinner then? Where am I supposed to eat?'

'I believe the maids' dining room is up on the promenade deck, but you should ask Claudette. And Queenie, do try and mind your manners, won't you? The other maids would be horrified at your language.'

'Don't worry, miss,' she said. 'I'll be too keen on me food to do a lot of talking. I intend to eat all I can in case I feel sick later.'

I left her to put away my things and went along the passageway to find my mother. Mummy looked pleased when I went to see if she was ready for dinner. 'You look quite presentable for once, darling. You'll never be a great beauty like me, but you could turn some heads if you learned to make the most of yourself. This fresh-scrubbed look was fine before you came out, but you really should learn some make-up tricks. I'll have to teach you. Come over here and let me put on some rouge and lipstick.'

'No, really I'm all right,' I said, but Mummy was already brandishing a lipstick. So I was feeling rather self-conscious as we walked down the staircase to the first-class dining room. It was now full of people and the murmur of voices echoed from the high stained-glass ceiling and the gallery above. Lights twinkled from polished silver and glassware on the white-clothed tables. The maître d' bowed when he spotted Mummy. 'Miss Daniel, Lady Georgiana. The captain has requested that you do him the honor of dining at his table. This way, please.'

Mummy paused and posed prettily, to make sure the whole dining room was aware of her, and gave me a pleased little smirk as the maître d' led us down the full length of the dining salon. I glanced around, just in case Darcy was at one of those tables, but I saw no sign of him as I started after my mother. Unfortunately the fashionable and low-backed dress also had a very tight skirt. I had to take lots of little tiny steps in my unaccustomed high-heeled shoes to try and keep up with Mummy. It was unfortunate that I was halfway down the dining room when the ship gave an impressive roll. Suddenly I was tottering forward, going faster and faster and the only way of stopping myself was to grab on to the back of an approaching chair. Unfortunately also, the chair was occupied by a large bare back into which I careened with a thump. The poor woman had been about to take a sip of a cocktail and I had managed to thrust her face right into the glass. I suspect the cherry had gone up her nose as she gave a rather peculiar strangled sort of snort before she let out a gasp of indignation.

'I'm so sorry,' I gasped. 'I didn't mean . . .'

She spun on me, her face spattered with amber liquid. 'You clumsy, stupid girl,' she said in a clipped American accent. 'What sort of game do you think . . .'

Suddenly the maître d' was at my side. 'I'm so sorry, Your Highness. I should have escorted you personally, since we're going through a rough patch of water.'

For once I was not about to deny being a highness rather than a lady. The woman's face was now a picture of embarrassment. 'Oh, Your Highness. I had no idea,' she stammered. 'Of course I should have realized that the ship was rolling.'

'I really am terribly sorry,' I said. 'Is there anything I can do?'

'I'm sure I'll be fine as soon as I've wiped this off my face.'

'And I'll be happy to send you another cocktail to take the place of the spilled one,' said the maître d'. 'The captain is waiting to meet you, Your Highness.'

And I was whisked away, this time clutching his arm. We came to a central table for eight. Four people were already seated at it – the captain, looking resplendent in a uniform decorated with much gold braid, a striking Indian woman dripping with jewels, and a stout middle-aged couple – the wife wearing a rather frumpy brown lace dress. The men rose to their feet.

'Miss Daniels, Lady Georgiana. Welcome. I'm Captain Harrison. Do take a seat.' The captain motioned for Mummy to sit next to him and a chair was pulled out for me beside the Indian lady. 'May I introduce our table companions: Princess Promila, daughter of the late maharaja of Kashmir, and Sir Digby and Lady Porter. Sir Digby is the head of the British Industries Development Board.' He gestured toward my mother and me. 'I'm sure you're familiar with Claire Daniels, former duchess of Rannoch, and her daughter, Lady Georgiana.'

'Claire Daniels. Of course,' Sir Digby said, looking at Mummy with keen interest. 'Saw you on stage back in the good old days before the war, when you were still acting, didn't we, old dear? Absolutely cracking performance. Absolutely cracking.'

Lady Porter managed a weak smile. I could tell that she had looked forward to being the leading light of the captain's table and was now already eclipsed by a princess, a famous actress and me. Princess Promila gave me a warm smile as I took my place beside her. 'You are a grandchild of the old queen, are you not?'

'Great-granddaughter,' I said.

'My father spoke so highly of her. He stayed at Osborne House when he was a young man and came home so impressed. Such a little woman, he would say, and yet she commands an empire that spans across the world. He was a great champion of the British, my father.' She spoke with a clipped, almost exaggerated English accent with no trace of Indian in it. She had either had an English governess or been educated at an English girls' school.

'Do you still live in India?' I asked.

'Some of the time. I have a flat in Paris which I vastly prefer, but one is required to go home from time to time.' She waved a dainty hand languidly in a way that Westerners never can. 'I must say I enjoy my freedom away from court. Too many restrictions for a woman in Kashmir. Have you ever been there?'

'No, never. This is my first time outside Europe,' I confessed.

'You should come out to India sometime. We do throw absolutely splendid parties. No expense spared.'

'I've heard,' I said. 'My cousin the Prince of Wales had a marvelous time on his official visit.'

'Yes. He came to stay with us. I happened to be home and helped entertain him. What a charmer. Is he ever going to get married, do you think? He must be nearing forty.'

'Yes, he is. And his parents keep hoping he'll do the right thing and marry. I'm not so sure.'

'They say he has a certain American woman, don't they? Quite notorious. On her second husband, or is it her third?'

'I'm not sure. But she certainly doesn't have the makings of a future queen.'

'Fortunately for Britain she is still married to one of these husbands, so that rules out that impossible situation, doesn't it? Have you met her?' she asked.

'Yes. I'm not madly keen on her.'

'Neither is anyone except the prince, so one hears. Sharp tongue and rapier wit. I'm going to America to visit old friends, how about you?'

'I'm keeping my mother company,' I said. I saw Mummy give me a warning frown and left it at that. A wine waiter had uncorked a bottle of champagne and was pouring it into our glasses.

'Ah, here are our other table companions now, I believe.' The captain had risen to his feet again. A stocky bear of a middle-aged man was coming toward us. He had a shock of gray hair and wore round wire-rimmed spectacles that gave him an owlish look. Beside him was an incredibly sultry and glamorous woman in silver lamé with a silver fox fur draped carelessly over one shoulder. I recognized her instantly, as did everyone else in the dining salon, I'm sure.

The captain turned to Mummy. 'Surely you have already met Mr. Cy Goldman, the impresario of Golden Pictures, and of course the film star Stella Brightwell?'

The man opened his arms in an expansive gesture. 'It's Claire Daniels,' he said in a booming transatlantic voice. 'At last, we meet. You don't know how I've been longing for this moment.'

Mummy went pink, looking pleased and flattered as by now the entire dining room was focused on her. 'How do you do, Mr. Goldman.' She held out her hand. 'I've heard so much about you.'

'And of course you know Stella. Everyone knows Stella.'

The glamorous raven-haired beauty displayed a row of perfect teeth as she sat opposite Mummy. 'We meet again after so long, Claire,' she said. 'I can see that the years have been as good to you as they have to me.'

She spoke in a deep, husky voice, her English accent now tinged with years of living in America.

Mummy stared at her, then she threw back her head and laughed. 'It's Gertie. My God. Little Gertie Oldham.'

She turned to the rest of us. 'We were in a pantomime together before the war. I was the principal boy, of course, and Gertie and her sister were the babes in the wood. It all comes back to me now. Gertie and Flossie, the Oldham Sisters. Absolutely adorable. They sang, they danced, they did acrobatics. So talented. You know, I thought I recognized you when I saw your latest film.'

Stella Brightwell didn't look too amused about being reminded of her days as Gertie Oldham. 'Gertie and Flossie. Can you imagine how awful that sounds now?' Stella Brightwell gave a tinkling laugh. 'Soon after you married your duke we dropped those names and became

Stella and Bella Brightwell.' She paused to take a sip from the martini that the waiter had placed in front of her.

'And what became of your sister?' Mummy asked.

'Left show business,' Stella said. 'She never quite had my looks and talent, did she? And I was smart enough to go to Hollywood to chance my luck in films. She didn't want to leave England. I haven't seen her for ages.' She reached across and put her hand over Mummy's. 'But it's so lovely to meet you again, Claire. You know, Cy, she might be the answer to our prayers.'

'You know, you may be right, honey.' They were both staring at Mummy.

'Which prayers are these?' Mummy asked, looking half amused.

'We'll talk about it later,' Cy Goldman said. 'I'm sure these other good people don't want to be bothered with show business talk.'

'Oh, but we find it fascinating,' Lady Porter said. 'Such a different manner of living when one's own life is confined to living in an English country town and organizing the Women's Institute.'

'You do a splendid job with your charity work, my dear,' Sir Digby said. 'And you are quite the star in your amateur dramatics.' He turned to us. 'She was outstanding in *The Pirates of Penzance*.'

'Oh, Digby. We don't want to talk about my little stage triumphs.' Lady Porter tittered, going very pink.

'Were you one of the pirates?' Princess Promila asked.

Mummy choked into her champagne and managed to disguise it with a cough.

'And I don't believe we've been properly introduced yet,

Miss Brightwell,' Sir Digby went on in his fruity voice. 'I'm Sir Digby Porter and this is my wife, Mildred.'

'And let me introduce Princess Promila,' I added. 'I'm Georgiana Rannoch, Claire Daniels's daughter.'

'Pleased to meet you, honey. And you too, Princess,' Cy Goldman said. 'My, but we are a royal table, aren't we? I'm feeling like the country bumpkin here.'

'If there's one thing you are not, it's a country bumpkin, Cy,' Stella said with a laugh. 'I'll wager your palace is bigger than any of theirs.' She was looking around as she spoke. 'I don't see Juan,' she said.

'Who's Juan?' Mummy asked.

'Juan de Castillo. A gorgeous young man we met in Spain,' Stella said. 'Cy was on one of his plundering trips, you know.'

'Plundering?' Lady Digby glanced at her husband.

'Cy is creating his own castle on a hill above the Pacific Ocean,' Stella said. 'He's furnishing it entirely with antiques from Europe. He goes around raiding convents and monasteries and bringing back their treasures.'

'I do not plunder,' Cy Goldman said in his booming voice. 'I pay a fair price. They need money. I need their candlesticks and refectory tables. We both end up satisfied. You should see the stuff I'm having shipped back this time: lovely wood paneling I found at this conventon near Seville. All carved oak. And stained-glass windows dating back to the fifteenth century, wasn't it?' He turned to Stella for confirmation.

'Sixteenth, Cy. I told you before that the fifteen hundreds are the sixteenth century.'

Cy laughed. 'It's all the same to me. Old is old. And if it's old I want it in my castle.'

Stella leaned toward us. 'And he's having an entire chapel

dismantled and brought across stone by stone, window by window,' Stella said, looking at Cy Goldman as if he were an impossible but adorable child. 'And his prize plundering this time is a pair of golden candlesticks absolutely encrusted with jewels.'

'And the painting, Stella. Don't forget the painting.'

'Oh yes, the painting. A Madonna by El Greco. Found it in a monastery chapel. Cy isn't letting those out of his sight.'

'Out of reach, honey. They're locked in the ship's safe.'

Stella turned away, her eyes scanning the dining room as mine had been. 'Where is Juan? Spaniards are always so late. I take it he's to fill that empty seat at our table?'

'No, Miss Brightwell. I'm afraid the last place at table is to be taken by an American lady,' the captain said. 'Ah, here she comes now.'

I looked up to see none other than Mrs. Simpson making her way toward us across the dining room. The men rose to their feet as Mrs. Simpson approached the table, looking glamorous and perfectly groomed as always in a long black beaded dress and white mink around her shoulders.

'I'm so sorry to keep you all waiting, Captain,' she said in that low voice with the slight Southern drawl. 'You should have started without me.'

'Oh, but we have,' Mummy said, raising the glass of champagne in Mrs. Simpson's direction.

'My, my. What a surprise. It's the actress and her little daughter off on a transatlantic jaunt,' Mrs. Simpson said. 'How lovely to see you again.'

'Lovely to see you too, Mrs. Simpson,' Mummy said. 'Are you traveling alone? No Mr. Simpson in tow this time?'

'No Mr. Simpson,' she said. 'I have a spot of business to

attend to in Baltimore and unfortunately no friends were free to accompany me.'

She made it quite clear that by 'friends' she meant the Prince of Wales.

'What a pity,' Mummy said. 'Still, I'm sure you'll soon make plenty of friends on the boat.'

'Ship,' the captain corrected.

The two women stared at each other with mutual loathing. They had taken an instant dislike to each other the first time they had met and absence had definitely not made their hearts grow fonder.

'And how are you, Georgiana honey?' Mrs. Simpson turned to me. 'Still not married? The family hasn't managed to hook you up with a dashing European prince?'

'I'm afraid not,' I said. 'It seems that the family isn't very good at hooking anyone up with a suitable spouse.'

I saw the momentary flash of venom in those dark eyes, then she smiled. 'My, my. The little one is growing up and developing claws.'

'You must let me introduce the rest of our table companions,' the captain said hurriedly. And he introduced them in turn. I noticed Sir Digby and Lady Porter now looked decidedly pink and uneasy. I suspected that the rumor of Mrs. Simpson's liaison with the Prince of Wales might have finally reached the outer suburbs, even though the newspapers had been banned from mentioning the topic so far, out of deference to the king and queen.

Dinner was superb. After months of good food at Kingsdowne Place I was less impressed than I might have been when I was one step from starvation and living on baked beans, but I still worked my way merrily through every course. Mrs. Simpson was remarkably quiet for once. She answered questions politely, but that was all. Cy Goldman held the fort with tales of his estate above Malibu and the wild animals he had imported to roam around.

'Isn't that a little dangerous?' Lady Porter said. 'I've heard that zebras can be as lethal as lions.'

'We only send the difficult guests to feed them.' Cy gave a big, hearty laugh.

Sir Digby tried to steer the conversation to his wife's prowess in the amateur theater, making Mummy and Stella exchange grins.

It turned out that Sir Digby and his wife were also crossing the Atlantic for the first time. 'Sir Digby was asked to give a lecture at Harvard University and it seemed like too good a chance to turn down,' Lady Porter said. 'I must say I was reluctant. We did a cruise on the Med once and I was not the very best sailor, was I, Digby.'

'Turned positively green,' Sir Digby said. 'Puking all over the place.'

Lady Porter turned to the captain. 'So tell me, Captain. Do ships like this sink very often?'

'Only once, Lady Porter,' the captain said with a straight face.

As we rose to retire to the Palm Court where a band was playing for dancing we saw a dashing young man coming through the crowd toward us. For a second I thought it was Darcy but then I realized that the black hair was slicked down and the skin was a Mediterranean tan, rather than Darcy's Black Irish coloring. The young man's dark eyes flashed with pleasure as he saw us, and Stella hurried toward him.

'There you are, Juan. We missed you at dinner.'

'You were invited to the captain's table,' he said. 'But I was put with ladies from Milwaukee. *Madre de Dios* – how they can talk. Where is this Milwaukee, anyway?'

'Not far from Chicago.'

'We will not be visiting this Milwaukee, I pray?'

'Don't worry. We won't be going there.'

'Thanks be to God for that,' he said, flashing impossibly white teeth as he smiled.

Stella turned back to us as if reveling in a new toy. 'Isn't he divine?' she asked. 'Cy discovered him near Seville when he was plundering another convent. He speaks such good English and has done some acting too. Cy is going to make him a star, in my next movie, in fact. He's going to play King Philip of Spain to my Mary Tudor.'

'Philip of Spain and Mary Tudor?' Mummy laughed. 'They were about the least appealing couple in history. She was old and ugly and religious and he never even slept with her, did he?'

'One doesn't need to keep strictly to history.' Stella smirked. 'It is Hollywood after all.'

'Here's good old Juan,' Cy boomed, pushing through to join us. 'Let's you and I head for the brandy and cigars, old fellow, and leave the ladies to their chatter, shall we?' He turned to us. 'Isn't he the real deal? Clark Gable will be eating his heart out. And you know who else is the real deal? You, Claire Daniels. You're still it. The quintessential English rose. I don't know why you've waited so long to be in pictures. But we're going to remedy that.'

'Don't be silly. I'm an old woman now. I have a grown-up daughter.' Mummy laughed, but I could tell she was flattered. 'Come on, Georgie. Let's go and find you some dance partners.'

She slipped her arm through mine and led me away. 'And don't take any notice of anything they say, darling,' she muttered as we went back up the stairs. 'Nobody says a thing they mean in Hollywood. It's all a lovely big fake.'

I turned to watch the gorgeous Juan disappearing with Cy Goldman. There was something about him that reminded me of Darcy, apart from the Mediterranean looks and flashing brown eyes. I realized it must have been he I had spotted on the quayside, hurrying to join the ship at the last minute, and not Darcy at all. I gave a little sigh of disappointment. It seemed I had let my imagination run away with me, or maybe my wishful thinking. Darcy was clearly not on board the *Berengaria*. He didn't even know I was on my way to America. I let my mother steer me in the direction of the Palm Court from which lively musical sounds were emanating. Mummy stood at the entrance, observing the couples on the dance floor and the people sitting at tables, drinking cocktails.

'Nobody here worth knowing,' she said, after her usual rapid assessment. 'All the men are still in the smoking lounge. I honestly don't think I'll bother to wait around tonight. Some dreary woman like that Lady Digby will corner me and tell me stories about her amateur dramatic society production of Gilbert and Sullivan. I'm going to turn in, Georgie. You can stay and see if you find anyone worth dancing with.'

'There don't seem to be many people my age,' I said, looking around and not even spotting the overly friendly Mr. Halliday.

'Not in first-class, no,' Mummy agreed. 'Most of the world can't afford this kind of little jaunt. You could always have a whirlwind affair with the handsome Spaniard.'

'Mummy, I'm not the sort who has whirlwind affairs. You know that.' I had to laugh. 'Besides, he didn't even notice I existed. If he was ogling anyone, it was you.'

'Really?' she asked innocently, then gave me a self-satisfied smile before heading to her cabin.

Chapter 6

On board the Berengaria
Friday, July 13, 1934

I awoke the next morning to a light tap on the door and instead of Queenie a steward came in with a tray of tea and biscuits.

'A brisk day, my lady,' he said. 'Would you like breakfast in your stateroom?'

'Thank you. That would be lovely,' I said. 'Just a boiled egg and some fruit after that large meal last night.'

As I sat up I noticed the cabin rolling. I got up, went to the window and looked out. It was a gray morning and there were whitecaps on the waves. I rang for Queenie, who staggered in looking rather pale.

'It ain't half going up and down now, miss,' she said. 'I hope I ain't going to be sick. I don't want to miss out on the food. It's bloody good, even in the maids' dining room.'

'I've been told the secret is to eat regular small meals, nothing too rich,' I said. 'And if you feel sick go outside into the fresh air and focus on the horizon.'

'I'm feeling a bit Uncle Dick right now,' she said.

'Uncle Dick?'

'Rhyming slang for sick,' she said with a weak smile. She actually didn't look at all well.

'I'll manage to get myself ready,' I said. 'Go out on deck and then have some tea and toast.'

'Very good, my lady,' she said, which was a good indication of how ill she was feeling.

I realized that I was not feeling at all queasy. I ate my breakfast with relish then went up on deck to explore. A few people were sitting on deckchairs with rugs over their knees. A steward was going around with a tray of hot consommé. A group of young men was bravely attempting a game of quoits. I recognized one of them as Tubby Halliday. He waved when he saw me.

'Come and join us,' he called. 'It's quite a challenge with the ship rolling around like billy-o.'

I hesitated but then decided why not? 'All right.' I went over and was handed a quoit. The facts that I had never played the game before and couldn't always control what my limbs did shouldn't matter, should it? My first throw released from my hand at the wrong moment, resulting in a quoit that rolled along the deck and had to be chased down before it went over the side. My second went straight up in the air instead of toward the pin. 'Whoops,' I said. The men were nice enough to put this down to the pitching of the ship. I managed to relax and soon the pitching and rolling was part of the fun. I even landed a quoit over the pin.

'Jolly good,' said a tall young man, clearly an American by the loud check of his jacket. 'I'll have to nab you as my partner in one of the deck tennis tournaments.'

'Oh, I don't think so,' I said. 'I'm not that good.'

'In case you haven't noticed there aren't too many women under forty on the ship,' he said with rather too much candor.

'Thank you. You make me feel so desirable,' I said, rather proud of finding a comeback for once.

He flushed. 'Sorry, that wasn't very diplomatic, was it, and my old man wants me to become an ambassador some-day. I'm sure you'd be a delightful partner and you've got a good strong right arm. I'm Jerry by the way. Are you staying in town or are you heading out?'

'A few days in New York, I believe, and then we're going across the country by train.'

'To California?'

'To Nevada, I think.'

'Interesting.' Tubby Halliday had moved closer to me. 'The only reason anyone goes to Nevada is to get a divorce.'

'We might be looking at buying land,' I said, giving him a cold stare.

'No land worth buying in Nevada,' Tubby went on. 'And I see that the famous Mrs. Simpson is on board. Rumor has it that she's going home to Baltimore for that very reason.'

'Buying land?' I asked innocently.

He laughed. 'Getting a divorce from Mr. Simpson.'

'Gee whizz. Then she does intend to marry the prince,' the young American said. 'Wouldn't that be a turn-up for the books. Imagine a Yankee queen. What would you Limeys say about that?'

'It couldn't happen,' I said. 'The Prince of Wales wouldn't be allowed to marry a divorced woman. When he's king he'll become head of the Church of England, which does not accept divorce.'

'We'll see,' the American said. 'From what I've heard, she's a lady who likes to get her own way.'

'Not against centuries of English tradition,' I said.

'There's a way around anything,' the American said, taking an easy drag on his cigarette. 'Go ahead. It's your turn.'

I tossed the quoit down the deck. He was right, of course. I had thought that I would not be allowed to marry Darcy because he was a Roman Catholic and I was in the line of succession to the throne – albeit only thirty-fifth. But it had been pointed out to me that all I had to do was renounce my claim to the throne and I was free to marry whom I pleased. Since I wasn't likely to be queen unless the Black Death swept through the country again, this would be an easy decision. We hadn't announced our plans to marry yet, since neither of us had a penny to our names.

Tubby Halliday had moved closer to me. 'So is your mother really going to get a divorce? Who is she actually married to?'

'It's really none of your business, Mr. Halliday,' I said.

'Tubby, please. We're all on first-name terms on a ship. I was just interested. She is a public figure, after all, and public figures are fair game, aren't they?'

'Why this morbid interest in everyone else's life, Mr. Halliday?' I asked. 'It's not quite done, is it?'

The young American chuckled and gave Tubby a shove. 'Don't you know – he's a newspaper reporter for the *Daily Mail*. It's his job to dig up scoops.'

I felt anger welling up inside me. I have been brought up to control my emotions (a lady is in control at all times; a lady never shows what she is feeling) but I blurted out, 'You should be ashamed of yourself. Pretending to be chummy with me just so you can print horrid things in your newspaper about my mother and my family. You can count me out of your quoits and any other game you want to play.'

And I stalked off. I heard Tubby say to the American, 'You've well and truly put your foot in it for me this time, old sport.'

'I think you did that pretty well yourself,' was the reply.

Thank heavens I hadn't succumbed to his easy friendliness enough to tell him about Mummy's Reno divorce trip. She'd never have forgiven me. I decided that she would be up by now and made my way to her stateroom. As I tapped on her door I thought I heard voices. I opened the door cautiously.

'Mummy, are you up?' I called.

'Come on in, darling,' Mummy called. 'I'm not only up, I have visitors.'

I came into the room to see Cy Goldman and Stella Brightwell sitting on the sofa opposite my mother. The room was heavy with cigar smoke. Mummy was sitting up, fully dressed, face made up perfectly, looking very prim and proper, not sprawled across the armchair the way she usually sat.

'You remember our table companions from last night, Mr. Goldman and Miss Brightwell, don't you, Georgie? It seems they have staterooms just down the hall from mine. I must say the accommodations are splendid on the ship, aren't they?'

'Cy finds them quite cramped.' Stella laughed. 'But then you should see the size of Alhambra Two.'

'Alhambra Two?'

Stella gave Cy Goldman a challenging look.

'She means the place I'm building above Malibu. Just because I'm incorporating parts of old Spanish buildings into it Stella has dubbed it Alhambra Two. Actually it doesn't have a name yet.' He looked up at me and patted the sofa beside him. 'You're just the person we need, young lady. Take a seat. We're trying to persuade your mother to be in our movie. But for some reason she's the one person in the world who doesn't want to be a movie star.'

'So silly, darling,' Mummy said. 'What would Max think? What would anyone think? They'd say I was a has-been, trying to make a comeback.'

'On the contrary,' Stella said. 'They'd be amazed that you still look so young and gorgeous.'

'Oh, don't be silly.' Mummy laughed but I could tell she was flattered. Perhaps she was playing hard to get. 'Besides, I have no time to be in Hollywood. This is only a short trip then I must return to dear Max in Germany. He hates it when I am away.'

'So where exactly are you going in the States?' Cy asked.

'Reno, if you must know,' Mummy said. 'I have been tied to an annoying husband who doesn't believe in divorce. But my current beau is insisting that we get married, and I've been told that a divorce can be arranged simply and easily in Reno.'

'Yes, but not overnight, honey,' Cy Goldman said. 'Ask Stella. She can tell you. She went through it when she got rid of Freddie.'

'English husband, darling. Quite impossible. Drank like a fish and went after anything in skirts that didn't play bagpipes.'

'So how long does it take, exactly?' Mummy asked.

'There's a six-week residency requirement,' Stella said.

'Six weeks?' Mummy looked aghast. 'I have to live in Nevada for six weeks? Why didn't anyone tell me that?'

'There are ways around it,' Cy said. 'Tell her, Stella.'

'Some people check into a resort and lounge in the sun and have a good time,' she said, 'I did. It was bliss. Lovely swimming pool and gambling at night. But if you're really against being stuck in the middle of nowhere you rent yourself a little house out in the boonies, make sure you're seen around and then pay someone to take your place.'

'I can pay someone to take my place?'

'Sure you can. You let them know that because you're a famous lady you're steering clear of any bad publicity. You arrange to have food delivered, and ensure you are seen in the distance from time to time. Then you show up again when you go before the judge. They don't ask too many questions in Reno. It's a primary source of income for the state.'

Cy thumped one fist against the other. 'And during those six weeks you make a picture with us. What could be simpler? We'll put you up at the Beverly Hills Hotel. You'll come out to my castle on the hill on weekends. You'll have a ball. So will the young lady. She'll meet movie stars instead of cowboys. Much more fun than dreary Nevada.'

Mummy was fiddling with her hair – a sure sign she was nervous. 'Is there no way around this six week business?'

'Sure. You can go to Guam. I hear they'll issue you with a divorce on the spot there.'

'Guam? Where is that?'

'On the other side of the Pacific Ocean,' Goldman said. 'A long boat ride. Primitive. Grass huts. Mosquitoes. And no luxury liners like this. Tramp steamers all the way with an Oriental crew who drink.'

'No thank you,' Mummy said with a shudder.

'Or you could hop across the border to Mexico, but not all states would recognize a Mexican divorce.'

I could tell Mummy was weakening. 'What part would I have to play in this picture? I won't be anyone's mother.'

'Honey, you'll be a sexpot leading lady. A great foil for my darling Stella. You're a true-blue British gal and a real actress and that's what I need. Not some Hollywood type trying to play British.'

'And you said this was a picture about Mary Tudor and Prince Philip of Spain?' She sounded dubious. 'Where do I come into it?'

'You'd be Mary Tudor, darling,' Stella said.

'And who would you be?'

'Her sister, Elizabeth. You know, the future Queen Elizabeth I. It's going to be called *The Tudor Sisters*, or something like that, isn't it, Cy?'

Mummy shook her head. 'I'm sorry, I don't quite see . . .'

'Simple, Claire, honey.' Cy Goldman rested his cigar on the ashtray and leaned toward her. 'The story is all about romance and rivalry. Rivals for the same man, see.'

'Elizabeth and Mary? Which man?'

'Philip of Spain. It goes like this: Phil comes over to marry Mary, but he sees her little sister Elizabeth and falls in love with her instead. So Mary's going to put Elizabeth in the Tower of London and have her head chopped off, but she meets Philip's right-hand man, Don Alonso, and she makes a play for him to make Philip jealous but she falls for him. Then Philip finds out that his guy is fooling around with his new wife and they fight a duel and Don Alonso realizes he can't kill the king of Spain so he dies valiantly. Philip is remorseful and goes back to his wife. Elizabeth is brokenhearted. Good story, huh?'

'Good story?' Mummy said, looking up at me. 'It's utter rubbish. First of all there was no romance between Mary and

Philip. It was entirely political and I don't think they even slept together, did they? And Elizabeth was much younger and I'm sure she didn't come into the picture at all.'

Cy threw back his head and laughed – that great big bear laugh of his. 'It's a movie, Claire honey. It's Hollywood, not a history lesson. When history is too dull, I say we spice it up. And Americans just love your British history with all those old queens and princesses.'

'Cy's actually going to direct it himself. Think of that,' Stella said.

Cy beamed. 'You won't find a better director than me, Claire honey. It will be a tremendous hit. You'll be a star. What do you say?'

'And that good-looking boy Juan is to play Philip?'

'Absolutely.'

'But he's not much older than my daughter.'

Cy leaned across and patted her knee. 'Thanks to the wonders of modern movie make-up artists you'll look as young and gorgeous as he does. I promise. Cross my heart.'

Mummy looked at me again, then shrugged. 'What can I say? It's certainly better than spending six weeks in a Reno motel.'

Chapter 7

On the Berengaria
Still July 13

Rather rough but I don't feel seasick yet. Mummy is going to be a film star. As if she needed any more adoration.

So it seemed that we were going to Hollywood. I must say I was rather excited. I mean, one hears so much about the glamour of that place, and it would be fun to watch my mother turn into a film star. Cy had sworn us to secrecy for now, until he could organize the big press announcement back in Hollywood by which time Mummy's proxy would be spending her days in a Reno motel. I warned them that Tubby Halliday was on board and not to say anything within his hearing.

'Oh, so that's his game, is it?' Goldman said. 'I saw him hanging around the bar last night and I thought he was taking too much interest in other people's business.'

'He was trying to get out of me why my mother was going to America,' I said. 'Luckily I didn't tell him.'

'I suppose you might hint to him that your mom was going to Hollywood,' Cy Goldman said. 'That will throw him off the scent of your real purpose.'

'Brilliant,' Mummy said. 'Yes, if he asks more questions, Georgie, say that I'm accompanying my old friend Stella Brightwell to Hollywood and leave it at that.'

By the end of the day we had sailed through the squall, the sea had calmed, and the evening was bright and clear. It seemed there was to be a costume ball on our third night at sea and the talk around the ship was on what everyone was going to wear. There was even a costume hire set up in one of the onboard shops.

'What do you think, Georgie? What should we go as?'

I shrugged. 'It seems rather silly to go when we've nobody to dance with.'

'Don't be such a fuddy-duddy,' she said. 'Really, your great-grandmother comes out in you too often. It's fun to dress up and I'm sure someone will ask you to dance.'

'Do you plan to hire a costume or invent something then?' I asked. 'I haven't brought anything suitable with me, unless we wrap our sheets around us and go as vestal virgins.'

'*You* could go as a vestal virgin,' Mummy said. 'But that really would stretch my acting abilities. Besides, nobody goes in make-do outfits. They either bring them along or rent them on board. We'll go down and see what they have before all the best ones have been snapped up. I remember leaving it too late once and having to go as a cavewoman. Not my style at all.'

I followed her down to the room behind the purser's office that was now full of racks of clothing. We spent a good hour browsing through the outfits, Mummy fighting off other women for any costume she thought she might want. In the end she settled for Cleopatra. She tried to persuade me to be a mermaid, but I certainly wasn't going to wear two little shells across my front. I also rejected the merry milkmaid with far too much cleavage.

'Come on, darling. You're being difficult,' she said.

'I could be a nun, I suppose,' I said, holding up a black-and-white habit.

'Darling, no daughter of mine is going to be seen as a nun. You are hopelessly stuffy. Really I do wish that Darcy had ravished you the first time you met.'

'He did try,' I replied, blushing as I remembered that and other times that we had come very close to 'doing it,' but something had always intervened. 'And I'm not actually against the idea. It's just there has never been a good time and place.'

'There's always Brighton, darling. There's always a way if you want it badly enough. Now put down that nun's costume. I simply forbid it. Here, try on the black cat. It looks rather fun.' Mummy held it out. 'And you do have lovely long legs to show off.'

So I agreed, reluctantly. At least nobody would recognize me with a black nose and whiskers. When we came down to dinner at the captain's table the ball was the main topic of conversation.

'We're dressing the divine Juan as a cowboy. So sexy. All the women will swoon,' Stella said. 'How about everyone else?'

'We brought our costumes with us,' Sir Digby said. 'My wife is a dab hand with her needle and we always win first prize at the local garden fete. Don't we, old thing? But we're not telling you what we're going as. It's a surprise.'

'I don't bother with such childish amusements,' Mrs. Simpson said. 'I have enough dressing up in real life.'

'Pretending to be queen, maybe,' Mummy mouthed across to me. I almost choked into my lobster bisque. Everyone was chatting merrily, apart from Princess Promila, who seemed subdued and withdrawn.

'Will you be coming to the ball, Your Highness?' I asked.

She shook her head. 'I don't think so.'

She answered the rest of my questions in monosyllables and I wondered if she had felt seasick earlier in the day and was still recovering.

'So tell me, honey,' Mrs. Simpson said to me when the other side of the table was involved in a discussion about the future of the Talkies, 'what are you going to be doing in America?'

'I'm just keeping my mother company. She hates to travel alone,' I said.

'And what is your mother going to be doing, I wonder? Traveling without the handsome German? Isn't he still in the picture or is she on the prowl again?'

'Max is busy with his factories in Germany and couldn't get away,' I said. 'That's why I was called upon.'

'So is this just a little pleasure trip? I heard you might be traveling out West? For what reason?'

I remembered the gossip on deck earlier in the day. 'Pretty much the same reason that you're traveling alone, I should imagine,' I said.

She looked at me, eyes narrowed, wondering how much I knew. 'I'm just going to settle some financial affairs,' she said. 'I wondered if your mama's trip had something to do with a movie.'

'Maybe,' I said. 'I hear that someone is anxious to make a movie of her life story.'

She gave her characteristic brittle laugh at this. 'My God. Wouldn't that be something. The censors would never allow it.'

Dinner went on. I was rather proud of myself. I was no longer tongue-tied in the presence of people like Mrs. Simpson. I really was growing up at last. The handsome Juan joined us in the bar afterward and danced with Stella and Mummy. I watched Cy's face when Stella was dancing and saw a deep frown between his eyebrows. Just what was his relationship with Stella, I wondered. Hadn't a Mrs. Goldman been mentioned?

The next day dawned bright and clear. The steward appeared with tea before Queenie staggered into my cabin, still looking rather green.

'You can't be feeling seasick now,' I said. 'The sea is perfectly smooth. It's a lovely day out there.'

'I still feel it going up and down, up and down,' she said.

'What you need is a good breakfast,' I said. 'I'll dress myself. You go and put eggs and bacon in your stomach.'

She groaned. 'Don't mention food to me, miss. I don't feel like I'll ever want to eat again.'

'Well, that will save on the food bills,' I said, maybe a little uncharitably, as I was feeling remarkably well myself. 'Buck up, Queenie. Go out into the fresh air. Walk around the deck once and then eat something, if it's only some tea and toast. I promise you'll feel better.'

She staggered off and I bathed and dressed. Mummy was a notoriously late riser so I went up on deck and immediately saw my American friend, among a group of younger men, playing quoits again. 'Come and join us,' he called.

I was glad to see no Tubby Halliday among them and went over to them.

'I say. You're Georgiana Rannoch, aren't you?' one of them exclaimed.

Oh Lord. Not another newspaper reporter, I thought.

He was tall and gangly with hair that flopped forward across his forehead and a rather silly, vacant-looking face. He bounded toward me like an over-keen puppy. At the very moment I realized I knew him he said, 'I'm Algie. Algie Broxley-Foggett. We met at a hunt ball during your season. At the Windermeres'.'

'Oh yes, I do remember now,' I said. 'Didn't you set the curtains on fire?'

He grinned. 'Oh that. Silly little accident with a cigarette I thought I'd put out. No harm intended, what? I'm afraid things just seem to happen to me. Accident-prone, y'know.'

He took the quoit that was handed to him and hurled it at the peg. Instead it went sailing up into the air and struck an elderly military-looking man, taking his constitutional around the deck with his wife, in the back of the head.

'What the devil?' he demanded, spinning around.

'Sorry, and all that,' Algie said with an apologetic grin. 'Sudden gust of wind, don't you know.'

He turned back to us again. 'See what I mean? The pater says I'm an utter disaster. That's putting it a bit strongly, I think. I'd say more like a disappointment, or maybe even a hopeless case, but not a complete disaster. But he got a bit huffy when I flooded the bathroom and the ceiling came down on some rather valuable paintings. So he bought me a one-way ticket to America and told me to go out West and make a man of myself.'

'What will you be doing?' I asked.

'His pa wants him to work on a ranch to toughen him up,' my American friend said. 'He'll probably stampede the whole darned herd.'

'I probably will,' Algie said easily. 'And be trampled in the process. Serve the old man right if his son and heir is flattened and the title dies out. Come on, Georgie. Your turn.'

Strangely enough I tossed the quoit remarkably well. Maybe it was knowing that there was someone on board who was more clumsy and accident-prone than I was that gave me reassurance. After that it was suggested that we go down for a swim. It was strange to be swimming in that echoing, cavernous place. There was something sinister about it, and when Algie did a cannonball on top of a large American lady and she made such a fuss that we beat a hasty retreat, I was glad to be back in the bright sunlight.

When I finally went to seek out Mummy, she was with her film people again, reading through the script. It seems that Stella had had the script for ages and they had been looking for someone to play Mary. 'And who is to play this Don Alonso with whom I'm to fall madly in love?' Mummy asked.

'We haven't cast him yet. But someone as rugged and handsome as Juan, I promise you,' Cy said.

'This might be fun after all,' Mummy commented.

When we went down to dinner there was no sign of Princess Promila.

'She was very subdued last night,' I said. 'I hope she's feeling all right.'

'It was as smooth as a pond today,' Sir Digby said. 'Nobody could feel seasick on a sea like this, could they, old dear?'

'I feel extremely healthy,' Lady Digby said, 'but then I think it's a question of mind over matter. I am very much involved with the health and beauty movement and the Girl Guides at home and the one thing I stress is plenty of exercise and fresh air. Sir Digby and I have walked around the deck five times today.'

After dinner we went up to dress for the costume ball. As soon as I put on the black cat costume I saw that it was a mistake. I'm quite tall and thin and the costume was tight fitting, making me look like a black drainpipe with ears and whiskers at the top of it.

'You look very nice,' Mummy said kindly, 'and I'm sure you'll have fun.'

She, of course, looked stunning as Cleopatra. The black wig accentuated her wide blue eyes around which she had now drawn a black line of kohl, and she was wearing a self-satisfied smile at the looks of appreciation she was getting until we reached the ballroom and found that Stella Brightwell was in an identical outfit.

'Really, that is too bad of them,' Mummy said. 'They ought not to rent out more than one of the same thing.'

'They don't care,' Stella said, 'and besides, we both look divine, don't we, Cy?'

'I'm brimming with pride over my two stars,' he said, putting an arm around each of them. He was dressed as Benjamin Franklin with a wig and round wire spectacles and really looked the part. When Juan came up to join us, both Stella and my mother gave a small noise, halfway between a groan and a sigh. If I thought I had any chance of his showing interest in a black drainpipe with whiskers

I'd have groaned too. He was wearing tight fringed trousers, boots with spurs, a leather shirt open to his waist and a black cowboy hat. He tipped this to Stella, then took her hand and kissed it.

'I'm sure cowboys don't kiss hands,' she laughed.

'You would be surprised what cowboys can do,' he said in his husky Spanish voice. We made our way across the ballroom to a table by the window. I watched the way my mother moved, the way heads turned as she passed. Why couldn't I have inherited more of her grace and looks, I wondered. Instead I had the look and build of my healthy Scottish ancestors. Still Darcy found me desirable, I reminded myself. Then of course I became rather moony. If Darcy had been on the ship with me, we'd have danced together. We'd have strolled along the deck in the moonlight. He'd have taken me in his arms and kissed me. . . .

I sighed. Was there ever going to be a time when we had enough money to marry? I was roused from my revelry by a loud clanking and looked up to see a knight crusader standing over me. 'I say there, Georgie, old bean,' said a voice from inside the visor. 'Care for a hop around the floor?'

Oh golly. It was Algie Broxley-Foggett. The full details of the last time I had been at a ball with him returned with horrible clarity. He had spun me around so violently that we had knocked over a statue, which had fallen with a frightful crash. He had trodden on my toes and the toes of every other female. Still, I couldn't come up with a good reason not to dance with him. We clanked onto the floor and took off at a great pace, leaving a chorus of curses, groans and yelps from everyone we passed.

'I think your sword keeps sticking into people,' I pointed out.

'Oh, sorry. Can't see a bally thing with this visor on,' he said.

'Then take it off.'

'But that would spoil the effect,' he said. 'I'm supposed to be a fearsome knight, don't you know.'

'Watch it, young man,' an elderly Roman senator warned. 'You nearly knocked over my wife.'

I was glad when the dance ended and luckily Sir Digby, dressed as King Charles II, invited me to dance. Lady Porter was not too convincing as Nell Gwyn in curly orange wig and showing considerable cleavage. I observed that she watched her husband like a hawk in case he held me too closely. There was no sign of Tubby Halliday, unless he was so disguised that I didn't recognize him. When the band struck up a quickstep the young American, Jerry, whisked me around the floor, and I found that there was a big disadvantage to my own costume too. It had a long black tail that seemed to take on a life of its own, flying to and fro, slapping other dancers on the behind as they passed me, making them turn to glare in indignation. So after that I thought it might be wiser not to dance again.

At least I had a good excuse not to hop around the floor with Algie. I noticed that other ladies had similarly turned him down and he was drowning his sorrows in what looked like a lot of cocktails. I was having my own problems in the drinking department. Cocktails go to my head rather easily and Cy Goldman kept buying rounds of drinks that I didn't want.

'Come on, honey. Drink up. Put hair on your chest,' he'd say as the glasses lined up beside me. I'd take a sip or two and wondered when it would be impolite to slip away to bed. I looked up in horror as Algie staggered toward me again. He had now taken off his visor and was looking rather bleary-eyed. 'I say, Georgie. Care to trip the light fantastic again?' he asked. 'It's a slow waltz this time. Nothing too violent.' But he pronounced the word as 'schlow,' and swayed as he said it, nearly knocking over our table.

'You know, I think it's time you went to bed, Algie,' I said. 'If you try to dance again it will be another of your disasters.'

'You may be right, old bean,' he said. 'The room is swaying around a bit. Is that me or the ship tilting?'

'It's you,' I said. 'Come on. I'll lead you out.'

We crossed the ballroom without any major mishaps. 'Which deck is your cabin on?' I asked.

'A deck.'

'Oh, so is mine.'

I led him down one flight of stairs and pointed him in the direction of his cabin. Without warning he grabbed me and I found myself on the receiving end of a horribly slobbery kiss. Actually it reminded me of a Labrador we'd had when I was little – but not as pleasant. I struggled to push him away.

'What do you think you're doing, Algie?'

'Only a little kiss, old bean. For old times' sake, don't you know?'

'Just because I was helping you to your cabin didn't mean that I was inviting that sort of behavior.'

He was still holding me round the waist. 'But dash it all, Georgie. You're a girl and I'm a healthy, red-blooded male and my pater is always telling me to seize the moment, so I did.'

I didn't quite know whether to laugh or be indignant. 'Sorry, but that doesn't include seizing me. Go on, off to bed.'

'Speaking of beds,' he said, eyeing me with what he hoped was a lecherous leer, 'I say. You wouldn't fancy a spot of the old rumpy pumpy would you? Seeing that our cabins are so close to each other.'

'Thanks awfully, but no,' I replied. This time I couldn't stifle the grin.

'That's what all the girls say. They tell me American girls are easier. God, I hope so.' And off he staggered, down the passageway.

I was going to turn in myself, but my own head felt a bit fuzzy from the cocktails so I went out onto the deck and stood at the railing. An almost full moon was shining on the black water, highlighting the whitecaps of the wake. Sounds of the orchestra playing that slow waltz floated out to me. I stood there, staring out to sea, feeling melancholy and with a deep ache of yearning inside me. Suddenly, out of the corner of my eye I caught a movement. I thought I saw something come flying out of the side of the ship. Something large, hurtling down toward the water. For a moment I didn't quite believe what I had seen and thought it might be a trick of the moonlight, but then I heard the splash as it hit the waves far, far below.

Chapter 8

On the Berengaria
Late night, Saturday, July 14, 1934

I couldn't believe what I had just seen. I leaned out as far as I dared and peered down into the blackness. The moonlight was playing tricks on the water but surely something was bobbing there in the bow wave – something that looked like a person's head? Wasn't that hair floating out? Long, dark hair?

I didn't know what to do. For a moment I stood there, frozen. I'd feel stupid if I raised the alarm and I was wrong, but then what if there really was a person in the ocean? I remembered the man yanking me back when I had leaned over the railing at the dockside. What if someone as drunk as Algie had leaned too far and fallen? I ran back inside. What was one supposed to shout?

'Man overboard!' I yelled into the stairwell. Then I remembered the long hair. 'No – woman overboard. I mean – person overboard. Help. Quickly. Someone fell into the sea.'

There were a few people heading down the grand

staircase, leaving the ballroom. They sprang into action. Two men came up onto the deck with me while a third went to find a crew member.

'I was standing just about here,' I said as one of the men opened the teak chest nearby, brought out life belts and started hurling them over the side.

'Not much hope of finding someone again in the darkness like this,' he said. 'Are you sure it was a person and not someone just throwing rubbish over the side?'

'Not sure at all,' I said, 'but I thought I saw hair floating on the surface.'

'But nobody cried for help? No splashing?'

'No. Nothing.'

An officer now arrived, accompanied by other crew members.

'This was the young lady who saw it happen,' the man who had thrown the life belts said.

'How long ago was this?' the officer asked, peering down into the black water below us.

'Not long. It just happened. A few minutes ago.'

'We're traveling at twenty-six knots,' he said. 'In a few minutes a person would be miles behind us. I'll tell the captain.'

We stood at the railing, staring helplessly into blackness, and sure enough we felt the ship's engines cut and then we were turning. A searchlight was brought out onto a deck below us and eerie light played onto the water. A lifeboat was lowered but I think we all knew it was pretty hopeless. How would you ever find someone again in the vastness of this ocean, when we had been traveling away from them at a mile every couple of minutes? I felt sick and found that I was shivering. One of the men noticed this.

'You're cold, young lady. Let's get you inside. There's nothing more we can do up here. We leave it to the ship's crew now. Come along. We'll get a brandy.'

The costume ball had ended and the ballroom was deserted. No sign of my mother and her party. The men escorted me through the ballroom to the Palm Court, sat me down and put a snifter of brandy in front of me. 'Drink that up. You'll feel better,' one of them said. Actually all I wanted was to go to bed and curl up in a little ball, but I suspected that someone would want to ask me questions at some point, and sure enough before I could finish my brandy a ship's officer came up to us and said that the captain would like to speak to me. I followed the officer down long passageways, until he tapped on a door at the end of the hall, then ushered me through and I saw that I was on the bridge.

'The young lady, sir,' he said.

The captain had been standing at the helm, while other crew members were at the windows, looking out.

'Take over for me, Higgins,' the captain said. 'One last circle then we have to call it quits.'

'Very good, sir.'

The captain turned to me, then I saw recognition in his eyes in spite of my cat costume. 'Ah, Lady Georgiana. It's you. I was just told a young woman, dressed as a cat. Please do take a seat. This must have been most distressing for you.'

I nodded. I was still shivering as I sat on the chair a crew member had brought over to me.

'So you saw someone fall from the ship and into the sea? Are you sure of this?'

'The problem is that I don't know exactly what I saw. It all happened so quickly. I just caught the movement out of the corner of my eye.'

'Did anyone else see it?'

'No. I was all alone on the deck at the time.'

'And you don't think you imagined it? The moonlight can play tricks out on the ocean, especially after a night of drinking and dancing, maybe?'

I shook my head. 'I definitely saw something.'

'Tell us exactly what you thought you saw.' He pulled up a chair beside me.

I frowned, trying to re-create what I had seen. 'I was standing up on A deck, looking out to sea and I thought I saw something come out of a window farther down the ship and I watched it fall into the sea. I heard a splash and when I looked down it seemed to me that long dark hair was floating on the surface.'

'You're sure it was a person that you saw?'

'Not at all sure. It could have been a big object. A big bundle.'

'A bundle, you say?' he asked sharply. 'What made you use that word?'

I shook my head. 'I don't know. It just came out.'

'And when you looked down into the ocean you didn't notice anyone struggling or splashing or calling for help?'

I shook my head. 'No movement at all.'

'No white face? White limbs?'

'No. Just a dark shape and the hair floating out.'

The captain glanced across at the officer who was standing beside me.

'Would you say that whoever or whatever this was fell straight down or maybe jumped out first?'

I thought again. 'I couldn't say. I just caught movement and had an impression of something falling. Something quite large and dark.'

'And where did it fall from, do you think?'

'I believe it must have been from my level,' I said. 'From A deck, quite a way to the right of where I was standing. I suppose it could have come from one deck below me, but I don't think so.'

'Toward the stern, you mean?'

'Yes.'

'So that would be a part of A deck where there is no promenade deck. Where the cabins have windows that open directly onto the side of the ship?'

'Yes, I think so.'

'Make a note of who has those cabins on the starboard side, Jones,' the captain said.

'Do you want to speak to their occupants right away, sir?'

The captain shook his head. 'No, I think not. If our search doesn't turn up anyone in the sea tonight and nobody is reported missing by morning then we'll have to take the next step, but at this moment I don't want to alarm the passengers unnecessarily. Brooks should be reporting back from the lifeboat any minute. Personally I think it highly unlikely that we'll find anything. Looking for a needle in a haystack would be an easy task compared to this.'

I had been feeling sick and scared ever since the incident, but now I was conscious of another feeling. Somebody was watching me. I felt a tingle go up my spine as I turned around, trying to see if there was anyone else on the bridge with us, but I saw nobody.

'I think you'd better go to bed, Lady Georgiana.' The captain patted my hand. 'Thank you for your quick action, but there's nothing more you can do tonight. In the morning you'll have to make an official statement.'

I got to my feet, a little shakily.

'Johnson, escort Lady Georgiana back to her cabin,' the captain said, 'and have her show you exactly where she was standing and what she saw.'

A young seaman took my arm. 'This way, my lady,' he said and led me from the bridge.

As I went I heard an officer say, 'What do you think, sir? Any connection?'

'Could well be,' I heard another voice say softly – a smooth, deep voice that spoke in little more than a whisper. 'If she says she saw something, then she did.'

'So we should check the princess's suite right away?'

'Absolutely.'

I turned back to look but the door closed as I was halfway down the steps and I heard no more. The princess's suite? I remembered that Princess Promila had not shown up at dinner. Surely they didn't suspect that she had met with foul play?

The young seaman led me out onto the A deck promenade and I pointed out exactly where I had been standing and what I had seen. Then he escorted me to my cabin. There was no sign of Queenie, which wasn't surprising as she hardly ever managed to stay awake for my late nights and had been moaning like Banquo's ghost every time she had put in an appearance. I managed to get out of the cat suit and took off the black nose and whiskers before I got into bed and pulled the covers over me. What a strange night, I thought. How awful if someone had fallen overboard by accident after a little too much to drink. But then why had there been no signs of a struggle if someone had fallen into the water? Why no shouts for help? Had someone decided to commit suicide and thus decided not to struggle as they sank into the waves? It didn't seem likely. And what if I'd only seen something completely harmless, like someone throwing an unwanted object out of the window? But what object could be that large? And what could have floated out like long human hair on the water?

The alcohol in those cocktails and the subsequent brandy were starting to make the room swing around. I closed my eyes and wished that sleep would come. I was just drifting off when I heard a tiny noise – the click of a latch being turned, or a key being turned in a lock. Someone was coming into my room. I was instantly awake and alert. Surely I'd locked my door, hadn't I? And only the steward had a passkey. A sliver of light showed as the door opened inch by inch, then a dark shape was silhouetted against the light. A tall man, dressed in dark clothing, was coming into my room.

In an instant I was on my feet, looking around for some sort of weapon. How annoying that everything was bolted down on a ship. There was no vase, no bedside lamp, no jug on a washstand. All I could think of was the fruit knife in the bowl of fruit on the table and that would be hardly sufficient to ward off a determined intruder. Nevertheless I reached for it and felt the coldness of the mother-of-pearl handle as my hand closed around it.

'Don't come any closer, I've got a knife and I'm not afraid to use it,' I said bravely.

I heard a deep chuckle as the intruder came at me, grabbed my wrist with the knife in it, holding it up while he pulled me to him with the other arm and silenced the scream I was about to give with a kiss. For a second I was too stunned to react. Then all resistance melted away in an instant. I knew those lips well. For a long moment I forgot to be annoyed with him, then I pushed away from him as his arms wrapped around me.

'What the devil do you think you're doing, scaring me half out of my wits?' I demanded.

Darcy was smiling down at me. I could see the glint in his eyes in the light shining in from the passageway.

'Sorry. I had to stop you from screaming somehow and this seemed like the best way.'

He went to the door and closed it as I switched on the light over the bed. He looked at my hand that still clutched the fruit knife and started to laugh. 'That was the knife you were going to defend your honor with?'

'It was the best I could do, given the circumstances,' I said. I sank down onto the bed and he came to sit beside me.

'What are you doing here, Darcy?' I asked. 'I thought I spotted you on the dock but I decided I must have made a mistake because I haven't seen you since.'

'Nobody's supposed to know I'm on the ship,' he said, putting up a finger to touch my lips in a gesture that sent shivers down my spine. 'I didn't even know you were on board until I saw the passenger list. Then, of course, I couldn't contact you, which was infuriating. I shouldn't have come here now but I wanted you to be forewarned in the morning when you're summoned to a meeting and find that I'm there.'

'But why the secrecy? Are you running away from the law or on some kind of mission?'

'Rather more of the latter,' he said, 'but I'm afraid I can't tell you about it at the moment. How amazing that it was you who saw the person go overboard. I nearly choked when I was on the bridge and saw you brought in. I had to duck down the steps in the corner so you didn't see me.'

'It's funny but I sensed you were there,' I said. 'I think after what I'd just experienced I might have fainted dead away if I'd seen you.'

He shook his head. 'Not you. You're made of sterner stuff.'

'The problem is that I really don't know what I saw, except it looked like long hair floating out in the ocean. Do you think a person went overboard?'

'We won't know until someone is reported missing,' he said. 'The captain has done a good job of retracing our course but I'm afraid anybody in the ocean could have drifted or been swamped by a wave or just given up by the time we got there. And if there was no sign of a struggle, as you said, then they may have been unconscious or even dead by the time they hit the water.'

I shivered. 'Don't. It's too horrible. One minute we're all having fun at a ball and the next something like this happens.'

He put an arm around my shoulders. 'So – you were having fun at a ball without me, were you?'

'If you really want to know it was awful. Mummy chose a black cat costume for me that made me look like a black drainpipe with whiskers, Cy Goldman kept trying to force cocktails down me and an awful chap called Algie Broxley-Foggett was dressed as a knight in fake armor and insisted on dancing with me, knocking over everyone in the process. So no, I was not exactly having fun.'

Darcy grinned. 'Broxley-Foggett? He was at school with me. Scrawny little chap when I was in the sixth form. Absolutely clueless sort of fellow. I believe he set the dorm on fire once, trying to practice smoking.'

'Yes, that would be Algie. He also set the curtains on fire when I was at a hunt ball with him once. He's being sent out to America to make a man of him.'

'Lucky America,' Darcy said. 'He'll probably bring about another Wall Street crash.' He stopped talking and gazed at me, smiling. 'It is so good to be here with you, if only for a few moments. What are you going to be doing in America? I had no idea. I thought you were still at Kingsdowne when last I heard.'

'I'm traveling with my mother. This is strictly hush-hush, but she's trying to get a divorce and now it appears she's going to be making a film with Cy Goldman and Stella Brightwell.'

'Is she, by George? So she sees herself as a film star now. What happened to the German?'

'He wants to marry her, and I don't know how he'll feel about his future wife on the silver screen. But I don't think she could resist the chance to be famous and adored again. Mummy does love being adored.'

'Don't we all.' He took my face in his hands, drew me toward him and kissed me. Then somehow we fell back together onto my bed and it was more than kissing. It was almost as if I was in a dream, a small voice somewhere in the background whispering that I should stop now before it was too late and yet knowing I didn't want to.

Suddenly a great shaft of light fell onto us and a big black shadow stepped into the room.

'I came to see whether you wanted undressing, miss,' said Queenie in a peeved voice, 'but I can see you're already undressed.'

Chapter 9

When the steward came into my cabin the next morning he acted as if nothing was amiss. I don't mean about Darcy and me. Darcy had left reluctantly but in haste after Queenie's arrival, warning her not to say a word about his presence on board or I would sack her on the spot. I had fallen asleep with a smile on my face, knowing that he was close by, on the ship with me.

'Good morning, my lady,' the steward said. 'Another beautiful day. We are having a most fortunate crossing this time.'

Most fortunate? Not for some unlucky person, I thought and wondered if anyone had been reported missing by now. I was just finishing my tea and biscuits when Queenie appeared, looking bleary-eyed.

'The one time I manage to stay awake is the one time you don't want me around,' she said, glaring at me with hands on her broad hips. 'I said to myself, "She'll never be able to get out of that blinking cat suit without help so I'd better make sure I don't nod off." So I sat up on me bunk until I heard the last waltz played. And then when I came in I saw you'd got the cat suit off very nicely by yourself. Or with a little help from the gentleman, maybe.' She gave me a knowing look as she came across the room and picked up the cat costume that was lying on the floor. 'Who'd have thought he was on board with us? That's a turn-up for the books, ain't it? Or did you know and weren't saying nothing?'

'I didn't know, Queenie, and you mustn't mention it to anyone. Mr. O'Mara is on some kind of secret mission.'

'Cor blimey,' she said. 'He don't half lead an exciting life, don't he?'

'Doesn't he, Queenie,' I corrected.

'Well, he do, don't he?'

I sighed. She was never going to learn.

'Shall I run your bath then?' she asked. 'And what do you want to wear?'

'I think the navy blue linen trousers and a white blouse, please.'

She went across to the closet. ''Ere, I'm sorry about barging in on you last night when you were in the middle of a bit of the old how's yer father.'

'Yes, I was sorry too,' I said.

'You should let me know in future when I'm not to bother you. Tie a ribbon on the door or something.'

'Queenie, I wasn't exactly planning something like that.'

'Nobody ever is,' she said. 'At least that's what my old mum tells me. She said she'd been to the pictures with my dad and they took the long way home by the canal and next thing she knew she was expecting me and they had to get married in a hurry.'

'I'll remember not to walk home via the canal,' I said.

The loudspeaker in my room suddenly crackled into life. 'Attention, all passengers. There is to be a lifeboat drill for all passengers at ten o'clock ship's time. That is ten o'clock at your lifeboat station for all passengers. You do not need to bring your life jacket. This is only a drill. Repeat, this is only a drill.'

'I wonder what that's all about,' Queenie said. 'We already had one lifeboat drill when we came on board. We can't have hit an iceberg, can we?'

I looked out of my window and saw people out on deck in short sleeves. 'I think it's highly unlikely,' I said.

As I took my bath I realized I knew the reason for the drill. They needed to know if anyone was missing without alarming the passengers. I dressed, went down to breakfast and heard plenty of expressions of annoyance that the morning was being interrupted by another ridiculous drill.

'It's not as if we're on the *Titanic*,' one woman was saying.

It was obvious that not many people had heard about the incident last night and I wondered if those who did know had been asked to remain silent about it. I managed to eat a hearty breakfast then went up to my lifeboat station on the top deck. My mother, Cy Goldman and Stella Brightwell joined me.

'What a stupid waste of time,' my mother said. 'How many lifeboat drills does one need?'

'I think they're up to something.' Cy peered over the side. 'I think they want us out of the way on the promenade deck.'

'Up to what?' Stella demanded.

'Well, why did they ask if we had thrown anything out of our cabin window or whether anything was missing?' Cy asked.

'That was certainly strange,' Stella agreed. 'I couldn't see what they were getting at. I said I may have tossed out a cigarette butt from time to time.'

I said nothing. At our lifeboat station they took a roll call and kept us waiting for quite a while. It was only when mutiny was threatened that they let us depart again. I was just returning to my cabin when I saw the officer from last night approaching.

'Lady Georgiana. The captain would like a word, if you don't mind.'

I was escorted back up the stairs to the officers' quarters at the stern of the sundeck. I was shown into a pleasant sunny cabin paneled in dark wood. A definitely masculine room. The captain rose to his feet as I came in. Another officer was standing behind his desk and I reacted as I saw Darcy was standing over by the window.

'Ah, there you are, Lady Georgiana,' the captain said. 'Good of you to come. May I introduce First Officer Higgins and I believe you are acquainted with Mr. O'Mara.'

'Yes,' I said, managing not to smile. 'Mr. O'Mara and I are acquainted.'

'Please take a seat.' He motioned to a leather sofa. 'You might have guessed what was behind that muster on the lifeboat deck just now.'

'Presumably you wanted to see if anyone was missing.'

'Quite right.'

'And what was the result?' I asked.

'All present and correct, apparently.'

'Then I must apologize for raising a false alarm,' I said. 'I did hesitate before I called for help. I was never quite sure whether what I saw in the water was a person or not.'

'I would have dismissed the incident as something quite

harmless had it not been for a piece of disturbing news given to us two days ago. You met Princess Promila at our table. You noticed she was not present last night. She is extremely upset by the apparent theft of a large and very valuable ruby she had in her possession. It is called the Star of Srinagar and is a priceless family heirloom.'

'She didn't give you the jewel to put in the ship's safe?' I asked.

He shook his head. 'She likes to wear her jewelry. Besides she felt quite safe in the knowledge that her jewels were either on her person or in her jewel case in her cabin.'

'Was she wearing the ruby when it was taken?' I asked.

He shook his head. 'It was in her jewel case, so she says. But she swears her personal servant never left her suite.'

'And could the servant maybe have been bribed to help with the robbery?' I asked.

'The servant is an old family retainer, so devoted that she sleeps at the bottom of the princess's bed.'

I looked across at Darcy. 'Do you think this is somehow connected to what I saw last night? Is that why you brought me up here?'

Darcy came over and perched on the arm of my sofa. 'It's possible,' he said.

'But if a jewel was stolen, the thief would hardly throw it over the side of the ship, would he? Not unless there was a boat waiting to pick it up below, and there wasn't.'

Darcy nodded. 'I agree it is perplexing. But the occupants of the cabins from which your object could have been thrown have sworn that they were not responsible for throwing anything out of their windows, and that nothing appears to be missing.'

'If you thought the item you saw thrown into the water

was a person it must have been quite large,' the captain said.

I nodded. 'It's hard to say how large as it was hurtling down toward the ocean when I noticed it, but it was a good size.' I held my hands apart to demonstrate.

'And shape?'

'No definite shape. Someone mentioned the word "bundle" and I think that describes it. Maybe various items wrapped in one bigger piece of cloth?'

Darcy shifted position on the arm of the sofa. 'It would make perfect sense if people's cabins had been robbed while a ball was going on, and the thief tossed down the items to be picked up by an accomplice, except that we are in the middle of the Atlantic Ocean, nothing has been reported stolen last night, and we have seen no sign of any other ship around.'

'To be out here in a small boat would be folly,' the captain said. 'A ship our size could easily obliterate a small craft without even noticing it. And how would it have got this far from land? No. I have to say that the scenario you suggest is impossible. So the question is if not to hand something over to an accomplice then why throw something out of a window?'

'Somebody trying to get rid of something incriminating,' I suggested.

Darcy shook his head. 'But what? What would you need to get rid of in the middle of the ocean that couldn't easily be thrown out in New York Harbor?'

'If someone thought that cabins would be searched?' I said.

'Searched for the missing ruby, you mean?' Darcy asked. 'Unfortunately it is extremely easy to hide a precious stone on a ship this size. Shove it among the life jackets, stick it into a potted palm. Our best hope is searching every passenger at disembarkation – and what a stink that will cause.'

'But the very act of throwing out the object has now brought about that very thing,' the captain said. He looked across at Darcy. Darcy put a hand on my shoulder, an action that gave me an instant electric shock and made me forget what we were talking about for a moment.

'Georgie, what you don't know is that one of the reasons for the lifeboat drill was to search every cabin for the princess's jewel. Obviously we didn't have enough time to do the job really thoroughly but there were plenty of cabins we knew we didn't need to search. Those families traveling in second class, elderly clergymen, aged spinsters . . .'

'What about the crew's cabins? Did you search them too?'

'In this case it wasn't necessary,' Darcy said. 'You see the reason I am on this ship is that I'm on the trail of a notorious cat burglar, responsible for a string of jewelry robberies. We suspect he's a gentleman. He always leaves behind a black glove at the scene and the burglaries take place at society gatherings. Whoever he is, he's dashed clever, and daring. He's lifted things from under people's noses.'

'And left no trace, no evidence?'

'Not a thing, except that one of the gloves had the letters *BOB* written in ink on the label. Whether that was something put on by the manufacturer or the shop that sold it we don't know. Since our burglar is meticulous we can assume that if he wrote it there, he wanted us to know something. He was teasing us.'

'You keep saying "he,"' I said. 'You're sure this is definitely a man?'

'Since we suspect he can shin up drainpipes, cross ledges, open windows and perform various other athletic feats, it would have to be an exceptionally strong and agile woman. Also if it was one of the guests at various house parties, as we suspect it might be, a woman would be hampered by what she wore.'

'And you have reason to think he's on this ship?'

Darcy nodded. 'Two reasons, actually. We know an attempt was made to steal the princess's jewels once before in Paris. And we know that Stella Brightwell is on this ship.'

'Stella? You think she might be involved in this?'

Darcy leaned closer to me, his hand on my shoulder now squeezing tighter. 'This is not to go beyond this room, Georgie, but the only thing that links the burglaries is that Stella Brightwell was present at each of the gatherings.'

'Golly,' I said, forgetting to be sophisticated. 'You can't think she's the cat burglar. Why would she need to be? She's a film star. She's rich.'

'Stranger things have happened before now,' Darcy said. 'Some people turn to crime for the excitement, even when they don't need money. However, she has a watertight alibi for each of the robberies. When the crime was committed she was with a group of people, playing bridge, sitting at a dinner table, or in bed with Cy Goldman . . . all occasions on which it would have been noticed if she had left the room.'

'So it is true then,' I said. 'She's Cy Goldman's mistress? I thought they seemed awfully chummy.'

Darcy nodded.

'But doesn't he have a wife? I'm sure she was mentioned.'

'He does,' Darcy said. 'Mrs. Goldman spends most of the year in their penthouse in New York. She doesn't like the West Coast, apparently.'

'And she doesn't want to divorce him for carrying on with other women?'

'Some people find divorce is too tiresome,' Darcy said. 'And the current situation probably suits her just fine. She has all the advantages of being Mrs. Goldman. . . .'

'Except one,' First Officer Higgins commented.

I looked up and went bright red. Darcy grinned.

'As I was saying,' he went on, 'Mrs. Goldman has all the advantages of his wealth and position but she doesn't actually have to put up with him. I'm sure you've noticed he is not the easiest of men. I've been told he likes his own way all the time. He flies into temper tantrums if he's crossed. Like an overgrown two-year-old. But then men like him have what it takes to succeed. I don't know if he's told you his life history yet. He's very proud of it. He came to America as a young man at the turn of the century, after his village in Russia was burned to the ground. He came with nothing, did any job he could lay his hands on, met Thomas Edison, saved up and bought his own movie camera, then moved out West and started shooting pictures. Now he owns one of the most successful studios in the world. He can afford to be difficult.'

'So he would also have been present on each of the occasions that a burglary took place?' I asked.

Darcy grinned. 'I can't see him climbing through a window or up a drainpipe, can you? And burglary is not in his nature. I'm sure he has ruined plenty of men. I'm sure he could kill with his bare hands, but nothing sneaky. Everything he does is larger than life.'

'You say the thief attempted to rob the princess in Paris. Why did that not succeed? Was the thief seen?'

'No, unfortunately. The princess had a visitor who had brought her little dog. The dog started yapping and they found the bathroom window had been forced open. The burglar must have come around the side of the building on a ledge. I tell you, the chap has nerves of steel, I'll grant him that.'

'So what are you going to do now?' I asked.

'Search passengers when they disembark, but I suspect it's easy to hide a precious stone. Apart from that we can only hope that the thief is encouraged to strike again.'

'Encouraged, how?'

Darcy gave me a long look. 'I thought we might use you as bait.'

'Oh, I say. Steady on,' the captain interrupted. 'You can't do a thing like that.'

'Me? I'm known to be penniless. I have nothing worth stealing.'

'You are related to the richest people in England. What if you let slip that Queen Mary has given you a special piece of jewelry, a rare old family piece and you really should have left it in the bank, but it's so pretty that you wanted to bring it with you?'

'And you think the gentleman thief will believe that? Having never seen me wear anything more startling than a strand of garnets or pearls?'

'It's worth a try. The royal connection might be irresistible.'

'But shouldn't I be flashing this piece around?'

'Hint that you've left it safely in your jewel case in your cabin. Then see if the thief comes to take the bait.'

'And you want me to stay in my cabin to catch the thief? What about when I'm asleep?'

'Have your maid stay in the cabin when you're not there and we'll have it watched at night. It is the last night before we land. We don't have much time.'

'Queenie? You want Queenie to do something brave and responsible?' I had to laugh.

'She's been pretty brave before, Georgie. Hopeless in many ways but certainly she has spunk. Didn't she try to clobber me once when I was sneaking into your room?'

I went pink again and nodded. 'It's worth a try, I suppose.'

Darcy stood up, patting my shoulder as he did so. 'Good, then chat freely to your fellow passengers, especially at dinner, and we'll see.'

I was about to get up too when someone banged on the captain's door. A worried young officer came in. 'Captain, sorry to barge in like this, but a Mrs. Waldeck has reported a diamond ring missing. She knows it was in her jewelry case as she took it off after the ball last night. And when she went to put it on, after the lifeboat drill, it was gone.'

'So your thief has not been idle after all,' the captain said, looking at Darcy.

Chapter 10

On the Berengaria
Still July 15

I followed the captain and Darcy as we made for Mrs. Waldeck's cabin. She was a skinny, almost gaunt, American woman with a beaky nose that made her look like a bird of prey. And at this moment she looked ferocious enough to pounce on any of us.

'What kind of ship are you running here?' she demanded. 'You hire crew members who are criminals and thieves – send us up to the top deck for a completely unnecessary lifeboat drill, insist that our servants also leave their posts and then wonder that valuable jewels get stolen. What did we need another drill for, I'd like to know? We are not children. We learned our lifeboat stations on the first day out. And now here comes this stewardess saying, "Hurry up. Everyone wanted on deck," as if we were a flock of ducks.' She paused for breath then wagged a threatening finger at us – a finger dripping with rings. 'I expect you to search every cabin and have my ring restored to me before we dock in New York or there will be hell to pay. Believe me, Mr. Waldeck is not a forgiving sort of man. He will be furious. The ring came from his mother and is valued at over ten thousand dollars.'

'Mrs. Waldeck, I assure you we will do everything within our power to find your ring. Are you sure you didn't just drop it or mislay it?'

Those birdlike eyes glared at him. 'Captain, I am a most careful woman. I do not drop or mislay things.'

'I do apologize, Mrs. Waldeck. As I said . . .'

'Mrs. Waldeck,' Darcy interrupted, 'have you had any visitors to your cabin, apart from the steward? Anyone who could have noticed where you kept your jewel case?'

'Nobody – except that movie actress woman, Stella Brightwell. She did come in here one evening but I didn't let her in.'

'Stella Brightwell?' the captain said. 'Is she a friend of yours?'

'Never met the woman in my life. I heard someone trying my door handle when I was getting undressed. I opened it and there was Stella Brightwell. She was a bit tipsy, I think. She apologized and said she had an identical suite one floor above ours and she had come up in the elevator and must have pushed the wrong floor button.'

'Easy enough to do, I suppose,' the captain said.

'If one has consumed too much alcohol. I was in favor of prohibition, myself. And these actresses – they may look pretty but not a brain in their heads. In the old days it used to be the true upper classes who traveled on ships like this. Not so-called Hollywood royalty. I don't know what the world is coming to.'

The captain escorted me back up the stairs while Darcy

and other crew members searched Mrs. Waldeck's cabin. Having instructed Queenie that she was to stay in my cabin until told that she could go out, I went up on deck. Queenie had not been happy. 'But what if you don't come back and I miss me dinner?' she demanded.

'Until recently you were groaning that you could never face food again,' I pointed out.

'Ah, but I got me sea legs now and me appetite has come back. And bloody good food they serve here too.'

'I'll make sure you don't miss your dinner, I promise,' I said. 'But stay unobtrusive. Keep the curtains partly drawn so that nobody can see you're in the room. And if anyone tries to come in, call for help right away.'

'What exactly is this in aid of?' she asked.

'You are not to say a word to anybody, but someone may come to steal my jewels.'

This made her convulse in laughter. 'Gorn!' she said. 'You ain't got nothing worth stealing with yer.'

'I know that, but the thief may not. Try to get a good look at him.'

'What if I'm in danger and he clobbers me?'

'I don't think that will happen. If he sees you, he'll simply disappear.'

'Bob's yer uncle then,' she said.

I worried a little as I went out onto the deck. I worried whether she'd spill the beans, or whether she might get hurt. But first I had to do my part and spread the word about my valuable jewels. It seemed that the ship was buzzing with rumor. I saw Algie Broxley-Foggett with Tubby Halliday and a group of young men. Algie waved. 'Did you hear there has been a daring robbery?' he asked.

'I heard there had been several. All jewels,' a young

American said. 'Rather stupid not to keep the good stuff in the ship's safe, I'd say.'

'But such a bore if you want to wear it in the evening,' I said. 'I'm borrowing a divine bracelet from my cousin Queen Mary and I'm not keeping it in the safe. She said to me, "My dear, jewels are to be worn and enjoyed, not locked away," so I'm obeying. But my cabin is locked and my maid keeps an eye on it, so why worry?'

'Presumably this woman who had the diamond ring stolen has a maid and a locked cabin,' Tubby Halliday said. 'I do hope they catch the blighter.'

My opinion of him rose a little until he added, 'It will make a terrific scoop for me. Burglar caught red-handed on luxury liner. Your correspondent witnesses arrest – or better still aids in the capture.'

'Then you'd better start prowling the halls to see if the thief strikes again,' Algie said, 'not wasting your time playing quoits with us loafers.'

Darcy did not show his face all day. Nothing untoward happened and the only visitor at the cabin was a stewardess who knocked on the door with a pile of clean towels, asking if I had telephoned to request extras. I said I hadn't and she went again. Evening came, my last evening on the ship. It should have been a romantic occasion – a final ball at sea and my beloved on board to dance with me. But my beloved and I were both occupied with trying to catch a thief and this would be a last chance for that thief to strike. I had butterflies in my stomach as I told Queenie to lay out my white silk evening pajamas. There was to be a black-and-white ball after dinner and for once I'd be dressed in something fashionable. I put them on and added a jet ornament to my hair and a jet bangle. Then I went the whole hog and put on a touch of bright red lipstick and a little rouge.

Mummy nodded in approval when I went to find her. 'The duckling is finally growing into a swan,' she said. 'The outfit suits you. Did you hear about the burglaries? I've been closeted with Stella and Cy all day and my maid has only just told me. Thank God I never travel with my good jewels. How stupid can you be to bring valuable stones on board a ship?'

She was wearing a backless black evening dress that accentuated her still wonderfully slim and boyish figure and sported long white gloves and a delightful little white feather cap on her head. Over one glove she wore a sparkling bracelet. Seeing it gave me an idea. 'Mummy, can I possibly wear that tonight? The jet is a bit drab.'

'It's only costume jewelry, darling.' She pulled it off. 'Here, have it.'

I slipped it on. Hoping but not hoping that the thief would think it was real. Off we went to dinner and for once I enjoyed heads turning as we passed. Still no sign of Princess Promila. Mrs. Simpson wore the black beaded dress again, proving that she had nobody on board she needed to impress. The talk was naturally all about today's robbery.

'They called us all on deck, and of course the robber took that opportunity to strike,' Sir Digby said. 'Thank God Lady Digby leaves her good jewelry in the bank when we travel.'

'I can't imagine anyone traveling with real jewels,' Mrs. Simpson said. 'I have paste copies made and leave the real ones at home.'

'Exactly what I do,' Mummy said. 'I mean, whom does one need to impress on a ship?'

'I couldn't agree more,' Mrs. Simpson said.

The two women looked at each other, for one rare occasion on the same side and in agreement.

At a table close by we heard Mrs. Waldeck loudly lamenting her stolen diamond. Dinner ended and we made our way up to the ballroom for the black-and-white ball. Everyone looked rather splendid and seemed to be having a good time. I looked around, hoping that Darcy might have come out of hiding. Instead I saw Algie, heading toward me with a look of determination on his face.

'Care to hop around the floor, old bean?' he said. 'It's a slow number so I won't tread on your toes too often.'

Pity overtook regard for the safety of my feet. Off we shuffled onto the crowded dance floor.

'So where will you go when we step ashore?' he asked me.

'A couple of days in New York, I gather, and then a train across the country and ending up in Hollywood where my mother might be persuaded to take part in a film. Who knows what she'll do?'

'Crikey,' he said. 'Whizz-bang, what? It will be dashed exciting, watching a film being made. I don't suppose they'll need any good-looking young British extras, will they?'

'I doubt it,' I said.

'No, of course not. Dashed stupid idea as usual.'

'So where will you go?' I really was feeling sorry for him now. How would someone so hopeless survive in the cutthroat world of America?

'Not sure, actually. Where they have ranches, I suppose. Where is that? Texas? Kansas? I really have no idea. And frankly I'm not sure any ranch would want me. I do ride rather well, so that might be in my favor.' He sighed. 'Oh well, if nothing works out, I'll come and visit you in Hollywood.'

Oh golly. I couldn't very well say, 'Not if you were the last man on earth,' could I?

The dance ended and the slow foxtrot turned into a fast-paced jive.

'Oh jolly good. The jive. My favorite American dance. I've been practicing,' he said.

'Oh, no, I don't think . . .' I started to say when my partner started flinging me around the floor. I became a lethal weapon, hurtling toward other couples like a bowling ball toward ninepins.

'Algie, stop. Do stop,' I tried to shout over the blast of trumpets.

'You're doing fine, old bean,' he yelled back. 'Isn't this fun?'

Since I had just knocked an elderly couple off the floor I could hardly agree, but Algie had turned into a wild thing and kept grabbing me and hurling me before I could collect myself. When someone equally uncoordinated careened into Algie's back he did let go of me and I went flying across the floor, out of control. The doors out onto the deck were open and I hurtled toward them, past surprised faces and out into the night.

'Whoa, Georgie, what are you doing?' Darcy appeared from the darkness of the deck and grabbed me before I could bounce off the ship's rail.

'I'm so glad it's you,' I said, feeling his arms around me. 'That idiot Algie Broxley-Foggett was dancing the jive with me. He's quite lethal.'

'Then let's hightail it away before he comes looking for you.' Darcy put an arm around me and shepherded me toward the prow of the ship. Suddenly we were alone in the darkness. Strains of music floated out across the water.

'This is nice.' I beamed up at him.

The music turned into a slow waltz. 'Would you care to dance?' Darcy said and took me in his arms.

We waltzed together in the darkness, and although I usually had to think of the steps when I danced, suddenly my feet weren't touching the ground. I was conscious of the warmth of his body against the thin silk of my outfit and his arms holding me so close that I could feel his heart beating. I nestled my head against his chest, enjoying the feeling of safety and contentment. I was sad when the music ended.

'I shouldn't really be out here.' Darcy looked around, but the foredeck was deserted, apart from us. He went over to the railing and looked out. I followed him and he pulled me close to him again. 'But frankly at this moment I don't care. If the gentleman thief doesn't know I'm on his trail by now then he's not as smart as I thought he was.'

'Princess Promila wasn't at dinner again tonight,' I said. 'She must be very upset.' Then another thought struck me. 'I suppose she really is Princess Promila? The burglar couldn't have snuck on board, killed the real Princess and dumped her body over the side?'

I felt Darcy holding me a little tighter. 'You're suggesting that my jewel thief is a woman and has killed the real Princess Promila?'

'It's a possibility,' I said.

He frowned. 'But the princess's faithful retainer would surely notice the difference.'

'Unless her faithful retainer is also a fake?'

'But the number of passengers adds up – unless?' He paused. 'We didn't count on a stowaway when we did our cabin check. I suppose stowing away wouldn't be impossible on a ship of this size.' He was staring out past me, trying to assess the situation, or visualize the princess's suite.

'Couldn't you check up on the princess after she leaves the ship? Follow her? Make sure she's genuine?'

'I could. I believe she said she's going to stay with the Astors. They'd certainly know if she was a fake.' He stared out to sea. 'So did you spread the word about your valuable jewels?'

'Yes, I did. And I stayed in my cabin most of the afternoon but no visits from the burglar. So I thought I should make the bait more tempting. I borrowed something flashy from my mother. It looks quite real, doesn't it?' I held up my arm, then I said, 'It's gone.'

There was no longer a sparkling bracelet on my wrist.

'When did you see it last?' Darcy asked.

'Before I started dancing with Algie. But he was flinging me around a lot. It's possible it just got knocked off from my wrist and is lying somewhere on the floor.'

'Possible,' Darcy said. 'Do you remember anyone dancing too close to you? Bumping into you?'

'Actually I was bumping into other people,' I said. 'Algie's idea of the jive was quite dangerous.'

'We'd better go back and look,' Darcy said. 'I don't really want to show my face in there, but would you go in again and look for the bracelet? Let people know it's missing. Seem upset. Watch reactions.'

'I suppose so,' I said. 'Why does something always seem to come in the way when we're together? Are we destined to have no more than two minutes alone and in peace?'

Darcy stroked back a curl that had fallen across my face then ran a finger down my nose, resting it on my lips. 'We just have to be patient for now. I'm trying my hardest to make some money – to make up for everything my father lost. One day I'd like to buy back our family home. And the racing stables. Big dream, I know. But I can't marry you and set you up in a horrid little flat.'

'Darcy, I don't need much.'

'You are the daughter of a duke, granddaughter of a princess. I'm going to provide for you properly or not at all.' He gave me a quick kiss on the forehead. 'Now go in there and see what you can do.'

I held his arm. 'When will I see you again?'

'I really don't know. I don't think I can show my face at disembarkation, just in case . . .'

'Will you stay in New York? We're going to be there for a few days.'

He sighed. 'I can't tell you, Georgie. I have no idea where I'll be going after this, or whether I'll be summoned straight back to England. I'll have to wait for instructions. You won't be long in America, will you?'

'Who knows? If Mummy gets a taste of Hollywood stardom our trip may drag on.'

'So you'll be going to Hollywood with Stella and Goldman?' He started to say something, hesitated, then said, 'Look, I don't want you to do anything in any way dangerous, but you could keep an eye on Stella Brightwell for me, couldn't you? Nothing silly like searching her room or anything, but seeing if there are any more burglaries . . .'

'Seeing if she wears the princess's ruby?' I asked, grinning.

He shook his head again. 'No, forget it. It's all too ridiculous. It has to be someone else. Let's just hope we find something when the passengers leave the ship. The New York police will be coming on board and they'll have the authority for a thorough search of anyone we might suspect.

Not that it will be pleasant. In fact I suspect there will be an awful fuss.' He grinned then touched my arm lightly. 'You should go or the ball will be over.'

Inside the ballroom the band now broke into a quickstep. I gazed up at Darcy, memorizing every feature, the way his eyes crinkled at the side when he smiled, the way a lock of dark curl always flopped forward across his forehead, the little cleft in the middle of his chin.

'I'll see you soon,' he said. 'I promise. I do love you, Georgie. You know that.'

I nodded, feeling tears welling up. 'I love you too.'

He drew me to him, kissed me hard on the lips, then let me go. Reluctantly I went back into the ballroom. I went over to where I had been sitting beside Mummy and Stella. 'I'm afraid I've lost your bracelet,' I said. 'I had it on when I was dancing with Algie. Now it's not there.'

'Don't worry, darling. As I said, it's only a copy. And the clasp was always a bit loose.' She sighed. 'I think I'm going to bed. I thought there might be a man or two worth dancing with, but Stella is hogging Juan and frankly there is nobody else. And I do wish people wouldn't keep staring. Really it is so tiring being a celebrity. You'll notice Mrs. Simpson never bothers to show up at these things.'

She got up, picked up her white fur wrap and flung it carelessly over her shoulder. 'Coming?' she asked.

'Actually I think I'll stay a little longer. I might want to dance again.'

'After that outing with the clod-footed oaf I should have thought you'd had enough dancing for a while.'

I smiled. 'You never know.'

Off she went. Stella and Juan came back to join me. 'Your mama has gone to bed?' Stella asked.

I nodded. 'Nobody worth dancing with. But I have to look for my bracelet. It was rather valuable and now I've lost it. It must have come off my wrist while I was dancing.'

'We'll help you look, honey,' she said. 'Won't we, Juan?'

I watched her as she went around the room. She really appeared to be searching diligently. Would she have had a chance to remove my bracelet when we were sitting together, or as I got up to dance with Algie? It seemed too stupid to consider. I spotted Algie sitting alone with a glass of something green in front of him. I went over to him.

'You didn't happen to see my bracelet, did you? It must have fallen off when we were dancing.'

'Golly, no,' he said. 'That's a rum do, isn't it? Was that the valuable bracelet you were talking about? Must have fallen off when we were spinning around. Do you want me to help you look?'

So now he joined Stella. Soon the word got out and half the crowd was searching, but the bracelet didn't turn up. In the end I went to bed. As I opened my cabin door the first thing I heard was a fierce snort of some wild animal. I turned on the light to find Queenie, lying on my bed, mouth open and snoring. And the second thing I saw was my bracelet, lying on my bedside table.

Now I was really perplexed. Was it possible I had forgotten to put it on after all? No. I remembered showing it to people, mentioning how it had come from the queen and was a priceless piece. So how had it got here?

'Queenie?' I asked. I had to repeat her name, louder and louder, until she gave a final quick snort and opened her eyes. 'Oh, wotcher, miss. Had a nice dance then?'

'Queenie, did anyone come into the cabin while I was out?'

'I don't think so. I must have nodded off when it got late. But no one knocked on the door.'

It was a perplexing puzzle. Queenie helped me undress then went back to her own quarters. I half hoped that Darcy would come to visit me again, but he didn't.

Chapter 11

Monday, July 16, 1934

New York ahead. I must say I'm excited to see America for the first time!

Our last morning on board dawned with no new reports of burglaries and we had to busy ourselves with packing my belongings, ready to go ashore. I realized then that there was no way that everyone could be searched properly. A jewel could be stuffed into the toe of a shoe, wrapped among stockings, handkerchiefs or even cut into the pages of a book. A clever thief would have no problem getting the jewel past the police.

Outside my window I saw people assembling on deck. I went to look and there in the distance was the New York skyline. I left Queenie to finish the packing and went out to join the others at the railing.

'There she is,' I heard someone say. And there ahead of us, against a sky still streaked with dawn light, was the Statue of Liberty. What an inspiring sight with her lamp glowing.

I could understand why immigrants had watched her and wept. Beyond were the skyscrapers of the New York skyline. I had no idea that buildings could be so tall. We sailed closer and closer until we docked right under the shadow of those buildings. As I looked down at the dock I saw that it was swarming with policemen. Golly, I thought. Did they always search this thoroughly after a robbery? Or was it possible there was something to my suggestion that someone had done away with the real Princess Promila? Had the splash I had heard, the hair I had seen floating out, really been a person after all? A person who had been murdered first and thus had not tried to struggle when she hit the water? And a person with brown skin would not have been easily identifiable as such among black waves. I felt sick just thinking about it.

Gangways were laid down, and all those blue uniforms came aboard. We were instructed to proceed to the first-class lounge where there was a lot of complaining about being kept waiting and officious customs officials wanting to poke their noses into baggage. When our turn came, Mummy and I were given the most perfunctory of checks before we were allowed ashore. I kept expecting to be taken aside for questioning but nobody said anything or stopped me as I left the *Berengaria*. I wondered if I should say something about my suspicions and maybe have them give the princess an extra grilling, but I realized that was up to the captain and Darcy. They must know what they were doing.

I looked back at the ship, hoping for a final glimpse of Darcy, but he was nowhere to be seen, probably at a good vantage point, watching the passengers disembark. I wished I knew what his plans were now. It would have been reassuring to know he'd also be in New York. I wondered if there were things he hadn't told me about this assignment. I never knew with him.

On the dock we were swept into the hustle and bustle and soon were riding in a taxicab to the Plaza Hotel, where Stella and Cy and Juan would also be staying. Queenie, Mummy's maid, Claudette, and the luggage followed in a second cab. The drive was quite alarming along those narrow streets between towering buildings. I had never imagined that buildings could be so tall. It was hot and sultry and unsavory smells wafted in through the taxicab windows. Every street corner seemed to have shabby-looking men standing on it. We were aware that there was a great depression in London, but here it felt much worse. Then we moved to a cleaner, smarter part of the city, pulled up in front of the Plaza Hotel and suddenly it was as if a fairy had waved a magic wand and transported us to another world.

'Ah yes,' Mummy said as doormen rushed to open our taxicab doors and help us out. 'This is more like it. For one awful moment I thought we'd have to skip New York and head straight for the train station. But I think this will do nicely for a few days.'

Our rooms were lovely, overlooking Central Park, and the whole hotel felt fresh and clean as if it had been repainted just for us. What's more, it was cool – which was welcome after the oppressing heat of the city. That evening Cy hired a horse-drawn cab and we went for a drive in Central Park where the breeze off the lake made it bearable to be outside. I found that I couldn't help thinking about all those poor people lining up for bread or sitting out on their steps with looks of hopelessness on their faces. I had grown up shut away from the real world. Now I was becoming all too aware of what life was like for so many people. If ever I had money and a position, I'd try to do something about it, I decided.

We dined with Mr. Goldman, Stella and Juan, who were taking an aeroplane to Los Angeles in the morning. This gave me one last chance to help Darcy and play my part as a detective. I brought the missing jewels casually into the conversation with what I hoped was girlish enthusiasm.

'I wonder if those jewels will ever be found, don't you?' I said. 'In a way it was rather exciting to know there was a jewel thief on the ship.'

'Not if you were the one who had the jewels stolen,' Mummy said. 'Then it would have been decidedly tiresome.'

'Oh God, yes. Dealing with insurance companies is a nightmare,' Stella added. 'But what about that bracelet you lost last night. Was that stolen, do you think? Did you report it?'

I gave a little laugh. 'Oh no. It was silly of me. I just mislaid it and found it again later in my cabin.'

I watched her face and didn't detect even a flicker of wariness. Of course someone who could cross a ledge to reach a window would have nerves of steel, wouldn't they? But as I looked at that flawless face with her long dark hair spilling over her shoulders I found the whole notion absurd. Surely she couldn't be our gentleman burglar in spite of the coincidences? As a film star and Cy Goldman's mistress, what could she possibly need with other women's jewels?

'Well, I think I'll make it an early night, if we're to catch a plane in the morning,' Stella said as we finished our coffee. 'We'll see you in Hollywood then, Claire, darling.' She gave my mother a kiss a few inches from her cheek. 'You should consider flying, like us. I don't know why you're taking the train. So tedious and dusty and full of horrid little people.'

'Not for me, thank you,' Mummy said. 'Far too many crashes on planes, even if the train does take longer.' She stood up and looked around the room with satisfaction as Cy blew us both a kiss and followed Stella from the room. 'Well, this is nice, isn't it? A few days to shop and play by ourselves.'

On the way out of the dining room we bumped into Sir Digby and Lady Porter.

'We meet again, Miss Daniels,' Sir Digby said. 'How very pleasant.'

'What a surprise to find you staying here, Sir Digby,' Mummy replied, her voice displaying no enthusiasm.

'We decided to see New York for a few days before we go up to Boston,' Lady Porter said, 'and we were told this is the place to stay. Horribly expensive though. And I don't think we'll be staying long. I haven't liked what I've seen so far. So dirty and noisy, isn't it?'

'Lady Porter is a country girl at heart,' Sir Digby said. 'She doesn't like big cities, although we've heard that Boston is supposed to be relatively civilized.'

'Are those Hollywood people also staying here?' Lady Porter asked.

'They are taking an aeroplane flight in the morning,' I said.

'Heavens. How adventurous.' Lady Porter snorted. 'Dangerous things, aeroplanes. But what about Princess Promila? I understood she was supposed to be staying here. I expect she likes to eat in her room. Not terribly sociable, was she?'

So Princess Promila was also here? I waited until Mummy was busy with her various face creams and went down to the front desk.

'Princess Promila?' The clerk looked through his register. 'She did have a reservation but she canceled it at the last minute.'

Of course that made me wonder whether they had discovered that the princess on board was really an impostor and had been apprehended on leaving the ship. It was so frustrating not to know. And now Stella Brightwell would be out of my reach. I was just dwelling on that very thought when the elevator opened and Stella herself came out. She glanced around quickly then crossed the foyer.

I only hesitated for a second, then followed her. She was walking fast and with purpose. The streets were still full of people on this warm evening and I tried to keep her in sight without giving away my presence. She crossed a major boulevard and then turned north, along the side of the park. This was very different from the New York I had seen earlier today. We passed grand mansions with long sleek automobiles waiting at the curb. The sounds of jazz music and laughter floated from an open window. Stella kept walking fast and then turned in to a side street.

My heart was racing with excitement. She had claimed she was going to bed early and here she was, slipping out without Cy. I realized I might be on the verge of solving a crime. If only I knew where Darcy was. This street was a quiet backwater, lined with trees planted at intervals along the curb, and Stella's high heels echoed from the tall buildings. I tried to move quietly, dodging from tree to tree so that she didn't know I was following her. Then I became aware of something. Light footsteps behind me that paused when I paused. Someone was following me.

I glanced back but saw nobody. And yet I had been in danger often enough in my life to sense a prickle on the back of my neck now. Had Stella worried that I was poking my nose into her business and was I being lured right now into a dark and deserted corner? Was it her accomplice who was following me? I hesitated, trying to decide if I should give up and go back to the safety of the Plaza, when Stella turned a corner yet again and came to a halt outside a grand-looking apartment building. She glanced around and I leaped back behind a tree just in time. I watched her studying the row of names in the box beside the front door, then she stood looking up at the windows, frowning.

Was this another place she planned to rob? Was she casing the joint, as they would say? Then a doorman appeared. She exchanged a few words with him, nodded, then turned away, walking back quickly in my direction. I flattened myself against the tree trunk as she hurried past me. As soon as she had passed I went to follow, then let out a little shriek of fear as a dark shape stepped out from a stairwell, blocking my path.

'And just what do you think you are doing, wandering around New York alone at night?' said a very familiar voice with a slight Irish tinge to it.

Darcy's eyes were shining in the light of the streetlamp.

'Are you going to make a habit of scaring me out of my wits?' I demanded. 'I thought someone was following me.'

'I was supposed to be following Stella,' he said. 'You got in the way. And terrible shadowing, by the way.'

'Thanks a lot,' I said. 'I thought I was rather good.'

'If that was a real criminal type you were trying to follow, you'd be lying dead by now.'

He was smiling down at me.

'Well, I sensed that you were following me. So the same goes for you. I was rather worried that it might be Stella's accomplice, luring me to a dark street because I'd chatted about the jewel thief.'

'Why would you do that?'

'I wanted to see if I got a reaction from her.'

'One day you'll push your luck too far, my lady. I asked you to keep an eye on her, that's all.'

'I was. I was following her. And now we have to find out what she wanted with that building and why she didn't go in. Do you think she had some kind of assignation there or was trying to drop off the jewels?'

Darcy shook his head. 'I'm afraid it's simpler than that. She was keeping an eye on Mr. Goldman.'

'He's in this building? Why?'

'Because his wife lives here. I think Stella wanted to make sure he was only visiting his wife when he sneaked out, and not another woman.'

'Oh, no. How funny.'

Darcy put an arm around my shoulder. 'Come on. I'll walk you back to your hotel.'

'This is a nice surprise,' I said as we walked with his arm around me. 'I was wondering when I'd see you again.'

'I expect I'll keep turning up like a bad penny,' he said.

'So the jewels were not found on anyone leaving the ship?' I asked. 'Do you still suspect Stella?'

'They weren't found. And yes, Stella is still a suspect. That's why I've been observing her.'

'What about Princess Promila? She was supposed to stay at the Plaza and then canceled at the last minute. Isn't that fishy?'

'I understand that she has gone to Newport, Rhode Island, to stay with the Astors,' Darcy said. 'That should be easy enough to verify.'

'So you think she is the real thing?'

'Yes, I do.'

We crossed Fifth Avenue.

'It's a lovely night,' Darcy said. He took my hand and led me into the park. We passed other couples, sitting on benches, or walking arm in arm. When we came to a deserted bench we sat. Darcy took me into his arms and kissed me. The kisses were long and delicious and left me breathless. After a while I sat with my head against his shoulder. I wished the moment could go on forever. Then I remembered that I had crept out without telling my mother where I was going. She'd probably be worried.

'I really should go back,' I said. 'I left without telling Mummy.'

'Do you really think your mother would notice you were gone?' Darcy laughed.

'Probably not. But I should get back just in case.' I stood up and pulled him to his feet.

Our shoes crunched on the gravel path as we made our way back to the lights of the city. His hand was warm in mine. 'Do you think you might be following Stella out to California?' I asked. 'She's taking an aeroplane in the morning.'

'Who knows?' Darcy said. 'I'm waiting for a wire from London to see what they want to do next. And to see where the ruby might turn up.'

'I wish you were coming with me.' I looked up at him, taking in the familiar details of his face.

He paused. 'I'd better not be seen at the Plaza. Just in case. So I'll say good-bye here, Georgie. Take care of yourself and don't do anything silly, promise?'

'I might say the same for you,' I said. 'You know I worry about you.'

'I'll be just fine.' He brushed back a strand of hair from my cheek. Then cupped my head in his hands and kissed me again. 'It won't be too long. I promise,' he whispered. 'Now off you go.'

Mummy was lying propped against the pillows reading a magazine. She barely looked up as I came in. 'Been downstairs, have you? Anything fun going on?'

'No, rather quiet actually,' I replied. 'How long do you plan to stay in New York? Cy and Stella are leaving tomorrow.'

'I have to do a little shopping first, darling,' she said. 'I'm told there will be nothing in Reno. And one has a duty to see what New York has to offer.'

So after breakfast Mummy went off to attack the New York department stores and I went to sit by the fountain in Central Park. Suddenly I saw two familiar figures coming toward me: Algie Broxley-Foggett and with him Tubby Halliday.

'What ho, old bean,' Algie said. 'Fancy bumping into you again.'

'Oh, you're still here, I see. Not off to the Wild West then?'

'I'll get around to it when the money runs out, I suppose,' Algie said. 'But Tubby here has things to do in New York and his newspaper is paying for his hotel so I took advantage of his kind offer to share a room. Where are you staying?'

'The Plaza,' I said.

'My, my. Hear that, Tubby, old bean? She's staying at the Plaza. We'll simply have to come and visit.'

'I don't think you'd better,' I said hurriedly. 'We're leaving any moment and I'm with my mother.'

'Well, that's not too friendly of you,' Algie said. 'I've always wanted a tour of the Plaza.'

'I thought you were heading for Hollywood,' Tubby said.

I looked at him warily, trying to remember how much of this was common knowledge. 'For a short while, I think.' I stood up. 'I had better be getting back. My mother will wonder where I've gone to.'

I felt them watching me as I walked away. Why was Algie so keen to see inside the Plaza? And what was Tubby doing in New York?

Chapter 12

On a train to Reno
Friday, July 20, 1934

We stayed in New York for a couple of days – long enough for Mummy to shop at Bloomingdale's and declare everything a sad imitation of last year's Paris, to go to a show and Mummy to declare it lacking the polish of the West End – and then we boarded the Lake Shore Limited, bound for Chicago and eventually the Wild West.

The first part of the trip was delightful as we followed the Hudson River up its valley. We dined on rather a lot of unmemorable food, fell asleep to the rhythmic rocking of the train and awoke in Chicago. We had to endure rather tedious hours in the ladies' waiting room in the station before we could board the California Zephyr and off we went again. The next section was flat and uninteresting until we crossed the Mississippi River, had dinner, and darkness fell across a huge expanse of sky. I'd never seen a world in which there was just land, unclaimed, unused land, as far as the eye could see. And the sunset – we never had sunsets like that at home – as if the sky were twice as large as in England and had been painted with a giant paintbrush in primary colors. It was magical. I decided I was going to like it here. We were served breakfast in Denver and then a day of mountains and emptiness. Once we spotted a lone horseman, but I think he was the only person we saw for hours. We fell asleep in the middle of nowhere and awoke to find the train had stopped in Reno. Then we had to summon the maids, gather up the bags and make a rather hurried departure. We watched the train pull out, leaving us on an empty platform in the middle of nowhere.

'Where do you think the main part of the town is?' Mummy asked, looking around.

'I think this is it,' I replied, examining the straggle of clapboard shacks, a few low brick buildings and the feeling of a true Wild West town in the middle of empty brown scrub. It was extremely hot and dusty and a mirage hung over the track. We left the maids and the luggage and set off in a taxicab to the office of a lawyer Cy had found for my mother. Electric signs flashed from unlikely cottages, advertising speedy marriage and divorce – sometimes both at the same place. We turned into what must be the high street as it had a big sign across it advertising Reno as 'The Biggest Little City in the World.'

'If this is a city, then I'm Charley's Aunt,' my mother said. 'I've never seen a drearier place, have you? Thank God I don't have to really stay here for six weeks. I'd go mad.'

We found our lawyer – who looked almost like a caricature of a slick villain. He had a large paunch, a hair-thin mustache, smoked a big cigar, and talked out of the side of his mouth. 'Don't you worry your pretty little head one bit,' he said, putting a big hand on Mummy's shoulder. 'Cy

Goldman told me to take care of you and take care of you I will. "Take care of my new star," Cy says, and whatever Cy says, Cy gets. Know what I'm saying?'

He whisked us off to the Riverside Hotel, told us that a stay had been arranged in a bungalow at a dude ranch where they asked no questions, and that Mummy's stand-in would report for duty as soon as Mummy wanted to check out. I could tell from her face that she'd like to check out in the next five minutes. However, we did what we were told. The papers were filed with great ceremony. We walked up and down Virginia Street in the evening, visited casinos, and made sure that plenty of people noticed Claire Daniels.

'This is certainly not Monte Carlo,' Mummy said, coughing in the smoke-laden atmosphere as we walked between craps tables and penny slot machines. 'I hope Max appreciates how I'm suffering for him. At this moment I could be at the villa on Lake Lugano, at my own dear little house in Nice or in London at Brown's. I never believed I could feel so homesick and so far away.'

I shared her feelings. I lay listening to the mournful toots of goods trains as they rattled past and wondered what Darcy was doing at this moment and when I'd see him again. Had he caught his gentleman cat burglar? I wondered.

'Cor, miss, this is bloomin' awful, ain't it?' Queenie said. 'If this is America, give me good old England any day.' Since she came from the backstreets of Walthamstow, near the gasworks, it really must have been bad.

It was hard to sleep with the heat and the trains and I was glad when we moved away from the tracks, out of town, to a ranch in the middle of the dusty desert. At least it had a swimming pool and shading cottonwood trees. Mummy refused to swim and stayed out of the sun. 'I'm sure Queen

Mary Tudor did not have a tan,' she said. 'The English aris-
tocracy have always been noted for their porcelain white
skin. Look at you, darling. If you go in the sun you just
freckle. You turn into a revolting orange blob, darling.'

'Thanks, awfully,' I said. 'You really know how to boost
my confidence.'

She slipped an arm around my shoulder. 'Sweetie pie,
nature isn't fair, is it? Some of us are born beautiful and
some aren't. Take your Darcy, for example. I'm sure he was
a devastatingly handsome little boy, whereas you were such
a homely child.' She walked away then turned from the door
and added, 'I wonder sometimes what he sees in you.'

With a mother like her, I thought, who needs a Mrs.
Simpson to deliver catty remarks?

I was extremely glad when Mummy's awful lawyer paid a
visit, introduced us to Wanda, who was to play the part of my
mother while she was in Hollywood, and said that Mummy
was free to leave. Queenie and Claudette perked up at this
news and packed our things in record time. Then we were off
on a train again, first across the Sierra Nevada mountains to
San Francisco and then down the coast to Los Angeles.

'I'm having horrible second thoughts about this whole
thing,' Mummy confided to me in a rare moment of inti-
macy. 'I mean if that dreadful place can call itself the best
little city or something, then what do you think California
will be like? One hears about Hollywood glamor but will
it really be more dust and shacks and men spitting on the
streets, do you think?'

'Golly, I hope not,' I said.

The train ride across the mountains was spectacular. We
changed trains, caught a glimpse of San Francisco Bay, and
then we were off again on the Coast Starlight. The first part

of the trip was nowhere near the coast and all we saw were golden hills and more golden hills. We fell asleep and when we awoke there was the sparkling Pacific Ocean right beside us. We breakfasted and soon after we pulled into the Los Angeles station.

As we stood on the platform a young man with slicked-back hair, horn-rimmed glasses, and a worried look on his face came hurrying toward us. 'Miss Daniels, Lady Georgiana?' he said. 'I'm Ronnie, Mr. Goldman's assistant. He sent me to collect you. They are filming at the set and he couldn't get away, but he wants me to say that all is ready for you and I'm to take you to the Beverly Hills Hotel.' With great efficiency he whisked us across the station, made porters appear as if by magic, and in seconds had us seated in an impossibly long black motorcar, then directed the maids and luggage to a taxicab that looked nothing like a London taxi. As we drove away from the station I gazed out of the window in excitement. There were pastel villas dotting wooded hills and when I spotted the Hollywood sign up on top of a hill my heart gave a little leap. We were really here! Who couldn't feel excited about being in Hollywood?

Soon we were driving along Sunset Boulevard, lined with fine-looking new buildings in bright pastel shades. A tram-line ran down the middle of it and there were motorcars everywhere. The depression that had been so visible in New York clearly hadn't struck here. Mummy had perked up considerably since arriving, and when we turned into the driveway of the Beverly Hills Hotel she gave a little squeak of pleasure. It was a pink palace with palm trees and brilliant tropical plants turning it into a fantasyland.

'I think you'll be quite comfortable here,' Ronnie said with understatement.

Young men in crisp white uniforms rushed out to greet us. Instead of being taken into the main building of the hotel, we were led through the grounds, past a big sparkling swimming pool, to our own bungalow set amid more riots of tropical foliage. Bougainvillea spilled around the front door. Spiky bird-of-paradise and hibiscus lined the path. The sunlight and colors were dazzling and the air was heady with perfume.

'The first thing we shall need is sunglasses, darling,' Mummy said. 'I can't risk getting frown lines.'

'I'll have an optical store bring you a selection right away,' Ronnie said. 'Do you think you can survive here for the time being?' He opened the door to a sumptuous interior, gold and white wicker furniture and white filmy curtains at the windows. There were two bedrooms and two bathrooms, and a small maid's quarters behind.

'I think we'll manage,' Mummy said. Luckily I wasn't asked, or I might have said something childish like 'golly.' The contrast to one who has survived years of Fig's frugality and Castle Rannoch's damp cold was overwhelming.

'Great, then I'll have the sunglasses guy come over and anything else you need today? If not, get some rest and the car will come for you at six o'clock tomorrow.' Ronnie was already heading for the door.

'Six o'clock? For dinner?' Mummy asked.

Ronnie laughed. 'No, six a.m. Cy wants you on the set. We're already shooting. Your final script will be delivered later this afternoon with the scenes for tomorrow marked up.' He glanced at his watch. 'I'd better be going. Cy gets mad if I'm away too long. And order what you like from the restaurants and bars. Just sign for it.'

'Well,' Mummy said as the door closed behind him.

'This isn't bad, is it? Apart from having to learn lines by tomorrow. I don't think I'm going to take to films. On the set at six a.m.? Really not me. Thank God the theater is more civilized.' She sank onto the brightly upholstered sofa and picked up a peach from an enormous bowl of fruit on a rattan table. 'Frankly, darling, I don't know why I agreed to this. I mean, I don't need the money. I don't really want to become a film star. It must be Stella's fault.'

'Stella?'

She took a bite of peach then looked up at me. 'I suppose it was just that I wanted to prove to Stella that I still had it. You know, last time we worked together she was just a little nobody. I was the big star of the pantomime and Stella and her sister were the novelty act – skinny little girls with big eyes like waifs. They were quite good little dancers and acrobats, I seem to remember, and they adored me.' She sighed, remembering being adored, I suspected.

The luggage arrived with Queenie. She looked around with approval. 'This ain't half bad,' she said. 'I think I'm going to like California. They were telling me on the train that everybody's equal in America. None of this bowing and scraping and calling people "my lady."' And she gave me a disapproving stare.

'If you want to find you still have a job when we return to England, I suggest you don't get carried away by what is done in America,' Mummy said. 'Face it that you're hopeless, Queenie. Nobody else but my good-natured daughter would employ you. Now hurry up and unpack your mistress's cases. I'm sure she'd like to go for a swim while I study.'

Queenie stomped off.

'That girl is getting too big for her britches,' Mummy said. 'You may have to replace her whether you like it or not.'

'I know,' I said, 'but it's rather like taking in a stray animal that you know can't survive on its own. You're stuck with it.'

'Not me, darling. You must learn to be more ruthless. It's the only way.' She went to the window and looked out. 'We'll have to go shopping before anything else. Our clothes are simply too formal for California. Look at those women in shorts. And none of them has a good bottom.'

The sunglasses arrived. Mummy found some shorts and halter tops in the hotel shop then settled down to study her script while I was banished to the pool. It was surrounded by lounge chairs, nearly all occupied by impossibly tanned bodies. I had just found a free lounge chair when a rather splendid lady came to sit beside me. Unlike everyone in shorts, she was wearing a long silk gown and trailing flimsy scarves, one of which was tied around 1920s-style bobbed hair. It was hard to say how old she was, as she was wearing a lot of make-up and big sunglasses.

'Well, hello there,' she said. 'I never see skin as white as yours in California. Look at you – absolute porcelain white-ness. You must have come straight from England where I'm told the sun never shines.'

'Not very often,' I agreed.

'Ah, so I'm right. You are English.'

'Half Scottish, actually.' I found I was stumbling over my words in the way I always did in Queen Mary's presence. She was quite an overpowering lady. 'Actually a quarter Scottish and a quarter German.'

'Interesting,' she said. Then she wagged a finger, bedecked with rings and red-painted nails. 'I bet I know who you are. There was a whisper going around that a royal personage was coming to stay here. You must be she. Am I right?'

'No, I'm not exactly royal,' I said. 'Queen Victoria was my great-grandmother, so the king is my second cousin, or is it first cousin once removed?'

'See, I knew it!' The woman gave a cackling laugh. 'That's royal enough for us out here, honey. Say, do I have to call you "Your Highness?"'

'Oh, no,' I said. I was about to say that 'my lady' was the correct term of address but I remembered what Queenie had said about everyone being equal in America. I didn't want to start off on the wrong foot here. 'My name is Georgiana, but everyone calls me Georgie.'

The woman stuck out her hand. 'Welcome to America, Georgie, honey. I'm Barbara. Barbara Kindell. I live here at the hotel and if you need anything you just ask me.'

'Thank you very much,' I stammered. We in England were not used to such friendliness. 'Are you also part of the film business?'

'In a way, Georgie, honey. In a way,' she said. 'I'd better let you go for your swim while I make a telephone call.'

As I lowered myself into the pool I was conscious of a small, wiry dark-haired man sitting with his legs dangling into the water and watching me with interest. Of course then I was horribly self-conscious of my lack of swimming ability. I did a dignified breaststroke up and down the pool, then when I stopped the small man slid into the water beside me. He had an interesting face with dark, alert eyes. Not exactly handsome but there was something about him – a confidence, maybe, in spite of his small stature. He swam over to me with easy strokes.

'You want to watch what you say to Barbara,' he said, 'if you don't want it splashed across the front pages of every newspaper in Hollywood.' He grinned at my surprise. 'She's our leading gossip columnist, sweetie. She prowls these places like a shark.'

'Crikey,' I said.

The man burst into laughter. 'Now that's a word I haven't heard in many years.'

I noticed then that he had a trace of English accent in his American-sounding speech.

'I'm sorry,' I said. 'I know I should sound more sophisticated but words like that just slip out, especially when I'm nervous.'

'You shouldn't be nervous around me. I'm a real friendly sort of guy,' he said. 'And do you know you have lovely long legs. I adore women with long legs.' And to my amazement he ran a finger gently up my left thigh.

'I think I should go and see how my mother is getting along,' I said, making for the steps.

'I'll see you around then, you sweet creature. Someone completely unspoiled – now that's a rarity for Hollywood. What a challenge.'

As I got out of the pool, my face rather red, I suspect, I met Barbara Kindell coming back from her telephone call. She beckoned me over to her. 'Watch out for that one, honey,' she said. 'He eats little girls like you for breakfast.'

'Who is he?' I asked.

She threw back her head and laughed. 'You don't recognize him, sweetie? He's Charlie Chaplin.'

I looked back and saw that the little man was now sitting on the side of the pool again, looking at me with amusement in his eyes. He looked nothing like the comic figure I had seen on the screen.

I was about to make for our bungalow when I saw a sight that stopped me dead in my tracks. A large person in yards and yards of a red and white frilly bathing suit was coming toward me. On her head was a red flowery bathing cap. She looked like a buoy floating off the coast and it took me a second to recognize her.

'Queenie!' I stammered. 'What on earth do you think you're doing?'

'Going for a swim, miss. That pool don't half look good.'

'Queenie. You are a lady's maid. You simply can't swim in the pool with your betters,' I said.

'Why not?' She glared at me defiantly. 'This is America. We're all equal. I do my job when you need me and when you don't need me I can do what I like in my own free time. That's what they told me on the train.'

I think I gasped. 'Queenie, do you think the queen would let her maid go roller-skating up and down the halls of Buckingham Palace?'

'We ain't at Buckingham Palace, are we? We're in a different country with different rules and I don't see why I can't take a dip in a pool during my free time.'

I couldn't think of a good answer to that. It was quite possible that American maids did swim in pools with Charlie Chaplin. 'I'm sorry, Queenie, but this is something we need to talk about,' I said. 'At the moment it is not appropriate. Please go back to the bungalow.'

'A right old spoilsport you've turned out to be,' she said and stomped ahead of me toward the bungalow.

Chapter 13

> *Talk about the lap of luxury! I'm feeling a bit like a film star myself. I wonder what Belinda would say if she knew that Charlie Chaplin had been flirting with me. I wonder what Darcy would say. . . .*

I was completely shocked. I remembered having the same feeling when I adopted an adorable kitten from the stables as a child and one day it scratched me. Not that Queenie was adorable. I followed her back into the bungalow to hear an imperious voice saying, 'My sister? She is not my sister. She is the spawn of a whore, a nobody.'

Mummy looked up in annoyance as we came in. 'You're not back already? I was just getting the feel of the character. Quite a challenge to make her appealing when she really is such a bitch. In fact I . . .' She looked up and those large eyes opened even wider. 'My God. What is that?'

'What is what?' I asked.

She pointed at Queenie. 'That. Your maid.'

'It's my swimming costume, madam,' Queenie said. 'I was going to go swimming but your daughter won't let me.'

'Queenie, in the first place I suspect that maids don't swim in the pool at the Beverly Hills Hotel, and in the second I've never seen anything more hideous in my life. Where on earth did you find it?'

'I bought it a while ago. Just in case I ever got the chance to go swimming,' Queenie said defiantly.

'It is utterly hideous. You look like a beached whale wrapped in a barber's pole. Go and take it off, for God's sake.' And she started to laugh. 'Absolutely hideous. Never seen anything worse in my life. Oh my God. It will probably give me nightmares!'

Queenie went to say something, then glared and pushed past me into her room. I followed. 'You do understand, don't you, Queenie? There's a gossip columnist at the pool. The press would love to print pictures of you, and then the queen would see them and be mortified.'

She looked like a deflated balloon and as usual I felt sorry for her. 'Maybe we'll find a way to go to the beach soon. I'm sure nobody would mind if you swam in the ocean there.'

'Well, I don't want to wear my uniform,' she said. 'It's too ruddy hot for this weather and I sweat something terrible.'

'I understand,' I said. 'I had no idea we'd be away long in a climate like this. I'll arrange for a lighter uniform. I'm sure Ronnie can make one appear by magic for you.'

'And I don't have to stay in my room in the bungalow all the time, do I? There's not enough space to swing a cat in here.'

'No, I think you could take a walk and explore the sur-roundings when I don't need you,' I said, sure that Queen

Mary would have told a servant that of course it was her place to stay close to her mistress in case she was needed. I feared I'd never be a good mistress of a stately home one day. I went to change and was just coming into the living room when there was a light tap at the front door. Since Claudette was nowhere to be seen I went to open it. A woman stood there, her face layered with an overwhelming amount of make-up, her hair the brightest blonde I had ever seen, and she was wearing a strapless peacock blue top over which a considerable amount of flesh was bulging.

'You must be the young royal lady,' she said. 'Barbara just told me about you and I thought I should do the friendly thing and come over and welcome you to our country.' And she dropped a really awkward curtsy, making me cringe with embarrassment and wonder if the rest of her breasts were about to appear from the strapless top.

'Oh please. That's not necessary,' I said. 'I'm actually only a lady, not a princess. And I'm told that in America everyone is equal.'

She laughed. 'Who told you that? We have our own kings and queens, you know, only here it's who has the most money.' She held out a chubby hand. 'I'm Dolores. Dolores Hanford.'

'And I'm Georgiana Rannoch,' I said. 'Are you visiting Beverly Hills too, Mrs. Hanford?'

'No, honey. My husband and I are residents of this lovely city. We have a mansion up in the hills above Sunset Boulevard. My husband is a real estate developer and making more money than we know what to do with. I come down to the hotel to have lunch and meet friends almost every day. This is the place where everyone gathers. Everyone who is anyone, that is. Would you care to join us for lunch?'

I glanced back at my mother, who was now strutting around the room gesturing. 'Why not?' I said. 'Thank you.'

Several women were already seated around a table in the restaurant and Dolores produced me as if I were a prized exotic pet. 'This is the young royal lady that Barbara was telling us about,' she said. 'Cousin of the king. Imagine that. And wait till you hear her accent. Go ahead, honey. Say something.'

'I'm very pleased to meet you,' I muttered. 'I'm Georgiana.'

They sighed as if I had just sung an aria. 'Isn't that just the bee's knees?' one said. 'So refined. So royal.' She patted the chair beside her. 'So come and sit down and tell us what you're doing in little old Beverly Hills and what it's like at the palace.'

I sat. They peppered me with questions – about my mother, the Prince of Wales, rumors they had heard. I tried my best to be discreet and answer vaguely, but it was rather like being at an inquisition. They also consumed an alarming amount of alcohol and all of them smoked. They only picked at their food, of which there were huge portions, and I was fascinated to see one of them using her hands to eat a bun with beef in the middle. Lettuce and juices squirted out of it as she attempted to get it into her mouth. Not a pretty sight. I had ordered a chicken sandwich, which at home would be a thin slice of chicken between slices of white bread. When it came up I was horrified to see it was half a chicken sitting on a roll. After the initial grilling Dolores and her crowd forgot about me and lapsed into their usual gossip. They were noisy, witty and terribly catty. It was shocking to someone like me to hear them describing the bedroom behavior of various celebrities without batting an eyelid.

'Three of them, honey. No, of course they were men. He can't stand women.'

What a wild and wicked place the world was outside of Castle Rannoch and Buckingham Palace. Frankly I was rather relieved when I could make my escape and go back to the bungalow. We had dinner delivered as Mummy didn't want to stop working on her lines. She was determined to be perfect on the first day on the set. Ronnie stopped by to see how we were getting on and told me that I'd be welcome to come to the set later in the day and he'd send a car for me. I was glad of this as I didn't want to find myself alone at the mercy of Dolores and the catty women, or risk bumping into Charlie Chaplin again.

The next morning Mummy woke me up at five with all her banging, clattering, and swearing and departed before six. I found I couldn't get back to sleep with the sun streaming in. I ordered breakfast, then wrote postcards to my grandfather and to Belinda. If she was still working at Harrods she'd need cheering up. Then I went for a walk to see if I could find Queenie a cooler uniform, but the only shops did not have clothing suitable for maids.

The car came for me at eleven and off I went to the studio, feeling very grand and rather excited. The gatekeeper saluted as we drove under the big sign saying GOLDEN PICTURES. People in strange costumes crossed in front of us. We passed what looked like an old-fashioned town square, then a European village. They were filming at the latter, with young men dressed in lederhosen and girls in dirndls. The car swung around into a narrow alley between buildings and stopped. Ronnie came out to meet me, carrying a clipboard.

'Great. You made it. Come on in. We're about to start shooting.'

He led me into a big dark box. At one end was a set of a palace room, and my mother, in a costume more sexy and revealing than Bloody Mary ever wore, stood at a table, while Juan, in tights and doublet, stood facing her. The first thing that struck me was how young and beautiful she looked, and not for the first time I marveled that I could be her daughter and look so little like her. Ronnie put a finger to his lips. 'And action,' shouted a voice from the darkness.

'How dare you, Philip,' she said. 'You may be king in your country, but here I am the queen. Don't ever forget that.'

He walked over, grabbed her wrist and pulled her toward him. 'But you are also my wife. And the wife is at the mercy of her husband. Do not ever forget that either.' Then he kissed her – very passionately.

'And cut!' shouted the voice. 'Great stuff, Claire, honey. Juan, we need less of an accent from you. Tone it down and don't lisp.'

'I can't help it,' Juan said. 'This is the way I talk. This is the way Spanish men talk. You wish me to play King Philip of Spain, do you not?'

'Sure you should sound Spanish but the people in Peoria need to understand you. Try again.'

Make-up women darted out to dab at Mummy's face. She went back behind the table and the scene was played again. And again. When they broke for lunch she came over to me. 'Now I know why I prefer the theater. We have gone over the same little bit thirty-four times. Of course Juan isn't going to lose his accent overnight. He'll have to work with a speech coach for weeks. Cy isn't pleased.'

Cy Goldman himself came over to join us. 'Come and

eat in my private dining room,' he said. 'You're doing great, Claire. So believable. What an actress your mother is, Georgie. I'm going to make her a big star.' He led us at break-neck pace across the lot, where a real-looking castle had now been built, and into a small dining room. 'But Juan,' he said. 'I'm having second thoughts about him. It's the accent, isn't it? He's not ready for the big time yet. He's got the looks and the sex appeal all right, but the audience has to understand him. It's just not the voice of a macho guy. So I'm bringing in an alternative. I've asked him to join us for lunch.'

And as if on cue the door opened and in came someone whom I recognized instantly. Even if I had hardly seen a film in my life I knew Craig Hart. Everyone in the civilized world knew Craig Hart. Women threw themselves at his feet. And in real life he was as tall, dark, handsome and rugged in the extreme as he was on the screen.

'Craig. Good to see you.' Cy pumped his hand. 'Come on in and meet my new star. Claire Daniels.'

Craig sauntered across the room, moving with animal grace, and held out a big hand to my mother. 'Well, hello there, gorgeous. I am delighted to meet you,' he said in his deep, rumbling voice that had reduced millions of females to a trembling jelly.

'Well, hello, yourself,' Mummy said, her eyes lighting up with pleasure. 'I think I'm going to enjoy working with you, Craig.'

Oh dear, I thought. Now we might never go home to Max. Then, to my amazement, Craig turned his attention to me. 'And who is this enchanting young woman? Another new discovery, Cy?'

He took my hands in his. His dark eyes held mine and I felt my own heart beating faster.

'This is Claire's daughter, Craig,' Cy said. 'The one I told you about.'

'I thought it might be. What a little charmer.' And he smiled down at me. 'What is your name, you adorable creature?'

'It's Georgie.' I could hardly stammer out the words.

'I am really glad to meet you, Georgie,' he said. 'Really glad.' He was still holding my hands but he looked past me to Mr. Goldman. 'You know, Cy, I think this is going to work out very well all around, don't you?'

At the time I didn't know what he meant. I was still in shock that Craig Hart was paying attention to me and not my mother. After a lunch when I could hardly swallow a thing we went back to the set. Mummy was giving me curious and amused glances. I'm sure my face was still beet red.

'Isn't Craig being kind to you,' Mummy said. 'What a nice man, making you feel special like that.'

She went back to make-up before returning to the set. I was about to go in when Ronnie stopped me. 'Not a pretty scene in there at the moment,' he said. 'Cy has just told Juan that he's not playing Philip any longer. Juan is upset. Stella is furious.'

Even as he said it the door burst open and Stella stormed out, dressed in full Elizabethan costume with long red hair flowing over her shoulders. Cy came hot on her heels.

'I can't believe you.' She turned on him like a tiger. 'You promise him the moon and then you let him down like that.'

'He wasn't good enough, Stella. Be reasonable,' Cy shouted, grabbing her arm and whirling her back to face him. 'He didn't make the grade. He was nothing. A Spanish peasant. He should be damned grateful I brought him here.'

'He's not a peasant. He comes from an old, old family

with a castle, parts of which you tried to buy, if I remember rightly. You take everything you want from Spain, don't you?' Stella demanded. 'The great Cy Goldman. Just because you have money you think you can buy everything. Well, you can't buy me.'

He pulled her close then so that their faces were only inches apart. 'Don't forget, sweetheart, without me you're done for. You were a has-been. Your voice isn't really good enough for the talkies, is it? Who else would give you a starring role in a picture, huh?' He released her then. 'Maybe you're getting just a little too fond of the Spanish peasant, huh? You want to watch your step, Stella baby. There's plenty more where you came from. Now get back in there and try a little harder, because you know what? Claire Daniels will out-act you in every scene.'

Stella tossed her red hair and stalked back into the studio. I saw Cy give a little smirk as he followed her. It wasn't a comfortable afternoon on the set. Cy had appeased Stella by letting Juan try out for Don Alonso, the dashing Spanish advisor. We moved on to a scene between Stella and my mother, and I could see what Cy meant. Mummy shone, the way she always did on stage. Stella's voice had an annoying sharp quality to it and even with all that make-up she still looked older than the eighteen-year-old girl she was supposed to be playing. And the more I saw of the script, the more stupid I thought it was. It wasn't just that the history was completely wrong. The dialogue was peppered with Old English words and phrases like 'forsooth,' 'gadzooks' and 'fie, my lord, fie.'

When we were finally driven back to the hotel Queenie was remarkably subdued. I suppose my talking-to had made her realize that she had behaved inappropriately. Or perhaps

Claudette had made her see sense. Either way she laid out my dress for dinner, and took my day clothes to be pressed without a word or a single 'Bob's yer uncle.'

At seven o'clock there was a knock on our door. I opened it cautiously, dreading Dolores or her chums. Instead Cy Goldman and Craig Hart stood there. Cy's arms were full of flowers. 'We've come to take you lovely ladies out to dinner,' Cy said. 'Come on. Put your dancing shoes on.'

Mummy acted pleased and flattered. As we walked to a waiting car I heard Craig mutter to Cy, 'Yes, I think she'll do nicely.' And I got the feeling they were talking about me. Was I about to be discovered and turned into a film star? Then I grinned. That would be too absurd. Craig drove us in an enormous white convertible. We were whisked down Wilshire Boulevard at great speed to another fine hotel called the Ambassador and walked past palm trees to a club called the Cocoanut Grove. A negro jazz band was playing and the place was full.

'Everybody's here tonight,' Cy said. 'Hi, Norma, honey.' He kissed a cheek. 'Norma Shearer,' he said to us. 'And Errol, you old devil.' He turned to us. 'You haven't met Errol Flynn yet, have you?'

Another gorgeous dark man eyed us both appraisingly. 'You and I have to dance when the music gets going,' he said to my mother.

Craig put an arm around my shoulder. 'Watch out for that one,' he said. 'He likes his girls pure and innocent.'

'How do you know I'm pure and innocent?' I heard myself asking and surprised myself.

Craig laughed. 'Honey, when you've been around as long as I have, you know. That's what's so appealing about you.'

I knew I should say 'I do have a boyfriend,' but I didn't

want to spoil the moment. I had Mummy and Cy to keep an eye on me, didn't I?

We dined. A man called Bing Crosby got up and sang. Mummy went off to dance with Errol Flynn. Craig asked me to dance and held me close. It was all rather heady. I couldn't wait to write about it to Belinda. Cy insisted that we leave at ten as we had to be on the set early next morning and Craig had to study his lines, so I didn't have a chance to see what might have happened later. Neither did Mummy. She and Mr. Flynn were getting along remarkably well. I could tell she was in her element here and wondered if being Frau von Strohheim still had its appeal. And I did wonder what I would do if Craig made advances to me.

The next day the car came to take me to the set again. 'Lots of tension,' Ronnie muttered as he escorted me inside. 'Stella and Cy. She hasn't forgiven him. Juan is doing badly and muffing his lines and may well be out altogether.'

'Oh dear,' I said. 'Is making talkies always like this?'

'Worse, sometimes. We haven't had a real catfight yet, although Stella has clearly decided that having your mother in the film was not such a good idea after all. She wanted an older woman so that she could look young, but I must say your mother looks magnificent. And she can act too. I wouldn't be surprised if she didn't end up as a big film star.'

'I think she's intending to go back to Europe after this picture,' I said.

'Cy won't let her. He'll sign her to a contract if it's the last thing he does.'

We got through a long and tense day. There was no mention of dinner this evening. It was hot and muggy as we drove home and all I longed to do was go for a swim.

'Queenie. Help me out of this,' I called as I came into my bedroom. No answer. I bet she had fallen asleep again. At least it wasn't on my bed this time. 'Queenie?' I opened her door. The bed was made. The room was tidy. I came out into the living room.

'Claudette. Queenie's not here. Don't tell me she went for a swim again.'

Claudette shook her head. 'She 'as gone. I tried to talk to her but she doesn't listen to me. She is *fou*, that one. Mad.'

'What do you mean, gone?' I asked.

She pointed at the coffee table. 'She left you a letter.'

I picked it up. Written in Queenie's childish script:

Dear Miss,

I am sorry to say that I am leaving your employment. I have been offered a good job by Mrs. Hanford. She has always wanted an English maid and she offered me a lot of money to leave you. Since we haven't been getting along too well lately and you keep telling me off I thought I'd take my chances with her. Sorry to leave you in the lurch but you know how to take care of yourself quite well.

Yours faithfully,
Queenie Hepplewhite (your former maid)

I just stood there staring. I couldn't believe it. Queenie – hopeless little Queenie had landed herself a plum job. And I couldn't believe the sense of loss I felt. I knew I should have been relieved to be rid of her. Now I could find myself a proper lady's maid – one who wouldn't fall asleep on my bed, or iron holes in my evening gowns. But I found instead I was blinking back tears.

'Queenie's gone,' I said to my mother, who was sprawled

on the sofa with her script on her knees. 'She's left me. Got a better job.'

'Good luck to whoever's landed with her,' Mummy said, not looking up. 'Don't worry, darling. Claudette can take care of both of us. She has very little to do here. She won't mind a bit – will you, Claudette?'

'No, madame,' Claudette said, giving me a look that said the opposite.

'Now leave me in peace. I must work,' Mummy said.

I felt too upset to go to bed. I wandered the grounds. Suddenly I heard a man's voice saying, 'There she is at last.' And a hand reached out from the bushes and grabbed me.

Chapter 14

At the Beverly Hills Hotel
Wednesday, August 1, 1934

I was about to scream when a male voice said, 'Georgie, old bean. Steady on, it's me. Algie.'

His face came into focus in the light of the torches that lined the pool.

'Algie? What on earth are you doing here?' I asked. 'I thought you were supposed to be working on a ranch.'

'Well, old thing, you see it's like this. Tubby's newspaper wanted him to come out to Hollywood on some kind of secret mission thingy so I thought I might join him. Keep him company, you know. Dashed lonely for a chap in a foreign country like this. We've become rather good pals. And I knew you'd be here, what with your mother making a picture, don't you know. I thought you might be able to pull a few strings to get me a job on a film.'

'Get you a job on a film? What on earth could you do on a film, Algie?'

'I don't know. I'm an adaptable sort of chap. And I'm not

too proud to take lowly work. Assistant director or something. Anything would be better than chasing cows on a ranch.'

'Well, I suppose you could come with me in the morning,' I said dubiously.

'I say, you are a brick, old bean. What time?'

'The car will come when I call it. Say nine o'clock.'

'Could we make it closer to ten, do you think? I'm not exactly an early riser. They had to yank me out of bed by my feet every morning at school.'

I laughed. 'Then I don't think the film industry is for you, Algie. My mother has to be on set at six.'

'Six?' The word came out as a yelp. 'As in six a.m.? I've only ever seen six a.m. when I've been returning home from a party.'

'Well, that's when film directors expect you to show up. And I'm sure ranchers go to work before sunup too.'

He swallowed hard. I watched his Adam's apple go up and down. 'Well, I suppose I could learn anything if I really had to. All right. I'll jolly well do my best to be there at nine tomorrow. And thanks awfully, Georgie. I really appreciate this.'

As he turned to go, a thought struck me. 'Just a minute. How did you manage to find me?'

'Ah well. Old Tubby, you know. He's on the trail of your mama.'

I felt the blood draining from my face. If Tubby had been following my mother then he'd know all about the divorce and Reno and my mother's double. We'd be doomed. Homer Clegg would never divorce Mummy now. Mummy would never forgive me. 'Tubby has been following us? All the way from New York? That's absolutely despicable.'

'Steady on, old girl. It wasn't like that. Tubby's editor

cabled him in New York and said he'd got wind that Claire
Daniels was making a picture and he wanted him to go
out to Hollywood and try to get an exclusive interview –
"My return to stardom." You know the kind of thing. So
we hopped on the next train and here we are. It seems that
everyone here has heard about your mama and knew where
she was staying.'

'I see,' I said. 'Well, don't you dare bring Tubby to the
studio with us. He'll have to approach my mother himself if
he wants an interview, and let me warn him that she doesn't
like newspaper reporters.'

So off he went. I let myself into the bungalow. Mummy
was now reading her lines out loud, declaiming, 'Thou
daughter of a whore. Get thee from my sight!'

I tiptoed past her, undressed myself, hung up my own
clothes and went to bed with a heavy heart.

In the morning Algie showed up a little after nine, pleased
with himself, but looking awfully bleary-eyed and disheveled. I suspected he'd simply staggered out of bed, into his
clothes and out of the door.

'And you do understand, you're not to mention anything of
what goes on here to Tubby,' I said. 'My mother would be furious if she knew. I sincerely hope he hasn't sent you as a spy.'

I looked him straight in the eye. The fact that he didn't
blush and look uncomfortable convinced me that this wasn't
the case.

'Oh gosh no,' he said. 'Absolutely not. I just want to find a
job that isn't as beastly as mucking out cows.'

The gatekeeper saluted as we drove under the arch saying
GOLDEN PICTURES. Ronnie came out to meet me.

'How's it going?' I asked.

'Not well,' he said. 'Everyone is still very tense after yesterday.' He noticed Algie. 'Who is this? I'm afraid no guests are allowed on the set. Mr. Goldman's orders.'

Before I could introduce Algie he stepped forward, holding out his hand. 'Algie Broxley-Foggett. How do you do. I'm a childhood friend of Georgie's and come from a very old family connected to the Tudors. I've come out to California to make my fortune so I'm hoping that Mr. Goldman will find a job for me on his film.'

I looked at Algie with wonder. So the bumbling, clumsy, likable idiot could be quite devious if he wanted. He certainly wasn't a childhood friend, nor, I suspected, was he connected to the Tudors.

'Well, I guess that will be okay then,' Ronnie said uncertainly. He looked at me. I was tempted to say what I had been thinking but decided to give Algie the benefit of the doubt. He needed all the help he could get in life, I suspected.

We waited until the red light went off then followed Ronnie into the darkness of the studio. At the other end lights blazed over an interior palace set, this time with a four-poster bed front and center.

'And action,' shouted a voice and the clapboard snapped together.

'Get out of my sight, thou daughter of a whore,' Mummy said with venom.

'Cut,' came a voice from the blackness. 'Cy, we can't let her use the word "whore" if we don't want the picture to end up with an A rating.'

'Okay. Claire, sweetheart, you'd better say "prostitute" then.'

'Cy. Maybe not "prostitute." A little risqué for the censor,' said the voice.

'What the hell do you want her to say. "Daughter of a naughty wench"?'

'Cy,' Mummy interrupted. 'Trollop. How about if I say "trollop"?'

'Great idea, Claire. Nobody will know what a trollop is. Go ahead with it. And Stella, you're supposed to be an innocent young girl and these are the talkies, remember? That voice wouldn't convince anyone you were a British princess. Listen to how Claire sounds . . . or better still, wait until her daughter gets here and listen to her. Maybe she can give you coaching.'

'I have made thirty-five pictures, Cy. I do not need coaching,' Stella said in a frosty voice.

'But they were mostly silent, weren't they, honey. You've got great expressions for the silent screen, I'll give you that . . . but I wouldn't mention those thirty-five pictures. They give away your age.'

'Fine, if you don't want to do my script, I can always take it to another studio,' Stella said angrily.

'Not while you're under contract to me, honey.' Cy laughed. 'You aren't going anywhere, baby. You know which side your bread is buttered on. Now let's get on with it.'

Mummy delivered her line about the daughter of a trollop. I could tell she was feeling rather pleased with herself, knowing that she'd scored a point over Stella. There was no such thing as bosom friends in the acting profession, I decided.

We moved away from the door to find seats. 'I say, old bean, that's not right, is it?' Algie whispered to me. 'I mean Mary and Elizabeth didn't ever love the same man. I don't think Mary loved anybody!' I put a finger to my lips just as Algie stumbled in the blackness and kicked over a chair.

'Cut!' Cy Goldman yelled, then wheeled around and spotted Algie. 'What's this guy doing here?'

Ronnie stepped forward before we could answer. 'He's a childhood friend of Lady Georgiana and from a real distinguished British family with connections to the Tudors themselves. He's hoping he might be useful to you on the picture.'

'The first thing he'd better learn is that nobody talks or moves around when we're shooting.' Cy glared. 'What do you do, young man?'

'Do? Well, not too much until now. Just came down from Oxford. Oh, I see what you mean – what job could I do on the film. Well . . . I rather fancy myself as an actor,' Algie said. 'It might be ripping fun to be dressed up like that in tights and a doublet and with a sword.'

'Have you had much experience?'

'Oh, rather. My Lady Macbeth got rave reviews.'

'Lady Macbeth?'

'In prep school. You should have seen my sleepwalking scene, my hands covered in blood and saying, "Out, damned spot. Out, I say."' He swung out his arms in a dramatic gesture, knocking one of the lights. It teetered and would have fallen, had not two of the crew leaped to grab it.

There was a cross between a moan and a cry from the set. 'He quoted from the play we never mention,' Mummy wailed. 'The Scottish play. Now we are cursed, doomed. Something terrible will happen.'

'It will be fine, Claire,' Mr. Goldman soothed. 'The boy doesn't know any better. But I don't want him on set upsetting my stars. You say you're related to the Tudors?'

'Oh, absolutely. Oodles of Tudors in the old family tree,' Algie said. He went to lean nonchalantly against a rough stone wall, only to find it was a flat that teetered and again he had to be grabbed by a stagehand.

'Well, I guess we could use an extra script consultant, seeing that you know the Tudors personally,' Mr. Goldman said, eyeing him dubiously. 'And that you're a longtime friend of our Georgie.'

'Can we get on with this?' Stella snapped. 'How am I supposed to stay in character if we keep being interrupted every second? And I know it must be tough for Claire too, playing such a young woman.'

A few days ago Mummy was her bosom friend, I thought. I wondered why this sudden hostility now? Perhaps Juan was showing interest in my mother. Perhaps Stella had suggested my mother for the part because Mummy was older and a has-been and thus not a threat. But now it was clear that Mummy was a better actress and looked better too. They went back to work but the tension level was still extremely high. Were they all thinking what Mummy had said about the curse of *Macbeth*? I knew theater people were terribly superstitious.

We broke for lunch in the cafeteria. It looked so funny to see everyone in costume eating American food. When we came back to the studio after lunch there was still tension in the air. The afternoon dragged on. I was definitely wishing I was back beside the pool and wondering if I dared summon the car when the door opened, sending a shaft of light across the set. Mr. Goldman swore, yelled 'Cut!' and swung around. 'What now?' he bellowed.

Ronnie came toward him, looking more worried than usual. 'Real sorry to interrupt, Mr. Goldman, but I've just had your wife on the telephone.'

'My wife? What does she want now?' Goldman growled.

'She's heard about your shopping spree in Europe – buying stuff for the castle,' Ronnie said, wincing as he said it.

'So? What of it?'

'She thinks you've gone crazy and you're turning the place into a Gothic nightmare – her words, not mine, sir. She's flying out this weekend to see for herself.'

Mr. Goldman muttered a string of swear words, some of which I'd never heard before. Then he said, 'Well, maybe it's not such a bad idea after all. I'm not getting a good feeling here. It's not going well. Maybe we all need a break. Okay. Listen up, everyone. I've made up my mind. I'm taking you all up to the castle.'

'All of us?' Stella asked. 'And your wife too?'

'Sure. Why not? It's a big place. Plenty of bedrooms, Stella honey. Give you a chance to relax and settle down. It won't be wasted time. We can do some read-throughs and blocking with Craig. Is he still in his trailer?'

'I believe so, Mr. Goldman.'

'Then maybe Georgie would like to go and tell him the plan. He was asking about you, Georgie.'

'Craig? Mr. Hart, you mean? Asking for me?' I stammered. 'What did he want?'

'Missing you, I guess.' And he gave me a wink.

'Golly,' I said.

'Tell him we'll work here on set Friday morning, then drive up to the castle Friday afternoon. Got it?'

'I'll show you where the trailers are,' Ronnie said, escorting me to the door. I followed, rather stunned by everything that had happened and by the suggestion that Craig Hart – internationally adored heart-throb – wanted to see me. Surely not when my mother was available. When every woman between fifteen and fifty was available? I gave a little grin, but then I paused to think. These film stars were noto-rious womanizers. Was Craig Hart expecting to find me his next willing victim? Was he interested in the challenge of an English virgin?

'You'd better come with me to the trailer,' I said to Ronnie. 'Protocol at home would demand that I didn't go into a gentleman's trailer alone.'

Ronnie laughed. 'How refreshingly quaint,' he said. 'Lady Georgiana, I think you should know . . .' He broke off as he saw Craig himself coming toward us.

'Well, hello there, you lovely creature,' he said in that deep, rumbling voice that had melted a million women's hearts. 'I was just coming to find you to tell you I'm taking you out to dinner tonight. Have the driver take you home early enough so you can make yourself beautiful, okay, sweetheart?'

I saw a look of amusement cross Ronnie's face. Was he relishing Craig's next conquest? Still I didn't want to say no. What girl would? But I wasn't quite so naïve these days. I did know that when men invited me up to their room to show me their etchings it wasn't a discussion on art that they were after. I'd go to a restaurant with him but that would be all. And I'd make sure to tell him about Darcy. Of course I would. . . .

I realized as I was driving back to the hotel that I'd left Algie to fend for himself. He'd probably bring the scenery crashing down on top of the stars. Still, it would serve him right for telling such fibs. A dear childhood friend indeed, and I'd be willing to bet that there wasn't a single Tudor in his family. Let him find his own way home on the tram.

It was strange to go into an empty bedroom and real-ize that there was no Queenie. I'd half expected that her American employer might have thrown her out by now and she would have returned with her tail between her legs, but it hadn't happened. I took off my clothes, went for a quick swim, ran a bath and then changed into my dark blue backless evening gown – the one in which I looked almost sexy. Was this wise? I asked myself as I examined my reflection in the mirror. Did I want to encourage a man like Craig Hart? But then I didn't want to look like a frump, either.

'It's just dinner,' I told myself. 'An experience. Something I'll be able to tell Belinda about in my next letter.'

When Mummy heard about the dinner with Craig, her eyes lit up. 'Oh, isn't he a peach taking us to dinner again.'

'Not you, Mummy. Me. He's taking me to dinner.'

'Whatever for, I wonder,' she said. 'Maybe he has a thing for virgins. You want to watch yourself. The back seat of these American automobiles is big enough for a multitude of sins.'

'I'll be careful, I promise.'

'And you know what we used to say on the stage? If you can't be good, be careful, and if you can't be careful put a sixpence between your knees.' And she laughed.

Craig arrived for me at eight and off we went, to the Cocoanut Grove again. It was rather heady being the center of attention. Flashbulbs flashed. Gossip columnist Barbara Kindell came over to us. 'Well, here's a couple I'd never have expected to see together,' she said, grinning at my discomfort. 'And I hear we're off to Alhambra Two, right? Away from prying eyes.'

I'd forgotten that that was what Cy Goldman had called his castle.

'A whole group of us, Miss Kindell,' I said.

'I might just secure myself an invitation. Should be fun, especially since I gather that Mrs. Goldman is coming into town.' And off she went, presumably to write about us in tomorrow's newspapers.

Craig drove me home about ten. He was a perfect gentleman in the taxicab. 'I'll see you safely to your bungalow,' he said.

Alarm bells went off in my head. 'It's lovely,' I said. 'I share it with my mother and our servants.'

He smiled, slipping an arm around my shoulder. Go on, a voice whispered. Tell him about Darcy now. We walked past the pool. 'I've had a great time,' he said. He took me into his arms and he kissed me. I knew I should resist, but it was such a practiced, gentle kiss – and what girl would turn down the chance to be kissed by Craig Hart?

'Excuse me. Your ladyship,' a man's voice called from the darkness. 'Sorry to interrupt, but I've a young man at the front desk asking for you. I didn't like to send him out to the bungalow alone. Not at this time of night.'

Oh Lord. It was obviously the wretched Algie again. Probably Tubby had left and he was trying to cadge a place to stay now. Or it might even be Tubby himself, angling for that interview with Mummy. 'Tell him to come back tomorrow morning. I'm busy now,' I said.

'I can see that for myself,' said a second man's voice. One that I recognized.

And to my utter horror Darcy stepped into the torchlight.

Chapter 15

The Beverly Hills Hotel
Thursday, August 2, 1934

I broke away from Craig Hart, my mouth open with disbelief.

'Darcy. What on earth are you doing here?' I stammered.

'More to the point, what have you been doing here?' Darcy was staring at me coldly. 'No. Don't answer that. I can see for myself perfectly well. "Don't bother me now. I'm busy. While the cat's away, the mice will play." Well, you are certainly full of surprises, Georgiana Rannoch.'

Craig stepped up beside me. 'You know this guy, honey? Is he bothering you?'

'He's my' – I was about to say 'fiancé' when I remembered the rest of the world wasn't supposed to know that – 'boy-friend,' I said.

'Hey there, fella,' he said in his deep, rumbling voice. 'Just a friendly little kiss, you know. No harm done. And all's fair in love and war, they say.'

'Do they?' Darcy demanded. 'I've heard about creeps like

you, taking advantage of innocent girls. I should punch your pretty nose.'

'Darcy, no.' I stepped between them. 'Look, there was nothing in this. This is Craig Hart–'

'Oh, I know who he is.' Darcy gave a bitter laugh. 'He's rich. He's famous. You're naïve. No wonder you were swept off your feet.'

I was angry now, and just a little tickled too. Darcy was actually jealous. I savored the notion before I went on. 'I was about to say that Mr. Hart is kindly looking after me while my mother is filming. He took me out to dinner and was just escorting me back to my front door. Over here in Hollywood people hug and kiss all the time. It doesn't mean anything.' I turned back to Craig. 'I'm sorry about this, Mr. Hart. Thank you for a lovely dinner. I'll see you tomorrow.'

Craig grinned and touched my cheek with his finger. 'So long, sweetheart. Sweet dreams. And don't let this guy boss you around. You do what you want.'

He sauntered away, leaving Darcy standing there, still glaring at me.

'I'm sorry,' I said. 'But there really was nothing to worry about. I made it quite clear to him that I wasn't interested.'

Darcy was shaking his head. 'I'm trying to come to terms with this. I leave my sweet but innocent young lady, shy and awkward around men, for a couple of weeks. I come back and she is calmly dating one of the world's hottest heart-throbs and telling him she isn't interested. Has someone I don't know taken over Georgie's body?'

I laughed then. 'I don't understand it either. My mother and I were introduced to him and he made a beeline for me and not Mummy. So of course I wasn't going to turn down the chance to be wined and dined by him. It was such a feather in my cap when my mother is always telling me how plain and gawky I am.'

'She is?'

'All the time. "You poor child. Too bad you didn't inherit my looks." She even said, "I wonder what Darcy sees in you."'

'Then she's blind if she doesn't see it too,' he said. 'I knew she was completely self-centered, but I'd no idea she was catty too.'

'She's an actress. It goes with the territory,' I said.

'Your mother and my father. What a pair.' He grimaced.

'Have you seen him lately?'

'No, but I got a letter before I sailed. It said, "Isn't it about time you made something of yourself? You can't expect to inherit anything other than the title from me, and since I plan to live a damned long time you won't get that anytime soon."'

I slipped my hand into his. 'It's good to have horrid parents in common,' I said, 'but what are you doing here? You didn't come all this way just to see me, did you?'

'If I had the kind of money my father spent as a young man I would have answered yes to that. But as it happens I'm still on the trail of our jewel thief.'

'Golly,' I said before I remembered not to. 'So did you find the princess's jewel and that woman's diamond when we were searched leaving the ship?'

Darcy shook his head. 'We found nothing. I didn't think we would.'

'And the princess really was genuine?'

'I've no doubt about it.'

'And you didn't find any clue as to what was thrown overboard? Not a body?'

'We've still no idea about that either. Nobody seemed to be missing, unless it was a stowaway who met a bad end.'

'Or a stowaway who killed someone on the boat and took his place? Or her place?' I gave him a knowing look. 'Remember I suggested that at the time.'

Darcy frowned. 'If you're meaning the princess again, she was who she claimed to be. I'm sure.'

'Did you speak to her? I was rather tempted to go and visit the Astors myself but they were in Newport, Rhode Island.'

Darcy gave me an exasperated look. 'I contacted the Astors, who verified that she had arrived safely. I'm sure they'd know if she was an impostor. But if it was anyone else who was murdered and thrown overboard . . . I don't know how they'd ever find out. In the absence of a body that is now fish bait.'

'Don't.' I shivered. 'I keep thinking of that long hair floating out on the surface of the ocean.'

He touched my shoulder gently, giving it a little squeeze. 'Maybe you were mistaken. It was a long way down from where you were standing, wasn't it?'

I nodded and was silent for a moment before I asked, 'So what makes you think your thief has come out here?'

Darcy looked around at the gardens, now bathed in shadow. Then he lowered his voice. 'The answer is that I don't know. But I've a couple of things to go on. We found a fingerprint on the doorjamb of Princess Promila's suite. It was smudged but it looks as if it could belong to Stella Brightwell.'

'You still think she could be the thief? That doesn't make sense.'

'I agree, but your grandfather would tell you there is no

such thing as coincidence. And one of the few details we have to go on is that Stella Brightwell was present on every occasion that the thief struck. She is the only person who fits that bill.'

'If it was her fingerprint on Princess Promila's doorjamb, that doesn't really prove anything, does it?' I said. 'They were fellow first-class passengers. Tablemates. What was to stop Stella from popping in to see the princess for a chat or a drink?'

'Nothing, except the princess claims that Stella never visited her suite. Nobody did. She's a very private person.'

'Interesting. And what is the other clue that brought you here?'

'Someone tried to contact a major American gangster who is also a big-time fencer of stolen property. He's currently in Las Vegas, Nevada, and the letter to him came from Los Angeles, from someone who had a ruby to sell.'

'I see. Have you seen the letter? Any clues from it?'

Darcy shook his head. 'I haven't seen it yet. But it was typed on a standard sort of machine and no fingerprints, so I'm told.'

'So what's your next step? Can you lay a trap to pretend to be the fence and catch the thief that way?'

'We tried. Didn't work. Our burglar is not stupid. He or she must have sensed the trap and didn't show up.'

'So what now?'

'I want to know why the thief has traveled out to California,' Darcy said. 'One thought is that Cy Goldman has just bought a couple of valuable pieces from Spain.'

'Oh yes. The candlesticks encrusted with jewels and the El Greco painting.'

'He told quite a lot of people on the ship, apparently.'

'If your thief really is Stella Brightwell, there is no way she's going to steal from Cy Goldman. He's her lover.'

'Probably true. But if it was someone associated with Stella Brightwell? If she works with an accomplice, perhaps? I gather Goldman is taking these Spanish treasures up to his castle when he goes.'

'Which is this weekend,' I said.

'It is? Are you sure?'

'Mr. Goldman announced today that he was taking everyone to his castle on Friday. Mrs. Goldman is coming out to see what he's just had shipped from Spain. He's planning a house party. He didn't want to be up there alone with her, I suspect.'

Darcy grinned. 'So do you think you can secure me an invitation? I'd rather not let Goldman know the real reason, just in case he passes it along to Stella Brightwell.'

'I'll take you to the studio with me in the morning, if you like,' I said. 'They send a car for me.'

Darcy shook his head. 'I love the casual way you say that. Now I'll never be able to keep you in the style to which you've become accustomed.'

I reached up and touched his cheek, feeling the bristles of stubble where he hadn't shaved for a while. 'This is not the sort of life I'd ever want, trust me.'

His fingers closed over my hand. 'Oh, Georgie,' he said. 'Why is everything so damned difficult?'

'It will get better,' I said, slipping my arms around his neck. 'I could always have a prolonged affair with Craig Hart and allow him to ply me with diamonds.'

'You little minx.' He pulled me close to him. 'Was that really just a friendly "thank you for dinner" kiss? It didn't look like it to me.'

'On my part it was a "how do I get out of this without making a public fuss" sort of kiss. And actually it was quite chaste. Almost like a required stage kiss. Now your kisses, on the other hand . . .'

'Like this, you mean?' he asked and demonstrated. Things might have progressed a little further if a couple hadn't strolled past us, laughing at a private joke. We broke apart.

'Where are you staying?' I asked.

'An awful little fleapit near the train station,' Darcy said. 'I have only just arrived. And I don't think my expenses would cover this place.'

'I'd invite you to my bungalow, but I'm sharing with my mother.'

'A bedroom? With your mother? Never.'

'No, silly. We have a bedroom each but there aren't any spare beds.'

'I don't mind sharing.' His eyes were glinting in the torch-light, teasing me now.

'I wouldn't mind either, but there's a nasty newspaper reporter who was on the ship plus a Hollywood gossip columnist prowling around.'

'Don't worry. I can survive where I am – especially if you can get me included in the trip to the castle.'

'I'll do my best,' I said. 'I'll see you in the morning, then.'

He nodded. 'I'll be here.'

A sudden thought struck me. 'You could always have Queenie's bed.'

He laughed. 'Share with Queenie? No thank you. I'm not that desperate.'

'No. She's gone. Left me for greener pastures. Some woman who has always wanted an English maid offered her good money.'

Darcy was still laughing. 'Does she know what she's letting herself in for?'

'Who – Queenie or the woman?'

'Both, I should think. So thank you for your kind offer but I rather think it's wiser not to.'

He brushed my cheek with his lips, ruffled my hair and was gone.

Chapter 16

Friday, August 3, 1934
Off to Mr. Goldman's castle. It should be fun.

In the morning there was a tap on my door. I leaped to open it,
expecting it to be Darcy, but instead it was Algie.

'I thought I'd cadge a ride again, old sport,' he said.

'Weren't you supposed to be on set with the rest of them at six?' I asked, deciding that I now actively disliked him.

'Dash it all, Georgie. A fellow wasn't raised to go down a coal mine or to milk cows. Or to be on film sets at the crack of dawn. Besides, what kind of script consultation would they need at that ungodly hour?'

'Algie?' I shook my head. 'If they actually needed advice on their script do you know anything at all about the Tudors? Are you actually related to them in any way?'

He had the grace to blush. 'Well, you know, old thing, most old families can trace links to anybody they like. And I know that Henry the Eighth had eight wives.'

'Six wives,' I said.

'Did he? I thought it was eight.'

I suspected Algie wouldn't last long at his post. But at that moment my thoughts were turned elsewhere as I saw Darcy coming toward us. Algie frowned. 'What's that O'Mara chap doing here?'

'Coming with us to the studio, since he happens to be my young man and he's come all this way to see me. Isn't that romantic?'

Algie was still frowning. 'I thought they didn't allow visitors on the set,' he muttered.

'Darcy doesn't need to be on the set, but I do want him to come to the castle with me.'

'What oh,' Darcy called, coming up to us. He frowned as he noticed Algie. 'Broxley-Foggett, isn't it? Didn't you vomit all over the quad when you first came up to Oxford? Right in front of the master too?'

Algie winced at the memory.

'What are you doing out here?' Darcy asked, staring at Algie so that they looked like two aggressive dogs who had just met.

'He's the script consultant and expert on the Tudors,' I said.

'The Tudors? In what way?'

'Well, you know, old chap, family history and all that.'

'If anyone should be an expert then it's me. My great great great and many more greats grandmother was Henry the Eighth's sister.'

'We'll mention that when you meet Mr. Goldman,' I said, slipping my arm through his. 'It will be a good feather in your cap.'

'I say, won't that make him want to chuck me out?' Algie asked.

'Probably. Unless your great great and many greats grandfather was Henry the Eighth himself,' I said, giving Darcy a grin. 'I'll summon the car.'

We rode to the studio in uncomfortable silence. Algie was clearly put out by Darcy's appearance and I wondered if he might have secret designs on me. I remembered the unpleasant kiss on the boat. We reached the studio, sneaked in and stood in darkness near the door to watch Stella, Juan and Mummy in a particularly tense scene. Stella looked anything but an eighteen-year-old virgin. Juan kept stumbling over his words and Mr. Goldman was about to explode.

'Take a break,' he said at last. 'Get a coffee. Snort some cocaine. Anything to get this goddamned scene finished.'

He came stalking toward us and stopped short when he saw Darcy. I braced myself for another explosion when he said, 'And who is this?'

'The honorable Darcy O'Mara, son of Lord Kilhenny and my young man,' I said. 'What's more, a direct descendant of Henry the Eighth's sister.'

'Is he?' He was prowling around Darcy as if he were a new and fascinating antique. 'Interesting. That look – real aristocratic. He may be just what I'm looking for right now. Can you act, young man?'

'Act? I've never tried,' Darcy said, looking amused. 'Apart from acting as if I were fascinated at boring dinner parties.'

Goldman threw back his head and roared with laughter. 'Did you hear that voice? And those looks. Just what we need. Young man, I'm going to make you a star. Come with me.'

He dragged the surprised Darcy across the set to where Stella was having make-up reapplied, Mummy was sipping a coffee and Juan was sulking. 'Look what I found, ladies,'

Cy exclaimed. 'He's what we need for Don Alonso. A real thoroughbred aristocrat. You can't fake breeding.'

'But what about Juan?' Stella demanded. 'You can't just throw him out after bringing him all this way.'

'I'm not throwing him out. I think the boy will be a big star someday, but he needs polishing. Whereas one look at this guy tells me he'll be a natural.'

'I can't believe—' Stella began when she saw Darcy. I saw her eyes widen, then she smiled. 'I can see what you mean, Cy. He might be just what we're looking for.' She held out her hand. 'Well, hello. I'm Stella.'

'Of course you are. Only someone in the middle of the Amazon jungle wouldn't recognize you. I'm Darcy O'Mara,' Darcy said.

'Aren't you sweet? I'm delighted to meet you,' Stella said. She was doing everything but physically throwing herself at him. Juan clearly had been forgotten. I felt myself bristling, but tried to remind myself that Darcy had to play up to Stella at the moment.

'And me? You tell me that I am no longer in your picture?' Juan said, stepping forward now, dark eyes flashing. 'You do not want me?'

'It's that accent. The way you slur your words. That girly lisp,' Goldman said.

Juan's eyes flashed even more dangerously. 'You insult my mother tongue, my country? You call me girly? I come from the land of bullfighters. Of men who are men.'

'You still lisp,' Goldman said. 'It's an accent that won't go down well with the ladies in the theaters.'

'Then I will leave and go home now.'

'You're not going anywhere,' Mr. Goldman said.

'You think you can stop me?'

'You bet your sweet life I can. You signed a contract, remember. You belong to Golden Pictures just like Stella and Craig do. When I say "jump," they jump.' He thumped Juan on the shoulder. 'Don't worry. We'll have a part written in for you. We'll give you some exposure. Work with a voice coach. But you, young man' – he turned back to Darcy – 'I want you for my Don Alonso. Come up to the castle with us this weekend and we'll go through the script with you.'

'I say, that's jolly decent of you. Thank you very much,' Darcy said. I glanced at him with amusement. He really could act. He'd discarded any trace of Irish accent and was trying to sound like a typical young English aristocrat directly descended from Henry VIII.

I started to wonder. Did he really want to act in Mr. Goldman's epic? Did he really want to sign a contract with Golden Studios and be stuck in Hollywood, or was he just glad he'd found a way to be invited to the castle? I didn't have a chance to ask him as Stella and Mr. Goldman swept him away and I was left alone in the darkness.

I didn't have another chance to see him until we were in a motorcar being driven to Alhambra Two, Mr. Goldman's castle. Mr. Goldman announced that he didn't like taking drivers from the studio because then he'd have to pay them to hang around all weekend with nothing to do and we were perfectly capable of driving ourselves. We went in three cars, with Ronnie driving Mr. Goldman and Stella, Craig driving Algie and Juan, and Darcy driving Mummy, her maid and myself. Mummy was astonished that nobody else was bringing a personal servant and that her maid would have to ride with us.

'One can have too much of this equality, darling,' she said. 'Just think, if I'd stayed with Homer Clegg, I'd have had to do everything for myself too – and probably muck out horses and round up cattle.' She shuddered. 'Of course Stella and Cy both grew up on the wrong side of the tracks. Those little girls were as poor as church mice when I first met them in the theater. Their father was a Spanish waiter who deserted the family.'

I smiled to myself as I climbed into the car beside Darcy. Mummy too had grown up on the wrong side of the tracks. She had been born in a two-up, two-down row house, daughter of a Cockney policeman. But that past had been conveniently obliterated in her mind.

Once we were under way I turned to Darcy with the question I was dying to ask. 'Are you really going to play that part in Mr. Goldman's film?'

He was staring straight ahead, navigating the unfamiliar road and driving on the wrong side. 'Why not? You don't think I've got what it takes to be a film star?'

'I'm sure you have. It's just that . . .' What could I say? That I was scared he'd be a roaring success and would stay in Hollywood and have other women throw themselves at him? When I tried to form those thoughts into words they sounded petty and juvenile. I shook my head. 'No, of course if you really want to, I'm sure you'll be brilliant. Star of the film.'

Darcy grinned. The drive was spectacular, out on the road that hugged the Pacific Ocean. Steep golden sandstone cliffs rose to our right, blue water and white surf on the left. The colors were overwhelmingly bright, and in spite of all the tension of the last few days I began to look forward to this latest adventure, especially now that Darcy was beside me. After a few miles we left the paved road and began to climb into the hills up a narrow canyon. The dirt road twisted and turned until we came to a high wire fence with barbed wire around the top. A gate, similarly topped with barbed wire, barred our way.

'It looks like a prison,' Mummy muttered to me. 'Do you think we'll be allowed out again for good behavior?'

'When have you ever behaved well?' I turned to tease.

'Naughty child. You should spank her, Darcy.'

'Now that's a thought,' Darcy quipped back.

There was a small gatehouse built in the Spanish style. A man came out of this and the gate swung open. The gatekeeper saluted Mr. Goldman as his car sailed past. He kept saluting as we followed. We continued on, up a steep winding track between hills of parched golden grass, dotted with oak trees and scrub, until suddenly the landscape became more obviously cultivated with shade trees, flowering oleanders and bougainvillea, even rose bushes. Among the trees I caught glimpses of small cottages and wondered if the description of a castle had just been Mr. Goldman's private tease.

Then we came to a gravel forecourt, with a fountain in it, just like an English country estate, and behind it – for once I was justified in saying 'golly.' My mother muttered not quite such a polite word. Above us, perched on a bluff, loomed a huge edifice – a cross between Moorish castle and Gothic fantasy with medieval turrets, domes of bright blue tiles, archways, balconies. The front façade was sparkling white marble, while other parts were made of rough stone, to resemble a medieval castle. The white stone glowed pink in the early evening sun.

To the left of the castle was an enormous swimming pool, its clear blue waters sparkling in the pale light. It was edged by a line of Greek columns and arches. Classical statues stood between the columns and were dotted around the forecourt.

'No expense spared here,' Darcy muttered. 'It looks as if he's pillaged the Acropolis for this lot.'

Darcy parked the motorcar next to the others in front of a vast garage. As I climbed out I was greeted by the most heavenly smell – the herby scents of vegetation mingled with the sweeter perfumes of a thousand rose bushes and tinged with the fresh salty breeze from the ocean, which lay far below us, sparkling in sunshine. This really was a fantasy paradise. And to add to the illusion I spotted something moving among the trees in the parkland, and for a second I thought my eyes were playing tricks on me. No deer or cows but striped animals. They really were zebras. I blinked and stared again. And could that actually be a giraffe among those oak trees? Then I remembered that the wild animals had been mentioned in our conversations on the ship. I hadn't taken them seriously then.

'Oh my God. It's a bloody zoo,' my mother exclaimed as she exited from the motor. 'You don't think there are any lions, do you? I'm not leaving the house.'

'I shouldn't be at all surprised,' Darcy said. 'He probably feeds them with guests who have outstayed their welcome.'

Cy Goldman was standing on the steps waiting to greet us. 'Welcome to my humble abode,' he said in his big voice. 'I hope you enjoy your stay here. Feel free to use any of the facilities – swimming pool, gymnasium, riding stables – all at your disposal. And now I'd like you to come and get your keys. My guests never stay in the main house. Too much closeness for me. That's why I had the guest cottages built on the grounds. So let's see. Claire honey, you don't mind sharing a cottage with your daughter, do you? I've put you in Honeysuckle Hall – my English-style cottage – so that you feel at home.' He held out a key to her. 'And you young guys – Juan, Darcy, Ronnie and you – what's your name.' He pointed at Algie, making it quite clear that he hadn't expected Algie to come along. 'There's plenty of room for you all in the Hacienda. That's the low Spanish-style building just behind the main house. Ronnie will show you the way.' He held out a key to Ronnie.

'Craig, I wouldn't insult you by putting you with lesser mortals, so you get one of the poolside suites. Stella, it might be wiser if you took the other, seeing that Mrs. Goldman will be arriving soon.'

'I don't see why I shouldn't have my usual room in the house, Cy,' she said, staring at him defiantly. 'I come here more often than she does and all my things are there. Don't worry, I won't try to climb into bed with you, I promise.'

Cy shrugged. 'Suit yourself, but she's not going to like it.'

'Do I care?' Stella muttered as she turned away. 'I could always bunk in the Hacienda with the boys. I bet they'd find a way to keep me happy.' And she shot him a challenging look as she walked past him up the steps and into the main house.

Mr. Goldman cleared his throat. 'Alfredo will drive you down to your cottage, Claire,' he said. 'When you've settled in, come up to the house and I'll give you the grand tour. Drinks will be waiting beside the pool. Bring your costumes if you want to swim. Don't worry about the breeze. The pool is heated.'

A young and ruggedly handsome man started loading our luggage aboard a little motorized cart. It crossed my mind that he might be one of Mr. Goldman's discoveries who hadn't measured up and had been discarded like Juan. We climbed aboard and crunched across the gravel forecourt, along a flagstone path, finally stopping outside a cottage that looked as if it had been taken, brick by brick, from a quaint English village. Honeysuckle climbed over the porch. Inside was furnished to complete the illusion, with a tall Welsh dresser full of blue and white china, copper pots, low ceilings and wood beams. As we entered it even smelled old. The furniture was definitely antique – the sort of tables, sideboard, writing desk and high-backed armchairs you'd find in any English country house. Mummy was still grinning. 'I wonder if he bought the whole thing and had it shipped across from England,' she said. 'How horribly quaint. I'd rather have had the Spanish-style bungalow where the men are staying. At least that's close to the house. But I suppose he wants us to feel at home in a replica of Merrie Olde England.'

'At least it's a trifle better than that other cottage beyond this.' I pointed out of the window to where a replica of a cottage that might have housed Hansel and Gretel's witch stood nestled among tall oak trees. It had tiny paned windows, a ridiculously pointed roof and weathered shutters.

'No accounting for taste.' Mummy shivered.

Claudette unpacked for Mummy and I hung up my own things. I couldn't help imagining what Queenie's reaction to this place would have been and how she made me laugh as well as exasperating me. I wondered if I'd ever be able to afford another maid. I swallowed back the lump in my throat. When Mummy had changed into more casual wide-bottom slacks and blouse, tied her hair back with a red scarf and repaired her make-up, we followed the path back up the hill to the house. Of course we were among the last. Mummy never dresses in a hurry.

'I don't think I like the thought of walking up this path,'

she said. 'Where is the young man with his little cart when we need him? Did you notice a telephone in the cottage?'

'It's not too far and it's a nice evening,' I said.

Mummy looked around. 'I certainly don't intend to walk down it alone at night. What about the wild animals? I shall keep thinking we're being stalked by lions and tigers.' She latched on to my arm. 'I'm not even keen to meet a zebra face to face. I hear they've got nasty tempers.'

'I think wild animals are usually shy and avoid humans,' I said, staring up at the castle that loomed above us, gleaming in the setting sun. 'But isn't this place extraordinary? I've never seen anything like it.'

'It's certainly over the top, and completely tasteless,' Mummy said. 'He must have an awful lot of money to waste. I thought Max was rich, but at least he's sensible. I must write and tell him about this.'

'Your German must have improved,' I said.

She glared at me. 'He has a secretary to translate.' She looked around again. 'Drinks by the pool, didn't he say? I didn't bring my costume, did you?'

'No,' I said. There was no way I'd have wanted to reveal my body to a group that included Craig and Stella.

'It's a little nippy for a swim,' Mummy said, 'and I don't look my best with goose bumps.'

As we approached the pool we could see Cy Goldman and several other people already assembled amid the archways and palm trees. Stella was in a bright green, form-fitting bathing suit, sitting with her feet in the clear blue water, holding a martini in her hand. She was looking up at someone, laughing, and I couldn't tell if she was flirting with Juan or Darcy or both. Mr. Goldman beckoned us over and told us to order cocktails from the barman.

'Enjoy yourselves while you can before my wife gets here,' he said. Then he looked up and swore under his breath. Another motorcar was coming up the canyon. 'Too late,' Cy said.

The motor came to a halt. A chauffeur opened the back door and a large woman in black stepped out. She was dressed for New York not California in a two-piece suit with a diamond brooch on her lapel. Her hair was marcel waved into tight curls and her face was a mask of bright make-up. She looked around with disapproval then stalked over toward us. 'There you are, Cyrus,' she said. 'I was expecting you'd have had the courtesy to wait until I arrived. But no, you can't even be bothered to greet your wife when you haven't seen her in ages. I only saw you for a couple of seconds when you were in New York.'

'Nice to see you too, Helen,' Cy replied dryly. 'It wasn't my fault that you had your museum auxiliary meeting when I came to the apartment. Anyway, you're here now. Come and have a drink and meet everyone.'

She looked at us with disapproval. 'You've brought a whole slew of people here? How thoughtless. Didn't it occur to you that I'd want us to spend some time together?'

'You never did before,' Cy said. 'Anyway, we need to keep working on the picture we're shooting. It's just cast members and a few friends.'

'Well, I've brought some friends too,' she said. 'I ran into Barbara at the Beverly Hills Hotel and she was delighted to keep me company on the drive. So was dear Charlie. I gather you'd invited him and he was planning to drive up later, but then he decided to hitch a ride with us.'

I watched as Barbara Kindell and Charlie Chaplin emerged from the car.

'Charlie's okay, but what did you want to bring her for?' Cy hissed. 'You know that anything that happens here will be in the New York newspapers tomorrow.'

'Don't be so stuffy, Cy. She's an old friend. A good friend. A loyal friend, which is more than I can say for some people.' She reached out for Barbara Kindell and hooked her arm through Barbara's. Barbara gave us a small triumphant smile. Charlie Chaplin had headed straight for the bar, took a cocktail and then turned toward my mother and me, raising his glass to his lips.

'Ah, the flower of English womanhood,' he said.

He was about to come over to us when he noticed Craig and Darcy. 'Don't tell me I have competition this weekend,' he said. 'I'm not exactly worried about my boy Craig, but who are these other fellows?'

'My new stars, Charlie.' Cy Goldman moved across to put an arm around his shoulder. 'Juan is a Spanish matador and this guy O'Mara is a true-blue Irish lord. I'm going to make him the next Fairbanks. And Juan the next Valentino.'

'Good luck.' Charlie looked amused. 'So long as neither is a comic. But then they don't look very comical.'

Cy was looking past him, frowning. 'Did you bring someone else, Helen? Is that your new maid?'

Mrs. Goldman turned around. 'No, Cy. This is a charming young lady I met on the train. She was so helpful to me when I couldn't get my bag down from the rack. And when she told me she was an up-and-coming costume designer and she was actually on her way out to see you, I insisted that she come along. What's more she's a real blue-blooded descendant of the Tudor family and I heard it just happens you're making a movie about the Tudors.

So I thought she might be quite a help in designing your costumes for you.'

I was staring in amazement. Of all the surreal things I had seen today this was the most unbelievable.

'Belinda,' I exclaimed.

Chapter 17

At Mr. Goldman's castle, somewhere up the coast from Los Angeles
August 3

Belinda dropped her train case and rushed toward me, flinging out her arms. 'Georgie, darling. What a lovely, lovely surprise. Fancy meeting you of all people here.'

She looked back at Mrs. Goldman as she kissed my cheeks. 'This is my oldest and dearest friend in the world. Lady Georgiana, you know. Cousin to His Majesty the king. I'd heard that you were in Los Angeles but I had no idea . . .' She looked around the group, beaming. 'And your dear mama, and good heavens – there's Darcy too. It's like a family reunion.'

Mr. Goldman was looking bemused and for once speechless. 'Let me get this straight. This kid is another Tudor relation? Did they breed like rabbits?'

'The British aristocratic families are all related to each other in some way,' I said, although I was fairly sure that Belinda was in no way linked to the Tudors. I was giving her full marks for her acting ability. She knew very well that we were with Mr. Goldman and that the film was about the Tudors. 'This is Miss Warburton-Stoke. Belinda and I were at school together.'

Belinda turned the full force of her charm on Cy Goldman. 'How do you do,' she said, 'and how kind of you to include me at this lovely, lovely place.'

Of course then he could hardly say that he didn't want to include her. He scratched his head. 'Where are we going to put these people, Ronnie?' he asked.

'We can put Mr. Chaplin in the other poolside suite, if Miss Brightwell's not using it,' Ronnie said. 'And we can have Maria open up Trianon for Miss Kindell and the young English lady. Unless you'd like your new protégé to sleep in the big house, Mrs. Goldman?'

'Barbara can sleep in the big house with us,' Mrs. Goldman said firmly. 'I want to have her close by, just in case I need her.'

'I have an extra bed in my room. Belinda can share with me,' I said, smiling sweetly at her. 'It will be just like old times at school.' Belinda opened her mouth to protest but then decided not to. 'Thanks, Georgie,' she said.

'Well, that's settled then,' Cy said. 'You'd all better have a drink. And to what do I owe this honor, Helen?'

'I need permission to come to my own house now, do I?' She faced him defiantly.

'No, but since you haven't been here in years I thought you weren't interested.'

'I heard you bought a chapel from a Spanish convent and you're having it shipped over here, brick by brick,' she said. 'I wanted to see for myself.'

'It's not here yet,' he said.

'So where are you going to put it?'

'It's going to be my new bathhouse for the pool. Imagine taking a shower with all those saints looking down from stained-glass windows.'

I caught Charlie Chaplin's eye and he winked. I was beginning to like him in spite of the rumors. Belinda had returned to the group with her cocktail. She looked around. I saw her appraising Juan, then her gaze fixed on Craig.

'My goodness. That can't be Craig Hart, can it?' she said breathlessly and she made a beeline for him. 'I'd recognize you anywhere, Mr. Hart. I'm such a big fan. I loved you as a pirate in your last film.'

'Well, thank you very much, little lady,' Craig said. 'What was your name again?'

'Belinda,' she said, gazing up at him adoringly. It was lucky that I really had no interest in being Craig Hart's next conquest. I moved over to Darcy.

'Well, that's a turn-up for the books. What's she doing here?' he whispered. 'Did you invite her?'

'Of course not. I wrote to her from New York and told her about Mr. Goldman and the film. She must have taken the next boat. You know Belinda. She never misses a good opportunity. Perhaps she now wants to be a costume designer for the movies. She'd be good, I think.'

'I think she'd rather catch a rich film star,' Darcy muttered behind his cocktail glass. 'Look at her turning on the charm.'

The fog was now rolling in from the ocean and with it a chill breeze. Stella shivered and hauled herself out of the pool. 'I'm cold, Cy. Let's go inside.' She put on a toweling robe and slippers.

I didn't miss the daggers look that shot from Mrs.

Goldman. So she was all too aware of Stella Brightwell's role
in his life. I wondered what she must think about having his
mistress with him so openly.

'That's right,' Cy said. 'I promised these people a tour of
the house. Then these young British aristocrats can tell me
if it's better than their stately homes. It damned well better
be, the money I've spent on it.' He clapped his hands. 'Come
on, then. Follow me. House tour coming up.'

He led us up the long flight of marble steps and opened
a massive studded oak front door. We stepped into the cool
darkness of an entrance hall two stories high. Weapons
decorated the walls and the vaulted ceiling was hung with
ancient banners. The whole effect reminded me sharply of
Castle Rannoch.

'Follow me,' Cy said. Our footsteps echoed from the high
ceiling as we crossed that foyer. On either side there were
alcoves, decorated with classical statues that really didn't
go with the weapons hanging above them. Then Cy pushed
open a door and we entered a sitting room, rather like the
one I had left at Kingsdowne Place, with a great marble fireplace at its center.

'Recognize this?' Cy said with a triumphant grin. 'It came
from one of your British houses. Lord something or other.
You should have seen the job they had getting it up the hill.
Took a team of oxen to pull it.'

One magnificent room after another followed. There were
paintings on oak-paneled walls, statues in corners, suits of
armor, archways, beamed ceilings. . . . And the interesting
thing was that none of it really belonged together, almost
like items laid out ready for an auction. It was as Mummy
had said, a Gothic fantasy. Cy was beaming like a proud
child. 'Designed the whole thing myself,' he said. 'Not bad

for a boy who came to the States with nothing. Who was glad to get a job selling newspapers.'

'Cyrus,' Mrs. Goldman said in her strident voice. 'So what about those other things that you told me you'd found in Spain? Didn't I hear you'd bought candlesticks? And an El Greco?'

'So you're suddenly interested in antiques? Or did you hear how much they're worth?' He looked back at her, almost gloating in his expression. 'I got them for a steal, if you're worried about how much I paid – this convent had no idea what they were. That El Greco was hanging behind a side altar in their chapel. Their roof was leaking and their plumbing wasn't working and they were happy to get those things fixed. But you wait until you see them, Helen. Exquisite.'

He quickened his pace, and led us into a narrow side hall. I gasped as I saw a figure looming over me with an ax raised. Then I realized it was only another suit of armor. 'Watch out for that guy,' Cy called jovially. 'He's my guard. He dispatches people I don't like.' He went ahead and opened a door at the end. 'My prize possession,' he said. 'My library.'

'Prize possession. That's rich. You don't even like reading,' Mrs. Goldman said.

'I like books. I like the look and smell of old books,' he said. 'Do you know who owned this library before me? Another English lord. Probably one of your relations.' (He looked at me, then Darcy.) 'He was having financial troubles, so I bought the whole thing, lock, stock and barrel. Had the shelves shipped over here and reassembled just as it was. I even found windows from an old country house in England.'

I noticed then that the windows had been set into alcoves, to give the impression of thick castle walls, I supposed. Each of the alcoves was hung with heavy red drapes. The windows were clearly very old, maybe even Tudor – small panes of imperfect glass between heavy oak frames.

'There. That's the El Greco,' Cy said, drawing our attention away from the windows and the stunning view beyond. He went over to a small painting now propped up against one of the shelves. It was a Madonna and Child with the painter's characteristic long faces and elongated hands. It was done in muted reds and blues and the woman looked incredibly sad, but it was lovely in its own way.

'Looks rather dreary to me,' Mrs. Goldman said. 'Couldn't you have found something more cheerful?'

'You wait until you find out what it's worth, honey. Then you'll suddenly decide it's lovely and you have to have it in your living room in New York to show to the Hadassah ladies.'

'I don't think they'd take kindly to a Madonna and Child,' she said. 'Even if they are by El Greco.'

Cy put down the painting then moved over to the polished library table. 'I thought I might put the candlesticks in here on the table so I can enjoy them when I'm working,' Mr. Goldman said. A plain wooden case now lay on it. He opened this and took out a candlestick. There was a gasp from the group. It was amazing – a little too ornate for my taste, but brilliant nonetheless. It was about eighteen inches tall, and around its base was a complete country scene all in gold, with young girls dancing among trees. Curled garlands of golden flowers rose up its sides. And dotted everywhere were precious stones – ruby and emerald centers for the flowers, while diamonds, sapphires, topaz, and lapis adorned the girls and the trees, all sparkling in the light of the chandelier that hung from the ceiling.

'Pretty, huh?' He held it up to us.

'I hope you've got it properly insured,' Helen Goldman said. 'That thing's worth a fortune.'

'There's a pair of them, Helen. But don't worry. I'll get them insured. Besides, who can break into this place?' Cy said. 'I'll have the fence electrified if you're worried.' He put the candlestick back in its case and closed the lid. 'Now let's go and see where we're going to hang the El Greco. If I put it next to the Goya it will be overshadowed. It needs just the right lighting.'

We followed him out of the library. 'You're like a little boy.' Helen drew level with him now. 'Can't get enough new toys, can you? Well, don't forget that it's my money too that you're wasting like this.'

'There's plenty more where that came from,' he said, 'and if you don't like the way I live you can always divorce me, you know.'

'You don't want a divorce,' she said. 'You wouldn't want to pay all that alimony and you know I'd drag all the sordid details of you and your mistresses through the courts. Believe me.'

'Oh, I do believe you. You always did have a vindictive streak,' he said.

'I'm sure the newspapers would love to read about you and dear Stella – or are you looking to move on to someone a little younger, perhaps? You're not wearing well around the edges, Stella honey. I'd say this is your last hurrah as a movie star.'

'You're a bitch, Helen, did anyone tell you that?' Stella said.

'Frequently. And I enjoy it. It's one of my few pleasures since my husband abandoned me.'

'I abandoned you?' Cy demanded. 'I like that. Who wanted her own bedroom from day one? And kept the door locked?'

'You always were too demanding. You should have given me more time. Like a great ape, you were.'

The rest of us were trapped in the corridor with them, absolutely squirming with embarrassment. In England such a scene would never have happened. Fighting in public was just not done among our sort of people. It was Charlie Chaplin who took control. 'I think we'll go change for dinner and leave you to it, Cy,' he said. 'I enjoy a prizefight as much as anyone, but I hate seeing good antiques get smashed. Come on, gang.'

We followed him back down the hallway and out into the mist that had risen from the Pacific Ocean to take over the landscape. Trees were now blurred and indistinct shapes.

'Where on earth are we going?' Belinda asked.

'We have one of the guest cottages,' I said. 'Look. Down there in the trees.'

'We have to walk back here in the dark?' Belinda said.

'I agree,' Mummy said, 'and with the wild animals too.'

'Wild animals. That's funny.' Belinda laughed.

'You didn't see any on your way up here?' Mummy said. 'Those woods are teeming with giraffes and zebras and God knows what.'

Belinda peered into the trees, still not sure if we were pulling her leg. 'And there may be lions. We haven't seen them yet,' I added, still feeling rather cross with her. 'What are you doing here, Belinda? You really have a nerve.'

'Darling, I got sacked from Harrods when this obnoxious

Frenchwoman told my boss that I wasn't really French. And your postcard arrived the same day. I said to myself it must be fate, so I used my last paycheck to buy a ticket. And another piece of absolute luck – I met Mrs. Goldman on the train. Helped her with her case, actually. I had no idea who she was until she told me. So it really had to be fate, didn't it?'

'Yes, but what do you want to do here?'

'I told Mrs. Goldman I was a costume designer. Well, I could be, easily. You have to admit I have a flair.'

'Yes, you do.'

She glanced around, then pulled me closer to her. 'But now I'm thinking I might have found my sugar daddy instead. Isn't Craig Hart divine? Did you see how attentive he was to me? Is he married?'

'Not at the moment, I don't think. But he's fickle.'

'He was pursuing Georgie until you arrived,' Mummy said. 'I can't think why.'

'He even kissed me last night,' I said with a grin. 'Darcy saw and was not amused.'

'And what's Darcy doing here then? And isn't that Algie Broxley-Whatsit? What a little creep he always was – he groped one at hunt balls.'

'They are doing exactly the same thing as you, Belinda dear,' Mummy said. 'Using my fame to get themselves a job on a film.'

'How screamingly funny.' Belinda laughed loudly. There was a stirring in the bushes and some kind of antelope bounded out. 'Ye gods,' Belinda said. 'You weren't joking about the animals.'

While we dressed for dinner I told Belinda about Queenie. 'Well rid of her, darling. She was a millstone around your neck,' Belinda said. 'Now, if Darcy plays his cards right and becomes a film star you'll be able to marry him and afford a real maid.'

I was surprised at the jolt of horror I felt as she said this. Did I want my future husband to be a film star? I knew it would make him a lot of money, but it would mean a life very different from the one I had visualized. And women throwing themselves at him. Darcy was only human and I'd seen the way Stella was already ogling him.

'Tell me, Georgie,' Belinda went on. 'Do you think I might really have a chance with Craig Hart?'

'For one night, maybe. Isn't that how film stars behave? He was kissing me yesterday.'

'But when he experiences the incredible sex I have to offer, isn't it possible that he might want an aristocratic English wife?'

'But you don't even know him. He may be horrible under the façade. He may have tantrums and act like a spoiled little boy.'

She shrugged. 'It doesn't matter. He'd have enough money to keep me happy.'

I sat on my bed and looked up at her. She already looked older than me. 'Is that what you really want, Belinda? Just lots of money, no matter how you get it?'

'Money and sex, darling. That's about it.'

'What about love?'

She looked out of the window. 'I don't think I'm destined for love,' she said. Then she peered harder. 'What do you think that Stella Brightwell is doing among the trees? Feeding the animals?'

I went over to join her. It was hard to see through the fog in the fading light, but it really did look like Stella Brightwell,

with something dark draped around her shoulders, moving
quickly through the trees. I wondered if she'd arranged to
meet Juan, perhaps. Or if she was running away in a huff
after that tiff in the corridor. In which case Mr. Goldman
was not pursuing her.

Chapter 18

At Mr. Goldman's castle
The evening of August 3

> *I am still rather annoyed with Belinda although in a way I'm glad she's here. She is so good at crashing other people's parties. Actually I suppose I'm jealous. I wish I had her nerve.*

By the time we had waited for Mummy to change her clothes and adjust her hair and make-up and had walked back to the main house, we were among the last to assemble in a long gallery that looked as if it had been lifted from Versailles. One wall was lined with mirrors. The furniture was brocade and gilt. There was a great marble fireplace in the middle of one wall. In the far corner Charlie Chaplin, Craig and Darcy stood at an impressive cocktail cabinet shaped like a Spanish galleon. Algie was hovering near them, hoping to be included in their conversation. Stella Brightwell was standing alone staring out of the window. She was toying with a strand of hair in a nervous manner. Barbara Kindell was sitting pretending to read a magazine but actually taking in the scene. There was no sign of Juan or Ronnie or the Goldmans.

Belinda made a beeline for the men at the cocktail cabinet. Mummy went over to Stella. I followed and saw what Stella was looking at. Juan was outside alone, walking up and down, puffing on a cigarette, glancing from time to time up at the castle.

'It's not right.' Stella looked up at Mummy. 'Cy discovers him in a small Spanish town, promises him the Earth. Drags him all this way, far from his home, and then tells him he's not a star after all. Now Juan doesn't know what to do. I think he'd like to go home but Cy has him under contract. He has us all under contract – me, Craig . . . we're all his puppets, you know.'

'Could Cy's change of heart have more to do with your interest in Juan than his accent?' Mummy asked. 'I get the feeling he doesn't like to share his possessions.'

Stella and Mummy exchanged a glance. 'I must admit I am tempted,' Stella said. 'I mean, I'm eternally grateful to Cy for everything, but you have to admit it. He's old. And Juan – I mean, my God, what a body. I bet he's a raging bull in bed.'

They looked back and saw that I'd overheard. I pretended to find a magazine and went to sit on a sofa but I could still overhear perfectly well.

'That was one of the things Cy accused me of in our little dust-up just now,' Stella said. 'Thank God you left. It wasn't pretty. I think "catfight" probably describes it. God, that woman is poison. I think she just came here to make trouble – I can't think why else. She hates the West Coast.' She paused to light a cigarette, then took a long draw on it before she went on. 'She won't live with him. She won't share his bed but she won't let him go. Someone should push her off a cliff and have done with it.'

'Or feed her to the lions?' Mummy asked.

She and Stella exchanged a wicked smile.

Then the Goldmans came in together, giving every appearance of being a happy couple. 'Ready for dinner, everyone?' Cy boomed in his loud voice. 'Eat hearty tonight because tomorrow it's going to be work, work, work for most of you. I want this movie shot on time. I promised Claire I'd be done with her on schedule and by God I intend to be. Come on. This way.'

He led us through double doors at the end of the Versailles room. A long dark wood table stretched the entire length of the chamber. Along it were tall candlesticks, each flickering with light. Two chandeliers hung from a wood-paneled ceiling. Small-paned windows looked out onto the hillside. It was like stepping back into medieval times. There were banners and crossed weapons on the walls. Yet another suit of armor in the corner.

'Take a seat,' Cy commanded. 'How about this table, huh? I got it from a monastery last time I was in Europe. And the candlesticks. They had them in the chapel but I think they look better here.' He sat at one end of the table, Mrs. Goldman at the other. Place cards indicated where the rest of us should sit. Stella was in the middle with Craig facing her. I was on one side of him, Belinda on the other. Charlie Chaplin and Mummy were on either side of Mr. Goldman. Ronnie on the other side of me. He had been sent to fetch Juan, who sat, silent and glowering, next to Mrs. Goldman.

'Okay, Maria, you can serve now,' Mr. Goldman called and a pleasant-looking Mexican woman came in carrying a tray of oysters to the table. She was just about to offer them to Mr. Goldman when Mrs. Goldman let out a yell. 'What were you thinking, Cyrus? There's thirteen at dinner. Don't you know how unlucky that is?'

'I don't believe in luck, personally. Besides, people have arrived who weren't in my final count. People you brought, Helen. You brought the bad luck, not me.'

Mrs. Goldman glared and fell silent. The dinner was simple by our English standards but very tasty. After the oysters there was a spicy soup with vegetables and crunchy bits, then quail, then big slabs of prime rib, served very rare. The meal finished with ice cream and fruit. I would have enjoyed it more if I hadn't sensed the clear atmosphere of tension around me. Mr. and Mrs. Goldman exchanged barbs the full length of the table. Charlie was flirting across the table with my mother, who was not exactly repelling his advances. Belinda monopolized Craig. I turned to Ronnie. 'Is it always like this here?' I asked.

Ronnie smiled. 'You should know by now, Mr. Goldman feeds off drama. There has to be high stress around him. And Mrs. Goldman – she's hardly ever here, especially not when he's got guests like this. And between ourselves she's not exactly the gracious hostess.'

He looked past me to where Belinda was now hanging on Craig's every word.

'I see I've been discarded,' I whispered to Ronnie.

'Your friend is practically throwing herself at him,' Ronnie agreed. He smirked. 'I wonder if she'd be so eager if she knew.'

'Knew what?'

He leaned closer. 'I was going to tell you yesterday, to save you from getting the wrong idea and further embarrassment.' He paused then muttered, 'Craig Hart is . . . well, you know. He is not exactly interested in the female sex, if you know what I mean.'

'Crikey. One of the leading heart-throbs in the world and he's a fairy?' I whispered.

Ronnie nodded. 'It's a closely guarded secret. I suspect that's why Mr. Goldman introduced him to you. He's made it clear to Craig that he needs to marry somebody and marry quickly. Marriage to a young lady with royal connections would look good in all the picture papers, wouldn't it?'

'How awful,' I said. 'Luckily I have Darcy or I might have been swept off my feet and said yes.'

'You'd better warn your friend in a discreet way,' Ronnie said.

'Yes.' I was watching them. It would be interesting to see how things progressed.

Dinner ended and Mr. Goldman stood up. 'I fancy a good cigar. Any of you guys care to join me?'

'You'd better go and smoke in your library then,' Mrs. Goldman said. 'You know how I hate the smell of cigar smoke. It gives me a headache.'

'Fine with me,' Mr. Goldman said. 'Brandy and cigars in the library, guys. Anyone coming?'

'I will.' Darcy got up to follow him, as did Archie, Craig and Ronnie. Charlie Chaplin started to follow them, then turned back. 'I think I'd rather get to know this young lady with the long legs,' he said, making a beeline for me. 'I want you to tell me all about yourself.'

'There's really not much to tell,' I said, blushing as the others watched while he escorted me from the room.

'I believe Maria's put out coffee in the rotunda,' Mrs. Goldman said. She led us through double doors to a round open area, just off the main foyer. It was decorated more in the Spanish style with leather sofas and chairs, and heavy dark wood tables. Coffeepots and cups had been put on a low central table.

'Now come and sit next to me, you sweet young thing, and I'll attempt to corrupt you,' Charlie Chaplin said.

'I've been warned about you, Mr. Chaplin,' I replied, safe in the knowledge that I was surrounded by people and Darcy was nearby. Also that two minutes ago he'd been flirting with my mother, who now looked slightly miffed.

'No doubt by our dear Barbara.' He flashed her a wicked smile. 'All lies.'

'You know I only ever speak the truth, Charlie,' Barbara said. 'Nobody has ever managed to sue me for libel yet, especially not you.' She went to sit beside Mrs. Goldman.

'I should help pass around the coffee,' I said, dodging past him to where Belinda was already handing around cups. Belinda was looking pleased with herself.

'Did you see how he didn't take his eyes off me once all through dinner?' she whispered. 'I think this may be it, Georgie. I've finally struck gold.'

I debated whether to tell her, but decided it was none of my business. I finished handing around coffee then sat on the sofa beside my mother. Charlie immediately came over and squeezed in beside me. 'Now isn't this cozy,' he said as he rested one hand casually on my knee. 'So tell me all about the royal family. All the juicy scandals with the Prince of Wales.' And he walked his fingers up my thigh. I wasn't sure whether to slap his hand or not and decided to pretend that it didn't bother me that one of the most famous men in the world was now trying to seduce me. Two of them in two days. I rather wished that Fig could see me now.

We were still drinking coffee when Ronnie came back to join us.

'So what do we do in the evenings?' Mummy asked. 'I don't see a bridge table, or a gramophone.'

'Mr. Goldman doesn't go in for parlor games and such,' Ronnie replied. 'He has a full cinema in the basement where he'll be happy to show you his latest successes.'

'I don't feel like watching a film at this hour,' Mummy said.

'We could play some kind of game if you'd like to organize it, I'm sure,' Ronnie said. 'Charades? Twenty questions?'

'I don't feel like that either.' Mummy gave a bored sort of sigh. 'I need a little excitement. It's been horribly dull since I came here. Come to think of it, Homer Clegg turned out to be as dull as ditchwater. Is it always horribly dull in America?'

'I have a little something in my purse that might make you feel better, if you like.' Stella moved over to Mummy and whispered in her ear, just loud enough for me to over-hear. 'I'm willing to share if you want to go through to the kitchen. God knows I need cheering up too. It's been a hell of a day.'

'Darling, I can't take drugs in front of my daughter. What would she think of me?' Mummy said. There was an awk-ward sort of silence. I noticed Barbara Kindell watching Stella and Mummy with interest. Presumably she had also overheard. I wondered if Stella's cocaine use would show up in tomorrow's gossip columns.

'Cy always was a rotten host,' Mrs. Goldman said. 'Of course he grew up with no sort of refinement. I've tried to educate him but he's never even bothered to learn bridge. But then . . . he has found other less savory games to play.' And she stared pointedly at Stella.

We went back to sipping coffee, hoping there would not be a repeat of this afternoon's uncomfortable scene. I think we were all glad when Darcy came back in with Craig. They went over to the coffee tray but Stella intercepted. 'It will be cold by now. I'll have Maria make you some fresh.'

Darcy came to perch on the arm of my sofa, giving my shoulder a reassuring touch. Craig went over to the window. 'Too cold for a swim tonight, I'm afraid,' he said. 'The fog has come in.'

'Oh, I don't know.' Belinda looked up at him. 'I'm always game for a late-night swim.'

'Did you bring your costume?'

'No, but does it matter?' Her eyes flirted outrageously. I was always rather impressed and secretly envious of this skill.

'All right. Come on, then. What are we waiting for?' Craig held out his hand to her. 'Anyone else care to join us?'

'Not me,' Mummy said. 'Watching my nipples turn blue with cold is not my idea of fun.'

So off they went.

'What's Cy doing now?' Mrs. Goldman demanded.

'I don't know. I thought he was following us,' Darcy said.

'Probably playing with his new toys one more time.' She sniffed. 'Just like a two-year-old. Pathetic. Well, if you'll excuse me, I think I'm going up to bed. It's been a long and tiring day.' She got up and headed for the stairs.

'Do you want me to come up with you, Helen, honey?' Barbara Kindell asked. 'Are you okay?'

'I'll be fine,' Helen Goldman said. 'I should never have come. Stupid. Absolutely stupid.' And she stomped off, across the tiled foyer.

There was an awkward silence, then Ronnie and Darcy

went off to talk in a corner, the latter glancing back at me as Charlie's hand rested on my knee while he whispered something silly and rather risqué in my ear. I grinned at Darcy to let him know he didn't need to worry. Maria arrived with more coffee and handed around cups.

'Where's Juan?' Stella asked suddenly.

'He went to bed right after dinner,' Ronnie said. 'I don't blame him. It hasn't been the easiest sort of day, has it?'

'I wonder if I should go and see if he's all right. Give him some moral support,' Stella said. She started for the front door.

'Is that what you call it these days?' Mummy had a glint in her eye.

Suddenly there was an almighty crash. Coffee cups were hastily put down. We leaped up. 'What was that?' Stella demanded. 'It came from the direction of the library.'

We crossed the entrance hall and turned into the side corridor. The suit of armor was lying sprawled on the tiled floor. Suddenly a tall apparition wearing a helmet and visor staggered out at us, making Stella, who was first in line, scream. Darcy grabbed it. Then he said angrily, 'Broxley-Foggett, what the devil do you think you're doing?'

'I say, get this bally thing off me, will you?' a muffled voice said.

It took two of them to wrench the helmet off Algie's head. He looked suitably sheepish. 'Sorry about that, everyone,' he said. 'Dashed silly of me, I know. I saw the suit of armor and I realized I was rather keen to be an extra in the film and wondered what I'd look like and whether Mr. Goldman might decide to make me a star too. So I put the helmet on and the blasted visor dropped and I couldn't see where I was going. I must have knocked the whole bally thing over.'

'I'm surprised Mr. Goldman hasn't bawled you out for knocking over one of his prized possessions,' Ronnie said. 'Where did he go?'

'He was still in the library when I came out,' Algie said. 'But I went to spend a penny and it took me hours to locate a loo. Almost left it too late, don't you know? Had to put on a bit of a sprint. Do you know that even the lavatories have banners hanging in them?'

Ronnie stepped over the armor and pushed open the library door. The smell of cigar smoke still lingered in the air. 'Mr. Goldman, sir?' he began. Then he said, 'He's not in there. That's strange. Wouldn't we have noticed if he had come out?' Then he said, 'The candlesticks are missing.'

'What?' Darcy pushed past him into the room. I followed and saw the foot at about the same moment he muttered, 'Oh my God.'

Chapter 19

Cy Goldman was lying between the big library table and the heavy drapes that were now closed around the window alcove. One of his candlesticks lay on the floor beside him, matted with hair and blood. I didn't want to look but with that morbid fascination one has for anything gruesome I couldn't help myself. The back of his head had been smashed in.

'Everyone stand back,' Darcy said. 'Out of the room now and nobody touch anything. Someone should call the police.'

'The police? That's not going to be easy,' Ronnie said. 'We're under the jurisdiction of Ventura County, not any particular city. That would mean the sheriffs and I don't believe they have anyone stationed anywhere near here, or anyone who is equipped to investigate a homicide. Perhaps they request assistance from Los Angeles – or even from Ventura. I don't know how it works. I've never had to deal with anything like this before.' His usually worried face was now creased into a deep frown and he looked white enough to pass out any second.

'Do we have to?' my mother asked. 'Call the police, I mean. Couldn't we say it was an accident and he fell and hit his head? It probably was an accident, wasn't it? He drank too much at dinner and he fainted, or had a heart attack. And if we call the police, think of the scandal.'

'This was no accident.' Darcy stared at her. 'I think I can guarantee he was murdered.'

'Murdered? My darling Cy?' Stella's voice trembled. 'Who would do that to him? We were all his friends. We all adored him. Let me go to him.' She struggled as Darcy kept her away.

'I suppose he is actually dead?' Algie said, trying to sound flippant, but his voice trembled a little. 'I mean he didn't just faint or something?'

'I don't think anyone survives his head being bashed in like that,' Darcy said grimly. 'This was done with considerable force.'

'Come on, everyone,' Ronnie said. 'Back into the rotunda, I suppose. And I'll see if I can round up any kind of law enforcement, though I've no idea where.'

He grabbed Stella's arm, attempting to pull her away. She resisted, trying to get back to Cy Goldman's body. 'He must have interrupted a burglar,' Stella said, her voice now choking with emotion. 'The other candlestick is missing. But I don't understand it. I mean, we were all here. Only a few yards away from him. How could anyone have come in here unnoticed? There's only one way in to this estate and it's through that gate. And our gatekeeper, Jimmy, would never let in anybody he doesn't know.'

'We have to presume that the gatekeeper is all right,' Darcy said, 'and an intruder didn't bash him over the head to get in here.'

'Jimmy has an alarm button he can push from inside his cottage if he needs help,' Stella said. 'And he can telephone through to the main house. And our groundsmen are armed.'

'I expect someone could cut the wire fence if they were determined enough,' Charlie said. 'And there must be places where trees have grown up close enough to the fence to make it possible to climb over.'

Ronnie swallowed hard. 'I'll go and put through a call to Jimmy at the gate, make sure he's all right and tell him not to let anybody in or out until the police get here. And I suppose we ought to have the groundsmen drive around the perimeter to check if the fence has been cut. Oh God. And someone will have to go and tell Mrs. Goldman.'

'I'll do it, honey.' Barbara patted his arm. 'It should be someone she knows and trusts.'

'Are you sure?' Relief flooded Ronnie's face. 'And she'd better get dressed and come down right away if the police are going to be here.'

One by one they staggered out, stepping over the suit of armor.

Stella paused at the doorway and looked back. 'It's like a bad dream,' she said. 'I can't believe he's gone.'

Darcy remained standing behind the body, and, fighting back my revulsion, I went to join him. He was staring down at Mr. Goldman with a sort of horrified fascination. 'And to think we were in here with him less than half an hour ago. It doesn't seem possible.'

I put a hand on his arm. 'It's horrible,' I said.

'If it were any other young lady, I'd have you escorted from the room instantly before you swooned over the evidence,' he said, 'but you're probably more familiar with this sort of thing than I am.'

'I don't go looking for dead bodies,' I said. 'They just sort of happen to me. But we should take this opportunity to think things through before the police get here.'

'You realize what this means, don't you?' Darcy said, dropping his voice so that he couldn't be overheard. 'It had to be one of us.'

'Oh crikey,' I said. 'I suppose you're right. What a horrid thought. Unless . . .' He looked up at me. 'Unless it really was your cat burglar from London. You had a hunch he might be here, didn't you? If anyone could find a way in here, it sounds as if he could.'

Darcy nodded. 'Or she,' he said. 'But this doesn't fit with what we know of him or her. The burglar takes enormous risks, we know that. He's walked along ledges and gained access from rooftops, so he might have been able to find a way into the estate. I don't think the front door was locked, so he could have waited until we were all at dinner and slipped into the house and waited to take his chance. But the manner of death doesn't seem right. At home they refer to him at Scotland Yard as the gentleman thief. It's always been suspected that he is an aristocrat, or at least moves in their circles.'

'And you don't think aristocrats kill people?'

He smiled. 'Yes, but not bash their heads in. A stiletto through the heart – I'd go along with that. But our thief works with finesse. This killing is brutal, violent, and I don't think our thief is a violent person. There have been occasions in the past when he was interrupted during a burglary and he just melted away. He might have killed someone then, but he chose to abandon his attempt.'

'He was interrupted, you say? So he has been seen?'

'No. He always managed to slip out of a window or down a hall as someone approached. We know he's slim and probably dark, but someone did glimpse his shadow. That's all.'

'It was definitely someone who came here to commit robbery,' I said, 'because the other candlestick is missing. The thief was going to take both of them, but Mr. Goldman must have interrupted him and was hit over the head before he could call for help.'

Darcy shook his head. 'And then the thief left the second candlestick because it now had blood on it? He must be a thief with sensibilities. Why not make off with both, especially when one can be identified as the murder weapon. It might even have telltale fingerprints on it. And I notice he hasn't touched the El Greco painting, which must be a lot more valuable.'

The painting still lay propped against a shelf. The colors glowed in the soft light.

'Well, your suspicions about Stella Brightwell certainly don't apply this time,' I said. 'Didn't you notice? She was devastated by his death. And presumably she could have taken the candlestick anytime she chose, and would never have killed her lover to do so.'

Darcy sighed and nodded. 'It does appear that way.' He looked around the room. 'We'd better get out of here and not risk touching anything until the police arrive.'

I pulled back the drape cautiously. 'I wonder if the window is closed or if the murderer got out that way.'

Darcy took out a handkerchief. 'It doesn't appear to be latched.' He pushed the window cautiously. It swung open.

I took a tentative step toward the window and peered down. Light shone out, illuminating a sheer marble wall and what looked like rocks below it. 'But I don't think anyone could climb out through it,' I said. 'It's an awfully long way down and I wouldn't want to risk falling onto those rocks.' Outside I heard the roar of a motor and one of the small carts went speeding past. I thought I saw a rifle slung across the back of the person who was driving it.

As I stepped back into the room I noticed something. 'Look at that, Darcy,' I said, and I pointed to a bloody fingerprint on the window frame. 'That should help the police identify the culprit easily enough.'

'Well, one thing is for sure,' Darcy said. 'He'll have a hard time getting away.'

'If you really think it was one of us, then he'll stay and hope to bluff it out,' I said. 'And if it was your clever burglar then he's probably already long gone.'

'You know, the awful thing, Georgie,' Darcy said as he ushered me from the room, 'I'm not exactly surprised, are you? There was so much tension in this place. Mrs. Goldman arriving out of the blue. That unpleasant fight before dinner . . . the dust-up with the Spaniard – Where is he, by the way? I haven't seen him since dinner and he hardly said a word then.'

'He went off to bed right after dinner. He's been upset all day.'

'So he was someone who wasn't accounted for when Cy Goldman was murdered.'

'Yes, but . . . he's sleeping in one of the cottages, isn't he? If he'd come in through the front door, he'd have had to cross the foyer to get to the library corridor and we would have seen him.'

'Someone should go and wake him. He'll need to be awake and alert when the police get here.' He closed the library door and we stood in the darkness of that hallway. 'I have a bad feeling about this, Georgie. I've heard enough about the American way of justice to know that it's often shoot first and ask questions afterward. A rural sheriff isn't likely to have the skills to solve this. I rather fear that it's up to us.'

'Up to us? How can we solve it? I mean we can hardly question our fellow guests, can we?'

'We can do some preliminary thinking – work out who was where, who had a motive, who had the opportunity.'

'As to that, who could it be? You men were all together smoking cigars with Mr. Goldman. Perhaps the sheriff will try to suggest that you were in a conspiracy and you all killed him together.'

'That's not even funny, Georgiana. He may well think that.'

'Oh golly. I didn't mean it seriously. Sorry. I don't think even a sheriff could believe that Craig Hart killed Mr. Goldman. Craig's a big star. Mr. Goldman made him one. They needed each other. And had no quarrel as far as I could see.'

'Anyway, Craig has to be in the clear. He and I left the library together. Ronnie left before us.'

'And Algie?' I asked.

'He must have left when we did. Yes, I believe he followed us down the hallway. You know what he's like – never quite part of the conversation, always hanging around the periphery, hoping to be included.'

'I must say it's refreshing to have someone more accident-prone than I for once,' I said. 'But think, Darcy. If he hadn't had that accident with the suit of armor, we might not have discovered Mr. Goldman's body for hours. It would have been more difficult to gauge when he died and the killer could have made an escape with ease.'

'That's true. Stupid young oaf. It's a wonder he didn't bump into the killer and wind up dead himself.'

'Darcy' – I paused at the doorway, staring at the armor still lying on the floor – 'I suppose Algie really is as dense and clumsy as he seems? I mean could it possibly be a clever ruse so that nobody would ever suspect him?'

Darcy frowned, then shook his head. 'I've known him for years and he's always been a complete twit. When he was a child and we were at a house party together he fell into the lake when he was trying to walk along a wall. I had to dive in and pull him out. He couldn't swim, of course.'

'Maybe he lost his clumsiness when he grew up but he found it useful to keep up the illusion.'

He grabbed my arm, his fingers digging into me. 'Georgie – are you saying that you think Algie could be the gentleman burglar?'

'It's a possibility, isn't it? He's tall and slim and he's an aristocrat and he wangles himself invitations to parties and things. He's always hanging around on the edge of conversations so he must hear interesting snippets. Was he attending any of the functions where the robberies took place?'

'I didn't actually study the guest lists myself but his presence obviously never raised red flags to the English police. I could send a cable to Scotland Yard and ask if his name appears on any of those lists. If I'm allowed to leave this place tomorrow, that is.' He walked down the hall and picked his way over the suit of armor. 'I suppose we'd better not touch this either. It does prove that Algie had the best opportunity to do the deed. We have no idea how long he was alone in this hallway, playing with the suit of armor. One thing we know – nobody could have entered or left while he was there. Which makes the window of opportunity for killing

Goldman even slimmer.' He shook his head. 'I can't see Algie hitting someone over the head like that, can you? He'd probably miss and smash some priceless object instead.'

'If he really is who he pretends to be,' I said. 'But he did look rather green about the gills when we discovered the body, didn't he? And if he did kill Mr. Goldman, then why draw attention to himself by knocking over the armor and putting the helmet on his head? He could have just slipped in to join the group and probably nobody would have noticed.'

'Unless, as you say, he was being rather too clever. He wants us to say that it couldn't possibly be him, because he was staggering around with a helmet stuck on his head, being idiotic as usual.'

We looked at each other.

'Darcy, how can we ever figure out who did this?'

'Well, if it was Algie, his fingerprints will be on the candlestick,' Darcy said. 'Actually the same goes for the rest of us. Nobody is wearing gloves. . . .'

'Or carrying a handkerchief? Wouldn't that do just as well?'

Darcy took me into his arms. 'You are a cold-blooded little thing, aren't you? Calmly discussing methods of murder.'

'I'm not always cold-blooded.' I smiled up at him. 'And if we ever get a chance I'll prove it to you.'

He kissed me on the tip of my nose. 'I can't wait.' Then he slipped an arm around my shoulder. 'I suppose we should go in with the others and face the music.'

Chapter 20

I had expected to find a bigger group in the rotunda, but I saw only my mother and Stella, sitting side by side holding hands on the sofa, and Charlie Chaplin and Algie, over at the bar with what looked like glasses of scotch, all stiff and silent as if posing for a portrait. Ronnie's voice could be heard, raised and strained, from a telephone in some alcove in the foyer. 'Yes, I'm sure it's Mr. Goldman. I know what my employer looks like.' And then, 'How soon? Well, I suppose we have no choice. Of course, I understand that. But you realize this will be a high-profile case. Your men will be in the spotlight. You're going to need to get it right.'

The telephone was slammed down and Ronnie's feet echoed from the ceramic tiled floor as he crossed the foyer toward us. 'Damned fools,' he muttered. 'They say their men are needed at a suspicious fire up in hills above the Simi Valley. That's miles from here. The sheriff is going to try and make it over here himself but he says nothing must be touched until he gets here. Does he mean touch nothing in the library or the whole rest of the house? What are we supposed to do, then. Not move?'

'I gather you spoke with the groundsmen,' Darcy said. 'We heard those little carts outside.'

'I did. They are going to tour the whole property. And Jimmy at the gate says nobody has entered except us. Only people he knows.'

'Is there any way someone could have climbed over the gate or found a way to open it when he wasn't looking?' I asked.

Ronnie shook his head. 'The gate has the same barbed wire on top of it as the rest of the fence and the only way to open it is a switch inside the gatehouse.'

'I hope they find the fence damaged somewhere,' Mummy said, 'because that will mean the killer has escaped again.'

'You want him to get away?' Stella demanded.

Mummy shrugged. 'I don't like the thought of him trapped close by with us. We have to sleep in that lonely little cottage tonight.'

Stella stood up suddenly, making us all jump. 'Oh my God. Juan. He's all alone and asleep. I should go and see if he's all right.'

'We'll go,' Darcy said. 'I don't want you walking around alone in the dark. Want to come with me, Algie?'

'Me?' It came out almost as a squeak. 'But what if the killer is prowling out there?'

'There are two of us,' Darcy said. 'Come on.'

Algie put down his drink, most unwillingly. 'I'm the heir to Broxley-Foggett estate. There will be a frightful stink if I'm bumped off.'

'And while you're out there you should tell the lovebirds in the pool,' Mummy said dryly. 'They won't thank you for disturbing them, but they'll have to be here when the sheriff arrives.'

'I'm not sure that I want that task,' Darcy said. 'You think they'll still be in the pool or will they have retired somewhere more private?'

'Craig has one of the poolside suites,' Stella said.

'Right.' Darcy looked as enthusiastic about interrupting them as Algie had done about going out in the dark. Surely Algie couldn't be the killer, I thought as I watched them go. He looked positively terrified. Certainly not like a killer who dared to kill when all of us were within earshot. I wanted to call out, 'Be careful' to Darcy but it seemed silly, and Darcy knew how to protect himself. Besides, who could be lurking around out there? If it was the thief, he'd be well away from the house by now. And if it was one of us – well, we were all here, weren't we?

Then I realized that no, we weren't. Juan had been absent since dinner. And Mrs. Goldman had gone to bed before the crime happened. That made me pause and consider. There was clearly no love lost between her and her husband. They had lived apart for years. And she never came out West. Stella said she hated this castle. Had wanting to see the candlesticks merely been an excuse to come out here and kill him? Presumably she was now a very rich widow.

I went over to the group of sofas and tried to see if the stairs were visible to those of us who were sitting facing that way. They were. But not the actual entrance to the passageway leading to the library. Had we seen Mrs. Goldman going upstairs in the first place? I wondered. Maybe she had never done so and hidden in an alcove behind one of the statues until the right moment. After all, she had refused Barbara Kindell's offer to accompany her. I shuddered. Murder is horrible enough, but when someone kills a person they are supposed to love, then that's even worse. Had they been in love to begin with, like Darcy and me? If so, when did love turn sour?

I jumped as Mummy touched me. 'Don't worry about him, darling. He can take care of himself. Come and sit down. Or better yet, get your old mother a drink.'

'What would you like?' Charlie asked. 'I'm acting as bartender.'

'Oh, I think it better be a large brandy,' Mummy said. 'I shall need fortification to face policemen.' She reclined in a dramatic pose of the distressed damsel. 'I don't know what I was thinking, coming here in the first place. I should never have accepted Mr. Goldman's offer. Why would I want to be a film star, at my age? So silly. And now it will be in the papers and Max will hear about it, and he loathes scandal. And what's more, Homer Clegg will find out about it and all will be lost.'

'Homer Clegg?' Charlie Chaplin asked with interest.

'Mummy's husband. The one she's trying to get unhitched from without his knowing.'

'Oh, honey, I've been through that hundreds of times. And every one of them was a nightmare. I hope you're doing it in Reno?'

Mummy nodded.

'Then at least you have a chance of things going smoothly. Anyway, if you want expert advice just ask me.'

'You're very sweet,' Mummy said. 'And you are extremely talented too. An absolute genius. I wouldn't have minded making a picture with you.'

'It would have been fun, I'm sure. But I rather fear that I'm a has-been. My day was over the moment they invented the talkies.'

'No, surely not. You've made some talking pictures,' Mummy said.

'Yes, but my brand of comedy was made to be silent. Not everybody makes the transition smoothly.' And he looked across at Stella's back. 'She's only hanging on by her fingertips because Cy kept her going.'

'So you think his death means the end of her career?' I asked in a low voice.

'Let's put it this way. Her star is definitely on the wane.'

Stella turned back from the window, making me wonder whether she had overheard. 'I hope they are all right,' she said. 'They are taking their time, aren't they?' Then she let out a sigh of relief. 'That's good. Someone's coming.'

The front door opened, allowing the cold fog to creep in, and we saw that it wasn't the men at all, but Belinda and Craig. Belinda was now wearing a jumper that was several sizes too big for her and Craig looked extremely romantic in a silk dressing gown, his hair still wet and tousled.

'What's all this about?' he demanded. 'We're having fun in the pool and suddenly someone's yelling at us to get dressed and into the house as the police are coming.'

'You didn't hear the news yet?' Ronnie asked. 'Mr. Goldman is dead.'

'Dead? Oh my God. Poor old guy,' Craig said, shaking drops of water from his dark curls as he ran his fingers through his hair. 'Heart attack? I'm not too surprised. He always was a heart attack waiting to happen, wasn't he?'

'I hardly think it was a heart attack,' Ronnie said. 'Someone hit him over the head with one of his new candlesticks and stole the other.'

Craig went almost as white as Ronnie had done. 'Murdered, you mean? We've got a killer on the premises? Then let's get the hell out of here while we're all safe. I'll go and pack. Someone get the automobiles out of the garage.'

'Nobody is allowed to leave until the sheriff gets here,' Ronnie said.

'Then where does Goldman keep his firearms? We need to arm ourselves just in case there's a gang of them.' Craig looked distraught now. 'There are mobsters in the area, you know. They'll gun us down without thinking twice.'

'I don't think a whole gang could sneak past us and get into the library without anyone hearing them, Craig,' Stella said angrily. 'And mobsters would have taken the second candlestick, even if it did have blood and hair on it.'

'Then what are you suggesting? A single burglar?'

'Has to be,' Stella said. Then she paused, thinking. 'That's strange. We had one of those on the *Berengaria* coming across the Atlantic. A ruby was stolen and then a diamond ring and as far as I know the thief was never caught.' She turned to look at my mother and me. 'You don't think that same thief followed us here, do you?'

'Anything is possible,' Mummy said.

I observed Stella with interest. Darcy must have had good reason to suspect her and yet she was bringing up the very events that might throw suspicion onto her. But I still couldn't believe she could have killed Cy Goldman. She owed her current and continued stardom to him, and she was his mistress as well. Why upset the applecart? Unless Mr. Goldman had decided, following that row before dinner, to break up with her. Maybe he'd had some kind of threat from his wife – a divorce with lots of alimony? I stared across the room at Stella's elegant back, now draped in a dark mink stole. I simply couldn't imagine her as the infamous cat burglar, crawling along ledges, leaping over rooftops, fearless, willing to take any risks. Impossible, I thought.

'Get that down you, old man. You'll feel better.' Craig

accepted the glass of scotch that Charlie handed him. Belinda shook her head and came to sit beside me.

'Mr. Goldman really was murdered?' she whispered.

I nodded. 'No doubt about it.'

'Just my luck,' she said. 'When I think I'm getting somewhere a door slams in my face. And I don't think I seem to be going anywhere with Craig either.'

'He said you were having fun in the pool.'

'His sort of fun, maybe.' She made a face, then she wrapped her arms around herself. 'I'm freezing,' she said, 'and all my clothes are down at your little cottage. I'm not going down there in the dark. But I must look a complete fright.'

I smiled at her. How typical of Belinda that she was worrying about her looks when a murderer was on the loose. 'Craig's jumper actually rather suits you. Very sexy.'

'You think so?' she asked. 'It didn't seem to turn on Craig.'

'So he didn't try to get fresh with you?'

She leaned close to me and whispered, 'Darling, we both stripped off and he has a body like a Greek god and he dived into the pool like Tarzan and I got in too and then guess what?'

'I don't know. What? Is it fit for my innocent ears?'

'He challenged me to a swimming race. Can you believe it? Me, of all people. You know how I swim. I hate getting my face wet.'

'Did you take on the challenge then?'

'I did point out that we were alone and naked and he said this wasn't the time or place, out of respect to our host, who was also his boss.'

I tried not to smirk.

'I did mention Mr. Goldman brought his mistress with

him, quite openly. But Craig said that they were always very discreet and he expected his stars to be models of decorum.'

'Oh dear,' I said, 'how very frustrating for you.'

'You can say that again. I was all ready for a good old roll in the hay. Dying for one, you might say. And with a body like his?' She shook her head in bewilderment. 'Georgie, do you think there may be a chance that I'm losing my touch? Am I destined for a life of spinsterhood and crochet and keeping cats?'

In spite of everything I did laugh now. 'No, Belinda. I really don't think that will happen to you.'

'So where is everybody else? Where's Darcy? Not out searching for the murderer alone, I hope.'

'He and Algie went to wake Juan. Remember he went to bed right after dinner and he'll need to be here when the police arrive.'

We looked up as we heard the sound of high heels tapping on the tiled floor. Mrs. Goldman was coming down the stairs, holding on to Barbara Kindell's arm as if it were a lifeline.

'Where is my husband's body?' she demanded. 'I have to see my husband's body.'

'Honey, do you really think you should? It will only distress you even more,' Barbara said to her.

'I have to see him. He was actually killed with one of those damned candlesticks, was he? I told him his stupid obsession with antiques would be the death of him one day, but I didn't mean . . . I never meant . . .' She gave a big wrenching sob that was quite unexpected.

'He's in the library, honey. I'll come with you.'

'No, I want to go alone,' she said. 'I need to say good-bye to my husband alone.'

'Make sure you don't touch anything,' Ronnie said.

Mrs. Goldman turned to glare at him.

'This is my house. I'll touch what I want.'

'Instructions from the sheriff, Mrs. Goldman.'

'Oh God,' she said and turned on her heel. I wondered if someone should follow her to make sure she didn't touch anything, but I realized it wasn't my place to interfere. But it did start me thinking: What if she had killed him and wanted to make doubly sure that she had left no telltale evidence?

'I think I'll pop to the nearest lavatory before we have to face the police,' I said casually.

'There's one in the last alcove on the right,' Stella said.

I sauntered down the hall and hugged the wall until I was out of sight of the rotunda. Then I slipped across to the hallway leading to the library. Well, I had proved one thing – I had managed this without being seen. As I tiptoed carefully over the pieces of armor toward the library I heard something. It sounded almost like an animal either breathing heavily or snarling and my thoughts went instantly to the wild beasts that roamed the grounds. The door was half open and I peered in. Mrs. Goldman was standing with her face in her hands, sobbing her heart out.

Chapter 21

Feeling embarrassed and guilty, I backed away, only just avoiding stepping into an armored leg that blocked my path. Was the awful remorse I had just seen because she loved her husband or because she had killed him in a moment of temper and now bitterly regretted it? I found the cavernous bathroom, decorated, as Algie had reported, with banners. When I returned there was still no sign of Darcy and the other men.

'Is my poor Helen still in the library?' Barbara asked.

I nodded. 'I could hear her crying.'

'Poor thing. She's devastated,' Barbara said.

'Devastated?' Mummy looked surprised and amused. 'I thought they loathed each other.'

'Oh, no. They were devoted.'

'They had a funny way of showing it,' Mummy said.

'I suppose they did. They fought like cats and dogs since day one, I gather, but they always made up and she adored him in her own way.'

'She lived in New York and he in Los Angeles? That didn't sound like too much adoration to me,' Mummy said, leaning forward to stub out a cigarette in the crystal ashtray on the table.

'He was taken in by her family the day he stepped off the boat as an immigrant from Europe,' Barbara said. 'I think he was very handsome when he was young and he's always had a presence. He went to work for her father's boot factory but he was ambitious right from the start. He persuaded Mr. Edison to give him a job in his movie company in New Jersey, and when he thought he'd learned enough, he headed out to Hollywood and started making his own movies. But Helen never liked the West Coast. She wanted to be in New York, near her family, and far away from his long string of mistresses—' She paused, looked up and stared at Stella. But Stella was staring out of the window and apparently quite unaware of her so the gesture was wasted.

'Did they ever have any children?' I asked.

Barbara shook her head. 'She had one miscarriage and the doctor said she shouldn't have any more pregnancies. I think that was a blow to both of them. But he's always lived for his work – like a maniac, never taking a moment to rest, as you've seen. I don't think he even noticed that Helen wasn't there.'

She broke off as Mrs. Goldman came back into the room. She was white-faced but one could no longer see that she had been crying. Her make-up had been repaired and she looked ready to address a meeting of volunteer ladies back in New York. Had she ever gone to bed? I wondered. If so, she had dressed again and put on her make-up very quickly. I studied her, wondering if her grief was a little overdone. Of everybody she had the best opportunity for murdering her husband. I now knew she could have crept around the rim of the foyer without being seen from the rotunda. She also had several good motives for murdering her husband – jealousy of his mistress, being excluded from his life, and who knew what kind of financial restraints he was trying to put on her. Someone would have to talk to Mr. Goldman's lawyer and tax accountant to see if he'd planned to cut off his wife's allowance, or at least trim it back. And then there might be a large life insurance policy, recently taken out. . . .

'Come and sit by me, honey,' Barbara said, patting the sofa beside her as Mrs. Goldman came into the rotunda. 'Would you like a drink? Charlie will fix you one.'

Mrs. Goldman shook her head. 'Nothing,' she said. 'Nothing will ever matter again.' Then she looked up at us. 'Who could have done this to him?'

Nobody answered her.

'The sheriff is on his way,' Mummy said. 'I'm sure everything will be sorted out in good time.' She was the only one who seemed unaffected by what had happened, other than being a little annoyed that it had disrupted her own schedule for the evening. But then that was typical of her. If it didn't concern her personally, it didn't matter. Just like a cat.

Feet crunched on the gravel outside.

'You see. There he is now,' Mummy said, but instead a draft of cold air wafted in as Darcy returned with Algie and a disheveled Juan, who stood blinking in the light. He was wearing striped pajamas and had a blanket wrapped around his shoulders. He was shivering and looked decidedly uncomfortable.

'The sheriff not here yet?' Darcy asked.

'No,' I replied. 'Did you see anything suspicious out there?'

'Not a thing. Of course it's quite foggy so anybody could be hidden within a few feet of us. And it would be very easy to escape into the parkland without leaving any kind of trail.'

'I thought I heard something,' Algie said. 'Something like a sinister growl, or a groan. Or maybe a snarl. Or a snort.'

'That was Juan clearing his throat.' Darcy gave him a withering look. 'I told you at the time. When you grabbed me and nearly yanked me over backward.'

'It sounded jolly sinister to me,' Algie said. 'Like an animal, you know.'

'How are you feeling, Juan?' Stella went over to him and guided him to a big armchair.

'How do you think I feel, eh?' he demanded indignantly. 'I am in a deep sleep. Suddenly I am rudely awoken. Now my head throbs.'

'He bally well was in a deep sleep,' Algie said. 'Talk about the sleep of the dead. We had to shake him before he finally surfaced.'

'I must have drunk too much wine with dinner. When I am depressed I drink too much wine,' Juan said. 'It does not agree with me.'

'You'd better have some coffee.' Stella picked up the pot. 'Oh, it's gone cold again,' she said. 'I'd better have Maria make more. Has anyone told her yet about Cy? Oh God. She'll have hysterics. She worshipped the ground he trod on. You should do it, Mrs. Goldman.' And she tried to hand Helen the coffeepot.

'Helen is in no fit state to go anywhere,' Barbara intervened. 'You're the one who is here more than anybody. You do it.'

'I don't think I could bear her weeping and wailing all over me,' Stella said. 'I'm only just holding my own emotions together at this point. Ronnie, sweetheart, would you be an angel?' And she handed him the coffeepot.

Ronnie looked at it in his hands and tried to come up with a good reason why he shouldn't go in to face Maria. Then he sighed. 'Oh, very well,' he said. He set off in the direction of the kitchen.

And an interesting thought struck me as I watched Stella go over to perch on the arm of Juan's chair. I would have said that she was with us in the rotunda all the time, but she had left once before when she went to ask for more coffee. So really only my mother, Charlie Chaplin and I had never left this area after dinner. Craig and Darcy had come in together, which cleared both of them. But all of the others had been alone and unaccounted for at some moment. I looked around the room. It was hard to picture any of them sneaking up on Cy Goldman and hitting him over the head with his own candlestick. Maybe it was a slick and agile intruder after all. When the groundsmen returned perhaps we'd know more.

Almost immediately we heard the predicted weeping and wailing coming from the kitchen. Actually more of a cross between shrieks and eerie keening. I pitied Ronnie. Everybody gave him the unpleasant jobs and he just accepted them. I supposed that it was the lot of a secretary to be the general dogsbody. He returned soon after, empty-handed.

'I don't think we're likely to get more coffee in the immediate future,' he said. 'I warned her that the police would want to talk to everybody and that just made the hysterics worse. She's gone to find Francisco. I'd go and make the coffee myself but that stove is a temperamental monster and only Maria knows how to work it.'

'It is no matter. I do not need coffee,' Juan said. 'I just want to return to my bed.'

'Well, you can't do that until the sheriff gets here,' Darcy said. 'I wonder when the men will come back from checking the fence?'

'It's an enormous property,' Stella said. 'I forget how many hundred acres. And a lot of it is rough terrain, steep hillsides, rocks, gullies. I doubt they'll be able to check every inch of that fence.'

'Then the murderer could be long gone,' Craig said. I could see the relief in his face.

We all froze as the telephone rang. Ronnie went to answer it. 'Yes, of course,' he said. Then he returned to us. 'That was Jimmy at the gatehouse. He said he had the sheriff there and wanted to know if it was all right to let him in.'

'You see how conscientious he is about his job,' Stella said. 'Nobody could have got past him at the gate. If they don't find anything wrong at the fence we have to presume the murderer is still on the premises.'

'Or is one of us,' Charlie Chaplin said with obvious relish.

There was a gasp from around the room. 'You're joking, surely, Charlie,' Stella said. 'Which of us would ever want to hit Cy over the head to steal a candlestick? It doesn't make sense. If any of us was inclined to take the dratted thing all we'd had to do was sneak in sometime during the night, not go into the library when we knew Cy was still there.'

'I have to disagree with you there, Stella honey,' Craig said. 'When Darcy and I left Cy he said he was going to put the candlesticks in the safe for the time being. Mrs. Goldman had asked him to do this since he didn't have them properly insured yet.'

'That's right. I did,' Mrs. Goldman said. 'I told him he was an idiot to have such valuable objects just sitting there on a table when the house was full of people. And what about the Mexican servants, I said. How do you know whether you can trust them or not? The candles could be over the border in no time at all and mean a lifetime of luxury for one of them.'

'Oh, come now,' Stella said angrily. 'Maria and Francisco worshipped him and they have been with him for years.'

'Yes, but what about those guys who work on the grounds? How much do you know about them, huh?'

'That's a good point, I suppose,' Darcy said. 'The sheriff will want to interview all the outside employees, Ronnie.'

'So whoever took that candlestick had to take his chance before Cy locked it away.' Barbara gave Mrs. Goldman a knowing look. 'And I agree. I'd like to take bets it was one of those Mexican gardeners. I have to keep a close eye on my Mexican maids. I know one of them has been helping herself to the sugar.'

She broke off as we heard the scrunch of tires on the gravel. Ronnie was on his way to the front door when there was thunderous knocking.

'Good evening, sir,' we heard him say. Then a rough gravelly voice responded. 'This better be good, son. If I find out it's you movie people's idea of a joke and it's some kind of dummy crime scene you've got in here, I'll have you all locked up in the slammer.'

'No joke at all I'm afraid, Sheriff,' Ronnie said. 'Mr. Cy Goldman, head of Golden Pictures, has been murdered.'

A big man, unshaven, with heavy jowls, lumbered into view. He was wearing a Stetson hat and cowboy boots. To my outsider's eyes he looked like a caricature of a Wild West sheriff. He was staring at us with contempt.

'Sheriff Billings,' he said. 'Ventura County Sheriff's Department. And who have we here?'

Ronnie cleared his throat nervously. 'Well, we have Mrs.

Goldman, Mr. Goldman's widow. And then we have Stella
Brightwell, Claire Daniels, Craig Hart, Charlie Chaplin . . .'

'You making fun of me, boy?' the sheriff demanded.

'I assure you he's not,' Charlie said. 'I'm Charlie Chaplin.'

'You mean to tell me that you're really Mr. Chaplin?' the
sheriff demanded. 'You don't look a bit like him.'

'Do you want me to stick on a false mustache, put on a
porkpie hat and do my funny walk with a cane to prove it
to you?' Charlie asked. He didn't seem in the least put out,
almost as if he was enjoying himself. 'Or would you rather
see my driver's license?' He fumbled in his pocket, produced his wallet and handed it to the big man, who glanced
at it, turned a little pale, then handed it back. 'Sorry, Mr.
Chaplin, sir. You can't blame me for being too careful, can
you? These movie types – they leave Hollywood for the
weekend and think it's amusing to play little jokes on the
country bumpkins. And we're stretched thin as it is, trying
to cover a county of this size. We've already got a suspicious
fire out of control in the hills above Simi so I've had to leave
most of my men there. But I've got volunteer deputies on
their way with the medical examiner.'

'Volunteer   deputies?'   Mrs.   Goldman   demanded.
'Amateurs? What good can they do? This is a murder case,
Sheriff. You need trained professionals. Shouldn't you call
Los Angeles and see if they've got some real detectives they
can lend you? Or even Ventura?'

The sheriff drew himself up to all of his six feet in height.
'Ma'am, we may be a rural force but we get just as good
training as any city slicker. Now, if we can get down to business, one of you can take me to the body. The rest of you stay
put until I tell you that you can move.'

'This way, sir,' Ronnie said.

'And are you a movie star too?' the sheriff asked. 'Don't recognize you.'

'No, I'm Mr. Goldman's secretary,' Ronnie said. 'Ronald Green.'

'And is everybody in the house together in that room? I want everyone in one place, where I can see them until my men have searched the house.'

'We assembled everyone for you, in anticipation of your arrival,' Ronnie said. 'Apart from the servants.'

'How many of them?'

'There's only Maria in the house. She cooks and cleans. Local women come in to help when we have a big party here. Her husband, Francisco, helps with the heavy work. We have four groundsmen but they are out driving around the fence to see where an intruder could have gotten in. They should be back soon. And there's Jimmy on the gate. You met him.'

'Yeah. I met him all right. Nearly booked him for obstructing justice.' He scowled in the direction of the door as if he could see all the way down to the gate. 'Wouldn't let me in even when I showed him my badge. Well, as soon as those guys show up I want to talk to them. And the cook and her husband.' He turned away. 'So which way to the body?'

'Over here, Sheriff.' Ronnie went ahead of him.

'I hope nobody's touched anything.' We heard the sheriff's voice echoing from the high ceiling. 'And what's this dang fool stuff all over the floor?'

'It's armor, sir. The suit of armor fell down and we didn't think we should move it. Just in case.'

'Suit of armor? You movie types live in a fantasy world, don't you?' And the sheriff's voice got fainter as he entered the library.

But that was another interesting thing. We had heard him quite clearly when he was beside the suit of armor. Would we have heard a loud exchange, a shout for help, a cry coming from the library? Wouldn't that mean that Mr. Goldman knew his attacker and didn't think he needed to shout for help?

Chapter 22

The sheriff's face was somber when he returned to us. I noticed he still hadn't taken off his hat. The dowager duchess Edwina, with whom I'd been staying, would have been affronted but here nobody seemed to mind.

'Someone made a nasty mess of his head, didn't they?' he said. 'That blow was administered with a lot of force. But don't worry. I have no doubt we'll find the perpetrator soon enough. He was stupid enough to leave a bloody fingerprint on the window frame. Then he must have jumped out and run off into the woods. If he's a known thug, we'll find him.'

'And if he's not?' Stella asked.

'He won't get far, will he? If the fence runs all the way around the property and he can't get past that gatekeeper of yours, I'd say he was stuck here, hoping to hide out until we all leave. But don't you worry. We'll bring in dogs in the morning. They'll flush him out.'

'I don't think dogs would be a good idea on this property, Sheriff,' Stella said.

'Oh, and why not?'

'Not unless you want a stampede of zebra, giraffe and

wildebeest.' Stella said the line deadpan. 'For all I know there are a few lions patrolling the grounds as well.'

'Are you trying to be funny again?' The sheriff's bulldog face flushed red.

'Certainly not,' Stella said. 'Mr. Goldman kept a menagerie of African animals. Just as exotic decorations, you understand. But I believe that a giraffe can easily kill a dog. Or a man, for that matter.'

'Was the man completely mad? He builds a castle like something out of a horror movie, then he stocks the grounds with dangerous animals.'

'He did it because he could,' Mrs. Goldman answered before Stella could. 'He came up from nothing and when he became successful he was like a small boy in a candy store. He was always trying to see what his money could buy next – seaplane, racing car, Paris apartment . . . he's tried them all. And look where it got him. I always warned him, but he never listened to anyone. Thirteen at dinner tonight, you know.'

'I take it you're the widow,' Sheriff Billings said.

'I am.' She gave him a hostile stare. 'I never thought I'd hear that word applied to myself. I believed he was immortal.'

'And since my men aren't here yet, I'd like to get started on the questions. I don't suppose you want to be here all night any more than I do.' He pulled up a straight-backed wooden chair. 'Now, you just said you were thirteen at dinner. I see twelve of you in the room right now so I guess you were all there. And Mr. Goldman was alive and well then?'

'He was,' Mrs. Goldman said. 'After dinner he wanted to smoke one of his disgusting cigars and I told him he'd have to do it where I couldn't smell the smoke. So he said he'd go to the library and most of the men went with him.'

'Who didn't?'

'I didn't,' Charlie said. 'I'm not keen on cigars and I wanted to get to know this fascinating young lady better. It's so rare to find someone regal and virginal in Hollywood. You can't blame me for being intrigued.'

'And your name, miss?' The sheriff licked his pencil.

I thought this might be a good time to make the sheriff aware of my rank. 'I'm Lady Georgiana Rannoch,' I said. 'I'm here with my mother who was about to shoot a film with Mr. Goldman.'

'What's more she's a cousin of the king of England,' my mother added.

'English royalty, huh?' He looked rather impressed, which was gratifying. I decided to go on. 'And this is my good friend Belinda Warburton-Stoke, and my young man, the honorable Darcy O'Mara. Both English aristocrats.'

'And they came out here with you?'

'They just popped in to see me,' I said sweetly. 'But Mr. Goldman was rather struck with Mr. O'Mara's looks and wanted to use him in his picture.'

Even as I said the words they sank in. There wouldn't be a picture now. Darcy was in no danger of becoming a film star. I felt terribly relieved.

I watched the sheriff scrutinizing first Belinda and then Darcy. Then his gaze fell on Juan, who was still huddled in his blanket, looking miserable.

'And you're one of the hired help? What happened – did you fall in the pool?'

Stella stood up, looking regal. 'This is Señor Juan de Castillo from Spain – from a very old family. They used to own large estates near Seville. His aunt is mother superior of a convent.'

The sheriff was now focusing on her. 'You're Stella Brightwell,' he said in a hushed voice. 'I'd recognize you anywhere. I've seen all your movies, Miss Brightwell. And yours too, Mr. Hart. Two of my favorite stars. Maybe I could get your autograph when this nasty little business is over – for the kids, you know.'

'Of course, Sheriff.' Stella gave him her most charming smile. 'Happy to oblige your children.'

'So Señor Castillo is over here visiting one of you? What's the connection?'

'Mr. Goldman discovered him in Spain on his recent trip to buy more antiques. We were planning to shoot a movie about King Philip of Spain so Mr. Goldman thought Juan would be perfect for the part.'

'Only then he tells me I am no good enough because my Spanish accent is too strong,' Juan said peevishly. 'So I come all this way and then he doesn't want to make me movie star after all. Now all I want is to go home to my village and my people.'

'Well, that seems to be everybody,' the sheriff said.

'You've forgotten me, Sheriff,' Barbara Kindell said testily.

'My apologies, ma'am.' He tipped his hat to her then studied her hawkish middle-aged face. 'Don't tell me you're Mary Pickford.'

'Very droll,' Barbara said. 'I am a dear friend of Mrs. Goldman.'

'And your name, ma'am?'

'Barbara Kindell.'

His head jerked upright. '*The* Barbara Kindell?'

'The very same,' she said.

'But you write all those columns – secrets of the stars. My wife's your biggest fan. So if I could get your autograph too, ma'am?'

'The sooner you solve this crime, the sooner we can give you our autographs, Sheriff,' Charlie said. 'We're all dying to go to bed and poor Juan here is fighting hard to stay awake. So can we please get on with it?'

'Certainly, Mr. Chaplin, sir. I'm working as fast as I can. These things can't be rushed, you know. Too easy to over-look something.' He licked his pencil again. 'Now you say that the men went off to smoke in the library. I take it that's where the body is now lying?'

'It is,' Ronnie said.

'What happened then?'

'We smoked cigars. We had a cognac,' Darcy said. 'We discussed Mr. Goldman's new antiques. He passed them around so I'm afraid our fingerprints will be on the candlesticks.'

'You said "candlesticks" in the plural?' Sheriff Billings asked. 'I only saw one – lying on the floor beside him.'

'There were a pair. The other is missing.'

'So it was a robbery gone wrong, you think? Why didn't the thief take the second candlestick?'

'Presumably because it had blood and hair on it?' Darcy said, glancing across at me.

'Criminals aren't usually that squeamish,' the sheriff said. 'He could have wiped it off. Instead he's left us the murder weapon and if we tie in prints on the candlestick with that bloody print on the window frame, we'll have us a murder conviction.'

He looked around the group as if he wanted everyone to know he had just made a good point. 'So those candlesticks were valuable, right?'

'Extremely,' Ronnie said. 'They were solid gold, deco-rated with real jewels.'

The sheriff whistled. 'I thought that would just be gold plating. Solid gold, huh? Must be worth a fortune.'

'The strange thing is that an El Greco painting was also in the room and I presume it must be a lot more valuable than the candlesticks but that wasn't touched.'

The sheriff looked at him with pity. 'Golden candlesticks can be melted down, boy,' he said. 'It's not as easy to fence a stolen painting.'

He tilted back in his chair to a point that I thought he might topple over backward. 'So let's get back to where we were. You were smoking and drinking and examining these candlesticks. Then what?'

'One by one we left the library,' Darcy said. 'I think Ronnie went first, then Craig and I followed him and then Algie . . .'

'Who?' the sheriff demanded. I realized we'd all overlooked Algie again. He had sat silent and unnoticed in the shadows.

'Me,' Algie said in a squeak. 'Algernon Broxley-Foggett. Another English aristocrat over here helping Mr. Goldman with the script of the picture. And a close friend of these other English people.'

I looked at Darcy, who was about to open his mouth to deny this, but then he changed his mind.

'So how come I missed you before when I was going around getting names?' the sheriff asked angrily.

'Happens all the time, I'm afraid,' Algie said. 'The trouble is I'm rather forgettable. Always been my misfortune to be overlooked. Just a likable, ordinary chap, I suppose. Easy to overlook me among all these glamorous types.'

'So you were the last to leave the library?'

'I wandered out behind O'Mara and Craig Hart,' Algie

said. 'Then I lingered on because I was interested in the suit of armor and it looked about my size. Unfortunately I got the helmet stuck on my head and knocked over the whole bally thing. Typical of me, I'm afraid.'

'And what about Mr. Goldman? Did he stay in the library after you left?'

'He did,' Craig said. 'He told us to go ahead and he'd better put the candlesticks in the safe or there would be hell to pay from his wife. So we left him there and went to join the others in this room.'

'So would you say you were the last to see Mr. Goldman alive?'

'It looks that way,' Craig said. 'Unless anyone else went into the library after us.'

'They'd have had to pass this young fellow playing with the suit of armor, wouldn't they?' the sheriff asked.

'Ah, well,' Algie cleared his throat nervously. 'I wasn't there the whole time. You see I needed to spend a penny.'

'Spend a penny?'

'You know. Take a widdle. Visit the loo, old man.'

'What's a "loo, old man"?' the sheriff demanded.

I looked at Belinda and we started to giggle. We couldn't help ourselves. The sheriff was glowering.

'He means he went to find a lavatory,' Darcy said, also trying hard not to smile.

'Oh, you mean take a piss.' The sheriff nodded now. 'So anyone could have snuck down that hallway while Mr. Goldman had his back turned, and struck him over the head.'

'Yes, only we were all here together,' Stella said. 'Except for Mrs. Goldman, who went up to bed right after coffee.'

'But before her husband was killed?' the sheriff asked.

'Probably,' Stella said, her face calm and sweet.

'We have no idea when my husband was killed,' Mrs. Goldman said. 'All I can tell you is that I was upset and tired and I went up to bed sometime during the evening.'

'So everybody else is accounted for except Mrs. Goldman?'

'Actually this young lady and I went for a swim together,' Craig said, managing to imbue that phrase with hidden implication.

'You went for a swim – in the dark?'

Craig gave that devastating smile. 'The pool is lighted and heated, Sheriff. It was very pleasant – wasn't it, Belinda?'

'So you and the young lady were absent for a while?'

'But together,' Craig pointed out. 'And outside.'

'And everyone else was in this room, apart from Mrs. Goldman, who had gone to bed?'

'And Juan,' Algie pointed out.

Juan shrugged. 'I am sleeping in my bed, señor. After dinner the wine does not agree with me. They do not understand wine in America. Too many years of prohibition, I think. So my head hurts and I go straight to bed and fall asleep.'

'We can vouch for that,' Algie said. 'We had a devil of a time waking him.'

'So it appears that you can all vouch for each other?' the sheriff said. 'How convenient.'

'If you're trying to suggest that it was a conspiracy between us to kill Mr. Goldman, I think you're barking up the wrong tree,' Stella said, coldly now. 'We all owed everything to him. Without him our lives are in tatters.'

The sheriff rocked uneasily in his chair. I wondered how many murder investigations he'd had to conduct before and decided he wasn't quite sure how to proceed. 'We can't do much until the doctor ascertains the time of death,' he said.

'We can tell you that, pretty accurately,' Darcy said. 'It must have been within a fifteen-minute window from the time Craig and I left to the time when we heard the crash of that suit of armor. So between ten thirty and ten forty-five.'

'That's just your word for it, sir. We'll have to see if the medical examiner agrees with you. They shouldn't be too long now, I hope, although it's quite a drive in the fog.'

Almost on cue the telephone rang. Ronnie looked inquiringly at the sheriff, then went to answer it. 'What?' I heard him say. 'Yes, the sheriff is here. Of course, bring him up.' Then his eyebrows raised and he said, 'Her? It's a woman?'

He came back to us. 'That was one of our groundsmen, calling from the gatehouse. They caught someone.'

'Trying to escape?'

'No, trying to break in. They can't quite understand her and she fought like a wildcat but they are bringing her up to the house right now.'

The sheriff looked pleased. 'The accomplice, mark my words,' he said. 'She was probably waiting with the getaway car.'

The tension in the room was palpable as we waited. It seemed to take forever but at last we heard the sound of a motor and the crunch of tires. Then there was a raised woman's voice, some male grunting and a couple of curses as Ronnie went to open the front door.

'Get yer bleeding 'ands off me,' said a strong Cockney accent. 'This ain't no way to treat someone what's connected to your guests and royal people at that.'

And a red-faced and very disheveled Queenie was shoved, struggling, into the foyer.

Chapter 23

I stood up as Queenie looked around, blinking like an owl in the electric light. 'A fine welcome you give people in America, that's all I can say,' she said.

'We caught her trying to force her way through the gate,' the groundsman said. 'We couldn't quite understand what she was saying but she was clearly up to no good.'

'I was trying to get in and the blooming gate wouldn't open,' Queenie said angrily. 'And then suddenly these men start shouting and grabbing me. I told them I'm with Lady Georgiana Rannoch what's staying here as a guest of Mr. Goldman.' Her gaze fastened on me. 'Oh, there you are, miss. Thank God. I'm so glad to see you. Tell these people who I am. They've been treating me like I'm some kind of criminal or something. Manhandling me something shocking.'

'What are you doing here, Queenie?' I asked. 'A social call at almost midnight? No wonder the gatekeeper was suspicious of you.'

'It's taken me this long to hitch a ride out from Beverly Hills,' Queenie said. 'There ain't no buses. I had no idea it was so far and hardly any motorcars come this way. And it's bleeding cold too. Then the sodding gate wouldn't open and I thought it was stuck and I was trying to push it when these two great gorillas came out and grabbed me. I told them who I was but they seemed not to understand me.'

'That's because they are Mexican and you speak with a Cockney accent,' I said. I wanted to smile but I was determined not to. For once I was going to play the indignant employer. 'So what exactly are you doing here?'

'Well, I should think that was ruddy obvious,' Queenie said. 'I've come back to you. I decided I'd rather work for you for no money than the old cow who was paying me well.'

'You got the sack, you mean? You set fire to her dress or broke her perfume bottle?'

'I bloody well didn't,' she said. 'If you want to know I was doing quite well, apart from melting her undies when I ironed them. How was I to know about a stuff called rayon and what happens when you iron it? But the old cow had no idea how to treat servants. She wanted me to clean her toilets. "I can't do that,' I said. "I'm a lady's maid." And do you know what she said then? She said, "I'm not paying servants to have them sit around doing nothing. I don't need someone to dress me but I do need clean toilets. In America we work for our living." So I told her that I was used to working for quality and no amount of money was worth being treated like dirt and I walked out. I went back to our bungalow at the hotel and they said you'd come up here. So here I am.'

'You want to come back to work for me?' I said. 'Isn't that rather presumptuous? Didn't it occur to you that I might have found a new maid?'

'Gorn,' she said with a grin. 'Where would you find a

proper maid here? If they thought I was worth snapping up and paying in Beverly Hills there can't be too many maids around.'

I thought this was an insightful comment. 'Well, I suppose you'll have to stay now, Queenie,' I said, 'because you would not be allowed to leave. There has been a murder and this policeman has just started his investigation.'

'Blimey,' she said. 'You don't half get yourself involved in a lot of murders.'

The sheriff was looking at me with interest.

'What does she mean?' he asked.

'I've just had the bad luck to have been staying in places where someone died. Nothing to do with me, I assure you. Just an innocent bystander.'

'And this young woman is your maid?'

I sighed. 'Yes, I suppose she is.'

'Well, keep an eye on her. I'm still not happy about someone trying to break in.'

'Don't worry. She's quite harmless apart from damaging everything within reach,' I said.

Craig had also risen from his seat and went over to the men who were lingering near the front door, looking uncomfortable at being inside the house. 'You're the groundsmen, right? So did you find any evidence of a break-in along the fence?'

'No, señor,' one of them said. 'The fence looks fine. We drove all the way around and didn't see nothing unusual.'

'And the man at the gate? Nobody has tried to get in or out apart from this young woman?'

'No, sir. Jimmy says the only people he's let in all day have been Mr. Goldman's guests. People he knows.'

Craig looked around at the rest of us. 'Then we have to

presume that the killer is among us here, don't we? It simply can't be an outsider.'

'Unless the outsider is still hiding among the trees and rocks,' Mummy said in her usual bored way, stretching languidly on the sofa as if this were any cocktail party and not a murder inquiry. 'It seems to me it would be quite easy to hit poor Cy over the head and then melt into that fog until an opportune moment came for someone to open the gate.'

'So maybe you guys could start patrolling the grounds now,' the sheriff said.

'In the dark? What could we see in the dark?' one of the groundsmen demanded. 'Someone hears us coming and slips behind a tree or a rock. It's impossible.'

'Then we'll get dogs brought in in the morning, wild animals or not,' the sheriff said. 'My men will be arriving soon with the medical examiner, and then we'll do a complete search of the house for clues. And in the meantime I'll be questioning each of you in turn in the library.'

'In the library?' Mrs. Goldman demanded. 'But my husband's body is still there. Surely that's not appropriate and most insensitive.'

'They can move the curtains around the body if you do not wish to look at him,' Juan said. 'But I think you will not wish to interview me. I was not there. I left after dinner.'

'I told you. Nobody is touching anything,' the sheriff boomed. 'And I want to speak to everybody.'

'Then why do you want us in the library, if we're not supposed to touch anything?' Barbara said in a testy voice. 'Won't that risk contaminating the crime scene?'

It was clear we were all getting tired and feeling the strain.

'I have my reasons,' the sheriff said. 'And since you all

were in that room this evening at some point, then it would
be natural to find your prints there anyway, wouldn't it?'

I realized then what his reasons were. He wanted to see
how we reacted to trying to speak normally in the presence
of Mr. Goldman's body. Perhaps he hoped that the killer
would show signs of uneasiness under the strain. But from
my experience killers can remain completely cool in such
circumstances, can lie without batting an eyelid. That's why
they kill in the first place – they have the sort of personality
that spurs them to take risks the rest of us couldn't imagine.

'Let's start with the widow,' Sheriff Billings said. 'And the
rest of you stay put. Nobody is to move from this room.'

'You want us to stay here?' one of the groundsmen asked,
looking at his colleague.

'I'll want to speak with the employees separately. Go and
round up your pals and the household servants and I'll be
speaking to you shortly.'

'In here? In the house?' He looked at us uneasily.

'Better make it the kitchen. And perhaps someone could
put on a pot of coffee. I've been on the job since seven this
morning,' the sheriff said. After they had gone out of the
front door, muttering to each other in Spanish, the sheriff
turned to Mrs. Goldman. 'Come along, Mrs. Goldman.
Follow me.'

We watched them walk away, Mrs. Goldman walking as
if she were a zombie. Barbara Kindell stood up as if to follow
and assist her friend, but then sat down again. 'It's not right
to put her through this after she's just lost her husband,' she
said. 'That man is a bully and a brute. His wife may be a big
fan of mine, but that won't stop me from telling it like it is in
my column this Sunday. And on my radio show too.'

'I suppose he's just trying to do his job,' Darcy said. 'He

wants to catch us with our guard down to see if anyone
cracks under the pressure of being in a room with the body.'

'I shall find it horrible,' Stella said. 'It's a sadistic thing to
do, that brute grilling us with questions when he knows that
poor Cy is lying there.'

'It will not bother me,' Juan said. 'I have nothing to hide
and I have seen bodies before. In Spain we are used to death
in the bullring.'

'That's also horrible,' Stella said. 'I went to a bullfight
once with Cy and swore I'd never go again. Spain is such a
cruel country.'

'Oh and America is not?' Juan demanded. 'Here you
shoot each other with guns, no? Al Capone and the gangsters? At least in Spain we fight with honor.'

'Easy, old man.' Craig put a hand on Juan's shoulder.

'What should I do, miss?' Queenie shifted awkwardly
from one foot to the other. 'Should I go up to your room and
wait for you?' She had been standing away from the group,
half in the foyer as if she didn't know where she belonged.

'The sheriff said that nobody should leave and I presume
that includes you,' I replied. 'You'd better find a chair and
come and join us.' I was still feeling ambivalent about her
arrival. In a way I suppose that I had grown fond of her and
was glad to have her back, but I wasn't ready to forgive her
deserting the ship at the first opportunity.

Belinda moved closer to me on the sofa. 'I'm freezing,' she
said. 'I didn't get a chance to dry off properly. And I really
wish I hadn't come here.'

'Your own fault,' I said.

'I know. Stupid, really. I do these impulsive things, hoping
that something good will come out of them, but it never
does. I went down to Kingsdowne Place when you were

staying with the Eynsfords and look what happened there. The problem is that you are a disaster magnet, Georgie. I should learn to stay well away from you.'

By now I was also tired and grouchy and I'd had enough for one evening. 'Face it, Belinda, you don't come to see me. You come because you hope to take advantage of people I know.'

One of the good things about Belinda is that she is frightfully easy-going. She nodded. 'You're right. I'm a horrid, shallow person and I only think about myself. But I have to add that my actions are born partly out of desperation. It's not easy trying to survive with little money in this world.'

'I'm certainly aware of that,' I said, 'but I would never land myself on people claiming to be something I'm not, in the hope of snagging myself a rich man.'

'No, of course you wouldn't. You have Queen Victoria's blood running through your veins. You are eminently respectable and moral. You'll marry and have oodles of children and live in a drafty old country house and be supremely happy. I like the good things in life, unfortunately.'

I glanced across at Darcy. He caught my gaze and winked, making me feel so much better. This might be a horrible situation but I was in the same room as a man who loved me and whom I hoped to marry someday. Poor Belinda looked for love in all the wrong places, and while she lived a glamorous life from time to time, she had no security. I patted her hand. 'Your turn will come, I'm sure.'

'I'm not so sure anymore. Craig Hart invites me for a skinny dip and then rejects me? There must be something wrong with me. I'm getting old and haggard and unattractive.'

'Belinda, you're twenty-three and devastatingly beautiful.

In fact if you wanted to stay on here and make a career in films, I'm sure you could.'

The flicker of a smile crossed her face. 'Do you really think so? You're very kind, Georgie. A sweet person. You deserve happiness.'

I leaned closer. 'And when we're alone I'll tell you something else that will make you feel better,' I whispered.

'Oh God. I wish he'd hurry up,' Mummy said in her stage voice that echoed around the cavernous rooms. 'All I want right now is my bed. And to be back in Germany with Max or at my villa in Lugano. Or my dear little place in Nice. Or at Brown's Hotel in London. Anywhere but here. This was such a stupid idea in the first place. And a ridiculous movie. Bloody Mary and the Virgin Queen fighting over King Philip of Spain – I ask you.'

Silence fell again.

'I don't know about anyone else but I'm going to have another drink,' Charlie said. He went over to the drinks table and sloshed cognac into a glass. We looked up as Mrs. Goldman returned and sank onto the sofa next to Barbara. She pushed an imaginary strand of hair back from her face, even though her hairstyle and make-up were still immaculate.

'So many stupid questions,' she said. 'So unnecessary. Somehow he latched on to the fact that we didn't live together. As if that gave me a motive for murder. Trying to put words in my mouth. I told him that life suited us perfectly the way things were but he wouldn't give up.'

'Here, you need this more than me, Helen.' Charlie handed her his drink. 'Get that by you.'

'I don't normally, but right now I really do need one,' she said and took a big gulp. 'He wants Stella next,' she said and there was a glint of malicious glee in her eyes. I suspected she'd taken delight in giving Stella an excellent motive for his murder. Stella looked pale but regal and resolute as she walked from the room. I watched her go, still wondering. Darcy obviously still had reason to suspect her or he'd never have come here. And she had left the room to order another pot of coffee. How long had she been gone? Long enough to sneak into the library and bludgeon her lover to death? And then make off with one candlestick? I shook my head. This made no sense to me. If she wanted to steal the candlesticks she had ample opportunity. Presumably she knew the combination to Mr. Goldman's safe. She could drive up alone whenever she wanted. And as for killing him in such a brutal manner – there was no reason that I could see. They had been very chummy on the ship. She was still the star of his pictures. They had driven to the castle in the same car. And she didn't seem the volatile type. But then who else in this room would have wanted Cy Goldman dead – apart from his wife?

I looked around them, one by one.

'Do you want me to go up to your room, miss, and get your nightclothes ready?' Queenie asked.

'I don't think you can do that,' I said. 'We're not staying in the house. We're all in bungalows dotted around the grounds.'

'Well, I expect I can find the right one if you show me where it is,' Queenie said. 'Someone will have a torch, won't they?'

'Queenie, we're a long way from the house and the grounds are full of wild animals,' I said.

'Go on.' She nudged me. 'You're pulling my leg.'

'I'm certainly not,' I said. 'Mr. Goldman imported exotic

animals for his park – giraffes, zebras, and God knows what else.'

'Cor blimey,' she said. 'And to think I was trying to get in through that gate. I might have come face to face with an elephant. So what do you want me to do? It don't feel right for me to sit here among your lot.'

'I suppose you'd better join the other servants in the kitchen,' I said.

'And how do I find where the kitchen is in this 'ouse of 'orrors?' she demanded. 'I'll be bound to get lost and meet a boa constrictor or something.'

I looked up and saw one of the groundsmen still lingering near the front door. I beckoned him over. 'Could you possibly drive my maid over to the cottage where I'm staying?' I asked. 'She's afraid to walk on her own in the dark.'

'Of course,' he said. 'Follow me, miss.'

Queenie gave me a pleased grin. He was rather good-looking in a Latin way. I watched her go then saw my mother and Belinda watching me.

'You really are too soft,' Mummy said. 'You should have refused to take her back.'

'Mummy, I could hardly leave her to fend for herself in California, could I? I brought her out here, and hopefully she's learned her lesson.'

Mummy sighed and got up. 'I think I need another drink, Charlie darling.'

'Of course you do. We all need a little something right now to cheer us up, don't we?'

'I know what might cheer me up.' She walked slowly over to him and I watched him watching her. I had a feeling that she wouldn't be spending the rest of the night in our bungalow, if we were ever released to go to bed. And again I marveled that I could be her daughter. Perhaps I had been switched at birth with Belinda.

I realized that I could do with a drink too, but Mummy and Charlie were now being horribly chummy at the drinks table and I dared not interrupt. So I was glad when we heard the sound of heavy footsteps outside and then rapping on the front door.

Ronnie went to answer it and several men entered the hallway. They looked to me like a gang of desperadoes who might have come to raid the bank in any Wild Western film. 'Where's the sheriff?' one of them asked. 'We got word of a body being found here?' He was unshaven, wearing a sweaty shirt and a cowboy hat he hadn't bothered to remove.

'The sheriff is in the library where the body is also located,' Ronnie said. 'Are you one of the deputies?'

'No, I'm the doctor,' the scruffy individual said. 'The deputies came to get me when I'd just returned from a horseback ride. So take me to him. I'm dog tired and want to get home.'

After prim and fastidious English doctors, I didn't put much faith in this one. It was interesting to observe that under the thin veneer of glamor in Beverly Hills this was still the untamed West. The deputies moved into the front hall, looking around with awe as if they'd suddenly found themselves on a strange planet. We turned at the sound of tapping feet and Stella came across the hall, followed by the sheriff. She made a beeline for the cocktails.

'Odious man,' she muttered. 'One minute he's asking me personal questions about my relationship with Cy and the next he's asking for my autograph for his wife.'

'So you finally got here,' the sheriff said as he joined his men. 'What news on the fire?'

'Won't be contained for a few days at least,' one said.

'They've got fire crews come in from all over the place but it's moving so damned fast they can't stop it.'

'Right. Nothing more we can do there anyway. In the hands of the fire marshal now,' he grunted in his deep, gravelly voice. 'Doc's with the body now. I need you boys to do a thorough search of this house. And did one of you bring a fingerprinting kit?'

'Out in the truck, Sheriff.'

'Then go get it. We've got us one fine bloody print that should make it easy to identify our killer.'

One of them slouched out again, walking with that strange rolling gait that comes from a life in the saddle.

'So what are we supposed to be looking for?' another of them asked.

'Clues, boys, clues. Any more fingerprints – oh, and a golden candlestick covered with precious stones. Not too easy to hide, I'd have thought.'

'Surely nobody would be stupid enough to hide the candlestick in the house,' Belinda whispered to me. 'But then I can't think that anyone would be stupid enough to steal the candlestick in the first place. Certainly not one of us. And if I were trying to steal it and Mr. Goldman caught me at it, I'd bluff my way out, saying I wanted to take a closer look in good light. I wouldn't bash him over the head.'

'I know,' I said. 'That's why I think it has to be an outsider. One of us would have a good excuse for being in the library and wouldn't have panicked if we'd been caught with the candlestick.'

'I wish we could go to bed,' Belinda muttered. 'I am incredibly tired. Of course I could have livened up no end if there had been a good reason to stay awake. But alas, I seem to have lost my sex appeal.'

I had just decided to spill the beans to her when we heard running footsteps on the gallery up above and then someone yelled, 'Sheriff. Up here.'

The big man took the stairs with surprising grace. Then we heard him say, 'Well, I'll be . . .'

He returned to the head of the stairs. 'Okay, who is currently sleeping in this room to the left at the top of the stairs?'

'That's my room, Sheriff,' Stella said coldly.

'Then perhaps you'd like to come up here, Miss Brightwell,' he said. His eyes had a triumphant gleam to them.

'Oh really,' she said. 'What have they found now? My frilly underpants from Paris?'

'Oh, no. Much more interesting than that,' he said.

Stella stalked across the foyer and up the stairs. 'Mrs. Goldman was right when she said we should try to bring in detectives from Los Angeles,' she said. 'Your incompetent louts are keeping us awake for nothing.'

'Incompetent louts?' the sheriff demanded. 'You counted on us being really stupid, did you? Or you'd have found a better hiding place for this.'

There was a scream. Darcy was up the stairs in an instant. So were Craig and Ronnie, followed closely by me. We clustered at the doorway of a bedroom that would have been right at home in Castle Rannoch – huge four-poster bed, tapestries on the walls, old chests, candlesticks . . . and one candlestick, more beautiful than the rest, lying in the middle of Stella's bed.

Chapter 24

Stella was standing there, her mouth open, pointing at it. 'How did it get there?' she demanded.

'That's what we'd like to know, Miss Brightwell,' the sheriff said.

'Someone must have put it there,' Stella said, sounding angry now. 'Someone is trying to frame me.'

'Oh yeah?' The sheriff was still gloating. 'Or maybe you killed your lover and decided to take one of the candlesticks as a little souvenir. Only the body was found quicker than you'd hoped and you had nowhere to hide it properly. So your bed seemed a fairly safe place – unless you decided to invite someone else to join you tonight.'

'How dare you!' Stella said. 'In case you've forgotten, I am a famous actress. I could afford to buy my own candlestick if I wanted one. If I'd asked Cy for it, he'd have probably given it to me as a present. He adored me. I adored him. And if that old cow had given him the divorce he wanted, we'd have been married by now.'

'But she didn't, did she?' the sheriff said. 'Perhaps you just found out he never planned to divorce his wife. Perhaps he was about to ditch you and move on to someone new and you didn't like that.'

'So I hit him over the head with his own candlestick?' she snapped. 'Don't be ridiculous. I abhor violence, Sheriff.'

'We'll find out soon enough, Miss Brightwell,' he said. 'When my man has had a good look at that fingerprint. If I were you I'd pack some clothes. You may be on your way to jail before the night is over.'

'I bet she was the one who did this,' Stella said, her voice now cracking with emotion. 'That cow, his wife. She always hated me, even though she didn't want Cy for herself. What's the betting she bashed his head in and then planted the candlestick on me. Killing two birds with one stone. How very neat. You want to question her more fully, Sheriff. Find out if she's taken out a large life insurance policy on her husband recently.'

'Don't worry, Miss Brightwell. We'll be doing that. Trust me. But when I was a young lawman my boss said to me, "Always go for what you know. Go for the obvious first then work outward." And what I know right now is that you could have a good reason for killing a former lover and the evidence was found in your bed.'

'Hardly a former lover,' she said. 'We had a quickie after we arrived this afternoon, before the dreadful wife got here.' And she smirked. 'And as to having the opportunity to kill him – ask the others. We came into the rotunda together after dinner and we didn't leave until Cy was found dead. Isn't that right?'

I hesitated, wrestling between telling the truth and betraying someone. Then I decided I had no reason to be loyal to Stella. Darcy had followed her across the country, suspecting her of being a notorious jewel thief. I had to tell what I knew.

'You did leave the room once, Stella,' I said, then blushed when all eyes turned on me. 'You went to ask for more coffee when Darcy and Ronnie joined us.'

'Oh yes. So I did.' Stella gave a little laugh. 'But two seconds going down to the kitchen and back hardly constitutes enough time to sneak into the library, kill Cy and rush upstairs with a candlestick, does it? Everyone would have seen me going upstairs, for one thing. And Maria can vouch for my presence in the kitchen. I'm not Peter Pan. I can't fly around the house in seconds.'

This, of course, was true. Even if she'd been out of our line of vision we'd have heard her feet going upstairs.

'I'm not going to caution you officially yet, but I want you locked up with a guard on you until we know more. Which of these rooms can be locked from the outside?'

'The library,' Stella said, 'but I take it even you wouldn't be insensitive enough to lock me up with Cy's body.'

'No. Of course not. And we'll want to conduct a further search on this room.' He looked around, unsure what to do next. 'What other rooms?'

'The poolside cabanas can all be locked from the outside,' Ronnie said, 'but they are currently occupied. As are some of the cottages. In fact Stella is the only person sleeping in the house, apart from Mrs. Goldman.'

'And Barbara Kindell,' Stella said. 'Mrs. Goldman wanted her friend close to her, remember?'

Instinctively we turned around but Barbara had not joined us at the top of the stairs. Neither had Mrs. Goldman, nor Algie. The sheriff looked around at those of us clustered in the doorway. 'So who would have known that this was Miss Brightwell's room?'

'Nobody apart from Mrs. Goldman and possibly Miss

Kindell,' Stella said. 'Most of them were visiting for the first time and Cy never liked his guests to sleep in the main house. He liked his privacy. That's why he had the cottages built. So they'd have had no way of knowing where I was sleeping.'

'Interesting.' The sheriff sucked through his teeth. 'Well, we've got to put you somewhere, Miss Brightwell. I can lock you in my truck for the night, but that's a little chilly right now. Or I can lock you in a bathroom. . . .'

'Oh, for heaven's sake. This is absurd.' Stella had remained remarkably composed until now but I could tell she was coming to the end of her tether. 'I believe some of the bedroom doors have old-fashioned locks and the keys must be somewhere. Ask Maria. She must know where they are kept. We've never thought of locking bedroom doors here.'

'Well, you wouldn't, would you?' the sheriff replied with a smirk. 'We've all heard what goes on in places like this.'

'Oh, really, this is pathetic,' she said. 'Lock me up and put a guard on me if you like, but I actually want to go to sleep. I don't know about you but I'm dead tired. And if you think I can fly away through the window then go and look out. On this side of the house there are rocks at the bottom of a large drop.'

'Very well,' the sheriff said. 'One of you men go and get the keys from the housekeeper, and you can find an unused room for Miss Brightwell – one that's already been searched, with no dangerous objects in it.'

'Come now, Sheriff,' Stella snapped. 'Do you expect me to go on another rampage with a candlestick?'

The sheriff ignored her. 'And Hansen, you remain outside the door.'

'It's not as if I can escape, Sheriff,' Stella said. 'There is only one way out of this property and that's through the gate that can only be operated from inside the gatehouse. And anyone walking alone in these grounds at night must be mad. I've no idea exactly what animals Cy keeps here but they are certainly not all friendly.'

'I'm not taking any chances, Miss Brightwell,' the sheriff said. 'Now if you'd like to go with my men . . .'

Stella turned back to look at us as she was led away. 'This is bloody stupid,' she said – showing how upset she really was. A lady never swears in public. But then she wasn't a lady, was she? She might be playing Princess Elizabeth in the movie but she had come from the lowliest of circumstances.

As we trooped down the stairs again we were greeted by the doctor. 'Ah, there you are, Sheriff,' he said. 'I hope one of your men can run me home. I've concluded my preliminary investigation,' he said. 'My initial observation is that Mr. Goldman died of trauma to the head, struck with a blunt instrument which one had to conclude was the candlestick, now lying beside him on the floor.'

'That was obvious to even the most stupid among us,' the sheriff said.

'Hold on a minute,' the doctor said. 'I have yet to autopsy the victim. We don't know, for example, whether he might have been knocked out in some other way first – poison perhaps, and then finished off with the blow to the head.'

'Hardly likely,' Darcy said. 'We were all talking and laughing with him fifteen minutes before he died.'

'And this was clearly a spontaneous act when the thief was interrupted in the middle of a robbery,' the sheriff added. 'One of the candlesticks was taken. Presumably the thief meant to take both of them but then couldn't bring himself or herself to take the candlestick matted with hair and blood.'

'That would prove he didn't die of poisoning or some other means first, wouldn't it?' I blurted out, finding this whole thing rather silly. 'I mean, there was an awful lot of blood all over the floor and if he was already dead, he would have stopped bleeding.'

They stared at me as if I were a newly arrived Martian.

'And how would you know that, little lady?' the doctor asked.

'I've been involved in a couple of murders in my life,' I said.

'She's helped to solve them,' Darcy added, moving closer to my side. 'She's quite a whizz, if you want to know.'

'Holy cow,' the doctor said.

'So let's hear it, then.' The sheriff turned to me with a sarcastic smile on his thick lips. 'Who did it? We're all dying to know and then we can go home.'

'Of course I have no idea who did it yet,' I said. 'But I really have to suspect that someone was trying to frame Miss Brightwell. I mean why hide the candlestick where it would so easily be found? She knows her way around this house. If she was planning to hide something, there must be hundreds of out-of-the-way corners and cupboards where nobody would ever look. She could even stash it inside a suit of armor—'

I broke off as I said this as a picture flashed into my head – Algie standing in the hallway with the suit of armor scattered around him. Right before we found the body of Cy Goldman. Was it possible that hiding the candlestick was exactly what Algie was trying to do, only he knocked over the armor and had to play the fool instead when we all came running? I couldn't wait to draw Darcy aside and tell him this. I looked around for Algie and he wasn't with us at the top of the stairs. I wondered if anyone was guarding the front door.

Before we could go downstairs another of the deputies came running up toward us. 'That fingerprint, Sheriff,' he said. 'I just tested it.'

'And?'

The silence was palpable.

'No go, I'm afraid. The person was wearing a glove. A leather glove.'

Chapter 25

Late at night on August 3

'Damn,' the sheriff muttered. 'Then that's what we're looking for next. A bloody glove, and its mate. No other fingerprints?'

'Plenty,' the deputy said. 'All over the candlestick, but then I gather it was passed around everyone here to take a look at.'

'That fingerprint was on the window frame,' the sheriff went on. 'So we have to conclude that either someone exited that way, or wants us to think they did. No sense in poking around in the dark, but as soon as it's light I want that outside area searched. Who would have thought it could be Stella Brightwell, of all people? My wife idolizes her. But don't they always say *Cherchez la femme*?'

'It would need someone with rope to have climbed down from the window,' Ronnie said dryly. 'In case you haven't looked out of the library windows, there is a sheer drop below. This house is built on a bluff, you know.'

'Then we'll be looking for rope as well as a glove,' the sheriff said.

'Now really, Sheriff,' Mummy's lovely voice echoed up the stairwell, 'can anything else really be accomplished tonight? We're all utterly exhausted and I'm sure you'd get more out of us in the morning. I'm equally sure you'd like a rest now and there are plenty of rooms all over the place. Help yourself.'

He looked down at Mummy, looking petite, frail and languid as only Mummy can. Then he said, 'Oh, very well. I suppose you can all go to bed, but I want everyone back here at eight o'clock sharp and don't get any funny ideas about leaving during the night. One of my men is staying in the gatehouse until this is over and that gate doesn't get opened unless I say so.'

'We wouldn't dream of leaving, Sheriff.' Charlie stepped out of the shadows to stand beside Mummy. 'We haven't had this much fun in ages. Usually it's quite a bore coming here but I must say I'm really glad that I did.' And he turned to glance at my mother. I had seen that look before and therefore I was not surprised when she said to me, in a breathless voice, 'You won't mind if I don't join you in that horrid little cottage tonight, will you? I think I need the protection of a nice strong man.'

'Does Mr. Chaplin count as a nice strong man?' I asked. 'He's rather small.'

'But wiry, darling, and he has such lovely eyes. Like a spaniel I once owned. So deep and trusting.'

'And I see you don't mind abandoning your own child to whatever monster might be prowling around out there tonight?'

She patted my arm. 'Oh, darling. You don't really think that, do you? It had to be Stella, didn't it? She and Cy had already had one tiff this evening. She lost her temper and clobbered him in a fit of rage. Didn't mean to kill him, of course, and then put a candlestick in her own bed to make it look as if someone was trying to frame her. She always was a quick-witted child.'

'What about your maid? What do I tell her?'

'You don't have to tell her anything. She's my maid. She sees nothing and thinks nothing. I'll tell her myself if it upsets your prudish side. Besides, I believe she came up to dinner in the servants' hall and I presume she hasn't been allowed to leave.'

She headed in one direction, to pass on the information to her maid. We headed for the front door. Belinda fell into step beside me. 'I don't want to walk all that way in the dark,' she whispered. 'Couldn't one of those strong men drive us? I'm scared we'd get savaged by an antelope or something.'

'I don't think antelopes go around savaging people,' I said, 'but I must admit I'm not too keen to walk there alone either. I'll ask the sheriff if we can be driven.'

Darcy was standing within earshot. 'Don't worry,' he said. 'You don't need to ask the sheriff. He's gone off to question the staff. I'll walk with you.'

'But will you be all right walking back alone?' I asked.

He smiled at me. He really had such a lovely smile. 'I can take care of myself.'

'Yes, but . . .'

He moved closer to me. 'Georgie – do you really think there is a murderer lurking in the undergrowth out there? It's obvious to me that one of us must have killed Goldman and my money is still on Stella Brightwell.'

'I'm not so sure about that,' I said.

'What are your thoughts then?' he asked as we stepped into the cold dampness of the night-time fog. Belinda latched on to one of my arms with an iron grip. I slipped the other arm through Darcy's and together we made our way down the flagstoned path.

'Well, Mrs. Goldman is the obvious one,' I said. 'Why did she come here when she normally avoids this place like the plague? I wouldn't be surprised if Mr. Goldman had announced that he planned to get a divorce and marry Stella. I really don't believe that they were a devoted couple, as Barbara Kindell insists, do you? And why is *she* here too? Was she in on the plot with Mrs. Goldman or is she simply hoping to get some kind of scoop?'

'There's nobody else who would seem to benefit from Mr. Goldman's death,' Darcy said. 'In fact they will all be out of a job if Golden Pictures folds.'

'Actually the one person I keep coming back to,' I said, 'is Algie Broxley-Foggett. He was on the ship. He turns up out of the blue and gets himself invited here. And when I suggested that the candlestick could have been hidden in a suit of armor I remembered him and his ridiculous claim about wanting to see how he'd look as a knight.'

Darcy walked on in silence for a few seconds, our footsteps echoing in the stillness of the foggy night, then he said, 'You might have something there. He was the only one unaccounted for after we left the library.'

'And he didn't run up the stairs with us when they found the candlestick in Stella's bed,' I added. 'Was that because he knew what they must have found?'

'Interesting,' Darcy said. 'So you think he could be the thief I'm tracking, don't you? I'd love to find out more about him – whether he was present at all the gatherings where jewelry was stolen. Whether Scotland Yard has any suspicions about him.'

'So how could you find that out?' I asked.

'I'll have to send a cable to London and that would involve driving into Los Angeles, I suspect.'

'Do you think the sheriff would let you leave?'

'I can ask in the morning. No telegraph office will be open before eight or nine, I'm sure. And I'm not ditching you tonight. In fact I may just sleep on your sofa, just to make sure.'

'Mummy's got other plans, so I gather,' I said. 'You could have her room.'

'Darlings, I don't want to be a killjoy,' Belinda said. 'Why don't I take your mother's room and you two can be cozy together.'

Darcy gave me a quick glance. 'If you don't mind . . .'

'When have I ever stood in the way of young love?' she said. 'Especially when it seems that I am destined to become an aged spinster who keeps cats and does good works.'

'What is she talking about?' Darcy looked amused.

'My dears, I was turned down by a man. Rejected. Spurned. I was naked and ready and so very willing and he wasn't interested. Let's face it – I've lost my sex appeal.'

'Belinda,' I said, trying not to grin, 'I shouldn't tell you this, since you tried to steal him away from me.'

'You? Craig Hart really was interested in you?'

'Strange though it may seem, yes he was.'

'But you've got Darcy.'

'I know that, but Craig didn't. He was very attentive to me until you arrived. I must admit I was flattered. I mean, Craig Hart. Who wouldn't be flattered?'

'I caught them kissing,' Darcy said.

'You see. I knew it. You have more sex appeal than I do.' Belinda's voice echoed through the fog.

'But it was the most uninspiring kiss I've ever had,' I said, 'and now I know why.' I lowered my voice, searching for the right words. 'He's one of them, Belinda. You know.'

'You mean Craig Hart is a queer?' She started to laugh. 'Are you serious?'

I nodded.

'And you knew that and let me go on thinking . . .' Darcy said.

'I only found out at dinner tonight,' I said. 'Ronnie told me. He said that Mr. Goldman had been pushing Craig to marry someone suitable and thus quell any rumors that could spoil his career. I suppose that's why he went after me. Marriage to a British aristocrat would make good publicity, wouldn't it?'

'Oh God,' Belinda said. 'And to think if I hadn't found out – I might have said yes to him and rushed off to Reno and found myself in a sexless marriage.'

'Ah, but think of the alimony when you divorced. You'd be set up for life,' Darcy quipped. 'They'd have paid you handsomely to stay mum.'

'True.' Belinda paused, then shook her head vehemently. 'Darlings – no amount of money is worth giving up sex for any length of time.' She released my arm and strode out ahead of us to where the fairy-tale shape of the cottage loomed out of the fog, a light glowing from a window. Darcy slipped an arm around my waist. 'And in case you think I have any intentions tonight, the answer is no. Not with Belinda and your maid in the next rooms,' he whispered. 'I'm only here to protect you.'

'That's good,' I said, feeling half relieved and half disappointed.

* * *

As we entered the cottage we were greeted by a worried-looking Queenie.

'Oh, miss. I ain't half glad to see you,' she said. 'I was scared out of me wits. I kept hearing noises outside, like someone or something prowling around and squeaks and heavy breathing. . . .'

'You're quite safe now, Queenie. There are three of us here and my mother's maid may be returning too.'

'Thank gawd for that,' she said. Then she noticed Darcy. 'So where's yer mum then?'

'My mother worried about being far from the main house, given the circumstances,' I said.

'Oh, that's lovely, ain't it. Real nice,' she said. 'Everyone else is scared to come down here, out of the way, but you send me down here alone.'

'That's because no killer would want to murder you, Queenie,' I said. 'Now you can go to sleep in peace. Mr. O'Mara will be staying.'

I noticed the twinkle in her eyes. 'Oh yeah?'

'To protect us,' I added.

I think I heard her chuckling as she went off to bed. I undressed in the bathroom, changing into my new silk pajamas, and came back to find Darcy had shed his dinner jacket and tie and was lying on one of the beds. One small table lamp gave the room a cozy glow.

'You look very smart,' he said. 'Did you buy those in case Craig Hart came to visit?'

'Shut up about Craig Hart,' I said. 'I do believe you were jealous.'

'Just a little.'

I went over and perched on the bed beside him. 'You never have to be, you know. There is only one man in my life.'

'And to think you're sitting on my bed, in baby blue silk pajamas and I'm going to refrain from doing anything more than kissing you good night – you must have turned me into a reformed character.'

I bent over him and kissed his forehead. 'You know I'd marry you now and be happy in a flat in Bayswater.'

'But I wouldn't be happy, and neither would you in the long run. You have a right to live the sort of life you were supposed to live, Georgie. Nice big house in the country. Plenty of servants. Your proper station in life. I'm not going to make you into a domestic drudge.' His arm came around my shoulder. 'That's why that role in the film seemed like such a great opportunity. I'd have been paid handsomely. Maybe I'd have become a film star and made enough to keep you in the style you deserve.'

'And every woman in the world would have thrown herself at you. I saw the way Stella was looking at you. These actors don't hold to the same moral code as people like us. Look at my mother! So I'm glad the film probably won't be finished now.'

'In a way so am I,' he said. 'I'd have looked really silly in tights.' He pulled me down beside him and I snuggled against his cheek. He leaned across and turned out the light. I gave a sigh of contentment. Then he said, 'Georgie, would you mind sleeping in the other bed. I have been a saint for too long. And you're lying against me in thin silk pajamas and I'm only human.'

'I really wouldn't mind,' I whispered.

'I would,' he said. 'We've waited this long. You've turned me down before because your conscience wouldn't let you, so I want to make sure that our first time is perfect – right time, right place and no interruptions.'

Almost on cue there was a banging at the front door.

'You see?' Darcy reached to turn on the lamp. 'I had a feeling this was not going to be a peaceful night.'

I followed him to the front door, wondering if Mummy had changed her mind about a night with Mr. Chaplin. Instead Claudette stalked in, her hand over her heart and gasping as if she'd been running. *'Mon Dieu,'* she said. 'I never wish to do that again, as long as I live. Nevair!'

'Do what, Claudette?'

'Find myself abandoned in the darkness. Madame says I am to come back 'ere as soon as those swine have finished asking me stupid questions. I leave the house and then I am lost in the fog. I do not know where I am. And something is breathing on me and it is some kind of large animal. I scream and nobody hears. I think I see the light of this cottage but when I get close the light goes out and I am in darkness again. I thought I had breathed my last and was about to be devoured by a lion.'

'Poor Claudette,' Darcy said. 'Well, you're safe now. We're here. You can go to sleep in peace.'

'Thank the *bon Dieu* for that,' she said and headed for her door.

'I should warn you that Queenie has returned and is sleeping in the other bed in your room,' I called after her.

'And you told me I could sleep in peace?' She turned back to scowl at us. 'She snores worse than a rhinoceros, that one.'

Darcy grinned at me as we went back to my room.

Chapter 26

Still at the castle, or rather in a quaint English cottage
Saturday, August 4, 1934

I opened my eyes to the twittering of birds and gray daylight filtering in through lace curtains. Darcy was already up and dressed, sitting on his bed, tying his shoelace.

'Good morning,' he said.

'What time is it?' I yawned and attempted to sit up gracefully.

'Still early. I thought I'd get going if the sheriff gives me the nod. I want to reach Scotland Yard during their working day if I'm to get answers quickly.'

'Do you want me to come with you?'

He shook his head. 'I think you'd be more use staying on here. Frankly I don't believe the bumbling sheriff will find out anything useful. He certainly won't arrive at the truth without a lot of luck or maybe someone breaking down and confessing.'

'All right,' I said. 'I'll stay. But don't be gone too long, will you? I feel much safer with you here.'

'I don't think you have anything to worry about,' Darcy said. 'This wasn't some random homicidal maniac. It was someone who wanted Mr. Goldman dead. Now he or she has achieved their purpose and it's just a matter of seeing if they can keep their composure and not lose their nerve. That's where you might come in. You're a good judge of character.'

'Unfortunately I've seen murderers who are as cool as cucumbers,' I said. 'And the person who did this must have nerves of steel to start with. Knowing that we were all within earshot if Mr. Goldman had cried out – knowing that he or she could have got blood on their clothing . . . someone took a terrible risk.'

'That's a good point,' Darcy said. 'Did we notice anyone whose clothing might have been sponged clean?'

I shook my head. 'Certainly not Stella. I noticed how lovely she looked when she was standing by the window. Not a hair out of place. Just perfect.'

'Speaking of looking lovely, do you know how delightful you look when you are asleep? Like an angel with blonde hair spilling over your pillow. When we're married I shall sit and watch you every morning.'

'Oh, Darcy,' I said, giggling with embarrassment because I'm not very good at accepting compliments, certainly not from handsome men and certainly not when I'm in my night attire. 'Won't that be lovely? I just wish I knew how long we'd have to wait.'

'Maybe we'll have to run off to Argentina or Australia and make our fortune there,' he said.

'I wouldn't mind. Anywhere would be fun with you.'

'Come here,' he said and pulled me up into his arms. 'Do you know how adorable you are?' And he kissed me. Properly this time.

'Cor blimey, miss. At it again?' said Queenie's disapproving voice from my doorway.

'Queenie, did I not teach you that you have to knock?' I said, feeling my cheeks burning.

'I don't knock when I bring in yer morning tea, do I? I tiptoe in and wake you gently. Well, I ain't got no tea, but I was going to lay out yer clothes for you, but I can tell I'm not wanted.'

'It's all right, Queenie,' I said. 'Mr. O'Mara and I were just about to go up to the main house for breakfast and then he has to go back to Los Angeles.'

'What, and leave us here alone with no bloke to protect us?'

'Queenie, I've told you. We'll be fine. Don't worry. I'm sure this whole mess will be sorted out today.'

'If you say so, miss.' She didn't sound convinced. 'And where am I going to have me breakfast? There ain't no food in this place. I already looked.'

'You'd better come up to the main house with us and I'm sure there will be food for you in the kitchen. Then perhaps you can bring something back for Claudette.'

'What? Me wait on another maid?'

'Queenie,' Darcy said firmly, 'I think you had better realize that Lady Georgiana is only taking you back out of the goodness of her heart, after you betrayed her and abandoned her. If you are going to continually whine and complain then you may find that she will leave you behind in America when she goes back to England.'

'Cor blimey, miss. You wouldn't do that, would you?' Her mouth dropped open.

'I might, unless you put your best foot forward and act the way a lady's maid should.'

She stared at the ground. 'I don't rightly know which is my best foot, miss,' she said.

'Hopeless. Utterly hopeless,' I muttered to Darcy as we started for the main house. There was no sign of Belinda. She was not the earliest of risers. I wondered how she had handled reporting for duty at Harrods. She wasn't exactly used to waking in her own bed either.

'I suppose it's all right to leave Belinda here alone.' I turned and looked back at the cottage.

'I think your friend Belinda can take care of herself,' Darcy said. 'She invited herself here, didn't she?'

He stood there, frowning. 'God, what a hideous-looking monstrosity this is,' he said. 'The man had no taste.'

'It was supposed to be an English country cottage,' I said. 'And the one over there through the trees is even worse. At least this one would be all right in an impossibly adorable English village, whereas that one could only be inhabited by the Brothers Grimm.'

Darcy grinned as he took in the sloping roof, gingerbread trim and small-paned windows. 'Who is staying there then?' he asked. 'Frankenstein's monster?'

'Nobody. We were given the English cottage to make us feel at home.'

As I went to follow Darcy I found myself staring at the other cottage. A thought that something was wrong came to me and departed again before I could latch on to it. I shook my head and followed Darcy up the path.

Fog still draped over oak trees and occasional bursts of birdsong echoed strangely so that it was hard to place where the sounds were coming from. The Gothic castle loomed up ahead of us and somewhere off to our right there was a weird flapping sound. I moved a little closer to

Darcy. I could well understand how frightened Claudette had been last night. I was rather glad to have Darcy beside me. But then I was always glad when he was near me. I sneaked him a little glance and he smiled, making me feel warm and glowing inside, as if nothing else really mattered.

As we stepped into the foyer of the castle there was no sign of anyone. No sheriff's man was guarding the front door, at any rate. I wondered if anything had happened while we'd been gone.

'It doesn't look as if you'll get any breakfast,' I said. 'Nobody's up yet.'

'Then let's find the kitchen and see if we can make ourselves some coffee,' Darcy said, going ahead of me down the main hall and into a narrow tiled hallway leading to the back of the house. As we came closer to the kitchen we heard sounds.

'You see. Someone's at work in the kitchen. We shall get breakfast after all,' he said, turning back to me.

The kitchen was surprisingly twentieth century compared to the rest of the house. There was a large shining gas range and even a refrigerator. When we entered we saw Maria at the stove. She spun around at the sound of our voices.

'Oh, you scare me. I not expect' – she put her hand up to her large bosom – 'and I apologize. I don't have your breakfast ready yet. That sonofabitch sheriff don't let us go to bed before early morning so I don't wake at my usual time.'

'That's all right, Maria,' Darcy said. 'We're up rather early, I know, but I want to drive into Los Angeles. Do you happen to have any coffee?'

'Coffee is in the percolator on the stove, señor. Help

yourself. And you tell me what you want me to cook for you
– eggs, ham, pork chop, pancakes . . .'

'Just some toast would be fine for me,' I said.

'That's all Miss Brightwell wants this morning,' Maria
said. 'Real cut up, she is. She normally has a good breakfast
but not today.'

'Miss Brightwell's up and around, is she?'

Maria shook her head. 'No, señorita. She locked up in
one of the rooms upstairs. Locked up like a common criminal. I ask you. They think she killed Mr. Goldman but
that's stupid. She wouldn't have done that. She loved him.
One of those men came down and said Miss Brightwell
wanted toast and tea, so I fix it for her. Now I'm waiting for
him to come back to take the tray up to her.' She indicated
the table.

'I'll take it,' I said eagerly. 'We don't want the toast and tea
to get cold, do we?'

'*Muchas gracias*, señorita,' she said, smiling shyly. 'I would
have taken it myself but these old legs are not good on the
stairs no more.'

'It's no problem.' I picked up the tray. 'Which room is it?'

'It's in that corridor to the left, second door toward the
back of the house. You can't miss it because it looks like the
door from another of those old churches.'

I picked up the tray and went carefully up the stairs. I
noticed then for the first time that each of the rooms had a
different door, taken from some old building. This one was
particularly solid and impressive, which was presumably
why they had chosen to keep Stella shut in there. I kicked
at the door with my foot and it was opened by one of the
sheriff's men, looking even more rough and haggard after a
sleepless night.

'I've brought up Miss Brightwell's tray,' I said.

'How kind of you, Georgie,' Stella said as I carried it into the room before he could take it from me. In contrast to her unshaven, unkempt guard, Stella still looked perfectly groomed. She was sitting in a high-backed armchair, wearing a black silk dressing gown trimmed with white feathers.

'There's no news, I take it,' she said as I put the tray in front of her. She sighed. 'I thought not. That horrid man has decided that I'm guilty and he's not even going to keep looking, is he?'

'We'll do our best to help,' I said. 'But it's not easy when the murderer must be one of us. You said that you suspected Mrs. Goldman.'

She glanced across at her guard, standing in the doorway watching us with a rather large weapon on the table beside him. 'Of course I do,' she said. 'She was the only one of us with means and motive, wasn't she? She said she went up to bed, but did anyone see her actually go up the stairs? And that poisonous Barbara Kindell might well be in it with her. They probably plotted together. Helen Goldman knew that Cy wanted to divorce her and marry me and he was going to cite denial of conjugal rights. Why else would she have come back here? She hates the place.'

She put some sugar in her tea, stirred it, then took a long drink. 'Ah, that's what I needed. I've lived in America for years but the need for a cup of tea is bred into one, isn't it?'

I nodded. 'It certainly is. A wonderful comfort when all else fails. In fact . . .' I stopped, staring at her.

'What's wrong?' she asked.

'I think I can prove that you didn't kill Mr. Goldman,' I said. 'I must find the sheriff. Where might he be found?' I asked the guard.

'He was outside, searching the grounds with our guys,' he said.

'Super. Thank you.' I ran down the stairs, across the foyer and outside. Cold air was coming up from the ocean, giving the day a clammy feel to it. I made my way around the house until I caught the sound of voices coming from among the trees. Sheriff Billings was standing there with another man, kicking at something on the ground with his foot.

'Careful how you pick it up,' he said, then looked up with a start as I came toward him.

'Lady Georgiana. What are you doing out here? A spot of sleuthing of your own?'

'No, Sheriff. I came to find you. I think I can prove that Stella Brightwell didn't kill Mr. Goldman,' I said.

'Oh really? Is that so?' He was smirking, which annoyed me. I hate it when men put on a superior 'I'm a man and you're only a woman' act.

'Yes, it is.' I gave him the stare I hoped I had inherited from my great-grandmother Queen Victoria. 'I want you to cast your mind back to the crime scene. Can you picture the body, lying on the floor?'

'Of course I can.'

'How would you describe the wound to Mr. Goldman's head?'

'Someone had struck him in the back of the head with considerable force, using a blunt object.'

'Correct. Was he struck directly in the back of the head? Right in the middle, would you say?'

The sheriff frowned. 'More to one side.'

'Which side?'

'The right. The wound was more to the right.'

Now I allowed myself to smile. 'I've just taken Stella

Brightwell her breakfast, Sheriff. I watched her put sugar in her tea, stir it and then pick up the cup and drink. And all using her left hand. Stella Brightwell is left-handed, Sheriff. That blow could not have come from a left-handed person.'

Chapter 27

At the castle
August 4

There was a silence. The sheriff's man shifted from one foot to the other, making the dried leaves crunch underfoot. Then the sheriff himself took a deep breath. 'You're right, little lady,' he said. 'That blow had to come from a right-handed person. Very astute of you. When that guy said you'd been involved in solving some murders, I didn't take him seriously.' He turned away, staring out into the trees. 'Well, dang me. Now it looks like we're back to square one. Unless you've some thoughts of your own?'

'I really don't know what to think,' I said. 'I don't know any of these people and why they might have wanted Mr. Goldman dead. But it had to be someone who hated Miss Brightwell, didn't it? Why else would one put the stolen candlestick in her bed?'

He nodded. 'Well, we're actually one step closer. We've just found the bloody glove.' He indicated what his man was now holding in a handkerchief.

'It's quite small, isn't it?' I said. 'Either a man with small hands or a woman. I wonder if it was dropped accidentally or deliberately. This isn't exactly on anyone's route to where they were sleeping last night, is it?' I looked up at the castle wall. 'But it must be below the library. Is it possible that someone *did* climb out of the window?'

'Meaning that it might have been an intruder after all? Someone who came to steal valuable objects and was surprised to be caught in the act by Goldman? But then how did the candlestick get in Miss Brightwell's bed? And how did the intruder get out without being seen?'

I shook my head. 'I know. None of it makes sense, does it? If it really was a robber, then why not take the candlestick or the El Greco painting, which is apparently even more valuable?'

'Perhaps someone tried to set this up to make it look like an outside robbery attempt,' the sheriff said. 'Dropping the glove out here where he knew it would be found. . . .'

'That is possible—' I broke off at the sound of footsteps coming toward us and heard Darcy's voice calling, 'Georgie? Are you out here?'

'Over here, Darcy,' I called back.

Darcy ran over to us. 'Thank God. I got worried when you didn't come back to the kitchen and then the front door was open and I couldn't find you.'

'This little lady has a good head on her shoulders,' the sheriff said. 'She's just shown me that Stella Brightwell couldn't have killed Mr. Goldman.'

'She's left-handed,' I said to Darcy. 'That blow was struck by a right-handed person.'

'Well done,' Darcy said.

'And we've found a bloody glove.'

Darcy stared at it. 'A black leather glove like the one our cat burglar wears.'

'What burglar is this, sir?' the sheriff asked, suddenly alert.

'I was sent from England on the trail of a jewel thief – someone who moves with ease in upper-class society, who knows their ways, who might be one of them. A valuable ruby was stolen on the ship crossing the Atlantic and the thief tried to negotiate its sale with a well-known gangster. The letter was intercepted and it was posted in Los Angeles. That's why I'm here. I suspected that Mr. Goldman's recent acquisitions might be of interest.'

'And you have your suspicions as to who this thief might be?'

'Between ourselves I suspected Stella Brightwell, but now Georgie has proven that she didn't kill Mr. Goldman. . . .'

'That doesn't necessarily prove she wasn't the thief,' the sheriff said, wagging a finger at us with animation. 'Perhaps we're looking at two different crimes here. She sneaked a candlestick up to her room. Someone else wanted Goldman out of the way, and knowing that a candlestick was missing it seemed like an opportune moment to strike – making it look as if the thief was also the killer.'

'You know, Sheriff, that's not bad,' Darcy said.

'So you reckon I should keep Miss Brightwell locked up a little longer?'

'I think it might be wise. And also might make the murderer let down his guard if he thinks he's not your prime suspect.'

'Right, then. Well, I appreciate your help, young man. And you too, Lady Georgiana.'

'And I may be able to help you even more,' Darcy said.

'There is one of the party that we're not sure about. He may be who he claims to be, and maybe not. If it's all right with you, I'd like to drive back to Los Angeles and send a cable to Scotland Yard. By tonight I should have an answer.'

'By all means.' The sheriff was now quite affable to us. 'I'll let the guys at the gate know that you have my permission to leave.'

'Right, then.' Darcy gave me a grin. 'I'd better get going.'

'I think I'll ride down to the gate with you,' I said as I accompanied him to the garage on the far side of the house. 'I'd like to take a look at the gate and the fence for myself. Just to see if it might be possible for a clever person to find a way in or out. You said yourself that your cat burglar could walk on ledges and cross roofs. Perhaps he can also scale barbed-wire-tipped fences?'

'You'll be all right walking back on your own?' he asked. 'It's quite a long way.'

'I could do with a good walk,' I said. 'And there is a road, after all. I expect the animals stay among the trees.'

'All right. Hop in.' Darcy opened a door for me and then went around to climb in beside me. The fog thickened as we drove down the hill, swirling in wisps across the road as if it were a live entity. Also I don't think I had quite taken in how far it was. I began to have serious second thoughts about this enterprise, but I was too proud to ask Darcy to turn around and drive me back to the house. I could always have the gatekeeper telephone to send one of the men down for me, I decided. We came at last to the fence and beside it a small building – square, unadorned, whitewashed with a Spanish tile roof. Darcy stopped the car as the gate swung slowly open. And I got out.

'Bye-bye,' I said. 'Good luck.'

'Same to you, and don't do anything silly while I'm away,' he said. 'No risks, understand?'

'Yes, dear,' I replied and he laughed. Then I closed the motorcar door, Darcy waved and drove off into the fog. The gate swung shut again. I stood looking up at it. Like the fence on either side it was about ten feet high and was topped with lethal-looking barbed wire. What's more, it fitted snugly against the metal posts so that there was no way to slip through the gap. And eyes were already upon me. I turned to see a dark-skinned man and one of the sheriff's deputies coming toward me.

'Can we help you, miss?' the deputy asked.

'I just rode down with Mr. O'Mara to keep him company and now I'm going to walk back to the house,' I said. 'I hate being cooped up for too long. And I wanted to see the fence for myself. It's quite formidable, isn't it?'

'Don't see nobody getting in or out over this fence,' the other man said.

'You must be Jimmy, the gatekeeper,' I said. 'I've heard about you.'

'Only good, I hope,' he said, and smiled, making a grim face suddenly friendly.

'They said the gate can only be opened from inside your little house, so presumably you know exactly who comes in and out.'

'Of course I do,' he said. 'I have to log them in in my book, don't I?'

'And I suppose that nobody has shown up recently whom you weren't expecting?'

'Nobody at all. Francisco came in with supplies two days ago, then yesterday it was just you people with Mr. Goldman. Three cars all following and then Miss Brightwell a bit later.'

'Wait a second,' I said. 'Miss Brightwell was with us. She was in Mr. Goldman's car, I'm sure.'

'No, miss. She came on her own, a half hour or so after the rest of you in her own little convertible.'

'Are you sure?'

He nodded. 'My job isn't exactly taxing. I know who comes in and out of this place.'

'Well, thank you,' I said. 'I'd better start walking back. I haven't had breakfast yet.'

'Watch out for the beasts,' Jimmy called after me. 'Some of them can be right mean.'

I nodded and the moment the gate was out of sight I found a stout stick lying by the side of the road and carried it for protection. And as I walked I tried to work out what Jimmy's revelation might mean. I remembered Ronnie saying that he was going to drive Mr. Goldman and Stella. Had I actually seen her get into the car? I thought I had but there was all the usual confusion about setting off on a trip as we tried to stow Mummy's luggage and Mummy's maid into the motorcar. I supposed it was possible that Stella had forgotten something at the last moment and told Cy Goldman to go on without her and she'd drive her own car up later. But it was all rather coincidental that the person now being locked in her room on suspicion of robbery, if not of murder, had chosen to arrive after everyone else. Was there possibly something in her car that she hadn't wanted anyone to see? I frowned as I strode out up the track, trying to make sense of this latest piece of news.

I'd gone about half a mile when a huge bird burst from cover on my right and ran across the road ahead of me. It took me a moment to realize it was an ostrich, and another long moment for my heart to stop beating rapidly. But I was glad to note that it appeared to be more frightened of me than I was of it. As I watched it disappear into a thick stand of bushes and trees on my left, I thought I saw something glinting among the leaves. Metal? I left the road and, sure enough, I spotted what seemed to be tire tracks in a soft patch of earth. I went on and found a small open-topped sports car, hidden among the bushes.

'Stella's motor,' I said to myself. But why had she hidden it here, unless she wanted to make a quick getaway? I searched the car but found nothing of interest in it, not even any identification or license in the glove box. Puzzled, I looked up to see a large antelope with impressive horns regarding me from a safe distance. When it snorted at me, I decided that discretion was the better part of valor and picked my way back to the road again, my stick clutched in my hand, at the ready. But no more wild animals appeared as I climbed the rest of the way up the hill and glimpsed the house standing on the bluff ahead of me. I confess I gave a sigh of relief. There was something strange and unnerving about this place, almost as if Mr. Goldman had created an illusion here where the rules of the rest of the world didn't apply.

As I approached my cottage the door opened and Belinda came out. She was still dressed in her bathrobe and slippers and her hair was tousled from sleep. 'Oh, Georgie. I'm rather glad to see you,' she said in her breathless voice. 'I woke up and found myself completely alone. Well, that's unusual enough to start with, isn't it? But then when you didn't come back I began to feel alarmed. I wondered if you'd all been spirited off or something.'

'We just went to get breakfast and then Darcy drove down to Los Angeles,' I said.

'Oh good. So all is well, then,' she said. 'I hoped that

letting Miss Brightwell go meant that they'd sorted things out.'

'What made you think they released Miss Brightwell?' I asked. 'She was locked up in her room when I left her a few minutes ago and the sheriff was showing no signs of wanting to release her.'

'But I saw her come out of that other cottage a little while ago,' Belinda said. 'I woke up, didn't know where I was and lifted the curtain to see out. And there was Stella Brightwell coming out of that door over there and creeping down into the trees.'

I stared at the fairy-tale cottage, trying to digest what she had just said. I hadn't been gone that long and when last seen the sheriff was out in the grounds, searching for more clues. And he still thought that Stella might be involved in the robbery, if not the murder. So how could she have made it as far as this and what could she possibly be doing in that cottage? Her things were still in the main house and that cottage had been unoccupied. . . . Then suddenly I realized what had struck me as odd when I looked at it earlier this morning. When we arrived yesterday there had been no curtains across that window, I was sure. Now the drapes were drawn. Someone had been in there overnight, and it couldn't have been Stella Brightwell. What's more, I realized I knew who it had to be.

Chapter 28

I stared into the trees that appeared like indistinct shadows among the fog. 'How long ago did she leave, Belinda?'

'Not long at all. Only a few minutes,' Belinda said.

'Come on, then,' I said, attempting to grab her arm. 'We must go after her.'

She shook herself free. 'What do you mean? Darling, I can't go after anybody. I'm still in my nightclothes.'

'We can't let her get away and I don't fancy following her alone. And we haven't got time to find anyone else.'

'But if the sheriff has let her go, then why are we going after her?'

'Because I think she may still be involved and there is something important we don't know.'

'You mean she may still be involved in the murder?'

'Possibly.'

'I'm not like you, Georgie. I don't actually enjoy chasing after murderers.'

'It will be all right with two of us.' I tried to convince myself as much as Belinda. 'Do come on, please, or I'll have to go alone and I really might be in danger.'

Belinda sighed. 'I don't know why I ever became friends with you in school,' she said. 'Yes, I do. I thought you were a sweet and innocent little thing who needed protecting out in the big bad world. How wrong I was. Somebody should have told me that you'd be involving me in a constant life of crime.'

'Well, if you're really not coming . . .' I started to walk away.

'Hold on,' she said. 'I'll put my shoes on. I'm not walking among wild animals in satin slippers.'

'Then please hurry up, and don't stop to put on your make-up or do your hair. . . .'

'Oh, Georgie, you are a bore.' She disappeared into the house while I waited, moving impatiently from foot to foot as I stared into the trees and listened for telltale sounds. But nothing stirred apart from wisps of fog that curled up, swirled and then melted. Belinda appeared remarkably quickly for her – now wearing a jacket instead of her dressing gown and with what to her might pass for sturdy shoes.

'Come on, then. Let's get this over with. I'm dying for breakfast,' she said as we set off down the hill and into the trees. 'I'm only coming with you because the sheriff can't think she's too dangerous if he let her go. . . . Oh my God. You don't think she escaped, do you? Is that why we have to catch her?'

'I'm not quite sure what to think yet,' I said. 'I think I can safely say that Stella Brightwell did not kill Mr. Goldman, if that makes you feel any better.'

'Let me see,' Belinda said, picking her way through scrub

and tall bleached grass. 'It might make me feel better about chasing Miss Brightwell, but it does little to reassure me about the various animals that are now lurking all around us.'

'I have a stick with me,' I said. 'I'll protect you.'

'A stick won't do much to protect me from a charging rhinoceros,' Belinda said.

'I don't think he has any rhinoceroses . . . or is it rhinoceri?'

'You don't know. He could have a pack of lions for all we know.'

'A pride of lions, Belinda. Get it right.'

'Oh shut up,' she said, then muttered a naughty word that no lady should know as her jacket caught on a thorny bush. 'I don't know why I agreed to do this. It's insane. And anyway, won't she hear us coming?'

'I want her to,' I said. 'I want her to know we're after her. It may make her panic. Come on.'

'Oh yes. A potential murderer who panics. That's very reassuring,' Belinda said.

We plunged on. The forest became denser. Belinda grabbed me with a gasp as two zebras trotted out of a bush in front of us and ran off.

'You see. I told you they were more frightened of us,' I said.

'How do you know that? I'd say I was quite frightened. Pretty bloody frightened if you want to know. My heart leaped right out of my chest.' Then she added, 'Look, Georgie. There she is.'

And we picked up a flash of a black jacket darting among the trees.

She was moving fast and branches clawed at my face as I hurried after her. Then, without warning, an impossibly tall shape stepped out between two large oak trees. I'd seen giraffes in the zoo, but up close like this and in a natural environment it seemed enormous. Miss Brightwell was nimble, watching where she put her feet, and she didn't seem to notice the giraffe coming straight at her until one of the great feet came down right in front of her. She looked up at it, gave a little gasp of horror, turned and ran straight into us.

'Hold her,' I shouted. I grabbed one arm, and Belinda, to my intense relief, grabbed the other.

'Let go of me,' she shouted, fighting like a mad thing. 'Get yer bleedin' hands off me before that bloody thing tramples us all to death.'

We hung on grimly. 'It was only trying to get away from you,' I said. 'See, it's gone off into the trees.'

'This place is like a madhouse,' she said, struggling less violently now. 'I wish I'd never come here.'

Although her face was familiar, her voice was not the polished, breathy film-star voice of Stella Brightwell.

'Wait a minute,' Belinda said. 'You're not Stella Brightwell.'

'I rather suspect that she's Stella's sister, Bella,' I said. 'Or, as she used to be known, Flossie Oldham. Am I right?'

'How the bloody hell did you know that?' she demanded, still trying to wriggle free from us.

'Her sister?' Belinda looked at the woman whose arm she was still holding. 'Yes, I can see now. There's a strong resemblance, but . . .'

'But not quite as pretty – right?' Bella spat out the words. 'Stella always had the looks and the talent, so they said, but I think I've done well enough in my own little way.'

'What does she mean?' Belinda asked.

'I think she means she's been a very successful jewel thief, slipping into posh house parties where her sister was a guest. Nobody would think it strange if they happened to bump into her, disguised as her sister.'

'Good heavens,' Belinda said. 'So you came here to steal the candlesticks?'

'You're too bleeding clever,' Bella said.

'But something went wrong and Mr. Goldman caught you, so you hit him over the head?' I asked.

'No, of course I didn't. I wouldn't do a thing like that. I've never hurt anybody,' she said, shaking her head so vehemently that I noticed she was wearing a wig. A wig that was identical to Stella's hairstyle. Aha! 'I found him lying there when I came into the library, didn't I? Lying there with his head all bashed in. I realized then that it would look bad for me if I was caught, so all I wanted to do was get away.'

'You could have left the candlesticks where they were. Why did you put one in your sister's bed? I take it that was you?' I asked.

She gave me an evil grin. 'Oh, they found that, did they? It was only to confuse things a bit and give me time to get away safely.'

'But your sister might even be charged with the murder – at the very least with the robbery,' I said. 'Don't you care about that? Why implicate her, of all people?'

'What's she ever done for me?' Bella spat out the words. 'I was only a kid when she said she was going to America and she didn't want me to come with her. I'd only hold her back, she said. So she left me to fend for myself. She became a big star, didn't she? I kept hoping she'd send for me but she never did. And then when I caught the flu in 1919, and nearly died, I wrote to her but she never bothered to write back. I couldn't work for a while, but then I kept myself going, in the chorus in pantomimes and seaside shows, but the funny thing was that everywhere I went people kept telling me I looked like Stella Brightwell. So I thought – why not? Why not use that resemblance to my advantage for once? And it worked. I've done very nicely for myself and I don't plan to stop now.'

'I should have thought a murder charge might put a stop to your little business,' I said.

'You can't pin anything on me. If they ask me I just came to get a glimpse of my long-lost dear sister. I've never even met that poor bloke. I had no reason to kill him.'

'So they won't find your fingerprints on the candlesticks?' I asked.

She snorted. 'Do you think I'm stupid? I always wear gloves.'

'I know,' I said. 'They found a bloody black glove in the grounds. And a bloody print made by that glove on the window frame. Did you really climb out of that window? It's an awfully long way to the ground.'

'I didn't go down. I went up. It was quite easy to lower myself down from Stella's window and then climb back up again. I do it all the time.'

'You really are amazing,' I said in spite of myself. 'Frightfully brave. The way you drove in through the main gate after everyone else, pretending to be Stella.'

'It's always worked before,' she said. 'No reason why it shouldn't.'

'But what if Stella had been driving another of the cars?'

'I watched you lot leave, of course. I saw the young bloke driving and the car's windows were tinted. I thought there was a good chance they wouldn't notice who the passengers were.'

We had been walking slowly up the hill, Belinda and I with a firm grip on her arms. The house came into view ahead of us. Bella started in alarm like a spooked horse and tried to back away.

'If you take me in there they'll think I killed him,' she said.

'I thought you were so confident a few minutes ago,' I said. I looked down at the watch on the wrist I was holding. It was her right wrist. 'Your sister is left-handed, like you,' I said.

'She is. So was our mum. I don't know about our dad. He left us when I was a baby. But what's that got to do with anything?'

'It should prove that you didn't kill Mr. Goldman,' I said. 'As it happens, the most they can cite you for is breaking and entering. You didn't steal anything. You just played a trick on your sister.'

'You think they'll go for that?' There was a slight tremble of hope in her voice and I realized that for all her brashness she was a frightened young woman alone in a strange country.

'I think they will believe it when a man sent over from Scotland Yard testifies that you have never committed any violent act, even when you could have done.'

'Blimey. There's someone come over from Scotland Yard after me, is there?'

'You've left quite a trail of robberies behind you, including the ones on the ship,' I said.

'Only one on the ship,' she corrected. 'The Indian princess.'

'What about the diamond ring?'

'I never took no diamond ring,' she said. 'That must have been someone else. Or what's the betting the passenger lied about the ring being stolen to claim on the insurance. They often do, you know.'

When I thought of the woman in question I realized this might well be true. 'But you did take the princess's ruby?'

She grinned. 'That was a piece of cake. But of course I shall deny this conversation if you mention it to anyone else. They've absolutely nothing on me. They can't even prove I was on the ship. I traveled on a fake passport.'

'So, the princess,' I went on, intrigued now. 'How did you do it? You dressed up like your sister and pretended you'd gone to her cabin by mistake?'

'How the devil did you know that?'

'I put two and two together,' I said, feeling rather pleased with myself.

'That was just to see where she kept things and how attentive the servant was,' she said. 'The good thing is that people like her never notice servants. I borrowed a stewardess's uniform and waited until the servant was dozing and the princess was out. Then I let myself in and helped myself.'

'And how did you hide the ruby when they searched the ship?'

She laughed then. 'Under my wig, of course. I always travel with extra wigs. I've a nice little compartment for stowing things – and one little ruby slips in easily.'

'Oh, I see!' I nodded with understanding. 'And you threw the extra wigs overboard when you thought they might search your cabin,' I said. 'I saw something fall overboard, heard the splash and then saw hair floating on the water. I thought someone was drowning.'

She laughed. 'Not someone. Many people. My other identities. The extra wigs, the duplicates of my sister's dresses. I always travel with those so I can look like her anytime I want. Actually I had my eye on a good diamond brooch and I thought I might help myself to it while everyone was at the costume ball, but I was seen by a real steward trying to get into a cabin. I know he alerted security and I thought I might have been followed. I couldn't take the risk of my cabin being searched so I bundled everything up and threw it overboard.' She looked at me appraisingly. 'You're quite smart, you know. Too bad you're a woman. You could be a detective.'

'The man who is following you from Scotland Yard is just as good,' I said.

'I can't get over that. Scotland Yard bothering to send someone after me.'

'You should realize that you're quite a celebrity,' I said.

She smiled then, making her look much younger. 'Go on.'

'Seriously. You are much admired at Scotland Yard for your daring exploits.'

'But that won't stop them from putting me in Holloway Prison if they get their hands on me, will it?' She stood there, staring up at the house again, and I could feel the tension in her arms as she tried to prevent us from leading her any farther.

'I'm afraid not,' I said.

'They'll have to catch me first, though.' And she gave me a defiant grin.

Chapter 29

Sheriff Billings looked up in surprise when Belinda and I entered the foyer with Bella Brightwell between us. 'What's going on now?' he said. 'Miss Brightwell – who the devil let you out?'

'This isn't Miss Brightwell,' I said. 'The real Stella is still locked up in a bedroom. This is her sister, Bella.'

'Nobody told me about a sister,' he said angrily.

'Nobody knew about her sister,' I said. 'I heard from my mother that Stella had a sister and that they had been in show business together. My mother had worked with them when they were little girls. So when people reported seeing Stella and I knew that couldn't be true I realized that her sister must be on the property too. And that the sister had a distinguished career of her own, as a jewel thief. And she could only be here for one reason – to steal the gold candlesticks Mr. Goldman had brought back with him.'

'So we've got the real killer at last.' He looked pleased with himself. 'Over here, boys!' he yelled.

'Hold on a minute,' Bella said. 'You can't prove any of this. I came here to visit my long-lost sister, Stella, that's all.

You won't find my prints on those candlesticks. You won't find them anywhere.'

'But it was your bloody glove print that we found on the library window frame,' I said. 'And the sheriff also found one bloody glove. I bet if we search hard enough we'll find its mate. Maybe it's even in your pocket at the moment.'

'I thought you were on my side,' she snapped at me.

'I'm on the side of justice,' I said, 'but you don't have to worry. You did nothing wrong this time in the eyes of the law. You drove in through the gate saying you were Miss Brightwell. That's true. You are Miss Brightwell. They let you in. They gave you permission to enter. And you went into the library, probably to take a look at the famous candlesticks, found Mr. Goldman lying there dead, got frightened and decided to put one of the candlesticks in your sister's bed as a cruel joke. Nothing criminal about any of that.'

'So you're saying she's not the killer?' Sheriff Billings asked.

'Look at her wrist, Sheriff.' I lifted the arm I was still holding. 'She wears her wristwatch on her right arm. That proves she's left-handed like her sister, don't you think?'

'Oh,' he said. 'Oh, I see. So she went into the library, intending to steal the candlesticks, but found Goldman on the floor instead.'

'I went into the library,' Bella said defiantly. 'And I didn't steal anything. You can't surmise my intentions. I might like books.'

'Enough of your cheek,' the sheriff said. 'You should realize that you are still in a very precarious position, young lady.' He wagged a threatening finger in her face. 'I could have you locked up for unlawful entry, trespass, any number of things. I know you were intending to carry off those candlesticks and you only chickened out because you stumbled over the body. But you can do yourself some good if you can help us throw any light on the murder. To start with, how did you get into that library? Everyone in the house swears that nobody was seen coming or going from that hallway.'

'Easy. I let myself into the house while you were all out by the pool, hid in an unused room, then went to Stella's room while you were all at dinner. I climbed down the wall to the library window.'

'You climbed down the wall?' He sounded incredulous.

'Oh, it's easy if you've got a rough, uneven rock wall like that,' she said. 'I do it all the time.'

'Well, dang me.' He shook his head. 'Now there must have been only a very brief time frame between the guests' leaving the library and Mr. Goldman being killed. You must have been in the best position to see or hear the killer. So think carefully – did you see or hear anything that could help us?'

Bella frowned. Then she shook her head. 'I don't think I saw or heard anything, or I wouldn't have tried to get into the room. As I said, I went upstairs while you were all at dinner. I waited in Stella's room because it was right above the library. I heard the men saying they were going to have cigars and brandy in the library, so I waited until the lights finally went out, then I climbed down the wall and let myself in through the window. The curtains were closed across the alcove. I stepped out and the first thing I did was to kick something. I picked it up and it was one of the candlesticks. I knew something was wrong then. I turned on my torch and I saw I'd got blood on my glove. That really spooked me. And then I saw him, of course – lying just on the other side of the curtain with his head smashed in.'

'You're sure you were alone in the room then?'

Bella shrugged. 'I've no idea. It was dark apart from my little torch. Anyone could have been hidden in one of the other alcoves or even in the shadows at the far end of the room.' She shuddered and hugged her arms to herself. 'Well, I just wanted to get out of there then. I knew I could take the candlesticks, but I also knew how bad it would look for me if I was caught with them. So I put back the bloody candlestick exactly where I had found it and then I decided I'd leave the other one in Stella's room, just to throw people off the scent. Give myself time to get away.'

'And where did you go after that?' the sheriff asked. 'Did you climb out of the window again?'

'I heard an almighty crash,' she said, 'then lots of running and shouting, so I decided I'd better make myself scarce. After I put the candlestick in her bed, I went across to the other side of the house where I could climb down onto the roof of the garage, then I stayed close enough to listen to what was going on. I realized there was no way I could escape from the estate that night, so I disappeared into the woods until I found an unoccupied cottage and I spent the night there.'

'Thank you, Miss Brightwell,' the sheriff said. 'I'm not sure what we're going to do with you at this point, but I suggest that we all get some breakfast and we'll see how things turn out. And please don't think of trying to escape. There's no way out of here except through that gate and my men are guarding it.'

'Thank heavens for that. I'm starving,' Belinda said.

'You can let go of her now.' The sheriff looked from Belinda to me. 'Nice work, ladies,' he said. 'Very astute of you, and gutsy too. You English ladies are not the prissy little wallflowers you are claimed to be.' He took Bella's arm. 'Come along, little lady. I want to keep you in my sight.'

'Prissy little wallflowers indeed,' Belinda muttered into my ear as we crossed the foyer. 'Odious man. I'm of a good mind to help Bella escape.'

'I don't think you'd better do that. Darcy wouldn't be pleased.'

We heard the sheriff's big boots echoing behind us until we reached the corridor leading to the library, where the sheriff paused. 'Before we go and eat I'd like you to take just one more look, Miss Brightwell,' he said. 'Just to see if anything else triggers your mind. You never know . . . any little thing.'

He ushered her down the narrow hallway ahead of him. I followed because I was curious. I too wanted to get another look at the library in daylight.

'I don't know about you but I'm off to breakfast,' Belinda called to me. 'I have no wish to see crime scenes or dead bodies. It would quite put one off one's scrambled eggs.'

The sheriff turned the key to unlock the library door. The heavy drapes were still closed and amid the smell of dust, old leather, and furniture polish there lingered the unmistakable smell of death. When you've smelled it once, you never forget it. The sheriff didn't open the drapes but instead turned on the electric light to reveal the body still lying where it had fallen, although now it was covered by a sheet. Bella gave a little gasp on seeing it. 'He's still there.'

'Yes, well we couldn't get our hands on the morgue wagon until this morning. It will be on its way now. And the doc wants to perform an autopsy, although the cause of death looks clear enough to me. So take your time. Look around the room. Is there anything you remember now that wasn't quite right? Anything to tip you off that someone else was still in the room – because I don't know how the hell he or she got out.'

'I don't think anyone could have climbed down the wall from here,' Bella said. 'That wall below is concrete and quite smooth. And it's a long drop. And they couldn't have climbed up, because I would have seen them.'

I was still staring with the same horrified fascination I had felt the night before. I remembered the scene with all of us clustered in the doorway, Mr. Goldman lying on the floor, all that blood . . . And the sheriff hadn't even finished interviewing the rest of us in the library, so presumably he had no way of knowing whether any of us might have cracked under the strain of seeing the body of the man they had just killed. But he had interviewed Mrs. Goldman here, even though she had strongly protested that it was inhumane to make her answer questions where her husband's body was lying.

And then I looked up, frowning as I tried to capture a thought that had crept into my consciousness. Something that had not seemed quite right at the time. Mrs. Goldman protesting that it was cruel to interview people where her husband was lying dead, and Juan saying, 'They can pull the curtains over the body if you do not wish to look at him.'

But how did he know that the body was lying half under the drapes in the window alcove? It was a big room. Mr. Goldman could have been lying anywhere. And Juan had been asleep when the rest of us had piled into the library and seen the body.

'Juan!' I burst out. 'It had to be Juan.'

'The Spanish guy who claimed he slept through the whole thing?' The sheriff looked surprised. 'What makes you think that?'

'Because he knew where the body was lying, but he couldn't have seen it if he'd been asleep in his own bed.'

'But why would he want to kill Goldman? Hadn't Goldman just brought him over from Spain to turn him into a movie star?'

'Yes. And then he appeared to change his mind,' I said. 'He told Juan he wasn't ready for the movies. He didn't like Juan's accent. In fact, he made fun of it.'

'But you don't go around killing people because of their accent.' The sheriff shook his head.

'I hardly know any of them,' I said. 'There may be another reason. Juan and Stella seemed to have an attraction to each other.'

'You reckon he maybe wanted to steal the candlesticks? Why else would he have come in here?'

'I don't know. Why don't you bring him in here and ask him? And when he comes in, see if his eyes go straight to the body. That would prove he knew where it was.'

'Okay, miss,' the sheriff said. 'Since you've delivered the goods so far I have to think that you know what you're doing. I'll send a couple of guys to fetch him.'

'And could I suggest one more thing?' I said. 'Tell him that you have proof that he killed Mr. Goldman.'

'But I don't. Only your word.'

'Please tell him you do. Tell him that Bella Brightwell came to steal the candlesticks and saw him. He won't know about her. That will throw him off guard.'

'I suppose I could do that. . . .' He looked doubtful. 'It's not what you'd call regular, but then this guy is a foreigner. He won't know.' He grinned then. 'Okay, let's get him.'

I have to admit that I began to have second thoughts while I waited for Juan to be brought to the library. It seemed he hadn't put in an appearance that morning yet and the sheriff's deputies had to go to the Hacienda to wake him. Bella and I stood outside the library beside the sheriff, shivering in the cold drafts coming through the open front door. She didn't look at me. I didn't look at her. Now that the first flush of excitement was over I was feeling slightly guilty that I had told the sheriff the truth about her. I wondered if she would be arrested here and then deported back to England. Then I reminded myself that she was a jewel thief. It was only right that she faced justice.

Now that I had time to think, I also began to worry that I might have made a mistake about Juan. Could he somehow have heard where the body was lying? Might Ronnie and Algie have described the scene to him when they hauled him out of bed? I didn't think they had told him much and he appeared to be half asleep when he was dragged into the house. But was it indeed possible that he had gone to bed and then managed to sneak back into the house without being seen when we were in full view of the front door all the time? Was I going to find myself in trouble for suggesting that he was Mr. Goldman's killer? The wait seemed an eternity. When my stomach gave a large growl I realized also that I was hungry. Belinda, as usual, was the smart one. She had gone to breakfast. I had somehow managed to involve myself in a crime yet again. When would I ever learn?

We all looked up at the sound of raised voices, the crunch of feet on the gravel outside. The two deputies appeared with an angry Juan between them.

'What is the meaning of this?' he demanded, stalking straight up to the sheriff. 'I am dragged from my bed once again? Why am I never allowed to sleep in peace, eh? I am told the sheriff wishes to speak with me. Okay, I say. First I must wash and shave and get dressed, but no. The say I must come now. You treat me without respect because I am a foreigner. I shall complain to your superiors.' He fished in his pocket, took out a cigarette and lit it, inhaling then blowing out smoke in what could only be described as an insolent manner.

'No, son, you've got it wrong.' The sheriff looked relaxed, as if he was about to enjoy what was coming. 'I treat you this way because I know you killed Mr. Goldman.'

'You know? How do you know?' Juan demanded. 'You try to pin this on me because I am foreign. I know how the police work in America. They like to find the – how you say – scapegoat. They don't care about the truth. But I say this – if I killed Mr. Goldman, where is your proof?'

'Well, as a matter of fact I have my proof right here,' Sheriff Billings said in his slow drawl. 'You see, someone saw you kill Goldman.'

'Who? Who saw me? What nonsense is this?'

'This young lady saw you,' the sheriff answered. He stepped aside to reveal Bella.

Juan appeared to notice Bella for the first time. 'Wait,' he said, frowning. 'You are not Stella. Who are you?'

'She's Stella's sister,' I said. 'She came here to steal the candlesticks. . . .'

'A common thief?'

'Better than a common murderer,' Bella said defiantly. 'And that's right. I was going to steal the candlesticks, but I saw you kill Mr. Goldman. I climbed down the wall and in through the window.'

'Down the wall? That is not possible. What are you, a fly?' He was still insolent, defiant.

'Do you want me to demonstrate?' Bella started for the window.

The color had drained from Juan's face, then his eyes flashed with anger. 'He deserved to die,' he said. 'He insulted me and my culture and my religion and my family. When I met him in Spain he was so polite, so excited. He would make me a big star, he said. And I thought this would solve our problems. My family is no longer rich. We can no longer afford to run our hacienda. I believed I would go home with money and fame. But when I came here, I found out he was a liar and a thief.'

'A thief? What did he steal?'

'He stole my heritage,' Juan said. 'Those candlesticks, they came from the convent where my great-aunt is mother superior. My family has always sent our women to that convent, for centuries now. They are simple women. Holy women. I am sure they did not realize the value of what they had. And the convent was badly in need of repair. Mr. Goldman offered them money and they sold their candlesticks. They sold an El Greco painting for pennies. To them it was a Madonna and Child, not an El Greco. And that devil boasted he had bought an entire chapel in Spain. He was going to have it shipped here, stone by stone, and rebuilt as his bathhouse. A holy chapel turned into a changing room? That's when I decided I would take back the things he stole from my great-aunt's convent. I would do justice on their behalf.'

'So you only pretended to go to bed after dinner?' the sheriff asked.

'Of course. I went to the front door, slammed it, then I went into the library ahead of them and waited behind the curtains in an alcove. When the last men left and Mr. Goldman was alone I decided it was the right time to confront him. I came out from behind the curtains. He was surprised to see me, but friendly. Not worried. "Hey there, Juan. Couldn't sleep after all? Have a brandy," he said. "Have a cigar. I won't be a minute while I put these candlesticks back in their box and into the safe."

'"You will not do that," I said to him. "I have come on behalf of the sisters of Santa Theresa to take back their property."

'He laughed. "My property now, son," he said. "Too late to change their minds. Besides, these'll look better on my dining table than in their gloomy old chapel."'

Juan paused, as if in physical pain. 'He turned away from me. I picked up the candlestick and I hit him, once across the head. He fell. I dropped the candlestick, appalled at what I had done. Then I crept out down the hallway and hid behind a statue in one of the niches. Then there was a great crash and everyone ran to see what had happened. I took my chance and slipped out and went to bed. And if you ask me if I am sorry – no. I told you. He was a man who deserved to die. I am proud to avenge the honor of my people and my country.'

'You won't be so cocky when you're facing the gas chamber,' the sheriff said.

'I spit on your gas chamber,' Juan said. 'And I spit on you.'

He spat on the marble floor. Then he turned and ran out of the open front door.

Chapter 30

For a moment I think we were all rather stunned. I know I was. The sheriff recovered first. 'Stupid fool,' he said. 'Where does he think he can go? He can't get out and he can't hide for long. We'll have dogs here soon and we'll track him down.'

We followed him to the front door. There was no sign of Juan, who must have already disappeared into the trees. The sheriff rushed over to the telephone, bawling out instructions. He looked satisfied when he returned to us. 'The truck with the dog handlers is already on its way,' he said, 'and I've alerted the guys at the gatehouse to have their weapons ready. Shoot to kill if necessary. Well, I guess that's all we can do for now. I don't know about you, but I need my breakfast.'

We followed him through to the dining room where Belinda, Ronnie and one of the deputies were tucking into a hearty meal.

'These pancakes are jolly good.' Belinda looked up as we came in.

I poured myself a cup of coffee, but I felt too sick to eat.

I'd heard the words 'shoot to kill.' Whatever Juan had done, he had felt he was justified. I suppose I might have felt that way if vandals had taken big chunks of Castle Rannoch. My problem is that I'm too soft-hearted. I can often see the criminal's point of view. I looked across at Bella, who had also helped herself to a plate of eggs, pancakes and bacon. She had no such sensibilities. I wondered what would happen to her now – would Darcy have the authority to take her home in handcuffs to face trial? I wondered how soon he would return and wished he hadn't gone on a wasted journey.

I was just managing to nibble a piece of toast when the telephone rang. One of the deputies went to answer it.

'That will be our boys arriving at the gate,' the sheriff said, a large hunk of ham poised on his fork.

But then the deputy came hurrying back. 'You're wanted on the telephone, sir,' he said.

We heard his big boots echoing on the marble floor. Then we clearly heard, 'Damn it. The goddamned fool. What does he think he can achieve with that? I'll get men onto it right away.'

And at the same moment the front door burst open and Craig Hart came in, still wearing a striped silk bathrobe. 'I smelled smoke,' he said.

'That damned Spaniard seems to have started a fire just inside the gate area,' the sheriff said. 'I don't know what he thinks he can do. Does he expect everyone to rush out of the gatehouse so that he can slip out?'

'I'd better go and call the fire department, and get the groundsmen onto it as soon as possible.' Ronnie stood up. 'Fire can spread real quickly at this time of year.'

He had scarcely left when Maria rushed in. '*Fuego*, señors,' she called. 'Fire.'

'Yes, we know, Maria. The guys at the gate told us and we've already sent someone to put the men onto it.'

'No, señor. Not at the gate. Up behind the house. Big flames.'

We ran to the front door. The air was already heavy with smoke. The wind had picked up, blowing away the fog and fanning the flames. We could see the orange glow below us and hear the crackle and roar as the fire spread.

'It can't have spread as fast as that,' Craig said. 'Look. It's already way over to the right.'

'And up above,' I shouted as I turned to see a tree go up in flames behind the house.

'He's ringed us with fire, the bastard,' the sheriff said in a horrified voice. 'How the hell are we going to get out?' He ran back to the telephone, jiggled it, then slammed it down. 'The line has gone dead,' he said. 'Let's hope those fire trucks get here in time to clear a way to the gate.'

Even as we looked, new bursts of flame appeared in the woodland. The ring of fire was now in place and it was coming toward us from all sides, feeding on dry grass and scrub.

'Go wake everybody up,' the sheriff said. 'Everyone should be ready to leave if we get a chance.'

'I'll go wake Algie,' Ronnie said.

'I'll go and get my mother.' I headed in the direction of Mr. Chaplin's suite behind the pool.

'And Maria, go and get Mrs. Goldman and her friend,' the sheriff barked.

'Francisco!' Maria wailed. 'Where is my Francisco? Francisco!' And she rushed off to the back of the house, shouting for him.

'The rest of you stay where I can see you,' the sheriff barked.

I didn't get as far as the pool. Mummy and Charlie Chaplin came running toward us, my mother's hair still in curlers – which shows you how frightened she was. Mummy never allowed a soul to see her without make-up and perfect hair.

'What is it?' she called. 'What's going on?'

'Juan's set some fires,' I shouted back.

'Juan? Whatever for?'

'A final act of malice, I'd say,' the sheriff responded. 'Doesn't want to face the gas chamber.'

'Juan killed Cy Goldman? I don't believe it.' Mummy reached us, breathing heavily after having run.

'He confessed. Kinda proud of it, I'd say. Avenging his heritage, he said.'

'Cy should never have made fun of his accent,' Mummy said. 'Has someone called the fire brigade? Shouldn't someone be getting out hoses and things?'

'The men should be onto it by now and the fire trucks have been called. But the nearest fire department is a long way from here. Malibu, perhaps, or even Oxnard. And I can't call again. The phone line is down.'

'Then what are we going to do?' Mummy demanded.

'Nothing much we can do,' the sheriff said. 'As you can see, that whole area in front of the gate is in flames. We'd never manage to drive through that.'

'Then how do we get out?'

'We should be okay here,' the sheriff said. 'There's a good gap between the house and the nearest foliage.'

As he spoke, flying embers fell crackling around us and we hurriedly stepped back inside.

'That's not good. Part of the house has a shake roof,' Ronnie said as he joined us with a terrified-looking Algie in tow.

'Oh my God. We're going to be burned alive,' Algie wailed. 'Somebody do something.'

'Do shut up,' Belinda said angrily. 'I'm going to rescue my things from the cottage. I've a couple of Chanel outfits I'd hate to lose.'

'Belinda, no.' I tried to grab her.

'Don't be silly. I'll be quite safe. The fire can't move as fast as that. I'll be in and out in a jiffy.' And she ran down the hill. I was half tempted to follow her, wondering if I had anything worth saving. Then I remembered one thing. 'Queenie. Queenie must be there, Belinda. And Mummy's maid. Get them out.'

We stood in the forecourt, waiting. Holding our breath while the swirling smoke stung our eyes and made us cough. We could see the flames rushing toward us from all sides. It really was quite terrifying. Suddenly a zebra burst from the trees, followed by another. A giraffe lumbered out at surprising speed. They stopped on the gravel, trembling, unsure where to go.

'I wish Belinda would hurry up,' I said. The flames were awfully close now. Suddenly there was a great whoosh and crackle and the Brothers Grimm cottage where Bella had spent the night went up in flames.

'Belinda!' I screamed.

And at that moment Queenie emerged from the trees, running up the hill with surprising agility for one so large, followed by Claudette and Belinda, each with items hanging from a half-shut suitcase.

'Oh, she's brought my things. How thoughtful of her,' Mummy said. 'She really is a gem.'

I noted that Queenie hadn't had the same sentiments about my stuff. She was running toward us like a charging hippo, her face red with determination.

'I had no idea fire could move that quickly,' Belinda gasped, brushing a strand of hair from a sooty face as she reached us. 'One minute we were fine and the next that horrid little German house went up, poof. Darling, I had to leave my favorite face cream behind, and do you know how much it cost in Paris?'

'Better than being cooked to a crisp or having your face so badly burned that you'd never need it again,' I said.

'You do have a point there, I suppose.' She wiped a smear of soot from her face again, but she was still looking longingly in the direction of the cottage.

'Cor swipe me, miss,' Queenie said. 'I thought I was a goner that time.'

'Why didn't you come up before?' I asked, feeling moved that duty had kept her to her post until instructed otherwise.

'Well, Claudette was in such a state about packing your mum's things that she wouldn't get out. So I thought I'd better help her or she'd find herself trapped. I almost had to drag her out of there in the end, and then she tripped over a fallen branch and I had to go back for her again. Bloody Froggies.' She made a face. 'It never struck me about packing up your things until it was too late. Sorry, but then your mum's clothes are better than yours, aren't they? And I thought she'd make a right old fuss if I didn't save them for her.'

The gardeners had now hooked up hoses and were making feeble attempts to prevent the wall of flame from reaching the house. But there were only two hoses and they were not long enough to cross the broad forecourt to the nearest of the trees. Antelopes burst from the forest and dashed past, only to be repelled by the flames behind the house. Smaller animals – a fox, squirrels, jackrabbits – joined them. Mummy's description of the place being a bloody zoo was now suddenly apt.

We could feel the heat now and the crackle of flames had become a roar. Smoke stung at my eyes so that I could hardly see.

'Maybe we should go back into the house,' Craig suggested.

'The fire trucks must get here soon.' Ronnie was staring down into the flames, almost willing himself to see fire trucks breaking through. 'I don't know if we're any safer inside.'

'Isn't the house made of stone?' Craig asked. 'That can't burn, surely?'

'The stonework is only a façade.' Ronnie's face was grim. 'The whole framework underneath is timber.'

'What are we going to do?' Algie demanded. 'Somebody go for help. We'll be burned alive.'

'We may be okay when it reaches the gravel and burns itself out,' the sheriff said, not sounding too confident about this. 'Isn't there a better outlet for those damned hoses?'

Suddenly there was a crackle above us and smoke rose from the roof.

'The roof has caught,' Ronnie shouted. 'Come on, let's try and put it out before it takes hold.'

Craig, the sheriff, and his remaining deputy followed Ronnie into the house. I hesitated, then decided I might be able to help too. 'Buckets. We need buckets,' I heard him shouting. 'Maria? Francisco?'

His voice echoed in the high-ceilinged foyer. At that moment Maria came flying down the stairs, followed by

Mrs. Goldman and Miss Kindell, clutching at each other and still in their robes.

'The whole place is on fire,' Barbara Kindell shouted. 'You can't go up there.'

'Someone should save the candlesticks.' Mrs. Goldman waved her arms frantically.

'Relax, honey. They're insured, aren't they?' Barbara tried to calm her.

'I don't know. Did he say he'd insured them or he was going to?'

I noticed that her concern wasn't for her husband's body.

Ronnie had grabbed some pots and pans and now ran up the stairs. I followed, reluctantly. We crossed the landing and were at the foot of the second staircase when Ronnie turned back, his face ashen. 'It's no use. The fire has come through the ceiling up there.' And even as he was speaking we heard the creak and crash of collapsing timber and exploding glass.

'Everyone into the pool,' Charlie Chaplin shouted as we appeared from the front door again. 'It's our only hope right now.'

We didn't wait to be urged a second time. Algie, Belinda and my mother made it first with surprising speed. I believe Algie knocked my mother out of the way to get down the steps first. The rest of us followed. Queenie hesitated as we jumped in. 'I can't swim, miss,' she called.

'Then get in the shallow end and duck under the water if the fire comes over us.'

The surface of that lovely blue water was already marred with ash and I wondered what we would do if the fire really did come over us. How long could we hold our breath under the water? Smoke was now billowing from the open front door and the roar and crackle echoed out. Suddenly from above us there was a horrible scream. I looked up to see Stella at an open window, high above us. We had forgotten all about her.

'My door is locked,' she screamed. 'I can't get out. Someone help me.'

Bella was out of the pool like a shot. 'Hang on, Gertie, I'm coming,' she shouted. She ran around the side of the house until she found a part of the wall that was made of rough stone. She went up this like a spider, then inched her way across on a ledge until she reached her sister's window.

'Come on, Gertie. You've got to trust me. Come on. Follow me.'

'I can't,' Stella wailed. 'I'll fall.'

'No you won't. Remember how we used to do that balance beam routine? You were good. Come on, ducks, or we'll both burn.'

Stella inched herself out of the window. The fire was right above them now. Painfully slowly they made their way along the ledge, past a window, then another. At last they reached the section of wall where Bella had climbed up. Bella went first, talking her sister down, showing her where to put her hands and feet. Charlie, Craig and Ronnie rushed over to them, standing ready to break a fall, then helping them down the last few feet to the ground. Bella took her sister's hand and dragged her into the pool just as flames erupted from Stella's window.

The heat became unbearable as fire engulfed the house. Burning embers and flying bits of timber rained onto us. On the far side of the house the garage caught on fire and we heard terrifying explosions as the petrol tanks blew up. A palm tree behind the pool ignited and went up in flames.

Animals stampeded around in blind panic, not knowing where to go. A couple of antelopes leaped into the pool with us, and in the forest others burned and screamed as they died. It was truly horrible, and it seemed to go on forever.

It wasn't until the fire in the parkland below finally burned itself out that we heard the sound of approaching fire engines.

'Better late than never, I suppose,' Mummy said and began to remove her hair curlers.

We hauled ourselves out of the pool as the first of the fire engines came through the blackened forest toward us.

'Let's get you out of here,' the fire captain said. 'Can't do anything to save the house, I'm afraid. It's gone.' He started to assist us up onto the truck. This wasn't a simple process as embers were still flying out from the burning house.

'My suitcase,' Belinda exclaimed and ran to retrieve it.

'No space for that, ma'am,' the fireman said. 'We'll bring it down later if we can. At the moment my priority is to get you away from here.'

'But I can't leave my things behind,' Mummy said. 'Look how tiny I am, Captain. I really don't take up much space and I could sit on my suitcase. . . .'

'Fine with me if you don't want to come,' the fireman said. Mummy hastily grabbed an armful of clothing from her case before nimbly hopping aboard. The firemen piled us onto the truck and drove us down to the gate. The area around the gate itself had escaped from the fire as it rushed up the hill. It was a shock to suddenly come upon green trees by the fence and a giraffe and several zebras cowering there. I was glad they hadn't all met a horrible end and found myself wondering about Juan. Had he also found a place of safety by the fence? I have to say that I no longer felt as charitable about him as I had done. Anyone who can condemn innocent people to being burned alive is truly despicable. I hoped the sheriff's men caught him and that he did have to face execution.

The sheriff's truck with the dog handlers had arrived and was waiting on the road.

'Keep an eye on the fence, boys. I don't want that bastard trying to slip past us,' the sheriff said.

We climbed down, shivering now in our wet clothing.

'How on earth are we going to get out of here?' Belinda asked. 'All the motorcars have been destroyed.'

'We'll take you back to our headquarters in the truck,' the sheriff said. 'It will be a bit of a tight squeeze but we'll manage. We'll need statements from all of you.'

I turned to see Stella looking at her sister with wonder. 'It really is you,' she said. 'I began to think it must be my guardian angel come to save me.'

'It's really me, all right,' Bella said. 'Maybe I am your guardian angel.'

'It's a miracle, Flossie. What were you doing here?' Stella asked.

'Come to visit my big sister. What else?' Bella grinned at her. 'It's been a long time, Gertie.'

'Too long. I've missed you.'

'Really? I thought you were too busy being famous.'

Stella smiled. 'We used to have good times together, didn't we? We only had each other.'

'You left me behind. You said I held you back.'

'I know. It was stupid of me. And hurtful. And now you saved my life. I'll try and make it up to you if I can.'

The sheriff helped her climb aboard. Bella watched her sister with a kind of fierce longing. Then it was my turn to join the others. The doors were shut and off we went. It wasn't until we finally reached our destination that we realized that Bella was not with us. She had somehow managed to melt away as we were busy boarding. I can't say I blamed her, and secretly I wished her well.

Chapter 31

The next few hours were a blur of being cold, hungry and in shock. We had to make statements. We were given blankets and mugs of coffee but all I wanted to do was to climb into a safe warm bed. I wished Darcy was with me, and wondered what he must be going through if he had arrived back at the estate to find it burned to the ground. At least the men at the gate could reassure him that we were safe, but he'd be worried nonetheless.

By mid-afternoon, taxicabs were ordered to drive us back to Beverly Hills. I had forgotten that so many of us were celebrities and was shocked, as we emerged from the sheriff's headquarters, to face a hail of flashbulbs going off in my face. Mummy, completely recovered and having changed into one of her retrieved outfits, posed as if nothing had happened and answered questions prettily. She joined us in a cab with the two maids.

'I do hope the firemen will remember to bring me my suitcase,' she said. 'It was so good of you to save that much, Claudette. I shall send you home on holiday as a treat.'

'You are too good, madame,' Claudette said.

'How fortunate it was only a weekend's jaunt and the rest of my things are safe and sound at the hotel.' Mummy examined her hair in the taxicab window.

'All right for you,' I said. 'The good clothes you bought me in London have gone up in smoke.'

'We'll just have to get you some more, darling. I expect they have passable clothing in Beverly Hills.'

'I've lost the rest of my things too, miss,' Queenie said. 'My spare knickers and all. I got new ones, special, 'cos we was traveling and I thought the ship might go down.'

The thought of Queenie's spare knickers suddenly made me laugh. We were safe. We had survived and all would be well. There were more reporters waiting as we drove into the Beverly Hills Hotel. I noticed Tubby Halliday among them. He had the nerve to wave. Then one man pushed his way through the mob and ran toward me. It was Darcy.

'Thank God.' He wrapped me in his arms, not seeming to notice that flashbulbs were going off around us. 'I've been out of my mind with worry. The telephone lines were down and when I got there . . .' He took my face in his hands and kissed me hungrily. And if the reporters were watching, I didn't care.

'Well, I suppose that is the end of my motion picture career,' Mummy said as we ordered drinks and sandwiches beside the pool. 'I can't see anyone else wanting to take over that particular picture. It really was awful, wasn't it? Absolute bosh. And I can't say I'm sorry. Max would have been furious, I expect, and I really enjoy a life of privacy and leisure these days.' She picked up a chicken sandwich and took a delicate bite. 'I suppose I was flattered that the world still saw me as a star. But now I look back on it I suspect that Stella only wanted me to take the part of Mary because she thought I would make her look younger and more beautiful.'

'She didn't succeed,' I said. 'You looked much better. And acted much better too.'

Mummy looked genuinely pleased. 'Well, aren't you the sweetest thing. What a nice daughter I have.'

I turned to Darcy. 'And I'm afraid that's the end of your movie career too,' I said. 'Unless you want to try your luck auditioning at some of the other studios.'

Darcy looked at me fondly. 'Can you really see me as a film star? I only agreed to take on the role because I thought it would give me a chance to observe Stella Brightwell. And then, of course, I realized that I might make enough money to enable us to marry. So now we're back to square one, old thing.'

'Not quite,' I said and filled him in on all that had been happening while he'd been gone.

'Her sister.' His face lit up. 'How very clever of you to work that out.'

'It made sense,' I said. 'Mummy had told me about their sister act when they were children and then people saw Stella Brightwell in places that she couldn't be. Just think how clever it was, Darcy. Bella slipped in to all the house parties where Stella was a guest, and if anyone saw her, they assumed she was her sister. But on every occasion Stella had a perfect alibi for all the actual robberies.'

'You don't think they were in it together?' Darcy asked.

'I'm sure they weren't. Stella was amazed to see her sister after all this time. They hadn't communicated for years. It was a touching reunion, actually. Especially because Bella saved her sister's life.'

'And where is this sister now? Do the police have her in custody?'

'I'm afraid not. I don't know where she is,' I said. 'There was a lot of confusion when we were being loaded into a truck and I think she took her chances to slip away then.'

'Pity,' Darcy said. 'So it looks as if I might go home empty-handed. They won't like that.'

'But you know who did it. The port authorities can be on the lookout for her if she returns to England – although I must warn you that she uses disguises and travels under a false passport.'

Darcy sighed. 'That's cheerful, isn't it? Fat chance of catching her, then.'

'I wonder if she might not give up her career in crime now that she has reunited with her sister,' I said. 'Stella certainly makes enough money to look after them both.' Although as I said it I wondered if Stella's career might now be at an end with Mr. Goldman's death.

I looked at Darcy and tried to sound casual. 'So you'll be going home now, I suppose.'

'I'll have to cable Scotland Yard and see what they want me to do and whether they want the American police to get involved. Since she hasn't stolen anything in America, that's not likely.'

'And what about us?' I asked Mummy. 'We can't stay here now, can we? Now that there is no film to shoot. I suppose we'll have to go back to that awful little house in Reno.'

'Not immediately, darling,' Mummy said. 'We need time to recover from our ordeal, don't we? Treating us to this hotel is the least Golden Pictures can do for us after we were nearly burned to a crisp. And I'll need to do some shopping for the items I lost. All my cosmetics, darling. I don't know how I'm going to replace them here. I suppose somebody in America knows how to make face cream.'

'There's always Helena Rubinstein or Max Factor,' Darcy said.

Mummy looked dubious. 'But they only make it for the masses and the movies, don't they. Not delicate skins like mine. I need things like monkey glands that aren't in normal cosmetics.'

I glanced across at Darcy and grinned. 'You could always ask Stella Brightwell. She looks quite good for a woman of her age.'

Mummy shook her head. 'Darling, she has wrinkles. It's the California sun. You notice that's why I never go out without a hat. Besides, she'll be in mourning for poor Cy. The whole world will be mourning him, won't they? He brought happiness into the lives of so many little people.'

I stifled a smile. Only my mother could get away with saying something like that.

She looked up suddenly. 'I've a brilliant idea! Why don't you two lovebirds rent a motorcar and take a little drive up the coast?'

'That sounds wonderful.' I turned to look at Darcy.

He nodded. 'I'm sure they won't expect me to take the very next train back to New York. I'll ask the reception desk to procure a car for us.'

'That's settled, then.' Mummy looked smug. 'You should find a delightful little wayside inn and have a night of unbridled passion.'

'Mummy!' I couldn't even look at Darcy and my cheeks were burning.

'Well, why not?' she said. 'I would. And poor Darcy's positively panting for it.'

'I'm not like you,' I said.

'And I don't think that I could justify a night of passion at an inn on expenses,' Darcy quipped, to spare me my embarrassment, I suspect. 'We'll settle for a day out alone, with no interruptions. Right, Georgie?'

I beamed at him. 'Perfect,' I whispered.

Mummy stood up and smoothed down her linen slacks. 'And if you do decide to spend the night along the way, don't worry about your poor, aged mother, left all alone here. I'm sure I'll survive.'

'No doubt Mr. Chaplin is in the neighborhood and he'd be delighted to keep you company,' I teased. 'By the way, what was he like?'

'Rather fun, actually. Only please, this must remain *entre nous*. Max wouldn't like it.'

Darcy and I exchanged a grin. He got to his feet too. 'I'd better send that cable to England right away. As soon as I know my instructions I'll be able to rent that car for us.'

'Heavenly.' I beamed at him. 'And speaking of cables – did you ever learn the truth about Algie Broxley-Foggett?'

'I did. He's exactly what he claimed to be – a silly young twit. The family is quite wealthy and he'll inherit a title one day. Hasn't exactly been a good boy all his life. Sent down from Oxford for cheating. No criminal record since. Father's a military man who despairs of him.'

'So he really was sent to America to make a man of him,' I said. 'I don't think it will work, do you? I think he's a dedicated sponger and con artist.'

'Good God. Speak of the devil,' Darcy said. We looked up to see Algie coming toward us, followed by Belinda. Their clothing was now dry, but they definitely looked like survivors of a shipwreck – as I had done when I first glimpsed myself in the mirror back at the hotel. Algie's white flannels were smudged with soot and horribly crumpled. His white V-necked pullover appeared to have shrunk. Belinda's normally perfect hair hung limp and straight and she was wearing no lipstick or rouge. For once she didn't look better than me!

'Oh, there you are. Jolly good show,' Algie said. 'We hoped we'd find you here. We're orphans in the storm, you see. No clothes, no money and nowhere to go. Don't quite know where to turn, either. Simply can't wire the pater for a handout.'

'I'm so glad to see you, darling.' Belinda went over to hug me. 'I thought we'd never leave that horrible little office in the middle of nowhere. And then when a car was finally procured and the driver said, "Where to?" we realized we had nowhere to go.'

'So we thought we might bunk in with you, if that's all right,' Algie said. 'Until we decide what we're going to do next. I'm bally well going to tell Golden Pictures that they owe me a job. I don't care if there is no Mr. Goldman, his studio will go on, won't it?'

'I don't know,' I said. 'I rather feel that he was Golden Pictures. We'll have to wait and see. Do you really think you're cut out for the motion picture industry, Algie?'

He looked rather hurt. 'Who, me? Jack-of-all-trades, you know. I sort of see myself as the next Douglas Fairbanks, but I'm willing to lend a hand at painting scenery or whatever.'

'And be on set at six in the morning?' I asked.

'If I bally well have to. I wonder who is in charge now? I wonder if we'll be paid a nice sum to compensate us for what we went through. After all, we were nearly killed, weren't we?'

'In the meantime you could always do what your father wanted and find your job on the cattle station,' Mummy said coldly. 'I still blame you for speaking the words we never speak from the play we never mention—'

'What, *Macbeth*, you mean?' Algie asked.

There was a horrified intake of breath from my mother. 'Someone get that boy out of my sight before I kill him personally.'

'Your friend Tubby Halliday still seems to be hanging around,' I said. 'He was among the journalists when we arrived. Why don't you see if you can bunk in with him? I don't think you're too popular around here.'

'Good old Tubby,' Algie said. 'Well, that should count as a scoop, shouldn't it? Claire Daniels rescued from death and all that. I must go and see him. He can interview me and I can give him all the dramatic details: How I survived a fire at a movie mogul's castle. Yes, that should finally make Tubby's name as a journalist, and maybe I'll get a fee for being interviewed.' He paused, and I could see the wheels of his brain turning over. I rather suspected that in his version of the story he might be the hero who saved us all from fiery death.

'I'd better go and hunt out old Tubby, then,' Algie said. 'As soon as I can round up some respectable clothing. At least the studio should have to spring for new togs, shouldn't they? I mean these were decent flannels, completely ruined. And my evening clothes, the lot, all gone. Actually that chap Craig Hart was being awfully decent. He said if I liked to come and see him, he'd take care of me.'

'You should definitely do that, then.' Belinda and I

exchanged a smile. 'Do you think you have a little corner for me, darling?' she said. 'Just until I fall on my feet again. I've decided to stay on in Hollywood for a while. I'm going to use the publicity from the fire to get myself hired as a costume designer. I had these brilliant designs with me that Mr. Goldman had requested, but unfortunately they all went up in flames.'

'What brilliant designs?' I asked, then I shook my head. 'Belinda, you are as bad as Algie.'

'We're survivors in a cruel world, darling. It's a pity I don't fancy him.'

'Oh, I say. I'm not that bad,' Algie said. 'You're not exactly my kind of girl, either. Now, Georgie, for example, she's a cracking girl. I wouldn't mind hitching up with her.'

'Sorry,' Darcy said. 'Already taken.'

'Really?' Belinda raised an eyebrow. 'At last.'

Chapter 32

> *There is a strange feeling of unreality after a traumatic event*
> *like the one we have just experienced. My feelings are suddenly*
> *very raw and all I can think of is going home to England, back*
> *to normality. I have had enough of film stars and palm trees!*

A trundle bed was put up in my bedroom for Belinda. Algie was sent, protesting, in search of Tubby Halliday. I rather thought those two deserved each other. Next day Mummy was magnanimous for once and took Belinda and me shopping for clothes. I was grateful for this even though we found nothing as glamorous as the backless evening gown and silk pajamas. I wondered if I would ever see their like again – ever be able to afford their like. Mummy even sprang for a new uniform for Queenie, even though she protested about this. 'I can't think why you ever took her back, darling. Utter disaster.'

'She did save Claudette,' I reminded her.

Darcy was gone all the next day, busy with the sheriff. Ronnie came to visit us, the usual worried frown on his face. It seemed the remaining wild animals had been rounded up and sent to the Los Angeles Zoo. After an extensive man-hunt for Juan, his charred body was finally found, pinned against the fence at the top of the property where he had been trying to get out. So he had been trapped by his own fire. Served him right. He might have had a grudge against Mr. Goldman, but he could easily have killed us all. And those poor animals too. Ronnie said that a date for the funeral had been set and Mrs. Goldman was going to stay on for a while, determined that the studio and all of Cy's hard work would survive. She seemed utterly devastated by his death.

On our third day back at the Beverly Hills Hotel a small package was delivered to me.

'This came for you, Lady Georgiana,' the bellboy said. 'By hand.'

I opened it. Inside was a small velvet pouch and inside that was a huge and gorgeous ruby pendant. I ran after the bellboy who had brought it to me. 'Wait. Who delivered this by hand?' I asked.

'I couldn't tell you,' he said. 'It was left at the front desk with the words "For Lady Georgiana. By hand." That's all I know.'

I handed it over to Darcy when he showed up that evening. He whistled as he looked at the ruby, sparkling red fire in his hand.

'So your friend Bella really must have decided to go straight,' he said. 'I'll have to deliver this back to Princess Promila. She will be pleased. And at least I'll have something positive to show for my journey here.'

'You aren't going to stay and hunt down Bella?'

'If this came by hand then she's still in the area and it's quite possible she's staying with her sister,' he said. 'I'll certainly follow up on that.'

'I think it's unlikely,' I said. 'She took the first opportunity to slip away from us at the estate. Her sister may know where she is, but I bet she won't tell, not after Bella saved her life.'

Darcy shrugged. 'It doesn't really matter, I suppose. I have no warrant for her arrest and no official jurisdiction anyway. And as far as we know she has committed no crime in America, apart from the diamond ring we presume she stole on the ship.'

I laughed. 'I forgot to tell you about that. Bella says she didn't take it and she suspected the woman said it had been stolen in order to claim on the insurance. She said people do it all the time.'

Darcy smiled. 'How interesting. I'll hand that tidbit of information over to the New York police. Not that they'll ever be able to prove anything. Pity. A woman like that should get her just deserts for once. And when I get home I'll give my report to Scotland Yard and they'll be on the lookout for Miss Brightwell if she ever decides to come home to England.'

I felt rather glad that Bella wasn't going to prison, at least not in the foreseeable future. And if she was with her sister, then I was glad of that too. Stella would need someone to comfort her with Cy gone.

I was plucking up courage to remind Darcy about our day out alone when he said, 'Look, Georgie. I should really deliver the ruby back to the princess right away.' He obviously read the disappointment in my face because he went

Rhys Bowen

on hurriedly, 'So we'd better make our day out tomorrow before I catch the night train back to New York. I'll go and see about that motorcar.'

It was a sparkling fine morning when we set off for the coast. Beverly Hills looked its pastel best with its palm trees shimmering in a light morning breeze.

I glanced across at Darcy and felt a great bubble of happiness inside me. I was in an open sports car with the man I loved beside me and a whole day ahead of us. Darcy had ordered a picnic basket from the hotel and a bottle of bubbly. Thank heavens for the end of prohibition!

'Someone suggested we drive as far as Santa Barbara to the north,' he said, 'but I'm not sure we want to waste the whole day together in a motorcar, are you?'

'Absolutely not,' I said. 'I say we find the first little cove and have our picnic there.'

So we turned north at Santa Monica, with its funfair and pier giving the place a festive feel. 'Too public,' Darcy said and we shared a grin. Then the road narrowed and hugged the shoreline as we retraced our route to Mr. Goldman's ill-fated castle. We had only gone a few miles when we saw the perfect spot. A narrow strip of beach below the highway with big rocks on one side, and nobody else in sight. Darcy pulled off the road. We took the picnic basket and climbed down the sandy cliff to the beach. It was a narrow half moon of sand, strewn with driftwood. A flight of pelicans drifted past. We found a spot out of the wind among the rocks and changed into our bathing suits.

'Do you want to go for a swim first?' Darcy asked.

'All right. Last one in is a rotten egg.' I ran toward the waves, reached them and stopped short with a yell. 'It's absolutely freezing,' I said.

Darcy joined me, laughing. 'Yes, I'm afraid California is never noted for its warm water,' he said. 'Even in summer.'

'I think I've changed my mind about swimming,' I said.

'Where's that rugged Scottish blood, Georgiana Rannoch?' Without hesitation he dived into an oncoming wave. Of course after that I could hardly back out. I took a deep breath and plunged in after him. A large wave broke over me, submerging me whether I wanted it or not and tumbling me over and over. I felt Darcy's hand gripping my arm and pulling me to the surface. 'Sorry, I should probably have warned you that the waves can be rather fierce too. But good for bodysurfing.'

'How do you do that?'

He dove into a breaking wave and rode it into the shore. 'Like that.'

I wasn't quite as successful, but I think I got the hang of it after a while. When we rode a powerful wave in together and it ended by flinging us up onto the beach we lay there gasping, side by side. Then, before I could recover, Darcy turned to me, swept me into his arms and started kissing me. His lips felt cold and salty and the salt tingled on my body as it dried in the sun. Waves rushed in past us and receded again, but I was only conscious of his body pressing against mine, his lips crushing mine, his tongue in my mouth. Oh golly, I wanted him badly. I had never felt a surge of desire like this. I had never known such desire to be possible.

Who knows what this might have led to but a loud honking and catcalls from the road above revealed that we were all too visible to passing motorcars. We broke apart, with a guilty smile. Darcy helped me up and hand in hand we went back to our towels. I wrapped my towel around me and sat there, watching him as he stood there, his dark hair tousled by sea and sand. I took in every inch of him, the muscular chest with just a little dark hair in the middle, the slim waist and then the bathing trunks below it. I think my eyes lingered there longer than they should. I looked up to find him eyeing me with amusement, and I blushed.

'I'll open the champers, shall I?' he asked, reaching into the bag and not waiting for a reply. He poured two glasses and sat beside me against a large boulder. It was warm in the sun and smelled of the sea. Darcy raised his glass to me. 'To us,' he whispered. 'Hoping it won't be too long.'

'Amen to that,' I said, clinking glasses with him.

We sipped and he laughed. 'I think you're actually quite a hot little piece, Miss Georgie,' he said. 'There is something of your mother in you after all.'

'Golly, I hope not too much. You want a wife who will be faithful to you forever, don't you?'

He looked at me long and hard. 'I know what I want,' he said.

I felt the shiver go all the way down my spine.

'We should see what they packed for us to eat,' I said uneasily and turned to open the hamper. There was a delightful assortment of sandwiches, fresh cheeses, fruit and biscuits. It's amazing how hungry swimming in a cold ocean can make one. We both tucked in, Darcy sitting close beside me.

'It's a good thing we started out early,' he said looking out over the ocean. 'It seems that the fog might be coming in again.'

And indeed what looked like a bank of dark cloud now lay over the horizon. We put away the picnic, then went for a walk along the beach, hand in hand, with me pausing to pick up shells and interesting pieces of driftwood. We talked about what kind of house we'd like and where it should be and whether we needed a place in town and what kind of servants would be ideal. It was all very silly, given that neither of us had a bean, but it gave us both hope. I kept thinking that I wanted to preserve this moment forever, to somehow catch it in a glass jar to be brought out when Darcy was far away.

'If only I'd been able to do that part in the film,' Darcy said thoughtfully, 'I might have been able to make this reality. Do you really think I have star quality?'

I laughed. 'Yes, but I'm biased.'

'Do you think I should stay on here and take my chances?' he asked.

'Do you want to be a film star?'

'Absolutely not,' he said, 'but I'm willing to do what it takes to get us together.'

'Then I say you should go home. And you should tell these people who hire you for mysterious assignments that you need a proper job with decent pay from them or you are not helping them out again.'

He laughed now. 'I'll take you with me. You've got Queen Victoria's air of authority when you say that.'

We made our way back to our things, had another glass of champagne and immediately felt sleepy. I lay against the rock with my head on Darcy's shoulder. I think we must both have drifted off because I awoke to something cold and wet hitting me. I sat up to find the dark clouds were now overhead and it was raining.

'Not fog after all,' Darcy said. 'I didn't think it rained in California in the summertime.'

'Maybe just a passing shower,' I said hopefully. As if in answer, the heavens opened and a deluge hit us. Immediately after there was a rumble of thunder out to sea.

'That's not good,' Darcy said. We leaped up, grabbing our things and slithering up the now-muddy cliff to reach the motorcar. Then we couldn't find a way to close the top, if it actually had one. We had to drive for several miles, with the rain stinging in our faces, before we found a small shack on the seashore and went inside for a hot cup of coffee. The rain showed no sign of abating so we were forced to drive back to Beverly Hills, feeling wet, miserable and disappointed.

'It's lucky we weren't planning to spend the night together in a wayside inn,' Darcy said, rain running down his face. 'A fine couple we'd have looked, turning up like this.'

As we turned into the forecourt of the hotel the clouds parted and the rain miraculously stopped.

'Just our luck,' Darcy said. 'We should have sat it out after all.'

'And been washed out to sea, I think. All that mud coming down the cliffs would have been horrible.'

He nodded agreement. We got looks of commiseration as we picked our way through the gardens, where hotel staff were now drying off lounge beds and sweeping up bits of foliage. As we opened the cottage door Mummy leaped to greet us.

'Thank God,' she said. 'I was going frantic because I had no way of reaching you.'

'We were fine, Mummy,' I replied. 'We just got a little wet. It wasn't dangerous or anything.'

'Oh, I know that,' she said. 'I wasn't worried about you. But I've had an awful telegram from Reno. It seems that Homer Clegg has shown up in person. We have to leave immediately.'

Chapter 33

Beverly Hills and then Reno
Tuesday, August 7, 1934

Darcy and I stood facing each other. 'I'd better go,' he said. 'I'll see you when you're back in England, then.'

'I don't know where I'll be,' I said. 'I really don't want to go back to Castle Rannoch and Mummy will be off back to Max.'

'You can always use my place, darling,' Belinda said. 'Since I'm going to be here for a while.'

We hadn't noticed her curled on the sofa.

She smiled. 'That sweet boy Ronnie came by this morning. He said that Golden Pictures will take care of everything we need and he's going to make sure I get an introduction to the costume department. This could be my big break, darlings.'

'I'm happy for you, Belinda,' I said. 'And can I really use your mews cottage for a while?'

'Absolutely. Feel free.'

'Golly,' I said. 'That's so nice of you.'

'Well, I have made use of you from time to time,' she confessed.

'Now you know where to find me,' I said to Darcy.

He stroked my wet hair back from my face. 'You had better go and take a bath. You look like a drowned rat. And I have to pack to catch that train.'

I walked with him to the cottage door. There were so many things I wanted to say, but couldn't. On the doorstep he kissed me gently. 'Take care of yourself,' he whispered.

'You too.'

His hand brushed mine. Then he was gone.

I went inside to find that Queenie had packed all my things and complained loudly about having to open the cases again for dry clothes. 'Just when I got them all nice and neat you go rummaging through them and messing them all up,' she said.

'Queenie, if you don't enjoy working for me, you're very welcome to stay here and find another American lady to work for,' I said, 'but if you come with me you've got to stop this complaining. I want a proper lady's maid, and one who does her job cheerfully and willingly. Is that clear?'

'Yes, my lady,' she said sheepishly.

I wasn't too hopeful.

Mummy had rented a car and driver to take us to Reno as quickly as possible. It was a spectacular journey over mountains, past lakes and forests until finally we came to the dry scrub and heat of Nevada. Mummy was a bundle of nerves all the way.

'I can't think how he found out about it,' she kept on saying. 'Now I'm finished. He'll never divorce me and Max won't be able to marry me and everything is ruined. Everything I hoped for gone, destroyed, vanished.'

You can see she was able to be dramatic and eloquent even in despair.

I sat in the little bungalow at the ranch while she went in search of Homer, awaiting the worst. But it wasn't long before I heard the tap of her high heels running up the path to the front door. Mummy burst in, her hair out of place, her face alight with joy.

'It's all all right, darling.' She was beaming. 'I saw Homer and everything is going to be wonderful. He didn't even know I was here, can you imagine? He came to Reno because he wanted to get a quickie divorce from me. He's found someone he wants to marry and suddenly he's not quite so religiously puritanical anymore. Isn't that brilliant? So we'll be divorced in a few days and free to go home.'

'What about Mr. Goldman's funeral? Aren't we supposed to attend that?'

Mummy shrugged. 'Oh, darling. There will be millions of people. Who would notice if we were missing – and it's not as if we were bosom friends or anything. And to be truthful, I've had enough of America. I want to be back home where there are no silly ideas of equality and I can buy a decent face cream. I can't wait, can you?'

Actually no, I couldn't wait.